Stay positive. 保持積極。

Stay optimistic. 保持樂觀。

Stay upbeat. 保持開朗。

　　背了這三句話，學會positive, optimistic, upbeat這三個同義字。背誦和使用過程中，潛移默化，無形中改變自己。

Keep going. 持續前進。

Keep running. 持續奔跑。

Keep moving. 持續前行。

　　可用這三句話來鼓勵努力工作的人，都表示「加油！」，一句比一句力道更大。

Change happens. 必然會改變。

Change improves. 改變能進步。

Change empowers. 改變獲能量。

我們要走出自己的「舒適圈」，
隨著時代的腳步改變。改變能夠進步
和獲得能量。

Never stop.　永不停止。

Never quit.　永不放棄。

Never surrender.　永不投降。

目標設定以後，只要自己喜歡，
對別人有益，就要堅持到底，必然能
夠成功。

「使用英文」是唯一的方法

　　經過50多年的研發，得到的結論是，英文要使用，才不會忘記。這真是一本奇書！適合所有人，不管你英文程度如何，都能背得下來，說得出來。天啊！三個字一句話，誰都學得會，也無形中增加了中文的程度。

背單字 → 沒有使用 → 早晚忘記
背句子 → 一句多義 → 不用就忘記

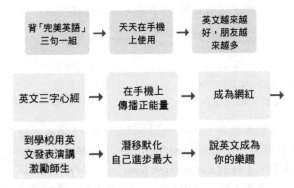

　　用這本書，到全世界各地傳播正能量，你就變成聖人了！

劉　毅

編者的話

♥英文三字經	中文三字經♥
Have a goal.	有目標。
Make a plan.	有計劃。
Set a target.	有願景。
Make it clear-cut.	要明確。
Make it achievable.	能達成。
Don't complicate it.	不複雜。

這六句話真是太美了，一般人最多只會說："Have a goal, plan, and target." 中文更是美到不行，感謝國學才女王宣雯修改。

我小時候，母親每天上午聽張澍教授廣播，影響我立志要當一位好的英文老師，這個目標 60 多年，都陪伴我生活，非常愉快！

♥英文三字經	中文六字經♥
Let passion lead.	讓熱情引導你。
Always be passionate.	永遠要有熱情。
Dream with purpose.	和目標同做夢。

Bailey 老師的原稿是 *Let passion guide.* (誤) 美國的教授 Laura E. Stewart 堅持要改成 Let passion guide you. 那又是四個字！折騰了好一陣子，才找到 ***Let passion lead***. (= *Let passion lead you.*) 英文就是這麼難，少一個字，多一個字都不行。我們發明「英文三字經」，不會背錯，因為都是三個字，說起來又有力量。

我 58 歲時被身邊的人要求退休，說我有錢不會用。60 多歲時，母親叫我不要再胡搞了。今年 78 歲，我非常愉快，因為—

Teaching English is my passion. 教英文是我的最愛。
Mastering English is my goal. 學好英文是我的目標。
Dream with purpose. 和目標一起做夢。

做自己喜歡做的事情，每天都過得有意義，不斷進步、成長，總感覺自己還沒有長大。

CONTENTS · 目 錄

📖 BOOK 1

目錄

📖 BOOK 2

目
錄

目錄

📖 BOOK 4

目
錄

目
錄

BOOK 5

目
錄

BOOK 1 \ PART 1

How to Be Successful
如何成功

PART 1・Unit 1~9
英文錄音QR碼

【開場白】

> *Hello, everyone!*
> 大家好!
>
> *Do you want to succeed?*
> 你們想要成功嗎?
>
> *Remember these nine things.*
> 要記住這九件事。

** successful〔sək'sɛsfəl〕*adj.* 成功的
　　succeed〔sək'sid〕*v.* 成功

UNIT ❶

First of all, you need *a* goal.
首先，你需要一個目標。

Have a goal.
有目標。

Make a plan.
有計劃。

Set a target.
有願景。

** —————————————

first of all 首先；第一 (*= first = firstly*
  = in the first place)
goal〔gol〕*n.* 目標
make〔mek〕*v.* 制定
plan〔plæn〕*n.* 計劃
set〔sɛt〕*v.* 設定 target〔'tɑrgɪt〕*n.* 目標

Make it clear-cut.

要明確。

Make it achievable.

能達成。

Don't complicate it.

不複雜。

** —————————

make〔mek〕*v.* 使

clear-cut〔͵klɪr'kʌt〕*adj.* 明確的；清楚的

achievable〔ə'tʃivəbḷ〕*adj.* 可達到的；
　可實現的

complicate〔'kɑmplə͵ket〕*v.* 使複雜

Let passion lead.

讓熱情引導你。

Always be passionate.

永遠要有熱情。

Dream with purpose.

和目標同做夢。

**

---

let〔 lɛt 〕v. 讓

passion〔'pæʃən 〕n. 熱情；愛好

lead〔 lid 〕v. 領路；帶路；領導

always〔'ɔlwez 〕adv. 總是；一直

passionate〔'pæʃənɪt 〕adj. 熱情的

dream〔 drim 〕v. 夢想

purpose〔'pɜpəs 〕n. 目的；目標

BOOK 1・PART 1

【Unit 1 背景說明】

要成功，一定要有一個目標。***First of all, you need a goal.*** 背誦密碼是 First of all（首先）和第一個字母 a 搭配。

這一段有三組：第一是「目標」，第二是「目標明確」，第三是「要有熱情」。結尾 Dream with purpose. 中的 purpose（目標）和第一句的 goal（目標）相呼應。「目標」的同義字有：goal-plan-target-purpose。

可以常說這九句話來激勵他人。

Have a goal.（要有一個目標。）也可說成：Know what you want to accomplish.（要知道你想要完成什麼。）

Make a plan.（要做一個計劃。）也可說成：Have a strategy.（要有策略。）Decide how you will do it.（要決定你會如何做。）

Set a target. 要設定一個目標。（= *Set a goal.* = *Make a goal.*）也可說成：Be clear about what you want to do.（要清楚你想要做什麼。）

Make it clear-cut.（要使它明確。）也可説成：It should be precise.（它應該要很精確。）Make your goal clear.（要使你的目標很清楚。）

Make it achievable.　要使它能夠達到。(= *Make it attainable.*) 也可説成：Your goal should be attainable.（你的目標應該要能夠達到。）

Don't complicate it.（不要使它太複雜。）也可説成：Don't complicate things.（不要使事情複雜化。）Keep it simple.（要使它保持簡單。）

Let passion lead.（讓熱情引導。）也可説成：Let passion lead you.（讓熱情引導你。）(= *Follow your passion.*)

Always be passionate.（一定要有熱情。）也可説成：Always be enthusiastic.（一定要有熱忱。）(= *Always be zealous.*)

Dream with purpose.　和目標同做夢；夢想要有目標。(= *Dream with intention.* = *Be intentional about your dreams.*)

UNIT ❷

Second, believe in yourself.
第二，相信自己。

Believe you can.
相信你能。

Believe you're capable.
信你能做。

Believe you're unstoppable.
所向披靡。

**
_____

believe〔bə'liv〕v. 相信

believe in 相信；信任

capable〔'kepəbḷ〕*adj.* 有能力的；能夠的

unstoppable〔ʌn'stɑpəbḷ〕*adj.* 擋不住的

Trust your abilities.

相信你的能力。

Trust in yourself.

相信你的力量。

Don't doubt yourself.

不要懷疑自己。

**

trust〔trʌst〕*v.* 信任；相信
ability〔ə'bɪlətɪ〕*n.* 能力
trust in sb. 信任某人；相信某人的能力
doubt〔daʊt〕*v.* 懷疑

Own your power.

掌握你的力量。

Know your worth.

了解你的價值。

Achieve your ambitions.

實現你的抱負。

**

own〔on〕*v.* 擁有；控制；支配

power〔'pauɚ〕*n.* 力量

worth〔wɝθ〕*n.* 價值（= *value*）

achieve〔ə'tʃiv〕*v.* 達成

ambition〔æm'bɪʃən〕*n.* 抱負

【Unit 2 背景說明】

***Second*, *believe in yourself*.** 中的 Second
（第二）和第二個字母 b 相呼應。很多人不敢學英
文，認為自己不行，你就可以說這九句話來激勵他
們。

***Believe you can*.**（要相信你能。）也可說成：
Believe that you can accomplish it.（要相信
你能做到。）

***Believe you're capable*.**（要相信你有能力。）也可
說成：Have confidence in your abilities.（要
對你的能力有信心。）

***Believe you're unstoppable*.**（要相信你是擋不住
的。）也可說成：Believe that no one can stop
you.（要相信沒有人能阻擋你。）Believe you
can do it.（要相信你做得到。）

***Trust your abilities*.** 要相信你的能力。（= *Have
confidence in your abilities*.）也可說成：
Believe that you can accomplish it.（要相信
你可以完成。）

Trust in yourself*.* 要相信自己的能力。(= *Believe in yourself.*) 也可說成 : Have faith in yourself. (要對自己有信心。)

Don't doubt yourself*.* (不要懷疑自己。) 也可說成 : Don't doubt your abilities. (不要懷疑你的能力。) Believe in yourself. (要相信你自己。)

Own your power*.* (掌握你的力量。) 也可說成 : *Take control of your power.* (要掌控你的力量。) Take control of your abilities. (要掌控你的能力。)

Know your worth*.* 要知道你的價值。(= *Understand your value.*)

Achieve your ambitions*.* (要達成你的抱負。) 也可說成 : Reach your goals. (要達到你的目標。) Attain your goal. (要達成你的目標。) Get what you want. (要得到你想要的。)

UNIT 3

Third, *try*, *try*, *try*!
第三，努力，努力，再努力！

Try your best.

盡力而為。

Do your best.

全力以赴。

Do your utmost.

竭盡全力。

**

try〔 traɪ〕*v.* 嘗試；努力

try one's *best* 盡力

do one's *best* 盡力

utmost〔'ʌt‚most〕*n.* (能力、努力的) 最
　大限度；極限

do one's *utmost* 做最大的努力；盡全力

Work like hell.

拼命工作。

Work like crazy.

盡力幹活。

Give your all.

全力以赴。

**

hell〔hɛl〕*n.* 地獄

like hell 拼命地

crazy〔'krezɪ〕*adj.* 瘋狂的

like crazy 拼命地 (= *like hell*)

give〔gɪv〕*v.* 付出

give your all 盡全力

Fully commit yourself.

全心投入。

Fully dedicate yourself.

全心奉獻。

Be totally focused.

全心全意。

＊＊────────────

fully〔'fulɪ〕*adv.* 完全地

commit〔kə'mɪt〕*v.* 使致力於

commit oneself 專心；全力以赴

dedicate〔'dɛdə,ket〕*v.* 奉獻；使致力於

dedicate oneself 獻身；投入

totally〔'totl̩ɪ〕*adv.* 完全地

focused〔'fokəst〕*adj.* 專注的

【Unit 3 背景說明】

<u>Third</u>, try, try, try! 爲了方便記憶，特別設計 <u>Th</u>ird 和 <u>tr</u>y 相呼應。

Try, try, try! 努力，努力，再努力！(= *Try, try, and try!*) 想要成功，一定要全力以赴，可以常用這九句話來鼓勵同學。

Try your best. (要盡力。) 也可説成：*Do your best.* (要盡力。) *Do your utmost.* (要盡全力。) Do all you can. (要盡全力。) Make every effort. (要非常努力。) Spare no effort. (要不遺餘力。)

Work like hell. (要拼命工作。) 也可説成：*Work like crazy.* (要拼命工作。) Work very hard. (要非常努力工作。) Work as hard as you can. (要盡量努力工作。) *Give your all.* (要盡全力。) Give it your all. (要盡全力。) Use all of your strength to do it. (要用盡全力去做。)

Fully commit yourself. (要全心投入。) 也可説成：*Fully dedicate yourself.* (要全心奉獻。) Apply yourself. (要全心投入。) *Be totally focused.* (要完全專注。) 也可説成：Put your mind to it. (要非常用心。)

UNIT ④

Fourth, *failure is inevitable.*

第四，失敗是無法避免的。

Don't fear failure.

不害怕失敗。

Expect to fail.

要期待失敗。

Failure isn't fatal.

失敗不會死。

** ────────

failure（ˈfeljə）*n.* 失敗

inevitable（ɪnˈɛvətəbḷ）*adj.* 無法避免的

fear（fɪr）*v.* 害怕

expect（ɪkˈspɛkt）*v.* 預期；期待

fail（fel）*v.* 失敗

fatal（ˈfetḷ）*adj.* 致命的；毀滅性的；極嚴重的

Failure breeds success.

失敗帶來成功。

Hardship yields progress.

苦難產生進步。

Adversity fuels strength.

逆境增強力量。

** ————————————

failure〔'feljɚ〕*n.* 失敗

breed〔brid〕*v.* 養育；培育

success〔sək'sɛs〕*n.* 成功

hardship〔'hardʃɪp〕*n.* 艱難；辛苦

yield〔jild〕*v.* 生產；引起；帶來

progress〔'prɑgrɛs〕*n.* 進步

adversity〔əd'vɝsətɪ〕*n.* 逆境

fuel〔'fjuəl〕*n.* 燃料 *v.* 加燃料於；
　加強；激起

strength〔strɛŋθ〕*n.* 力量

Forget about perfection.

拋卻完美。

Focus on progress.

專注進步。

Keep overcoming obstacles.

克服障礙。

** ——————————————

forget〔fə'gɛt〕*v.* 忘記

forget about 忘記（= *forget*）

perfection〔pə'fɛkʃən〕*n.* 完美

focus〔'fokəs〕*v.* 專注＜*on*＞

progress〔'prɑgrɛs〕*n.* 進步

keep* + *V-ing 持續⋯

overcome〔ˌovə'kʌm〕*v.* 克服

obstacle〔'ɑbstəkḷ〕*n.* 障礙；阻礙

【Unit 4 背景説明】

Fourth, failure is inevitable. 爲了幫助記憶，
特別編排 F̲ourth 和 f̲ailure 相呼應，都是 f 開頭的
字。很多人害怕失敗，可以説這九句話來激勵他們。

Don't fear failure. 不要害怕失敗。(= *Don't be
afraid of failure.* = *Don't be afraid to fail.*)

Expect to fail. (要期待失敗。) 也可説成：Know
that you will fail. (要知道你會失敗。) Don't be
surprised when you fail. (失敗時不要驚訝。)

Failure isn't fatal. 失敗不會致命；失敗不會死。
(= *Failing won't kill you.*) 也可説成：Failure
is not the end. (失敗不是結束。)

Failure breeds success. 失敗帶來成功。(= *Failure
leads to success.*) 也可説成：Success follows
failure. (失敗之後就是成功。)

Hardship yields progress. 苦難產生進步。
(= *Hardship leads to progress.*) 也可説成：
Difficulty helps you advance. (困難幫助你
進步。)

Adversity fuels strength. (逆境增強力量。)
也可説成 : Adversity makes you stronger.
(逆境使你更堅強。) Difficulty makes you
stronger. (困難使人更堅強。)

Forget about perfection. (要忘記完美。) 也
可説成 : Don't try to be perfect. (不要想要
完美。) Don't try to be flawless. (不要想毫
無瑕疵。)

Focus on progress. 要專注於進步。
(= *Concentrate on making progress.*
= *Concentrate on moving forward.*
= *Concentrate on advancing.*)

Keep overcoming obstacles. (要持續克服障
礙。) 也可説成 : Keep conquering anything
that stands in your way. (要持續征服任何的
阻礙。) Continue to solve problems and
advance. (要持續解決問題並向前進。)

UNIT 5

Fifth, seek feedback humbly.

第五，謙虛地尋求意見。

Ask for feedback.

尋求他人反應。

Get helpful advice.

獲得有用建議。

Never fear asking.

不要害怕詢問。

**

seek〔sik〕*v.* 尋求

feedback〔'fid,bæk〕*n.* 反饋；意見反應

humbly〔'hʌmblɪ〕*adv.* 謙虛地

ask for 要求

helpful〔'hɛlpfəl〕*adj.* 有用的；有幫助的

advice〔əd'vaɪs〕*n.* 勸告；建議

fear〔fɪr〕*v.* 害怕　　ask〔æsk〕*v.* 詢問

Swallow your pride.

不要驕傲。

Eat humble pie.

要很謙虛。

Accept any criticism.

接受批評。

** ————————————————

swallow〔'swɑlo〕*v.* 吞下

pride〔praɪd〕*n.* 驕傲

humble〔'hʌmbl̩〕*adj.* 謙虛的

pie〔paɪ〕*n.* 派

accept〔ək'sɛpt〕*v.* 接受

criticism〔'krɪtəˌsɪzəm〕*n.* 批評

Seek to improve.

要尋求進步。

Change with courage.

要勇於改變。

Improve to succeed.

進步能成功。

BOOK 1・PART 1

** ——————————

seek〔sik〕*v.* 尋求

seek to V. 尋求…；試圖…

improve〔ɪm'pruv〕*v.* 改善；進步

change〔tʃendʒ〕*v.* 改變

courage〔'kɝɪdʒ〕*n.* 勇氣

with courage 勇敢地

succeed〔sək'sid〕*v.* 成功

【Unit 5 背景説明】

Fifth, *seek feedback humbly*. 記憶密碼：
Fifth 和 feedback 相呼應。在字典上，feedback
的主要意思是「反饋」，在這裡是「意見反應」。想要
成功，就要不恥下問。

Ask for feedback. (要求別人給你意見；尋求他人
的反應。) 也可説成：Ask for suggestions.
(要求別人給建議。) Ask for comments and
suggestions. (要求別人給評論和建議。)

Get helpful advice. (要獲得有幫助的建議。)
也可説成：Get some useful suggestions.
(要獲得一些有用的建議。) Seek good advice.
(尋求好的建議。) (= *Seek good suggestions*.)

Never fear asking. 絕不要害怕詢問。(= *Never
be afraid to ask*.) 也可説成：Don't be afraid
to ask for help. (不要害怕請求協助。)

Swallow your pride. 吞下你的驕傲，也就是「不
要驕傲。」也可説成：Humble yourself. (要謙
虛。) (= *Be humble*.)

***Eat humble pie*.** 吃謙虛的派，也就是「要謙虛。」
(*= Be humble. = Swallow your pride.*)

***Accept any criticism*.** 要接受任何的批評。(*= Take any criticism.*)也可說成：Listen to all criticism.
(要傾聽所有的批評。)

***Seek to improve*.** (要尋求進步。) 也可說成：
Try to improve. (要努力求進步。) Work to better yourself. (要努力使自己更好。)

***Change with courage*.** 要勇於改變。(*= Be brave and change. = Be brave enough to change.*)

***Improve to succeed*.** (進步才能成功。) 也可說成：Better yourself in order to succeed.
(想要成功，就要使自己更好。) Do better so that you can succeed. (你要表現得更好才能成功。)

UNIT ⑥

Sixth, *stay patient*.
第六，要有耐心。

Stand your ground.
堅守立場。

Don't back down.
不要退縮。

Refuse to quit.
拒絕放棄。

** ―――――――――――

stay〔ste〕*v.* 保持
patient〔'peʃənt〕*adj.* 有耐心的
ground〔graʊnd〕*n.* 立場
stand *one's* **ground** 堅守立場
　(= *hold one's ground*)
back down 退出；放棄；打退堂鼓
refuse〔rɪ'fjuz〕*v.* 拒絕
quit〔kwɪt〕*v.* 放棄 (= *give up*)；停止

Always be patient.

要有耐心。

Always be determined.

要有決心。

Stick it out.

堅持到底。

** ─────────────

always〔ˈɔlwez〕*adv.* 總是；一直

patient〔ˈpeʃənt〕*adj.* 有耐心的

determined〔dɪˈtɝmɪnd〕*adj.* 堅決的；
下定決心的

stick〔stɪk〕*v.* 黏著；刺；戳

stick it out 堅持到底

Patience pays off.

忍耐值得。

Persistence pays off.

堅持值得。

Persevere to succeed.

堅忍成功。

** ────────────────

patience〔'peʃəns〕*n.* 耐心；忍耐；堅忍

pay off 取得成功；得到好結果；獲得回報

persistence〔pə'sɪstəns〕*n.* 堅持；
　堅忍不拔

persevere〔,pɝsə'vɪr〕*v.* 堅忍；堅持到底

succeed〔sək'sid〕*v.* 成功

【Unit 6 背景説明】

Sixth, *stay patient*. 想要成功，一定要不屈不撓，堅持到底。

Stand your ground. (要堅守立場。) 也可説成：Don't give in. (不要屈服。) Stand firm. (要堅定不移。) Persist. (要堅持。)

Don't back down. (不要打退堂鼓；不要退縮。) 也可説成：Don't surrender. (不要投降。) Be determined. (要堅決。)

Refuse to quit. (拒絕放棄。) 也可説成：Don't give up. (不要放棄。) Don't stop. (不要停止。)

Always be patient. (一定要有耐心。) 也可説成：Be tolerant. (要容忍。) Be persistent. (要堅持。) Endure. (要忍耐。) Persevere. (要堅忍。) Don't be impatient. (不要不耐煩。)

Always be determined. (一定要有決心。) 也可説成：Be resolute. (要堅決。) Be dogged. (要堅決。)

BOOK 1・PART 1

Stick it out. (要堅持到底。) 也可說成：Keep going. (要持續前進。) Don't give up. (不要放棄。)

Patience pays off. 忍耐很值得。(= *Patience is worth it.* = *Patience is worthwhile.*) 也可說成：Patience is rewarded. (忍耐會有回報。) You'll succeed if you are patient. (如果你有耐心，你就會成功。)

Persistence pays off. 堅持很值得。(= *Persistence is worth it.* = *Persistence is worthwhile.*) 也可說成：Persistence is rewarded. (堅持會有回報。) It's worthwhile to be persistent. (堅持很值得。)

Persevere to succeed. (堅忍才會成功。) 也可說成：Persist in order to win. (堅持才會獲勝。) Keep trying and you will succeed. (持續努力，你就會成功。)

UNIT ❼

Seventh, *be a sponge for knowledge.*

第七，要像海綿一樣吸收知識。

Be a sponge.

成為海綿。

Soak up information.

吸收資訊。

Learn without limits.

學無止境。

** ——————————

sponge〔spʌndʒ〕*n.* 海綿
knowledge〔'nɑlɪdʒ〕*n.* 知識
soak〔sok〕*v.* 浸泡；吸入；吸收
soak up 吸收
information〔ˌɪnfɚ'meʃən〕*n.* 資訊
limit〔'lɪmɪt〕*n.* 限制；極限；限度

Be constantly curious.

要保持好奇心。

Thirst for knowledge.

要能求知若渴。

Strive for self-growth.

追求自我成長。

**

constantly〔'kɑnstəntlɪ〕*adv.* 不斷地

curious〔'kjʊrɪəs〕*adj.* 好奇的

thirst〔θɜst〕*n. v.* 口渴;渴望

thirst for 渴望

knowledge〔'nɑlɪdʒ〕*n.* 知識

strive〔straɪv〕*v.* 努力

strive for 爲追求…而努力

self-growth〔ˌsɛlf'groθ〕*n.* 自我成長

Commit to learning.

致力學習。

Embrace lifelong learning.

終身學習。

Acquire knowledge everywhere.

無處不學。

** ————————

commit〔kə'mɪt〕*v.* 致力於＜*to*＞

learning〔'lɜnɪŋ〕*n.* 學習

embrace〔ɪm'bres〕*v.* 擁抱；欣然接受

lifelong〔'laɪf,lɔŋ〕*adj.* 終身的；終生的

acquire〔ə'kwaɪr〕*v.* 獲得；學得

knowledge〔'nɑlɪdʒ〕*n.* 知識

everywhere〔'ɛvrɪ,hwɛr〕*adv.* 到處

【**Unit 7 背景説明**】

  Seventh, ***be a sponge for knowledge***. 想要成功，一定要像海綿一樣吸收知識。

Be a sponge.（要像海綿一樣。）也可説成：Be a fast learner.（要快速學習。）（=*Be a quick learner.*）Learn a lot.（要學很多東西。）Be open to learning.（要願意學習。）

Soak up information.（要吸收資訊。）也可説成：Soak up knowledge.（要吸收知識。）Acquire a lot of knowledge.（要學會很多知識。）Learn all you can.（要盡力學習。）

Learn without limits.（要無止境地學習。）也可説成：Always keep learning.（一定要持續學習。）Don't limit yourself.（不要限制自己。）Learn everything you can.（要盡量學習一切。）

Be constantly curious. 要一直很好奇。（=*Always be curious.*）也可説成：Be inquisitive.（要充滿好奇。）

Thirst for knowledge. (要渴望知識。) 也可說
成 : Want to learn more. (要想學到更多。)
Want to learn as much as you can. (要想儘量
多學一點。)

Strive for self-growth. (要努力追求自我成長。)
也可說成 : Work to develop yourself. (要努
力發展自我。) Try hard to progress. (要努力
求進步。)

Commit to learning. 要致力於學習。(= *Commit
yourself to learning.* = *Dedicate yourself to
learning.* = *Be devoted to learning.*)

Embrace lifelong learning. 要擁抱終身學習,也
就是「要終身學習。」(= *Learn all your life.*) 也
可說成 : Never stop learning. (絕不停止學習。)

Acquire knowledge everywhere. (要到處學習知
識。) 也可說成 : Take every opportunity to
learn something. (要把握每一個能學習的機會。)
Learn new things everywhere. (要到處學習新
事物。)

UNIT 8

Most importantly, don't let good chances pass you by.

最重要的是，不要讓好機會擦身而過。

Opportunity strikes fast.

機會來得快。

Don't miss it.

不要錯過它。

Grab the chance.

要抓住機會。

** ————————————

most importantly 最重要的是
chance〔tʃæns〕*n.* 機會
pass *sb.* by 擦肩而過
opportunity〔͵ɑpə'tjunətɪ〕*n.* 機會
strike〔straɪk〕*v.* 敲打；來（= *come*）
fast〔fæst〕*adv.* 快地　　miss〔mɪs〕*v.* 錯過
grab〔græb〕*v.* 抓住

BOOK 1・PART 1

Challenge is everywhere.

處處有挑戰。

Opportunity is everywhere.

處處有機會。

Embrace the challenge.

要擁抱挑戰。

BOOK 1・PART 1

** ───────

challenge〔'tʃælɪndʒ〕*n.* 挑戰
everywhere〔'ɛvrɪ,hwɛr〕*adv.* 到處
opportunity〔,ɑpɚ'tjunətɪ〕*n.* 機會
embrace〔ɪm'bres〕*v.* 擁抱;欣然接受

Seize the opportunity.
要能抓住機會。

Seize the moment.
要能把握時機。

Seize once-in-a-lifetime chances.
把握難得機會。

**   ——————————

seize〔siz〕*v.* 抓住
opportunity〔ˌɑpə'tjunətɪ〕*n.* 機會
moment〔'momənt〕*n.* 時刻；時機
once-in-a-lifetime〔ˌwʌns ɪn ə 'laɪf‚taɪm〕
　　adj. 一生中難得一次的；千載難逢的
chance〔tʃæns〕*n.* 機會

【Unit 8 背景説明】

機會瞬間即逝，一定要把握機會。

Opportunity strikes fast. （機會來得很快，稍縱即逝。）也可説成：Opportunity comes without warning. （機會會毫無預警地出現。） Chances come suddenly. （機會會突然出現。）

Don't miss it. （不要錯過它。）也可説成： Don't miss your chance. （不要錯過你的機會。） Don't lose the chance. （不要失去機會。）

Grab the chance. （要抓住機會。）也可説成： Take the opportunity. （要把握機會。）

Challenge is everywhere. （挑戰到處都有。） 也可説成：Challenge is all around us. （挑戰就在我們身邊。） Everything is challenging in some way. （每件事情，就某方面而言，都具有挑戰性。）

BOOK 1・PART 1

Opportunity is everywhere. (機會到處都有。)
也可說成：Opportunity is all around us.
(機會就在我們身邊。) You can always find
an opportunity. (你總是能找到機會。)

Embrace the challenge. (要擁抱挑戰；要樂於
接受挑戰。) Welcome the challenge. (要歡
迎挑戰。) Accept the challenge. (要接受
挑戰。)

Seize the opportunity. 要抓住機會。(= *Grab
the opportunity*. = *Grab the chance*.)

Seize the moment. 要把握時機。(= *Seize the
chance*. = *Seize the opportunity*.)

Seize once-in-a-lifetime chances. (要抓住一
生難得一次的機會。) 也可說成：Grab the
rare chances. (要抓住稀有的機會。) (= *Grab
the rare opportunities*.)

UNIT 9

Finally, guide others to success.

最後，要帶領別人成功。

Be a leader.

成爲領導。

Be a mentor.

成爲良師。

Help others succeed.

幫人成功。

**

guide〔gaɪd〕*v.* 引導

success〔sək'sɛs〕*n.* 成功

leader〔'lidɚ〕*n.* 領導者

mentor〔'mɛntor〕*n.* 良師

succeed〔sək'sid〕*v.* 成功

Offer your support.

提供支持。

Offer your guidance.

提供指導。

Set an example.

樹立榜樣。

**

offer〔ˈɔfɚ〕*v.* 提供
support〔səˈport〕*n.* 支持
guidance〔ˈgaɪdn̩s〕*n.* 指導
set〔sɛt〕*v.* 設立；樹立
example〔ɪgˈzæmpl̩〕*n.* 例子；
　榜樣；典範

Share your knowledge.

分享知識。

Share your expertise.

分享專業。

Pave the way.

為人鋪路。

**

share〔ʃɛr〕*v.* 分享
knowledge〔'nɑlɪdʒ〕*n.* 知識
expertise〔͵ɛkspɚ'tiz〕*n.* 專業知識
pave〔pev〕*v.* 鋪（路）
pave the way 鋪平道路；創造條件

【Unit 9 背景説明】

　　成功以後，不要忘記，要帶領別人成功，樹立好的榜樣，爲人鋪路。

Be a leader*.*（要成爲領導者。）也可説成：Lead others.（要引導別人。）（ = *Guide others.*）

Be a mentor*.*　要成爲良師。（ = *Be a teacher.*）也可説成：Be an advisor.（要當個顧問。）Be a guide.（要當個引導者。）

Help others succeed*.*　要幫助別人成功。（ = *Assist others in being successful.*）也可説成：Assist others in reaching their goals.（要協助別人達到目標。）

Offer your support*.*（要提供你的支持。）也可説成：Offer to help.（要願意幫忙。）Provide help.（要提供協助。）Be supportive.（要願意支持。）Be helpful.（要樂於幫忙。）

Offer your guidance*.*（要提供你的指導。）也可説成：Provide advice.（要提供建議。）（ = *Offer advice.* = *Give advice.*）

Set an example. (要樹立榜樣。) 也可説成 : Be a role model. (要做一個模範。) Show how it's done. (要告訴別人該如何做。)

Share your knowledge. (要分享你的知識。) 也可説成 : Tell others what you know. (要告訴別人你知道的事。) (= *Tell people what you know.*)

Share your expertise. (要分享你的專業知識。) 也可説成 : Tell others how to do it. (要告訴別人如何做。) Tell others how to do what you do. (告訴別人要如何做你做的事。)

Pave the way. 要替別人鋪路。(= *Smooth the way.*) 也可説成 : Assist the progress of others. (要幫助別人進步。) Open the door for others. (要爲別人提供機會。)

【**How to Be Successful** 結尾語】

Thank you for being here today. 謝謝你們今天來。

I hope you enjoyed my speech. 我希望你們喜歡我的演講。

May your dreams come true! 祝你們夢想成真！

** enjoy〔ɪnˋdʒɔɪ〕*v.* 喜歡
speech〔spitʃ〕*n.* 演講
may〔me〕*aux.* 祝…；願…
dream〔drim〕*n.* 夢；夢想
come true 實現；成眞

【英語演講】

How to Be Successful

Hello, everyone!
Do you want to succeed?
Remember these nine things.

PART 1・Unit 1~9
英文錄音QR碼

BOOK 1・PART 1

First of all, *you need* ***a*** *goal.*

Have a goal.
Make a plan.
Set a target.

Make it clear-cut.
Make it achievable.
Don't complicate it.

Let passion lead.
Always be passionate.
Dream with purpose.

Second, ***b***elieve in yourself.

Believe you can.
Believe you're capable.
Believe you're unstoppable.

Trust your abilities.
Trust in yourself.
Don't doubt yourself.

Own your power.
Know your worth.
Achieve your ambitions.

Third, *try, try, try!*

Try your best.
Do your best.
Do your utmost.

Work like hell.
Work like crazy.
Give your all.

Fully commit yourself.
Fully dedicate yourself.
Be totally focused.

Fourth, *failure is inevitable.*

Don't fear failure.
Expect to fail.
Failure isn't fatal.

Failure breeds success.
Hardship yields progress.
Adversity fuels strength.

Forget about perfection.
Focus on progress.
Keep overcoming obstacles.

Fifth, *seek feedback humbly*.

Ask for feedback.
Get helpful advice.
Never fear asking.

Swallow your pride.
Eat humble pie.
Accept any criticism.

Seek to improve.
Change with courage.
Improve to succeed.

Sixth, *stay patient*.

Stand your ground.
Don't back down.
Refuse to quit.

Always be patient.
Always be determined.
Stick it out.

Patience pays off.
Persistence pays off.
Persevere to succeed.

***Seventh**, be a **sponge** for knowledge.*

Be a sponge.
Soak up information.
Learn without limits.

Be constantly curious.
Thirst for knowledge.
Strive for self-growth.

Commit to learning.
Embrace lifelong learning.
Acquire knowledge everywhere.

*Most importantly, don't let good chances
    pass you by.*

Opportunity strikes fast.
Don't miss it.
Grab the chance.

Challenge is everywhere.
Opportunity is everywhere.
Embrace the challenge.

Seize the opportunity.
Seize the moment.
Seize once-in-a-lifetime chances.

Finally, guide others to success.

Be a leader.
Be a mentor.
Help others succeed.

Offer your support.
Offer your guidance.
Set an example.

Share your knowledge.
Share your expertise.
Pave the way.

Thank you for being here today.
I hope you enjoyed my speech.
May your dreams come true!

BOOK 1・PART 1

How to Be Successful

Everyone would like to be successful, but few understand how to do it. It's actually very easy once you know how. *First of all*, you need the right goal. Your goal must be both clear and achievable. *Next*, you have to believe in yourself. Trust in yourself and know that you can do it. *Then* all you have to do is try. Commit yourself and work like hell!

Of course, some failure is inevitable. But failure isn't fatal, so don't be discouraged. *Instead*, seek feedback from others. Swallow your pride and accept any criticism. Only that way can you know how to improve. Soak up knowledge every chance you have. Be patient and try again. Remember that persistence pays off in the end. *More importantly*, don't be afraid to take chances. Opportunity strikes fast. You must be ready to grab it. *Finally*, once you have succeeded, share your knowledge and pave the way for others.

【翻譯】

如何成功

　　每個人都想要成功，但是很少人知道要如何做到。一旦你知道方法，其實非常容易。首先，你需要正確的目標。你的目標必須清楚，而且能夠達到。其次，你必須相信你自己。相信你自己的能力，知道自己能做到。然後你所必須做的，就是努力。要全心投入，並且拼命工作！

　　當然，有些失敗是無法避免的。但失敗又不會死，所以，不要氣餒，而是要向別人尋求意見。不要驕傲，要接受任何的批評。唯有那樣，你才會知道如何改進。要一有機會就吸收知識。要有耐心，再試一次。要記得，堅持到最後就會有回報。更重要的是，不要害怕冒險。機會來得很快，稍縱即逝。你必須準備好去抓住它。最後，一旦你成功，就要分享你的知識，並為人鋪路。

BOOK 1・PART 1

PART 1・Unit 1~9
中英文錄音QR碼

PART 1 總整理

Unit 1

Have a goal. 有目標。
Make a plan. 有計劃。
Set a target. 有願景。

Make it clear-cut.
要明確。
Make it achievable.
能達成。
Don't complicate it.
不複雜。

Let passion lead.
讓熱情引導你。
Always be passionate.
永遠要有熱情。
Dream with purpose.
和目標同做夢。

Unit 2

Believe you can.
相信你能。
Believe you're capable.
信你能做。
Believe you're
    unstoppable. 所向披靡。

Trust your abilities.
相信你的能力。
Trust in yourself.
相信你的力量。
Don't doubt yourself.
不要懷疑自己。

Own your power.
掌握你的力量。
Know your worth.
了解你的價值。
Achieve your ambitions.
實現你的抱負。

Unit 3

Try your best. 盡力而為。
Do your best. 全力以赴。
Do your utmost. 竭盡全力。

Work like hell. 拼命工作。
Work like crazy. 盡力幹活。
Give your all. 全力以赴。

Fully commit yourself.
全心投入。
Fully dedicate yourself.
全心奉獻。
Be totally focused. 全心全意。

Unit 4

Don't fear failure.
不害怕失敗。
Expect to fail.
要期待失敗。
Failure isn't fatal.
失敗不會死。

Failure breeds success.
失敗帶來成功。
Hardship yields progress.
苦難產生進步。
Adversity fuels strength.
逆境增強力量。

Forget about perfection.
拋卻完美。
Focus on progress.
專注進步。
Keep overcoming
　obstacles. 克服障礙。

Unit 5

Ask for feedback.
尋求他人反應。
Get helpful advice.
獲得有用建議。
Never fear asking.
不要害怕詢問。

Swallow your pride.
不要驕傲。
Eat humble pie. 要很謙虛。
Accept any criticism.
接受批評。

Seek to improve.
要尋求進步。
Change with courage.
要勇於改變。
Improve to succeed.
進步能成功。

Unit 6

Stand your ground.
堅守立場。
Don't back down. 不要退縮。
Refuse to quit. 拒絕放棄。

Always be patient.
要有耐心。
Always be determined.
要有決心。
Stick it out. 堅持到底。

Patience pays off. 忍耐值得。
Persistence pays off.
堅持值得。
Persevere to succeed.
堅忍成功。

Unit 7

Be a sponge.
成為海綿。
Soak up information.
吸收資訊。
Learn without limits.
學無止境。

Be constantly curious.
要保持好奇心。
Thirst for knowledge.
要能求知若渴。
Strive for self-growth.
追求自我成長。

Commit to learning.
致力學習。
Embrace lifelong
    learning. 終身學習。
Acquire knowledge
    everywhere. 無處不學。

Unit 8

Opportunity strikes fast.
機會來得快。
Don't miss it.
不要錯過它。
Grab the chance.
要抓住機會。

Challenge is everywhere.
處處有挑戰。
Opportunity is
    everywhere. 處處有機會。
Embrace the challenge.
要擁抱挑戰。

Seize the opportunity.
要能抓住機會。
Seize the moment.
要能把握時機。
Seize once-in-a-lifetime
    chances. 把握難得機會。

Unit 9

Be a leader. 成為領導。
Be a mentor. 成為良師。
Help others succeed.
幫人成功。

Offer your support.
提供支持。
Offer your guidance.
提供指導。
Set an example. 樹立榜樣。

Share your knowledge.
分享知識。
Share your expertise.
分享專業。
Pave the way. 為人鋪路。

BOOK 1　PART 2

How to Be Happy
如何快樂

【開場白】

Hi, everyone.
嗨，大家好。

Need more happiness?
需要更多的快樂嗎？

Here are nine tips.
以下有九個祕訣。

BOOK 1・PART 2

** ***Need more happiness?***
= Do you need more happiness?
tip〔tɪp〕 *n.* 祕訣

UNIT 1

First off, *advance to be happy.*
第一，進步才會快樂。

Advance in life.
生活中進步。

Make progress daily.
每天要進步。

Every step counts.
步步都重要。

** ———————————————

> ***first off*** 首先 (= *first* = *first of all*)
> advance〔əd'væns〕*v.* 進步
> progress〔'prɑgrɛs〕*n.* 進步
> ***make progress*** 進步
> daily〔'delɪ〕*adv.* 每天 (= *every day*)
> step〔stɛp〕*n.* 一步；步驟
> count〔kaʊnt〕*v.* 重要

Never stop improving.

不停進步。

Enhance your skills.

增強技能。

Grow your business.

發展事業。

** ───────

never〔'nɛvɚ〕 *adv.* 絕不

stop* + *V-ing 停止…

improve〔ɪm'pruv〕*v.* 改善；進步

enhance〔ɪn'hæns〕*v.* 提高；增進

skill〔skɪl〕*n.* 技能

grow〔gro〕*v.* 增長；發展；擴大

　(= *make bigger*)

business〔'bɪznɪs〕*n.* 事業

grow* *one's* *business 發展事業；擴展業務

Fulfill your desires.

實現願望。

Feel more successful.

感受成功。

Make life meaningful.

意義人生。

**

fulfill〔fʊlˈfɪl〕*v.* 實現；達到；使滿足

desire〔dɪˈzaɪr〕*n.* 慾望；願望

feel〔fil〕*v.* 感到；覺得

successful〔səkˈsɛsfəl〕*adj.* 成功的

make〔mek〕*v.* 使

meaningful〔ˈminɪŋfəl〕*adj.* 有意義的

【Unit 1 背景説明】

First off, ***advance to be happy***. 記憶密碼：
First off（第一）和第一個字母 a 相呼應。人生最
大的快樂，就是進步，就像小孩喜歡長大一樣。

Advance in life. 在生活中要進步。(= *Make
progress in life*.) 也可説成：Advance in
everything you do in life. (在生活中做什麼
事都要進步。)

Make progress daily. (每天都要進步。) 也可
説成：Take a step forward every day. (每
天都要向前走一步。)

Every step counts. 每一步都很重要。(= *Every
step matters*.) 也可説成：Every positive
action is important. (每一個積極的行動都很
重要。)

Never stop improving. (絶不停止進步。) 也可
説成：Keep on improving. (要持續進步。)
Keep advancing. (要持續進步。) Keep on
bettering yourself. (要持續讓自己更好。)

BOOK 1 · PART 2

Enhance your skills. (要增強你的技能。) 也可說成 : Improve your skills. (要改善你的技能。) Improve your abilities. (改善你的能力。) (= *Better your capacities*.)

Grow your business. 要發展你的事業;要擴展你的業務。(= *Develop your business*. = *Expand your business*.)

Fulfill your desires. (要滿足你的渴望。) 也可說成 : Get what you want. (要得到你想要的。) Do what you want. (要做你想做的。)

Feel more successful. (要覺得自己更成功。) 也可說成 : Feel more accomplished. (要覺得更有成就感。) Believe that you're getting ahead. (要相信自己快要獲得成功。)

Make life meaningful. 要讓人生有意義。(= *Make your life count*.) 也可說成 : Do something meaningful with your life. (用你的人生做有意義的事。) Have a purpose for your life. (要讓你的人生有目標。)

UNIT ❷

Second, social connections bring happiness.

第二，社交能帶來快樂。

Keep good company.

要結交益友。

Have close friendships.

有親密友誼。

Have meaningful relationships.

有重要關係。

**

social〔'soʃəl〕*adj.* 社交的
connections〔kə'nɛkʃənz〕*n. pl.* 聯繫
company〔'kʌmpənɪ〕*n.* 公司；朋友
keep good company 結交益友
close〔klos〕*adj.* 親密的
friendship〔'frɛndʃɪp〕*n.* 友誼
meaningful〔'minɪŋfəl〕*adj.* 有意義的；重要的
relationship〔rɪ'leʃənˌʃɪp〕*n.* 關係

BOOK 1・PART 2

Cherish loved ones.
珍惜所愛之人。

Hold family close.
保持家人親密。

Value friends dearly.
珍視朋友如金。

** ——————————————

cherish〔'tʃɛrɪʃ〕*v.* 珍惜

loved ones 親人；心愛的人

hold〔hold〕*v.* 使處於（某種狀態）

family〔'fæməlɪ〕*n.* 家人

close〔klos〕*adj.* 親密的

value〔'vælju〕*v.* 重視

dearly〔'dɪrlɪ〕*adv.* 充滿深情地；非常
　　（= *very much*）

Friendships bring happiness.

友誼帶來快樂。

Improve your health.

改善你的健康。

Increase your lifespan.

增加你的壽命。

** ───────────

friendship ('frɛndʃɪp) *n.* 友誼
bring (brɪŋ) *v.* 帶來
happiness ('hæpɪnɪs) *n.* 快樂；幸福
improve (ɪm'pruv) *v.* 改善；增進
health (hɛlθ) *n.* 健康
increase (ɪn'kris) *v.* 增加
lifespan ('laɪf‚spæn) *n.* 壽命

BOOK 1・PART 2

【Unit 2 背景說明】

__Second__, __social__ connections bring happiness. Second 和 social 都是 S 開頭。有好的朋友、家人陪伴，是人生極大的幸福。

Keep good company. (要結交益友。) 也可說成：Associate with good people. (要和好人來往。)

Have close friendships. (要有親密的友誼。) 也可說成：Maintain close friendships. (要維持親密的友誼。) Make some close friends. (要結交一些密友。)

Have meaningful relationships. (要有有意義的關係；要有重要的關係。) 也可說成：Develop deep relationships. (要發展深厚的關係。) Establish relationships that are important to you. (要建立對你而言很重要的關係。)

Cherish loved ones. 要珍惜心愛的人。
(*= Treasure the people you love*.) 也可說成：Treasure your friends and family. (要珍惜你的朋友和家人。)

Hold family close. (要使家人保持親密。) 也可
説成：Stay close to your family. (要和家人
保持親密。) Keep a close relationship with
your family. (要和你的家人保持親密的關係。)

Value friends dearly. (要非常重視朋友。) 也可
説成：Treasure your friends. (要珍惜你的朋
友。) Know the importance of your friends.
(要知道你的朋友的重要。)

Friendships bring happiness. (友誼帶來快
樂。) 也可説成：Having friends makes
one happy. (有朋友會使人快樂。) Having
friends will make you happy. (有朋友會使
你快樂。)

Improve your health. 改善你的健康。(= *Make
your health better*.) 也可説成：Get
healthier. (要變得更健康。)

Increase your lifespan. (增加你的壽命。) 也可
説成：Live longer. (要活得更久。)

UNIT ❸

Third, celebrate when you can.
第三，有機會就慶祝。

Spend time celebrating.
偷閒慶祝。

Grasp every opportunity.
抓住機會。

Relax and enjoy.
放鬆享受。

** —————————

celebrate (ˋsɛləˌbret) v. 慶祝
spend (spɛnd) v. 花費
spend + 時間 + (*in*) + *V-ing* 花時間…
grasp (græsp) v. 抓住
opportunity (ˌɑpɚˋtjunətɪ) n. 機會
relax (rɪˋlæks) v. 放鬆
enjoy (ɪnˋdʒɔɪ) v. 享受

Throw a party.

舉行派對。

Have a feast.

大吃一頓。

Have a banquet.

大快朵頤。

**

throw〔θro〕v. 丟；舉行
party〔'pɑrtɪ〕n. 派對；宴會
throw a party 舉行派對（= *have a party* = *hold a party*）
have〔hæv〕v. 有；吃；喝；舉行
feast〔fist〕n. 盛宴
banquet〔'bæŋkwɪt〕n. 盛宴；宴會

Celebrate your achievements.

慶祝成就。

Celebrate with friends.

和友同慶。

Toast to happiness.

舉杯而樂。

**

celebrate〔ˈsɛləˌbret〕v. 慶祝
achievements〔əˈtʃivmənts〕n. pl. 成就
　（= accomplishments）
toast〔tost〕v. 舉杯祝賀　n. 乾杯；舉杯祝賀
happiness〔ˈhæpɪnɪs〕n. 快樂；幸福

【**Unit 3** 背景説明】

  ***Third**, **celebrate when you can**.* 記憶密碼：
Third（第三）和第三個字母 C 相呼應。要把握機會
慶祝，生日、節日、大小喜事，都不要忘記。

***Spend time celebrating**.*（要花時間慶祝。）也可
 説成：Spend some time making merry.（要
 花時間盡情歡樂。）Spend some time having
 fun.（要花時間玩得愉快。）

***Grasp every opportunity**.* 要抓住每一個機會。
 （= *Take every opportunity*.）也可説成：
 Don't let any opportunities pass you by.
 （不要讓任何機會擦身而過。）

***Relax and enjoy**.*（放輕鬆，好好享受。）也可説
 成：Chill out and have fun.（要放輕鬆，並玩
 得愉快。）Rest and have fun.（要休息，並玩
 得愉快。）

***Throw a party**.* 要舉行派對。(= *Hold a party*.
 = *Have a party*.）也可説成：Host a party.
 （要主辦派對。）Hold a celebration.（要舉行
 慶祝活動。）

Have a feast. 要吃大餐。(= *Have a banquet.*) 也可說成：Have a big meal. (要吃很豐盛的一餐。)

Celebrate your achievements. (要慶祝你的成就。) 也可說成：Honor your achievements. (要表揚你的成就。) Recognize your accomplishments. (要認可你的成就。)

Celebrate with friends. (要和朋友一起慶祝。) 也可說成：Have fun with your friends. (要和你的朋友玩得愉快。) Make merry with your friends. (要和你的朋友盡情歡樂。)

Toast to happiness. 要為快樂而乾杯。(= *Drink a toast to happiness.*) 也可說成：Salute happiness. (要向快樂致敬。)

UNIT 4

Fourth, *freedom is happiness*.

第四，自由就是快樂。

Embrace your freedom.

擁抱你的自由。

Don't hold grudges.

不要懷恨在心。

Just move on.

只要繼續前進。

**

freedom〔'fridəm〕*n.* 自由

happiness〔'hæpinis〕*n.* 快樂；幸福

embrace〔im'bres〕*v.* 擁抱；欣然接受；

　（樂意）利用　hold〔hold〕*v.*（心中）懷有

grudge〔grʌdʒ〕*n.* 怨恨

just〔dʒʌst〕*adv.* 只

move〔muv〕*v.* 移動；走動

move on 繼續前進

Don't stay angry.

不要生悶氣。

Practice forgiving others.

要原諒別人。

Practice letting go.

要學會放下。

** ——————————————

stay〔ste〕*v.* 保持

angry〔'æŋgrɪ〕*adj.* 生氣的

practice〔'præktɪs〕*v.* 練習；實行

forgive〔fə'gɪv〕*v.* 原諒

let go 放開；鬆手；放下（ = *let it go* ）

Make a change.

做出改變。

Change your attitude.

改變態度。

You'll gain freedom.

重獲自由。

**

change〔tʃendʒ〕*n. v.* 改變
make a change 做出改變
attitude〔'ætə,tjud〕*n.* 態度
gain〔gen〕*v.* 獲得
freedom〔'fridəm〕*n.* 自由

BOOK 1・PART 2

【Unit 4 背景說明】

Fourth, *freedom is happiness*. 句中的 Fourth 和 freedom 都是 f 開頭。不要懷恨，不要生氣，放下才能獲得心靈的自由。

Embrace your freedom. (要擁抱你的自由。) 也可說成：Appreciate your liberty. (要重視你的自由。) Make use of your freedom. (要利用你的自由。)

Don't hold grudges. (不要懷恨在心。) 也可說成：Don't be resentful. (不要充滿怨恨。) Don't be bitter. (不要充滿憤怒。)

Just move on. (只要繼續前進。) 在此指「要克服負面情緒，忘掉不愉快的經驗。」也可說成：Just get over it. (就把它忘了吧。) Forget about it. (算了吧。) Put it behind you. (把它拋諸腦後。)

Don't stay angry. (不要一直生氣。) 也可說成：Forgive and forget. (【諺】既往不咎。) Let bygones be bygones. (【諺】過去的就讓它過去；既往不咎。)

Practice forgiving others. 要原諒別人。
(= *Forgive others*. = *Pardon others*. = *Excuse others*.)

> **practice** + 動名詞
> ①練習… ②實行…【可用來加強語氣】

Practice letting go. （要學會放下。）也可説成：
Let it go. （放手吧。）Forget about it. （算了；別再提了。）

Make a change. 要做出改變。(= *Change*.) 也
可説成：Do something different. （要做不同的事。）

Change your attitude. （要改變你的態度。）也
可説成：Have a different attitude. （要有不同的態度。）Have a different mindset. （要有不同的心態。）

You'll gain freedom. （你會獲得自由。）也可説
成：You'll be freer. （你會更自由。）

UNIT **5**

Fifth, you need to *exercise*.
第五，你需要運動。

Walk in nature.
要走進大自然。

Increase your pace.
加快你的步伐。

Take big steps.
要邁開大步走。

** ———————————————

exercise〔'ɛksə͵saɪz〕v. 運動
walk〔wɔk〕v. 行走；散步
nature〔'netʃə〕n. 大自然
increase〔ɪn'kris〕v. 增加
pace〔pes〕n. 步調；速度
step〔stɛp〕n. 一步　　*take a step* 走一步
a big step 一大步

Stretch every muscle.

伸展肌肉。

Hold each stretch.

保持伸展。

Make it routine.

養成習慣。

**

stretch〔strɛtʃ〕*v. n.* 伸展

muscle〔'mʌsḷ〕*n.* 肌肉

hold〔hold〕*v.* 保持；維持

make〔mek〕*v.* 使成為

routine〔ru'tin〕*adj.* 日常的；定期的；

例行的　*n.* 例行公事；慣例

Break a sweat.
要汗流浹背。

Increase your circulation.
要增加循環。

Strengthen your immunity.
強化免疫力。

**

break〔brek〕*v.* 打破;開始 (= *begin*; *start*)

sweat〔swɛt〕*n.* 汗;流汗

break a sweat 汗流浹背

increase〔ɪnˈkris〕*v.* 增加

circulation〔ˌsɝkjəˈleʃən〕*n.* 循環

strengthen〔ˈstrɛŋθən〕*v.* 加強

immunity〔ɪˈmjunətɪ〕*n.* 免疫力

【Unit 5 背景說明】

__Fifth__, you need to __e__xercise. 記憶密碼：
Fifth 和第五個字母 e 相呼應。運動會給你帶來
快樂。

Walk in nature.（要在大自然中散步。）也可說
　成：Go for a walk in a natural place.（要
　去自然風景區散步。）(= *Take a walk in a
　natural place.*)

Increase your pace. 要增加你的步調，也就是
　「要加快你的步伐。」也可說成：Walk faster.
　（走快一點。）Go faster.（要快點前進。）

Take big steps. 要邁開大步走。(= *Take large
　strides. = Take long strides.*)

Stretch every muscle.（要伸展每一條肌肉。）
　也可說成：Stretch all of your muscles.（要
　伸展你所有的肌肉。）Stretch all over.（要伸
　展全身。）

Hold each stretch. 要保持每一個伸展姿勢。
(= *Maintain each stretch.*) 也可説成：Keep
stretching. (要持續伸展。)

Make it routine. 要使它成爲慣例，也就是「要
養成習慣。」(= *Make it a habit.*) 也可説成：
Make it part of your life. (使它成爲你生活的
一部分。) Do it every time. (要每次都做。)
Do it regularly. (要定期地做。)

Break a sweat. 要開始流汗；要汗流浹背。
(= *Start to sweat.*) 也可説成：Perspire. (要
流汗。) Start to perspire. (要開始流汗。)

Increase your circulation. 要增加你的循環。
(= *Boost your circulation.*) 也可説成：Get
your heart pumping. (要使你的心臟像幫浦似
地持續上下跳動。)

Strengthen your immunity. 要強化你的免疫
力。(= *Boost your immunity.*) 也可説成：
Make your immune system stronger. (要
使你的免疫系統更強大。)

UNIT 6

Sixth, *see the world.*

第六，要看看世界。

Take a trip.

出門去旅行。

Take a journey.

展開新旅程。

Travel somewhere new.

旅行新地方。

** ——————————————

trip〔trɪp〕*n.* 旅行

take a trip 去旅行（= *go on a trip*）

journey〔ˈdʒɝnɪ〕*n.* 旅行；旅程

travel〔ˈtrævḷ〕*v.* 旅行；在…旅行；遊遍

somewhere〔ˈsʌmˌhwɛr〕*adv.*（在）某處

Join a tour.

參加旅行團。

Explore other cultures.

探索它文化。

See unusual places.

尋奇異之地。

** ───────────────

join〔dʒɔɪn〕v. 加入；參加
tour〔tʊr〕n. 旅行
explore〔ɪk'splor〕v. 探索
other〔'ʌðɚ〕adj. 其他的
culture〔'kʌltʃɚ〕n. 文化
unusual〔ʌn'juʒʊəl〕adj. 不尋常的

Open your mind.

可敞開心扉。

Expand your worldview.

拓展世界觀。

Create priceless memories.

創無價記憶。

**

open〔'opən〕*v.* 打開；使（思想等）開闊

mind〔maɪnd〕*n.* 心；精神；頭腦；想法

expand〔ɪk'spænd〕*v.* 擴大；拓展

worldview〔'wɜld‚vju〕*n.* 世界觀

create〔krɪ'et〕*v.* 創造

priceless〔'praɪslɪs〕*adj.* 無價的

memory〔'mɛmərɪ〕*n.* 記憶；回憶

【Unit 6 背景說明】

***Sixth**, **see** the world.* 背誦技巧：<u>S</u>ixth 和 <u>s</u>ee 都是 S 開頭。到新的地方去旅行，可以讓你得到快樂。

Take a trip. 要去旅行。(= ***Take a journey***. = *Go on a trip*. = *Go on a journey*.) 也可説成：Go on a vacation. (要去度假。) Go somewhere. (要去某個地方。)

Travel somewhere new. (要去新的地方旅行；要去沒去過的地方。) 也可説成：Go somewhere you've never been before. (要去你以前從未去過的地方。)

Join a tour. (要參加旅行團。) 也可説成：Sign up for a tour. (要報名參加旅行團。) Take a guided tour. (要參加有導遊的旅行團。)

Explore other cultures. (要探索其他的文化。) 也可説成：Investigate a different culture. (要調查不同的文化。) Learn about another culture. (要了解另一個文化。)

***See unusual places*.**（要看看不尋常的地方。）
也可說成：Visit some uncommon places.
（要去一些不尋常的地方。）Visit some
extraordinary places.（要去一些特別的地方。）

***Open your mind*.**（可敞開心扉。）也可說成：
Be open-minded.（可心胸開闊。）Be
accepting of new ideas.（會願意接受新的想
法。）(= *Accept new ideas*.)

***Expand your worldview*.**（可以拓展你的世界
觀。）也可說成：Broaden your view.（可以
拓展你的眼界。）(= *Broaden your mind*.)

***Create priceless memories*.**（可以創造無價的
回憶。）也可說成：Have memorable
experiences.（可以有難忘的經驗。）Do
memorable things.（可以做令人難忘的事。）

UNIT 7

<u>Seventh</u>, <u>s</u>eek opportunities to try new things.

第七，尋求機會嘗試新事物。

Take a risk.

冒險一試。

Take a chance.

勇於冒險。

Take a leap.

勇往直前。

** ───────────────

seek〔sik〕*v.* 尋求

opportunity〔͵ɑpɚˈtjunətɪ〕*n.* 機會

risk〔rɪsk〕*n.* 風險；危險　***take a risk*** 冒險

take a chance 冒險　leap〔lip〕*n.* 跳躍

take a leap 大膽試一試；踏出勇敢的一步；

放手一搏【源自 take a leap of faith（信仰之

躍），表示出乎信仰某事而做出大膽、冒險、

不計後果的舉動】

Change your routine.

要改變慣例。

Spread your wings.

要展翅高飛。

Pursue happiness boldly.

大膽追幸福。

** ———————————————

change〔tʃendʒ〕*v.* 改變

routine〔ruˊtin〕*n.* 例行公事；慣例

spread〔sprɛd〕*v.* 張開；展開

wing〔wɪŋ〕*n.* 翅膀

spread one's wings 展翅高飛；初試身手

pursue〔pɚˊsu〕*v.* 追求

happiness〔ˊhæpɪnɪs〕*n.* 快樂；幸福

boldly〔ˊboldlɪ〕*adv.* 大膽地；勇敢地

Seek new experiences.

尋求新經驗。

Explore the unknown.

探索未知事。

Risk brings reward.

冒險有回報。

**

---

seek〔sik〕v. 尋求

experience〔ɪkˈspɪrɪəns〕n. 經驗

explore〔ɪkˈsplor〕v. 探索；探險

unknown〔ʌnˈnon〕adj. 未知的

the unknown 未知的事物

　（= *unknown things*）

risk〔rɪsk〕n. 冒險

bring〔brɪŋ〕v. 帶來

reward〔rɪˈwɔrd〕n. 報酬；獎賞

【Unit 7 背景說明】

Seventh, *seek opportunities to try new things*.
記憶密碼：Seventh 和 seek 都是 S 開頭。冒險、嘗試
新經驗，都會給你帶來快樂。

Take a risk. 要冒險。(=*Take a chance*. = *Take a leap*.)

Change your routine.（要改變慣例。）也可說成：
Break your routine.（要打破慣例。）Do something
different.（要做點不一樣的事。）*Spread your
wings*.（要展翅高飛。）也可說成：Start to do new/
interesting things.（要開始做新的/有趣的事。）

Pursue happiness boldly.（要勇敢追求快樂。）也可說
成：Make happiness your priority.（要優先考慮自
己的快樂。）

Seek new experiences.（要尋求新的經驗。）也可說成：
Look for new things to try.（要尋找新事物來嘗試。）

Explore the unknown.（要探索未知的事物。）也可說
成：Do something you've never done before.
（要做你以前從未做過的事。）

Risk brings reward.（冒險會有獎賞；冒險會有回報。）
也可說成：If you take a risk, you will gain
something.（如果你冒險，你就會有收穫。）

BOOK 1・PART 2

UNIT **8**

Eighth, *everyone needs rest.*

第八，每個人都需要休息。

Remember to relax.

記得放鬆。

Recharge your body.

身體充電。

Reset your mind.

重啓思維。

** ————————

rest〔rɛst〕*n.* 休息

remember〔rɪ'mɛmbɚ〕*v.* 記得

relax〔rɪ'læks〕*v.* 放鬆

recharge〔ri'tʃɑrdʒ〕*v.* 給…再充電

body〔'bɑdɪ〕*n.* 身體

reset〔ri'sɛt〕*v.* 重置；重新設定

mind〔maɪnd〕*n.* 心；精神；頭腦；想法

Take hot baths.

洗熱水澡。

Soak your body.

泡泡身體。

Sweat it out.

出一身汗。

** ——————————————————

bath〔bæθ〕*n.* 洗澡

take a bath 洗澡；泡澡

soak〔sok〕*v.* 浸泡

body〔'bɑdɪ〕*n.* 身體

sweat〔swɛt〕*v.* 流汗；使出汗

sweat it out 揮汗如雨；做高強度的
　運動鍛鍊身體

Chat with friends.

和友暢聊。

Call loved ones.

打給愛人。

Talk it out.

說出心事。

**

---

chat〔tʃæt〕*v.* 聊天

call〔kɔl〕*v.* 打電話給

loved ones 親人；心愛的人

　（*= people that you love*）

talk out 透徹地討論；把（心裡話等）

　說出來

【Unit 8 背景說明】

Eighth, everyone needs rest. 記憶密碼：
<u>E</u>ighth 和 <u>e</u>veryone 都是 e 開頭。當你心情不好的時候，要休息。累了就要休息，泡個熱水澡，流一些汗，和好朋友聊聊天，都會讓你身心愉快。

Remember to relax.（記得要放鬆。）也可説成：
Don't forget to unwind.（不要忘了要放鬆。）
Don't forget to take a rest.（不要忘了要休息一下。）(= *Don't forget to take a break.*)

Recharge your body.（要替你的身體再次充電。）也可説成：Recharge your batteries.（要恢復體力。）Restore your energy.（要恢復你的活力。）

Reset your mind.（要重啓你的頭腦。）也可説成：Refresh your mind.（要提神醒腦。）Clear your mind.（要使你的頭腦清楚。）

Take hot baths. 要洗熱水澡。(= *Bathe in hot water.*) 也可説成：Bathe in hot water regularly.（要定期洗熱水澡。）

Soak your body.（要浸泡你的身體。）也可說成：Soak in a hot tub.（要在裝滿熱水的浴缸中浸泡。）

Sweat it out.（要揮汗如雨。）也可說成：Sweat a lot.（要流很多汗。）Perspire.（要流汗。）

Chat with friends.（要和朋友聊天。）也可說成：Talk to your friends.（要和你的朋友談話。）

Call loved ones.（打電話給你心愛的人。）也可說成：Call your family.（打電話給你的家人。）Call your close friends.（打電話給你的密友。）

Talk it out.（把心裡的話說出來。）也可說成：Talk about what is bothering you.（談論令你困擾的事。）Talk about what's on your mind.（要談論你的心事。）

UNIT **9**

Finally, but most importantly,
do good deeds every day.

最後，但最重要的是，要每天做好事。

Do good daily.

天天做好事。

Be kind always.

時時要善良。

Help others out.

常常助他人。

** ─────────────

most importantly 最重要的是

deed〔did〕*n.* 行爲

do good deeds 做好事　　*do good* 做好事

daily〔'delɪ〕*adv.* 每天 (= *every day*)

kind〔kaɪnd〕*adj.* 好心的；親切的；仁慈的

help sb. out 幫助某人度過難關 (= *help sb.*)

Share your abundance.

分享你的財富。

Share your blessings.

分享你的幸福。

Assist with generosity.

慷慨幫助別人。

**

share〔ʃɛr〕v. 分享

abundance〔ə'bʌndəns〕n. 豐富；大量
【在此指「你額外擁有的東西」(the extra
things you have)】

blessing〔'blɛsɪŋ〕n. 幸福；幸運的事

assist〔ə'sɪst〕v. 協助；協助他人
(= assist others)

generosity〔,dʒɛnə'rɑsətɪ〕n. 慷慨；大方

Offer kind words.

要會說好話。

Offer kind gestures.

做善意舉動。

Spread good vibes.

散播正能量。

** ——————

offer〔'ɔfɚ〕v. 提供；給予；出示

kind〔kaɪnd〕adj. 仁慈的；親切的；好心的

words〔wɝdz〕n. pl. 言詞；話

gesture〔'dʒɛstʃɚ〕n. 姿態；(心意的) 表示
  (= small acts)　　spread〔sprɛd〕v. 散播

vibes〔vaɪbz〕n. pl. (給人的) 印象；

　　情緒上的激動；氣氛【源自 vibrations 】

good vibes　正能量（ = *good thoughts*

　 = *positive vibes* = *positive energy*

　 = *positivity* ）

【Unit 9 背景説明】

我每天背這九句話，潛移默化，讓我進步又快樂。

Do good daily. 要每天做好事。(= *Do nice things every day.* = *Do something kind every day.*)

Be kind always. 要總是很善良。(= *Always be kind.* = *Always be nice.*) 也可説成：Always be considerate. (要總是很體貼。)

Help others out. 要幫助別人。(= *Help other people.* = *Assist other people.*)

Share your abundance. (要分享你的財富。) 也可説成：Share what you have. (要分享你所擁有的。) Be generous with your things. (要對你的東西很大方。)

Share your blessings. (要分享你的幸福。) 也可説成：Share your good fortune. (要分享

你的好運。）Be generous with what you have.（對於你所擁有的東西很慷慨。）

Assist with generosity. 要慷慨地協助他人。（ = *Help other people by being generous*.）

Offer kind words. 要提供好話，也就是「要說好話。」（ = *Say nice things*.）也可說成：Say compassinoate things.（要說深表同情的話。）

Offer kind gestures. （要做善意舉動。）也可說成：Do nice things.（要做好事。）Do compassionate things.（要做有同情心的事。）

Spread good vibes. 要散播正能量。（ = *Spread positive energy*.）也可說成：Create a good atmosphere.（要創造好的氛圍。）

【**How to Be Happy** 結尾語】

Thank you for listening.
謝謝你們的傾聽。

I hope it helps.
我希望演講的內容會有幫助。

Enjoy the day!
好好享受今天！

** listen〔ˈlɪsn̩〕*v.* 傾聽

　　hope〔hop〕*v.* 希望

　　help〔hɛlp〕*v.* 有幫助

　　enjoy〔ɪnˈdʒɔɪ〕*v.* 享受

【英語演講】

How to Be Happy

Hi, everyone.
Need more happiness?
Here are nine tips.

PART 2・Unit 1~9
英文錄音QR碼

First off, **_a_***dvance to be happy.*

Advance in life.
Make progress daily.
Every step counts.

Never stop improving.
Enhance your skills.
Grow your business.

Fulfill your desires.
Feel more successful.
Make life meaningful.

Second, *_s_**ocial connections bring happiness.*

Keep good company.
Have close friendships.
Have meaningful relationships.

BOOK 1・PART 2

Cherish loved ones.
Hold family close.
Value friends dearly.

Friendships bring happiness.
Improve your health.
Increase your lifespan.

Third, *celebrate when you can.*

Spend time celebrating.
Grasp every opportunity.
Relax and enjoy.

Throw a party.
Have a feast.
Have a banquet.

Celebrate your achievements.
Celebrate with friends.
Toast to happiness.

Fourth, *freedom is happiness.*

Embrace your freedom.
Don't hold grudges.
Just move on.

Don't stay angry.
Practice forgiving others.
Practice letting go.

Make a change.
Change your attitude.
You'll gain freedom.

Fifth, *you need to ***e***xercise.*

Walk in nature.
Increase your pace.
Take big steps.

Stretch every muscle.
Hold each stretch.
Make it routine.

Break a sweat.
Increase your circulation.
Strengthen your immunity.

Sixth, *****s****ee the world.*

Take a trip.
Take a journey.
Travel somewhere new.

Join a tour.
Explore other cultures.
See unusual places.

Open your mind.
Expand your worldview.
Create priceless memories.

Seventh, *seek opportunities to try new things.*

Take a risk.
Take a chance.
Take a leap.

Change your routine.
Spread your wings.
Pursue happiness boldly.

Seek new experiences.
Explore the unknown.
Risk brings reward.

Eighth, *everyone needs rest.*

Remember to relax.
Recharge your body.
Reset your mind.

Take hot baths.
Soak your body.
Sweat it out.

Chat with friends.
Call loved ones.
Talk it out.

Finally, but most importantly, do good deeds
every day.

Do good daily.
Be kind always.
Help others out.

Share your abundance.
Share your blessings.
Assist with generosity.

Offer kind words.
Offer kind gestures.
Spread good vibes.

Thank you for listening.
I hope it helps.
Enjoy the day!

BOOK 1・PART 2

【作文範例】

How to Be Happy

It's easy to be happy if you know how. ***First of all***, you have to advance in order to be happy. Make progress in your life every day and you will feel a sense of achievement. ***Then*** celebrate your achievements. Throw a party and celebrate with your friends. It's important to be social. Spend time with your loved ones and close friends whenever you can. Never stay angry with anyone. ***Instead***, practice letting go of negative emotions.

In addition, be open to new things. Change your routine and take a few risks. A great way to do that is to travel. Join a tour and explore another culture. It's vital to stay active by getting enough exercise, but don't forget to rest as well. You can take a hot bath or go to a sauna.

Relaxing will help you to recharge both your body and your mind. *Finally*, *but most importantly*, do a good deed every day. Always be kind and help others out. If you can do all of this, you are sure to be a happy person.

【翻譯】

如何快樂

如果你知道方法，要快樂很容易。首先，你必須進步，才會快樂。在生活中，每天都進步，你就會有成就感。然後要慶祝你的成就。舉辦宴會和朋友一起慶祝。善於交際很重要。一有機會，就要花時間和親人及密友相處。絕不要一直對任何人生氣，而是要擺脫負面的情緒。

此外，要樂於接受新事物。改變你的慣例，去冒一些風險，想這樣做，有一個很棒的方法，就是旅行。參加旅行團，探索另一個文化。有足夠的運動來活動身體非常重要，但也不要忘記休息。你可以泡個熱水澡，或是去洗三溫暖。放鬆能幫助你的身心恢復活力。最後一項要點是，要日行一善。一定要心地善良，並樂於助人。如果你能做到這一切，你一定會是一個快樂的人。

BOOK 1・PART 2

PART 2 總整理

PART 2・Unit 1~9
中英文錄音QR碼

Unit 1

Advance in life.
生活中進步。
Make progress daily.
每天要進步。
Every step counts.
步步都重要。

Never stop improving.
不停進步。
Enhance your skills.
增強技能。
Grow your business.
發展事業。

Fulfill your desires.
實現願望。
Feel more successful.
感受成功。
Make life meaningful.
意義人生。

Unit 2

Keep good company.
要結交益友。
Have close friendships.
有親密友誼。
Have meaningful
    relationships. 有重要關係。

Cherish loved ones.
珍惜所愛之人。
Hold family close.
保持家人親密。
Value friends dearly.
珍視朋友如金。

Friendships bring
    happiness. 友誼帶來快樂。
Improve your health.
改善你的健康。
Increase your lifespan.
增加你的壽命。

Unit 3

Spend time celebrating.
偷閒慶祝。
Grasp every opportunity.
抓住機會。
Relax and enjoy. 放鬆享受。

Throw a party. 舉行派對。
Have a feast. 大吃一頓。
Have a banquet. 大快朵頤。

Celebrate your
    achievements. 慶祝成就。
Celebrate with friends.
和友同慶。
Toast to happiness.
舉杯而樂。

Unit 4

Embrace your freedom.
擁抱你的自由。
Don't hold grudges.
不要懷恨在心。
Just move on.
只要繼續前進。

Don't stay angry.
不要生悶氣。
Practice forgiving others.
要原諒別人。
Practice letting go.
要學會放下。

Make a change.
做出改變。
Change your attitude.
改變態度。
You'll gain freedom.
重獲自由。

Unit 5

Walk in nature.
要走進大自然。
Increase your pace.
加快你的步伐。
Take big steps.
要邁開大步走。

Stretch every muscle.
伸展肌肉。
Hold each stretch.
保持伸展。
Make it routine. 養成習慣。

Break a sweat. 要汗流浹背。
Increase your circulation.
要增加循環。
Strengthen your
　immunity. 強化免疫力。

Unit 6

Take a trip. 出門去旅行。
Take a journey.
展開新旅程。
Travel somewhere new.
旅行新地方。

Join a tour. 參加旅行團。
Explore other cultures.
探索它文化。
See unusual places.
尋奇異之地。

Open your mind.
可敞開心扉。
Expand your worldview.
拓展世界觀。
Create priceless
　memories. 創無價記憶。

BOOK 1・PART 2

Unit 7

Take a risk.
冒險一試。
Take a chance.
勇於冒險。
Take a leap.
勇往直前。

Change your routine.
要改變慣例。
Spread your wings.
要展翅高飛。
Pursue happiness boldly.
大膽追幸福。

Seek new experiences.
尋求新經驗。
Explore the unknown.
探索未知事。
Risk brings reward.
冒險有回報。

Unit 8

Remember to relax.
記得放鬆。
Recharge your body.
身體充電。
Reset your mind.
重啓思維。

Take hot baths. 洗熱水澡。
Soak your body. 泡泡身體。
Sweat it out. 出一身汗。

Chat with friends.
和友暢聊。
Call loved ones. 打給愛人。
Talk it out. 說出心事。

Unit 9

Do good daily.
天天做好事。
Be kind always.
時時要善良。
Help others out.
常常助他人。

Share your abundance.
分享你的財富。
Share your blessings.
分享你的幸福。
Assist with generosity.
慷慨幫助別人。

Offer kind words.
要會說好話。
Offer kind gestures.
做善意舉動。
Spread good vibes.
散播正能量。

BOOK 1 \\ PART 3

How to Be Popular
如何受人歡迎

PART 3・Unit 1~9
英文錄音QR碼

【開場白】

> *Hi, friends.*
> 嗨,朋友們。
>
> *Want to be popular?*
> 想要受人歡迎嗎?
>
> *Here is some advice.*
> 這裡有一些建議。

** popular〔'pɑpjələ〕 *adj.* 受歡迎的
Want to be popular?
= Do you want to be popular?

UNIT ①

In the first place, *be a people person.*

首先，要做一個善於社交的人。

Greet others first.

先打招呼。

Give a smile.

展現笑容。

Start a conversation.

展開對話。

** ————————————

in the first place 首先 (= *first* = *first of all*)
people person 善於交際的人；與他人相處融洽
   的人　　greet〔grit〕*v.* 迎接；和⋯打招呼
first〔fɜst〕*adv.* 先　　smile〔smaɪl〕*n.* 微笑
give a smile 露出笑容；展現笑容
start〔start〕*v.* 開始
conversation〔ˌkɑnvəˈseʃən〕*n.* 對話

Don't be shy.

不要害羞。

Chat with people.

要會聊天。

Make a connection.

建立關係。

** ————————————————

shy〔ʃaɪ〕*adj.* 害羞的

chat〔tʃæt〕*v.* 聊天

connection〔kə'nɛkʃən〕*n.* 關連；關係

make a connection 建立關係

Say, "Hi there."

說：「嗨，你好。」

"How are you?"

「你好嗎？」

"How you doing?"

「你好嗎？」

**

hi〔haɪ〕*interj.* 嗨

hi there 嗨（= *hi*）

do〔du〕*v.* 進展

How you doing? 你好嗎？

（= *How're you doing?* = *How are you?*）

BOOK 1・PART 3

【Unit 1 背景說明】

　　在電梯中看到鄰居，我會先打招呼，笑一笑，開始對話。我們每天都有機會認識新朋友，他們或許是無價之寶，要好好把握這個機會。

Greet others first. 要先和別人打招呼。
(= *Say hello first.*)

Give a smile. (要展現笑容。) 也可說成：Smile.
(要微笑。) Show them your smile. (要對他們展現笑容。)

Start a conversation. 要開始對話。(= *Initiate a conversation.* = *Strike up a conversation.*)

Don't be shy. (不要害羞。) 也可說成：Don't be timid. (不要膽怯。) Don't be fearful.
(不要害怕。) Don't be introverted. (不要太內向。)

Chat with people. (要和別人聊天。) 也可說成：Talk to people. (要和別人說話。)

Make a connection. 要建立關係。(＝*Establish a relationship.*) 也可說成：Find something in common. (要找到共同點。)

Say, "***Hi there.***" 要說：「嗨，你好。」
(＝*Say,* "*Hi.*" ＝*Say,* "*Hello.*")

How you doing? (你好嗎？) 是慣用句，源自：How're you doing? (你好嗎？) 也可說成：***How are you?*** (你好嗎？) How are you getting along? (你近況如何？) (＝*How are things going with you?* ＝*How's everything?* ＝*How's it going?*) What's up? (你好嗎？) (＝*What's new?* ＝*What's happening?*)

【劉毅老師的話】

Memorize the sentences.
(要背句子。)
Rehearse them daily. (每天練習。)
Use them often. (常常使用。)

UNIT 2

Second, being polite is essential.

第二，有禮貌很重要。

Always be polite.

保持禮貌。

Have good manners.

有好風度。

Never be rude.

絕不無禮。

** ─────────────

polite〔pəˈlaɪt〕*adj.* 有禮貌的

essential〔əˈsɛnʃəl, ɪˈsɛnʃəl〕*adj.* 必要的；
非常重要的

always〔ˈɔlwez〕*adv.* 總是；一直

manners〔ˈmænəz〕*n. pl.* 禮貌

never〔ˈnɛvə〕*adv.* 絕不

rude〔rud〕*adj.* 粗魯的；無禮的

Hold the door.

為人開門。

Be on time.

準時赴約。

Apologize for mistakes.

錯時道歉。

**

hold〔hold〕v. 使保持;維持;支撐
hold the door 要撐著門;要讓門開著
on time 準時
apologize〔əˈpɑləˌdʒaɪz〕v. 道歉
apologize for 為了…而道歉
mistake〔məˈstek〕n. 錯誤

Use people's names.

要說出人名。

Say, "Hello, Pat."

說：「哈囉，派特。」

"Thank you, Pat."

「謝謝你，派特。」

** ───────────────

use〔juz〕*v.* 使用；說

name〔nem〕*n.* 名字

hello〔hə'lo〕*interj.* 哈囉

Pat〔pæt〕*n.* 派特

【Unit 2 背景説明】

要讓別人喜歡你，一定要有禮貌。粗暴一次，你的形象就會受損。__*Second*__, __*being polite is essential*__. Second（第二）和第二個字母 b 相呼應。

Always be polite. 一定要有禮貌。(= *Always be courteous*.)

Have good manners. 要有好的禮貌。(= *Be well-mannered*.)

Never be rude. 絕不要粗魯無禮。(= *Never be impolite*.)

Hold the door. (要讓門開著。) 也可説成：Hold the door open for people behind you. (要爲在你身後的人撐著門。)

Be on time. 要準時。(= *Be punctual*.) 也可説成：Don't be late. (不要遲到。)

Apologize for mistakes. (要爲了錯誤而道歉。) 也可説成：Say you're sorry when you make a mistake. (當你犯錯時，要說對不起。)

Use people's names. 要說出人名。(= *Say people' names*.) 也可説成：Address people by name. (要稱呼別人的名字。)

UNIT ❸

<u>Third</u>, <u>c</u>ompliment as much as you can.

第三，要儘量稱讚。

Often compliment others.

要常常誇獎人。

Say positive words.

要說正面的話。

Everyone likes compliments.

人人愛被稱讚。

**

compliment〔'kɑmplə‚mɛnt〕*v.* 稱讚
〔'kɑmpləmənt〕*n.*
as…as one can 儘量…；儘可能…
(= *as…as possible*)
positive〔'pɑzətɪv〕*adj.* 正面的；積極的
words〔wɝdz〕*n. pl.* 言詞；話
like〔laɪk〕*v.* 喜歡

Praise a friend.

稱讚友人。

Commend a stranger.

讚美生人。

Say something nice.

要說好話。

**

praise〔prez〕*v.* 稱讚

commend〔kə'mɛnd〕*v.* 稱讚（ = *praise*
= *compliment* ）

stranger〔'strendʒɚ〕*n.* 陌生人

nice〔naɪs〕*adj.* 好的

say something nice 說好話

Build others' confidence.

給人信心。

Make others happy.

使人快樂。

They'll like you.

人見人愛。

**

build〔bɪld〕*v.* 建立

others〔'ʌðɚz〕*pron.* 別人

confidence〔'kɑnfədəns〕*n.* 自信；信心

make〔mek〕*v.* 使

like〔laɪk〕*v.* 喜歡

【Unit 3 背景説明】

不要忘記，要常常稱讚，稱讚不花一毛錢，卻會給你帶來無價的回報。看到認識或不認識的人，有機會就要稱讚，誰都喜歡稱讚他的人。

Often compliment others. 要常常稱讚別人。
(= *Often praise others.*) 也可説成：Be generous with compliments. (要大方地稱讚。)

Say positive words. 要說正面的話；要說好話。
(= *Say nice things.* = *Say good things.*)

Everyone likes compliments. (每個人都喜歡稱讚。) 也可説成：Everybody likes to be praised. (每個人都喜歡被稱讚。) Everyone likes to hear positive things. (每個人都喜歡聽好話。)

Praise a friend. 要稱讚朋友。(= *Give a friend a compliment.*)

Commend a stranger. 要稱讚陌生人。(= *Praise a stranger*.) 也可說成 : Give praise to people you don't know. (要稱讚你不認識的人。)

Say something nice. 要說好話。(= *Say kind words*.) 也可說成 : Say something complimentary. (要說一些稱讚的話。)

Build others' confidence. (要建立別人的自信。) 也可說成 : Bolster others' confidence. (要加強別人的信心。) Make other people more confident. (要使別人更有自信。)

Make others happy. 要讓別人快樂。(= *Please other people*.) 也可說成 : Bring joy to others. (要帶給別人快樂。)

They'll like you. (他們會喜歡你。) 也可說成 : They'll appreciate you. (他們會欣賞你。) They'll think highly of you. (他們會對你評價很高。)

BOOK 1 · PART 3

(UNIT **4**

Fourth, dress yourself well.

第四，要好好地裝扮自己。

Dress for success.

為成功衣著。

Dress to impress.

為印象打扮。

Style is everything.

風格是一切。

** ————————————

dress〔drɛs〕*v.* 給…穿衣；穿衣；打扮

success〔sək'sɛs〕*n.* 成功

impress〔ɪm'prɛs〕*v.* 使印象深刻

style〔staɪl〕*n.* 風格；造型

everything〔'ɛvrɪˌθɪŋ〕*pron.* 一切事物；

最重要的東西

Clothing speaks volumes.

穿著識人。

Show your character.

看出性格。

Show your personality.

看出個性。

**─────────────────

clothing〔ˈkloðɪŋ〕*n.* 衣服【集合名詞】

speak〔spik〕*v.* 顯示;傳達;說 (= *say*)

volume〔ˈvɑljəm〕*n.* 音量;容量;

(書) 一冊;(*pl.*) 大量;許多 (= *a lot*)

show〔ʃo〕*v.* 展示;表現

character〔ˈkærɪktə〕*n.* 性格

personality〔ˌpɜsn̩ˈælətɪ〕*n.* 個性

Invest in quality.

投資品質。

Quality over quantity.

質重於量。

Keep it classy.

保持品味。

** ──────────────

invest〔ɪn'vɛst〕*v.* 投資 *< in >*

quality〔'kwɑlətɪ〕*n.* 品質

over〔'ovɚ〕*prep.* 比…重要

quantity〔'kwɑntətɪ〕*n.* 數量

keep〔kip〕*v.* 使保持

classy〔'klæsɪ〕*adj.* 時髦的；時尚的；
漂亮的；別緻的

【Unit 4 背景説明】

「人要衣裝，佛要金裝。」你只要花費你財產的萬分之一的錢，買到品質好的衣服，會給自己帶來快樂，因而得到更多的財富。買貴的衣服會穿很久，還是划得來。

Dress for success. 要爲了成功而裝扮。(= *Dress to succeed.*)

Dress to impress. 穿著要令人印象深刻。(= *Dress to impress others.*) 也可説成 : Dress in a way that will make a good impression on other people. (穿著打扮要令人留下好的印象。)

Style is everything. (風格很重要。) 也可説成 : Being stylish is important. (時髦很重要。) The way you look is very important. (你看起來的樣子很重要。) How you dress is very important. (你的穿著打扮很重要。)

Clothing speaks volumes. 衣服能説很多話，引申爲「衣服能傳達許多訊息。」也可説成 : Your clothes say a lot about you. (你的衣服透露很多關於你的訊息。)

Show your character. (展現你的性格。) 也可說成：Express your character. (表達你的性格。) (= *Express who you are*.)

Show your personality. (展現你的個性。) 也可說成：Express your personality. (表達你的個性。) (= *Express who you are*.)

Invest in quality. (要投資品質。) 也可說成：Buy good quality things. (要買品質好的東西。) Pay more for good clothing. (要多付錢買好衣服。)

Quality over quantity. 質比量重要。(= *Quality is more important than quantity*.) 是慣用句。也可說成：The quality of your clothes is more important than how much clothing you have. (你的衣服的品質比你擁有多少衣服更重要。) It's better to have a few good pieces than a lot of cheap clothes. (擁有幾件好衣服比有很多便宜的衣服要好。)

Keep it classy. (要保持品味。) 也可說成：Be elegant. (要優雅。) Be sophisticated. (要很有品味。) Be refined. (要很文雅。)

【比較】 classic〔ˈklæsɪk〕*adj.* 經典的
　　　　 classical〔ˈklæsɪkḷ〕*adj.* 古典的

UNIT 5

Fifth, enjoy giving.

第五，要樂於付出。

Be generous always.

總是慷慨。

Be generous everywhere.

到處大方。

Generosity is rewarding.

慷慨有報。

** ———————————

enjoy〔ɪn'dʒɔɪ〕*v.* 享受；喜歡

give〔gɪv〕*v.* 給與；付出

generous〔'dʒɛnərəs〕*adj.* 慷慨的；大方的

everywhere〔'ɛvrɪˌhwɛr〕*adv.* 到處

generosity〔ˌdʒɛnə'rɑsətɪ〕*n.* 慷慨；大方

rewarding〔rɪ'wɔrdɪŋ〕*adj.* 有報酬的；值得
做的；有益的

Give a gift.

送個禮物。

Offer your help.

提供幫助。

Sacrifice for others.

為人奉獻。

** ——————————

give〔gɪv〕v. 給與；送給

gift〔gɪft〕n. 禮物

offer〔'ɔfɚ〕v. 提供

help〔hɛlp〕n. 幫助

sacrifice〔'sækrə,faɪs〕v. 犧牲

others〔'ʌðɚz〕pron. 別人

Giving is profitable.

付出有利。

Sharing is beneficial.

分享有益。

Charity pays off.

慈善值得。

**────────────

give〔gɪv〕*v.* 給與；付出

profitable〔'prɑfɪtəbḷ〕*adj.* 有利的

share〔ʃɛr〕*v.* 分享

beneficial〔͵bɛnə'fɪʃəl〕*adj.* 有益的

charity〔'tʃærətɪ〕*n.* 慈善

pay off 取得成功；得到好結果；

　有回報；很值得

【Unit 5 背景説明】

　　人人都喜歡大方的人,小氣鬼大家都避而遠之。小氣、一毛不拔的人,往往吃最大的虧。

Be generous always. 要總是很慷慨。(= *Always be generous*.)

Be generous everywhere. (要到處都慷慨。) 也可説成:Always be charitable. (一定要慈善。)

Generosity is rewarding. (慷慨很值得。) 也可説成:Being generous will make you feel better. (慷慨會使你覺得更好。) (= *It makes you feel good to be generous*.)

Give a gift. (送個禮物。) 也可説成:Give someone a present. (送某人一個禮物。)

Offer your help. (提供幫助。) 也可説成:Be willing to help. (要願意幫忙。)

Sacrifice for others. (要為別人犧牲。) 也可説成:Give something up for the sake of others. (要為了別人放棄某樣東西。)

Giving is profitable. (付出是有利的。) 也可説成:You will profit if you give. (如果你付出,你就會獲利。)

Sharing is beneficial. (分享是有益的。) 也可説成:Sharing helps people. (分享對人們有幫助。)

Charity pays off. 慈善很值得。(= *Charity is worth it*.)

UNIT 6

<u>Sixth</u>, <u>socializing</u> pays off.

第六，交際總會值得。

Attend social events.

參加社交活動。

Go out often.

常常出門社交。

Expand your influence.

擴大你影響力。

**

socialize〔'soʃəl,aɪz〕v. 交際

pay off 得到好結果；很划算；很值得

attend〔ə'tɛnd〕v. 參加

social〔'soʃəl〕adj. 社交的

event〔ɪ'vɛnt〕n. 事件；大型活動

go out 出門參加社交活動

expand〔ɪk'spænd〕v. 擴大

influence〔'ɪnfluəns〕n. 影響力

Connect with people.

要會與人交流。

Talk to everyone.

要會與人說話。

Make people laugh.

要能引人發笑。

**

connect〔kəˈnɛkt〕*v.* 連接；連結；
　聯繫；建立關係
talk〔tɔk〕*v.* 說話
make〔mek〕*v.* 使
laugh〔læf〕*v.* 笑

Show your confidence.

展現你的自信。

Be absolutely unforgettable.

絕對令人難忘。

Build lasting connections.

建立持久關係。

**

show〔ʃo〕*v.* 展現

confidence〔'kɑnfədəns〕*n.* 自信；信心

absolutely〔'æbsə,lutlɪ〕*adv.* 絕對地；完全地
  (= *wholly* = *completely*)

unforgettable〔,ʌnfə'gɛtəbḷ〕*adj.* 令人難忘的

build〔bɪld〕*v.* 建立

lasting〔'læstɪŋ〕*adj.* 持久的

connection〔kə'nɛkʃən〕*n.* 關係；關聯

【Unit 6 背景説明】

Sixth, *socializing pays off*. 背誦技巧：<u>S</u>ixth 和 <u>s</u>ocializing 都是 S 開頭。不要老待在家裡，要出門參加社交活動，展現自信，想辦法讓別人喜歡你。

Attend social events. 要參加社交活動。(= *Go to social events*.)

Go out often. (要常常出門參加社交活動。) 也可説成：Socialize often. (要常常去交際。)

Expand your influence. (要擴大你的影響力。) 也可説成：Increase your power. (要增加你的力量。) Increase your influence. (要增加你的影響力。)

Connect with people. (要和別人建立關係。) 也可説成：Socialize with others. (要和別人交際。) Get to know people. (要認識別人。)(= *Meet people*.)

Talk to everyone.（要和每個人說話。）也可說成：
Speak to everyone you meet.（要和你見到的每
個人說話。）Chat with everyone.（要和每個人聊
天。）

Make people laugh.（要讓人笑。）也可說成：Be
funny.（要好笑。）Be entertaining.（要令人愉
快。）Be humorous.（要幽默。）

Show your confidence.（要展現你的自信。）也可
說成：Be confident.（要有自信。）Appear
confident.（要看起來有自信。）

Be absolutely unforgettable.（絕對要令人難忘。）
也可說成：Be memorable.（要令人難忘。）

Build lasting connections.（要建立持久的關係。）
也可說成：Establish relationships.（要建立關
係。）Keep in touch with new acquaintances.
（要和新認識的人保持連絡。）

UNIT ❼

<u>Seventh</u>, <u>stay humble</u>.
第七，要保持謙虛。

Always be modest.
永保謙虛。

Always be humble.
務必謙遜。

Live with humility.
謙卑過活。

** ———————————

stay〔ste〕*v.* 保持
humble〔'hʌmbl̩〕*adj.* 謙虛的
modest〔'mɑdɪst〕*adj.* 謙虛的
humility〔hju'mɪlətɪ〕*n.* 謙虛
【比較】humidity〔hju'mɪdətɪ〕*n.* 潮濕
with humility 謙虛地（= *humbly*）

Put others first.

要以人爲重。

Learn from others.

要向人學習。

Don't judge quickly.

不輕易批判。

** ————————————

put…first 把…放在首位

others〔ˈʌðɚz〕*pron.* 別人

learn〔lɜn〕*v.* 學習

judge〔dʒʌdʒ〕*v.* 判斷；評斷

quickly〔ˈkwɪklɪ〕*adv.* 快地

Accept your mistakes.

接受錯誤。

Learn from failures.

失敗中學。

Bragging isn't attractive.

吹噓沒用。

**

accept〔ək'sɛpt〕v. 接受
mistake〔mə'stek〕n. 錯誤
failure〔'feljɚ〕n. 失敗
brag〔bræg〕v. 吹牛；吹噓；自誇
attractive〔ə'træktɪv〕adj. 吸引人的

【Unit 7 背景説明】

見人説人話，見鬼説鬼話，看到流氓，要忍辱負重；看到大人物，要謙虛。

Always be modest. 一定要謙虛。(= *Always be humble.*) 也可説成：Don't show off. (不要炫耀。)

Live with humility. (要謙虛地生活。) 也可説成：Be humble. (要謙虛。) Be unassuming. (不要出風頭。) Don't be proud. (不要驕傲。)

Put others first. (把別人放在第一位。) 也可説成：Put other people before you. (把別人放在你的前面。) Put others' interests first. (把別人的利益放在第一位。) Think of others first. (要先想到別人。)

Learn from others. 要向別人學習。(= *Learn from other people.*)

Don't judge quickly. 不要太快下判斷。(= *Don't be quick to judge.*) 也可説成：Don't be judgmental. (不要動不動就批評人。)

Accept your mistakes. 要接受你的錯誤；要承認你的錯誤。 (= *Recognize your errors.*)

Learn from failures. (要從失敗中學習。) 也可説成：Learn lessons from your mistakes. (要從你的錯誤中學習教訓。)

Bragging isn't attractive. 吹嘘並不吸引人。 (= *Boastfulness is unappealing.*)

UNIT ❽

More importantly, stop arguing
for good.

更重要的是，要永遠停止爭論。

Always avoid arguing.

不要爭吵。

Always avoid drama.

不要激動。

Seek common ground.

尋求共識。

** ————————

argue〔'argju〕*v.* 爭論　　***for good*** 永遠
avoid〔ə'vɔɪd〕*v.* 避免
drama〔'dramə〕*n.* 戲劇；戲劇性場面；小題大作
seek〔sik〕*v.* 尋求
common〔'kamən〕*adj.* 共同的
ground〔graʊnd〕*n.* 立場
common ground 共同立場；共同點

Don't talk back.

不要頂嘴。

Don't take sides.

不要偏袒。

Choose your battles.

慎選戰場。

** ————————————————

talk back 頂嘴

side〔saɪd〕*n.* 邊；面

take sides 偏袒

choose〔tʃuz〕*v.* 選擇

battle〔'bætl̩〕*n.* 戰役

choose your battles 選擇你的戰役；
  慎選戰場

Don't blame others.

不要責備他人。

Don't belittle others.

不要貶低他人。

Find a solution.

尋求解決之道。

**

blame〔blem〕*v.* 責備；責怪
others〔'ʌðɚz〕*pron.* 別人
belittle〔bɪ'lɪtḷ〕*v.* 輕視；小看；貶低
solution〔sə'luʃən〕*n.* 解決之道

【Unit 8 背景説明】

争吵沒有贏家，解決争吵，唯一的方法，就是避開它。沒有人會喜歡愛吵架的人。

Always avoid arguing.（一定要避免争論。）也可說成：Don't argue.（不要争論。）Never argue.（絕不要争論。）

Always avoid drama.（一定要避免小題大作；不要激動。）也可說成：Don't get involved in turmoil.（不要捲入混亂。）（= *Don't get involved in a commotion.*）Don't cause a fuss.（不要小題大作。）（= *Don't make a scene.*）

Seek common ground. 要尋求共識。（= *Try to find something you can agree on.*）也可說成：Find a middle ground.（要找到中間立場；要各讓一步；要妥協。）Compromise.（要妥協。）

Don't talk back. 不要頂嘴。（= *Don't mouth off.*）也可說成：Don't argue.（不要争論。）Don't be rude.（不要無禮。）

Don't take sides. (不要偏袒。) 也可説成：Be neutral. (要中立。) Stay neutral. (要保持中立。) Don't get involved. (不要牽涉在內。)

Choose your battles. 要慎選戰場。(= *Pick your battles.* = *Choose your battles wisely.*) 也可説成：Only argue when you know you can win. (只有當你知道自己能贏時，才爭論。) Save your strength for the important battles. (把你的力量保留給重要的戰役。)

Don't blame others. (不要責備別人。) 也可説成：Don't say that others are responsible for your mistakes. (不要說別人應該爲你的錯誤負責。)

Don't belittle others. (不要小看別人。) 也可説成：Don't disparage others. (不要貶低別人。) (= *Don't put others down.*)

Find a solution. (要找到解決之道。) 也可説成：Find an answer. (要找到解答。) Solve the problem. (要解決問題。)

BOOK 1・PART 3

UNIT ⑨

Most important of all, never ever let your friends suffer losses.

最重要的是，絕對不要讓你的朋友吃虧。

Prevent others' losses.

防人吃虧。

Minimize their pain.

減低痛苦。

Relieve their burden.

減輕負擔。

** —————

never ever 絕不　　suffer〔'sʌfə〕*v.* 遭受
loss〔lɔs〕*n.* 損失
prevent〔prɪ'vɛnt〕*v.* 預防；防止
minimize〔'mɪnə,maɪz〕*v.* 使減至最低
pain〔pen〕*n.* 痛苦
relieve〔rɪ'liv〕*v.* 減輕；舒緩；解圍
burden〔'bɝdn̩〕*n.* 負擔

Help others win.

助人成功。

Lift their spirits.

提振士氣。

Inspire their hope.

激發希望。

**
_____

others〔ˊʌðəz〕*pron.* 別人

win〔wɪn〕*v.* 贏；獲勝；成功

lift〔lɪft〕*v.* 提振（精神）

spirit〔ˊspɪrɪt〕*n.* 精神

inspire〔ɪnˊspaɪr〕*v.* 激勵；激發；
使產生

hope〔hop〕*n.* 希望

BOOK 1・PART 3

Don't be stingy.

不要小氣。

Provide for others.

提供支援。

Gain more friends.

朋友變多。

** ―――――――――――

stingy〔'stɪndʒɪ〕*adj.* 吝嗇的；小氣的

provide〔prə'vaɪd〕*v.* 提供

provide for *sb.* 提供某人需要的東西

gain〔gen〕*v.* 獲得

【Unit 9 背景說明】

千萬記住，絕對不能讓你身旁的人吃虧，你才會有更多的朋友。

Prevent others' losses.（要防止別人的損失；要防止別人吃虧。）也可説成：Help other people avoid suffering.（要幫助別人避免受苦。）Stop others from getting hurt.（要阻止別人受到傷害。）

Minimize their pain.（要使他們的痛苦減至最低。）也可説成：Alleviate their suffering.（要減輕他們的痛苦。）

Relieve their burden. 要減輕他們的負擔。(= *Take away their burden.*) 也可説成：Solve their problems.（要解決他們的問題。）

Help others win. 要幫助別人贏；要幫助別人成功。(= *Help others succeed.*)

BOOK 1・PART 3

Lift their spirits. (要提振他們的精神。) 也可説成：Make them happier. (要使他們更快樂。) Make them feel better. (要使他們感覺更好。)

Inspire their hope. 要激發他們的希望；要使他們充滿希望。(= *Make them hopeful*.) 也可説成：Encourage their dreams. (要鼓勵他們追求夢想。)

Don't be stingy. (不要吝嗇；不要小氣。) 也可説成：Be generous. (要慷慨。) Be charitable. (要慈善。) Don't be ungenerous. (不要不慷慨。) Don't be selfish. (不要自私。)

Provide for others. 要提供別人需要的東西。(= *Give others what they need*.) 也可説成：Support others. (要支持別人。)

Gain more friends. (會得到更多的朋友。) 也可説成：Make more friends. (會交到更多的朋友。)

【How to Be Popular 結尾語】

Thank you for your attention.
謝謝你們專心聽講。
I know you can do it.
我知道你們會成功。
Good-bye and good luck!
再見,祝你們好運!

** attention〔ə'tɛnʃən〕*n.* 注意;專心

　　do it 做到;辦到;成功 (*= make it = succeed*)

　　luck〔lʌk〕*n.* 運氣

　　good luck 祝你好運

【英語演講】

How to Be Popular

Hi, friends.
Want to be popular?
Here is some advice.

PART 3・Unit 1~9
英文錄音QR碼

<u>In the first place</u>, *be <u>a</u> people person.*

Greet others first.
Give a smile.
Start a conversation.

Don't be shy.
Chat with people.
Make a connection.

Say, "Hi there."
"How are you?"
"How you doing?"

<u>Second</u>, *<u>b</u>eing polite is essential.*

Always be polite.
Have good manners.
Never be rude.

Hold the door.
Be on time.
Apologize for mistakes.

Use people's names.
Say, "Hello, Pat."
"Thank you, Pat."

Third, _compliment as much as you can._

Often compliment others.
Say positive words.
Everyone likes compliments.

Praise a friend.
Commend a stranger.
Say something nice.

Build others' confidence.
Make others happy.
They'll like you.

Fourth, _dress yourself well._

Dress for success.
Dress to impress.
Style is everything.

Clothing speaks volumes.
Show your character.
Show your personality.

Invest in quality.
Quality over quantity.
Keep it classy.

Fifth, *e*njoy giving.

Be generous always.
Be generous everywhere.
Generosity is rewarding.

Give a gift.
Offer your help.
Sacrifice for others.

Giving is profitable.
Sharing is beneficial.
Charity pays off.

Sixth, *s*ocializing pays off.

Attend social events.
Go out often.
Expand your influence.

Connect with people.
Talk to everyone.
Make people laugh.

Show your confidence.
Be absolutely unforgettable.
Build lasting connections.

Seventh, _stay humble._

Always be modest.
Always be humble.
Live with humility.

Put others first.
Learn from others.
Don't judge quickly.

Accept your mistakes.
Learn from failures.
Bragging isn't attractive.

More importantly, stop arguing for good.

Always avoid arguing.
Always avoid drama.
Seek common ground.

Don't talk back.
Don't take sides.
Choose your battles.

Don't blame others.
Don't belittle others.
Find a solution.

Most important of all, never ever let your
　friends suffer losses.

Prevent others' losses.
Minimize their pain.
Relieve their burden.

Help others win.
Lift their spirits.
Inspire their hope.

Don't be stingy.
Provide for others.
Gain more friends.

Thank you for your attention.
I know you can do it.
Good-bye and good luck!

BOOK 1・PART 3

How to Be Popular

Here is some advice on how to be popular. *In the first place*, you have to be a people person. Greet others first and start a conversation. Remember that socializing pays off, so attend lots of events and connect with people. *Second*, remember to be polite. Good manners are essential. *In addition*, give compliments whenever you can because everyone likes to hear praise. *Third*, dress well. Your clothing speaks volumes about who you are and you want to make a good impression.

Besides all that, be generous. Enjoy giving to others and making sacrifices. Never let your friends suffer any losses if you can. Step in to relieve their burden and minimize their pain. *More importantly*, don't argue. Don't blame others, take sides, or engage in drama. ***Above all***, be humble.　Be modest and don't brag about your accomplishments.　By following these tips, you can be popular with everyone you meet!

【翻譯】

如何受人歡迎

　　以下是一些關於如何受人歡迎的建議。首先，你必須是一個善於交際的人，要先和別人打招呼，並開始對話。要記得，交際是很值得的，所以要參加很多活動，和人建立關係。第二，記得要有禮貌。良好的禮貌很重要，此外，一有機會就稱讚，因為每個人都喜歡聽到讚美。第三，要穿得好。你的服裝能透露很多訊息，顯示你是什麼樣的人，而且你一定會想要給人留下好印象。

　　此外，要慷慨。要樂於為人付出與犧牲。如果可能，絕不要讓你的朋友吃虧。要介入，減輕他們的負擔，減低他們的痛苦。更重要的是，不要爭論。不要責備別人、偏袒，或捲入混亂的局面。最重要的是，要謙虛。要謙虛，不要吹噓自己的成就。遵循這些祕訣，你就會人見人愛！

PART 3・Unit 1~9
中英文錄音QR碼

BOOK 1・PART 3

PART 3 總整理

Unit 1

Greet others first.
先打招呼。
Give a smile.
展現笑容。
Start a conversation.
展開對話。

Don't be shy. 不要害羞。
Chat with people.
要會聊天。
Make a connection.
建立關係。

Say, "Hi there."
說：「嗨，你好。」
"How are you?"
「你好嗎？」
"How you doing?"
「你好嗎？」

Unit 2

Always be polite.
保持禮貌。
Have good manners.
有好風度。
Never be rude.
絕不無禮。

Hold the door. 為人開門。
Be on time. 準時赴約。
Apologize for mistakes.
錯時道歉。

Use people's names.
要說出人名。
Say, "Hello, Pat."
說：「哈囉，派特。」
"Thank you, Pat."
「謝謝你，派特。」

Unit 3

Often compliment others.
要常常誇獎人。
Say positive words.
要說正面的話。
Everyone likes compliments.
人人愛被稱讚。

Praise a friend. 稱讚友人。
Commend a stranger.
讚美生人。
Say something nice. 要說好話。

Build others' confidence.
給人信心。
Make others happy. 使人快樂。
They'll like you. 人見人愛。

Unit 4

Dress for success.
為成功衣著。
Dress to impress.
為印象打扮。
Style is everything.
風格是一切。

Clothing speaks volumes.
穿著識人。
Show your character.
看出性格。
Show your personality.
看出個性。

Invest in quality.
投資品質。
Quality over quantity.
質重於量。
Keep it classy.
保持品味。

Unit 5

Be generous always.
總是慷慨。
Be generous everywhere.
到處大方。
Generosity is rewarding.
慷慨有報。

Give a gift.　送個禮物。
Offer your help.　提供幫助。
Sacrifice for others.
為人奉獻。

Giving is profitable.
付出有利。
Sharing is beneficial.
分享有益。
Charity pays off.　慈善值得。

Unit 6

Attend social events.
參加社交活動。
Go out often.　常常出門社交。
Expand your influence.
擴大你影響力。

Connect with people.
要會與人交流。
Talk to everyone.
要會與人說話。
Make people laugh.
要能引人發笑。

Show your confidence.
展現你的自信。
Be absolutely unforgettable.
絕對令人難忘。
Build lasting connections.
建立持久關係。

Unit 7

Always be modest.
永保謙虛。
Always be humble.
務必謙遜。
Live with humility.
謙卑過活。

Put others first.
要以人為重。
Learn from others.
要向人學習。
Don't judge quickly.
不輕易批判。

Accept your mistakes.
接受錯誤。
Learn from failures.
失敗中學。
Bragging isn't attractive.
吹噓沒用。

Unit 8

Always avoid arguing.
不要爭吵。
Always avoid drama.
不要激動。
Seek common ground.
尋求共識。

Don't talk back. 不要頂嘴。
Don't take sides. 不要偏袒。
Choose your battles.
慎選戰場。

Don't blame others.
不要責備他人。
Don't belittle others.
不要貶低他人。
Find a solution.
尋求解決之道。

Unit 9

Prevent others' losses.
防人吃虧。
Minimize their pain.
減低痛苦。
Relieve their burden.
減輕負擔。

Help others win. 助人成功。
Lift their spirits. 提振士氣。
Inspire their hope.
激發希望。

Don't be stingy. 不要小氣。
Provide for others.
提供支援。
Gain more friends.
朋友變多。

BOOK 2 \ PART 1

Life Is Beautiful
人生很美

【開場白】

PART 1・Unit 1~9
英文錄音QR碼

BOOK 2・PART 1

> *Good to see you all.*
> 很高興見到大家。
>
> *Life can be a beautiful thing.*
> 人生可以很美麗。
>
> *Here's how to make it happen.*
> 以下就是如何實現的方法。

** happen〔'hæpən〕*v.* 發生
make it happen 成功實現;實現目標

UNIT ❶

First of all, *a*lways find the beauty in life.

首先，一定要找到生活中的美好。

Life is beautiful.

人生很美。

Life is sweet.

生活很甜。

Life is precious.

生命珍貴。

BOOK 2・PART 1

** ———————————

first of all 首先；第一

beauty〔'bjutɪ〕*n.* 美；美麗；優美

life〔laɪf〕*n.* 人生；生活；生命

sweet〔swit〕*adj.* 甜的；愉快的

precious〔'prɛʃəs〕*adj.* 珍貴的

Find the beauty.

找到美好之事。

Seek beauty everywhere.

遍尋美好之處。

Savor good things.

品味美好事物。

**

beauty〔'bjutɪ〕*n.* 美；美麗；優美

seek〔sik〕*v.* 尋求

everywhere〔'ɛvrɪˌhwɛr〕*adv.* 到處

savor〔'sevɚ〕*v.* (慢慢地)品嚐(= *relish*)；
(細細地)體會；欣賞(= *appreciate*)；
享受(= *enjoy*)

Dance through life.

舞動人生。

Have no regrets.

勿留遺憾。

Enjoy life fully.

好好享受。

**

dance〔dæns〕*v.* 跳舞

through〔θru〕*prep.* 遍及;整個…當中

regret〔rɪˋgrɛt〕*n. v.* 後悔;遺憾

enjoy〔ɪnˋdʒɔɪ〕*v.* 享受

life〔laɪf〕*n.* 人生;生活;生命

fully〔ˋfʊlɪ〕*adv.* 完全地;充分地;
　盡可能地

【Unit 1 背景説明】

Life is beautiful. ***Life is sweet***. ***Life is precious***.
這三句話意思相同。也可說成：Life is wonderful.
（人生很棒。）(= *Life is great*.) Life is valuable.
（人生很珍貴。）(= *Life is a treasure*.) Life is
enjoyable. (人生很愉快。)

Find the beauty. 要找到美好的事物。(= *Look for
the good/attractive/positive thing in a
situation/place*.)

Seek beauty everywhere. 要到處尋求美好的事物。
(= *Look for good/positive/attractive things
everywhere*.)

Savor good things. 要品味美好的事物。(= *Relish
the good/positive/wonderful things*.)

Dance through life. 要終生跳舞，引申為「要享受
人生。」(= *Enjoy life*.) 也可說成：Be carefree.
（要無憂無慮。）

Have no regrets. 不要後悔；不要有遺憾。(= *Have
no remorse*.) 也可說成：Don't regret anything.
（不要後悔任何事。）

Enjoy life fully. 要盡情享受人生。(= *Really enjoy
your life*.) 也可說成：Take pleasure in living.
（要樂於活著。）Take full advantage of life. (要
充分利用人生。)

UNIT ❷

Second, *be thankful for what*
*   you have.*

第二，要對你所擁有的心存感激。

Life's a blessing.

活著是一大幸福。

Appreciate your blessings.

要重視你的幸福。

Count your blessings.

想想自己多幸福。

**

thankful〔'θæŋkfəl〕*adj.* 感謝的 < *for* >
life〔laɪf〕*n.* 人生；生活；生命
blessing〔'blɛsɪŋ〕*n.* 幸福；幸運的事
appreciate〔ə'priʃɪ,et〕*v.* 感激；重視
count〔kaʊnt〕*v.* 數
count your blessings 往好處想；知足

Express gratitude daily.

每天感謝。

Gratitude is everything.

感激為上。

Always be thankful.

永遠感謝。

**

---

express〔ɪk'sprɛs〕*v.* 表達

gratitude〔'grætə,tjud〕*n.* 感激

daily〔'delɪ〕*adv.* 每天 (= *every day*)

everything〔'ɛvrɪ,θɪŋ〕*pron.* 一切事物；
　最重要的東西

always〔'ɔlwez〕*adv.* 總是；一直

thankful〔'θæŋkfəl〕*adj.* 感謝的

Don't be greedy.

不要貪心。

Enough is enough.

適可而止。

Always be content.

知足常樂。

**

greedy〔'gridɪ〕*adj.* 貪心的

enough〔ə'nʌf〕*adj.* 足夠的

always〔'ɔlwez〕*adv.* 總是；一直

content〔kən'tɛnt〕*adj.* 滿足的

【Unit 2 背景說明】

Life's a blessing. (生命是一項祝福。) 也可説成：
Life is a wonderful gift. (生命是一個很棒的禮
物。)

Appreciate your blessings. (要重視你的幸福；要
對你的幸福心存感激。) 也可説成：*Count your
blessings*. (要想想你有多幸福。) Be thankful for
what you have. (要對你所擁有的一切心存感謝。)

Express gratitude daily. 要每天表達感激。(= *Show
your appreciation every day*.)

Gratitude is everything. 感激是一切；感激最重要。
(= *Being thankful is the most important thing*.)

Always be thankful. 永遠要感謝。(= *Always be
grateful*.)

Don't be greedy. (不要貪心。) 也可説成：Don't
always want more. (不要總是想要更多。)

Enough is enough. 夠了就是夠了，引申為「要適
可而止。」也可説成：Having enough is good
enough. (擁有足夠的東西就已經夠好了。)

Always be content. (一定要知足。) 也可説成：Be
satisfied with what you have. (要對你所擁有的
感到滿足。)

UNIT ❸

Third, time is valuable.
第三，時間很珍貴。

Use time wisely.
好好利用時間。

Make time worthwhile.
讓時間有價值。

Make life meaningful.
讓生活有意義。

**

valuable (ˈvæljəbl̩) *adj.* 珍貴的
use (juz) *v.* 使用；利用
wisely (ˈwaɪzlɪ) *adv.* 聰明地
make (mek) *v.* 使
worthwhile (ˈwɝθˈhwaɪl) *adj.* 值得的；
　有眞實價值的
meaningful (ˈminɪŋfəl) *adj.* 有意義的

Value every second.

重視每一秒。

Cherish every moment.

珍惜每一刻。

Don't be idle.

勿遊手好閒。

** ———————————

value〔'væljυ〕*v.* 重視

second〔'sɛkənd〕*n.* 秒

cherish〔'tʃɛrɪʃ〕*v.* 珍惜

moment〔'momənt〕*n.* 時刻

idle〔'aɪdḷ〕*adj.* 懶惰的；遊手好閒的

Live passionately now.

現在就熱情地活。

Live fearlessly today.

今天無恐懼地活。

Embrace life's surprises.

擁抱生命的驚喜。

** ───────────────

live (lɪv) *v.* 活；生存；生活
passionately ('pæʃənɪtlɪ) *adv.* 熱情地
fearlessly ('fɪrlɪslɪ) *adv.* 無畏地；大膽地
today (tə'de) *adv.* 今天；現在
embrace (ɪm'bres) *v.* 擁抱；欣然接受
life (laɪf) *n.* 人生；生活；生命
surprise (sə'praɪz) *n.* 驚訝；令人驚訝的事

【Unit 3 背景説明】

Use time wisely. 要聰明地使用時間。(= *Use your time well*.)

Make time worthwhile. (要讓時間變得有價值。) 也可説成：Do something worthwhile with your time. (要用你的時間做值得做的事。)

Make life meaningful. (要讓生命有意義。) 也可説成：Do something meaningful with your life. (要用你的生命做有意義的事。)

Value every second. (要重視每一秒。) 也可説成：Appreciate every moment. (要重視每一刻。)

Cherish every moment. (要珍惜每一刻。) 也可説成：Treasure all the time you have. (要珍惜你所擁有的所有時間。)

Don't be idle. 不要懶惰；不要遊手好閒。(= *Don't be lazy*. = *Don't be inactive*.)

Live passionately now. 現在就要熱情地活。(= *Live with passion now*. = *Live with enthusiasm now*.)

Live fearlessly today. (今天要無所畏懼地活。) 也可説成：Be fearless today. (今天要無所畏懼。) (= *Have no fear today*.)

Embrace life's surprises. (要擁抱生命中的驚喜。) 也可説成：Welcome the surprises that come your way. (要歡迎來到你面前的驚喜。)

UNIT ❹

Fourth, *focus on the present moment.* 第四，要專注於現在。

Always be present.
活在當下。

Focus on now.
專注現在。

Live for today.
活在今天。

**

focus〔'fokəs〕*v.* 專注　　*focus on* 專注於
present〔'prɛzn̩t〕*adj.* 出席的；在場的；
　現在的
moment〔'momənt〕*n.* 時刻；現在
Always be present.（活在當下。）句中的
　present 作「留意的」解，等於 mindful。
always〔'ɔlwez〕*adv.* 總是；一直
live for 為…而活
today〔tə'de〕*n. adv.* 今天；現在

Don't rush anything.

勿操之過急。

Enjoy the journey.

要享受過程。

Take it in.

要好好體會。

BOOK 2 • PART 1

**

rush〔 rʌʃ 〕*v.* 倉促行事；急速做

enjoy〔 ɪn'dʒɔɪ 〕*v.* 享受

journey〔'dʒɝnɪ 〕*n.* 旅程【在此指「過
程」(process)，即在達到目標之前做的
事 (what you are doing while getting
to your goal)】

take sth. in 領會…；理解…；接受…

Breathe and observe.

活在當下。

Savor the moment.

品味當下。

Enjoy your life.

享受人生。

＊＊ ───────────

breathe〔 brið 〕*v.* 呼吸

observe〔 əb'zɝv 〕*v.* 觀察

savor〔 'sevɚ 〕*v.*（慢慢地）品嚐；

（細細地）體會；欣賞；享受

moment〔 'momənt 〕*n.* 片刻；時刻；

現在　　enjoy〔 ɪn'dʒɔɪ 〕*v.* 享受

life〔 laɪf 〕*n.* 人生；生活；生命

【Unit 4 背景説明】

Always be present.「一定要在場；一定要是現在。」引
申爲「一定要留意觀察身邊的事物；一定要活在當下。」
也可説成：Always be mindful.（一定要留意。）
Focus on what is happening right now.（要專注
於現在正在發生的事。）Live in the moment.（要
活在當下。）

Focus on now.　要專注於現在。(= *Focus on the
present*.) 也可説成：*Live for today*.（要爲今天而
活；要活在當下。）

Don't rush anything.（不要匆促做任何事。）也可説
成：Don't try to do things too fast.（不要想做事
做得太快。）Don't be in a hurry.（不要太匆忙。）

Enjoy the journey. 字面的意思是「要享受旅程。」
在此引申爲「要享受過程。」(= *Take delight in the
process*.) 也可説成：Take pleasure in what
you do every day.（要喜歡你每天做的事。）Take
pleasure in the steps you take to get to your
goal.（要喜歡你爲了達到目標所採取的步驟。）

Take it in. 要把它吸收進來，引申為「要好好體會。」
(= *Soak it up.*) 也可說成：Absorb it. (要吸收
它。) Appreciate it. (要欣賞它。)

Breathe and observe. 要呼吸並觀察，引申為「要
活在當下。」(= *Be present.* = *Appreciate the
moment.*) 也可說成：Relax and just watch.
(要放鬆並觀察。) Relax and take it in. (要放
鬆，並好好體會。)

Savor the moment. 要品味當下。(= *Enjoy the
moment.*) 也可說成：Appreciate the here and
now. (要重視此時此刻。) Focus on the present.
(專注於現在。)

Enjoy your life. (要享受你的人生。) 也可說成：
Delight in living. (要樂於活著。) (= *Take
pleasure in living.*) Have fun in life. (生活要
過得愉快。)

UNIT 5

Fifth, find true love.

第五，要找到真愛。

Love is beautiful.

愛是美麗的。

Love creates miracles.

愛創造奇蹟。

Life needs love.

人生需要愛。

BOOK 2 · PART 1

** ———————————————

fifth 〔 fɪfθ 〕 *adv.* 第五

true 〔 tru 〕 *adj.* 真的

love 〔 lʌv 〕 *n. v.* 愛

create 〔 krɪ'et 〕 *v.* 創造

miracle 〔'mɪrək!〕 *n.* 奇蹟

Learn to love.

要學會去愛。

Share your love.

分享你的愛。

Open your heart.

打開你的心。

**

learn〔lɜn〕*v.* 學習

love〔lʌv〕*v. n.* 愛

share〔ʃɛr〕*v.* 分享

open〔'opən〕*v.* 打開；使（心）打開；
  啟發（心靈）接受

heart〔hɑrt〕*n.* 心

open *one's* ***heart*** 敞開心扉

Care for others.

要關心他人。

Love your friends.

愛你的朋友。

Seek true relationships.

尋求真關係。

**

care for 關心;照顧;喜歡

others〔ˈʌðɚz〕*pron.* 別人

seek〔sik〕*v.* 尋求

true〔tru〕*adj.* 真的;真正的

relationship〔rɪˈleʃənˌʃɪp〕*n.* 關係

【**Unit 5 背景說明**】

Love is beautiful. (愛是美麗的。) 也可說成：
Love is wonderful. (愛是很棒的。) (= *Love is great*.)

Love creates miracles. 愛創造奇蹟。(= *Love can work wonders*.) 也可說成：Love is miraculous. (愛是很神奇的。)

Life needs love. (人生需要愛。) 也可說成：
Love is necessary. (愛是必需的。) Love is essential. (愛是必要的。)

Learn to love. (要學會去愛。) 也可說成：Find out how to love others. (要知道如何去愛別人。) Discover how to feel love. (要發現如何感受愛。)

Share your love. (要分享你的愛。) 也可說成：
Express your love. (要表達你的愛。)

BOOK 2 · PART 1

Open your heart. (要打開你的心。) 也可說成：

　Be open to love. (要願意接受愛。)

　Be compassionate. (要有同情心。)

　Have empathy. (要有同理心。)

　Be accepting of others. (要接受別人。)

Care for others. 要關心別人。(= *Care about other people*.) 也可說成：Take care of other people. (要照顧別人。)

Love your friends. (要愛你的朋友。) 也可說成：Value your friends. (要重視你的朋友。) (= *Treasure your friends*. = *Appreciate your friends*.)

Seek true relationships. (要尋求真正的關係。) 也可說成：Look for real friendships. (要尋找真實友誼。) Look for real friends. (要尋找真正的朋友。)

BOOK 2 · PART 1

UNIT 6

Sixth, *stay positive*.
第六，要保持樂觀。

Believe in positivity.
相信正面能量。

Choose happy thoughts.
選擇快樂想法。

Seek silver linings.
尋找一線希望。

** ─────────────────────

stay〔ste〕*v.* 保持
positive〔'pazətɪv〕*adj.* 正面的；樂觀的；
　積極的　　***believe in*** 相信；信任
positivity〔,pazə'tɪvətɪ〕*n.* 正面；積極
choose〔tʃuz〕*v.* 選擇
thought〔θɔt〕*n.* 思想；想法
seek〔sik〕*v.* 尋求　　silver〔'sɪlvɚ〕*adj.*
　銀色的　　lining〔'laɪnɪŋ〕*n.* 襯裡
silver lining（失望或不幸中的）一線希望
　（或一點慰藉）【源自諺語：Every cloud has
　a silver lining.（烏雲背後有銀邊；否極泰來。）】

Don't be negative.

不要悲觀消極。

Let negativity go.

放下負面情緒。

Never lose hope.

絕不失去希望。

** ————————

negative〔'nɛɡətɪv〕*adj.* 負面的；消極的

let go 放開；放下

negativity〔ˌnɛɡə'tɪvətɪ〕*n.* 負面；消極

never〔'nɛvɚ〕*adv.* 絕不

lose〔luz〕*v.* 失去

hope〔hop〕*n.* 希望

Change your outlook.

改變你的觀點。

Attitude is everything.

態度就是一切。

Perspective matters most.

眼光最為重要。

** ─────────────

change〔tʃendʒ〕*v.* 改變

outlook〔'aʊt,lʊk〕*n.* 觀點;看法

attitude〔'ætə,tjud〕*n.* 態度

everything〔'ɛvrɪ,θɪŋ〕*pron.* 一切事物;
最重要的東西

perspective〔pɚ'spɛktɪv〕*n.* 正確的眼光;
看法

matter〔'mætɚ〕*v.* 重要

most〔most〕*adv.* 最

【Unit 6 背景說明】

Believe in positivity. （要相信正面能量。）也可說成：Be optimistic. （要樂觀。）Believe that being optimistic will help. （要相信樂觀會有幫助。）

Choose happy thoughts. （要選擇快樂的想法。）也可說成：Choose to be happy. （要選擇快樂。）Don't engage in negative thinking. （不要有負面想法。）

Seek silver linings. 要尋求一線希望。（= *Look for a break in the clouds*.）也可說成：Look for the positive. （要尋找好事。）Look on the bright side. （要看事物的光明面；要樂觀。）

Don't be negative. （不要悲觀消極。）也可說成：Be optimistic. （要樂觀。）（= *Be positive*.）

Let negativity go. （放下負面情緒。）也可說成：Don't hold on to negative feelings. （不要一直有負面情緒。）Don't hold on to negative thoughts. （不要一直有負面想法。）

Never lose hope. （絕不失去希望。）也可說成：
Never give up. （絕不放棄。） Always have
hope. （一定要有希望。） Always be hopeful.
（一定要充滿希望。）

Change your outlook. （要改變你的觀點。）也
可說成：Change your attitude. （要改變你的
態度。）

Attitude is everything. （態度是一切；態度最重
要。）也可說成：Your attitude is very
important. （你的態度非常重要。）（= *Your
attitude is key*. ）

Perspective matters most. 看法最重要。
（= *Perspective is key*. ）也可說成：The way
you look at things is most important. （你
對事物的看法是最重要的。）

UNIT 7

Seventh, don't take life too seriously.

第七，不要把人生看得太認真。

Always keep calm.

常保持冷靜。

Don't stress out.

勿壓力過大。

Don't overdo it.

不要太累了。

** ———————————————

seriously (ˈsɪrɪəslɪ) *adv.* 認真地；嚴肅地

take* sth. *seriously 認真看待某事

always (ˈɔlwez) *adv.* 總是；一直

keep (kip) *v.* 保持　calm (kɑm) *adj.* 冷靜的

stress out 感到非常焦慮

overdo (ˌovəˈdu) *v.* 把⋯做得過分；把⋯做得

過火　***overdo it*** 做得過火

Keep life simple.

保持生活簡單。

Simplify your thoughts.

簡化你的想法。

Enjoy life's simplicity.

享受簡單生活。

＊＊ ——————————————

keep〔kip〕*v.* 使保持

simple〔'sɪmpḷ〕*adj.* 簡單的

simplify〔'sɪmplə,faɪ〕*v.* 簡化

thought〔θɔt〕*n.* 思想；想法

enjoy〔ɪn'dʒɔɪ〕*v.* 享受

simplicity〔sɪm'plɪsətɪ〕*n.* 簡單；單純

Always be relaxed.

務必放鬆。

Take it easy.

輕鬆一點。

Just chill out.

放鬆一下。

** ──────────────

always〔'ɔlwez〕*adv.* 總是；一直

take it easy 放輕鬆

relaxed〔rɪ'lækst〕*adj.* 放鬆的

just〔dʒʌst〕*adv.* 只；就

chill〔tʃɪl〕*v.* 變冷

chill out ①冷靜 ②放鬆一下

【Unit 7 背景説明】

Always keep calm. 總是保持冷靜。(= *Keep your cool.* = *Maintain your composure.*)

Don't stress out. 不要壓力太大。(= *Don't feel a lot of pressure.*) 也可説成：Don't get upset. (不要心煩意亂。) Don't get anxious. (不要太焦慮。)

Don't overdo it. 不要做得過火。(= *Don't do too much.*) 也可説成：Don't work too hard. (不要太努力工作。) Don't play too hard. (不要玩得太過火。) 依上下文決定意思。

Keep life simple. (保持生活簡單。) 也可説成：Simplify your life. (簡化你的生活。) Don't complicate things. (不要把事情複雜化。)

Simplify your thoughts. (簡化你的想法。) 也可説成：Don't worry too much. (不要太擔心。) Think calming thoughts. (要有使人冷靜的想法。)

Enjoy life's simplicity. (享受生活的簡單。) 也可説成：Appreciate the simple things in life. (要重視生活中簡單的事物。)

Always be relaxed. (一定要放鬆。) 也可説成：Always stay calm. (一定要保持冷靜。) Don't get stressed. (不要有壓力。)

Take it easy. 要放輕鬆。(= *Relax.* = *Unwind.* = *Let your hair down.* = *Loosen up.* = ***Just chill out.***)

UNIT 8

Above all, enjoy nature's beauty.

最重要的是，要享受自然之美。

Get lost outdoors.

到戶外亂逛。

Wander and wonder.

漫遊且好奇。

Find hidden treasures.

找隱藏寶藏。

** ───────────────

above all 最重要的是 (= *most important of all*)
nature 〔'netʃɚ〕 *n.* 大自然　***get lost*** 迷路；滾開
outdoors 〔'aʊt'dorz〕 *adv.* 在戶外
wander 〔'wɑndɚ〕 *v.* 四處走；流浪；徘徊
wonder 〔'wʌndɚ〕 *v.* 好奇；懷疑；想知道
hidden 〔'hɪdn̩〕 *adj.* 隱藏的
treasure 〔'trɛʒɚ〕 *n.* 寶藏

Appreciate nature's wonders.

欣賞自然奇景。

Savor the view.

細細體會美景。

Embrace every sunrise.

擁抱每個日出。

** ———————————

appreciate〔ə'priʃɪ,et〕v. 欣賞

nature〔'netʃɚ〕n. 大自然

wonder〔'wʌndɚ〕n. 奇景

savor〔'sevɚ〕v.（慢慢地）品嚐；（細細地）
體會；欣賞；享受

view〔vju〕n. 景色

embrace〔ɪm'bres〕v. 擁抱；欣然接受

sunrise〔'sʌn,raɪz〕n. 日出

Revel in nature.

享受自然。

Watch the sunset.

欣賞日落。

Go touch dirt.

接近自然。

** ――――――――――

revel〔'rɛvḷ〕v. 盡情地享受

revel in 盡情地享受（ = *delight in* ）

nature〔'netʃə〕n. 大自然

watch〔wɑtʃ〕v. 觀賞

sunset〔'sʌn,sɛt〕n. 日落

touch〔tʌtʃ〕v. 碰觸

dirt〔dɜt〕n. 泥土；爛泥；泥地

Go touch dirt. 去碰觸泥土。

（ = *Go and touch dirt.* ）

【Unit 8 背景說明】

Get lost outdoors. 要在戶外迷路，在此引申爲「要在戶外亂逛。」也可説成：Lose yourself in nature. (要讓自己迷失在大自然中。)

Wander and wonder. (要四處走動，充滿好奇。) 也可説成：Roam around and be amazed. (要四處漫步，並感到驚奇。)

Find hidden treasures. (要找到隱藏的寶藏。) 也可説成：Discover something amazing. (要發現令人驚奇的事物。) Go places and be amazed by what you see. (要到各個地方，並對所見所聞感到驚奇。)

Appreciate nature's wonders. (要欣賞大自然的奇景。) 也可説成：Recognize the wonder of nature. (要承認大自然的神奇。) Recognize how amazing the natural world is. (要承認自然界有多麼令人驚訝。)

Savor the view. (要品味美景。) 也可説成：Relish the view. (要欣賞美景。) Enjoy the view. (要享受美景。)

Embrace every sunrise.（擁抱每一個日出。）也可
說成：Welcome the sunrise every day.（要歡
迎每一天的日出。）Welcome every dawn.（要
歡迎每一個黎明。）

Revel in nature.（要盡情地享受大自然。）也可說
成：Delight in nature.（要喜歡大自然。）Savor
nature.（要品味大自然。）Relish nature.（要欣
賞大自然。）Enjoy nature.（要享受大自然。）
Appreciate nature.（要欣賞大自然。）

Watch the sunset. 觀賞日落。(= *Look at the
sunset. = Observe the setting sun.*) 也可說成：
Admire the sunset.（要欣賞日落。）

Go touch dirt. 字面的意思是「去碰觸泥巴；去碰觸
地面。」(= *Go touch the ground. = Get your
hands dirty.*) 在此引申為「去接近大自然。」
(= *Get in touch with nature.*)

UNIT ❾

Last but not least, a healthy life means everything.

最後一項要點是,健康的人生最重要。

Health empowers individuals.

健康給人力量。

Wellness breeds success.

健康創造成功。

Health comes first.

健康最為重要。

**

last but not least 最後但並非最不重要的是;
　最後一項要點是　　healthy〔ˈhɛlθɪ〕*adj.* 健康的
mean everything 意義重大
health〔hɛlθ〕*n.* 健康
empower〔ɪmˈpaʊɚ〕*v.* 使有力量
individual〔͵ɪndəˈvɪdʒuəl〕*n.* 個人
wellness〔ˈwɛlnɪs〕*n.* 健康
breed〔brid〕*v.* 養育;培育;產生
success〔səkˈsɛs〕*n.* 成功　　*come first* 最重要

Nutrition fuels longevity.

營養能促進長壽。

Eat healthy foods.

要吃健康的食物。

Always stay hydrated.

一定要補充水分。

**

nutrition〔njuˋtrɪʃən〕*n.* 營養

fuel〔ˋfjuəl〕*v.* 為…添加燃料；加強

　(= *provide energy for*)

longevity〔lɑnˋdʒɛvətɪ〕*n.* 長壽

healthy〔ˋhɛlθɪ〕*adj.* 健康的

stay〔ste〕*v.* 保持

hydrated〔ˋhaɪdretɪd〕*adj.* 攝入足夠水分的

Mental health matters.
心理健康很重要。

Think healthy thoughts.
要有健康的思想。

Healthy minds thrive.
心理健康才成功。

BOOK 2・PART 1

**

mental〔ˈmɛntḷ〕*adj.* 精神的；心理的
health〔hɛlθ〕*n.* 健康
matter〔ˈmætɚ〕*v.* 重要
healthy〔ˈhɛlθɪ〕*adj.* 健康的
thought〔θɔt〕*n.* 思想；想法
think~thoughts 心懷…想法
mind〔maɪnd〕*n.* 心；精神；頭腦；想法
thrive〔θraɪv〕*v.* 興盛；繁榮；成功

【Unit 9 背景說明】

Health empowers individuals. 健康使人有力量。
(= *Good health makes you more powerful.*)

Wellness breeds success. 健康創造成功。(= *Good
health leads to success.*)

Health comes first. 健康最重要。(= *Health is the
most important thing.*)

Nutrition fuels longevity. 營養能促進長壽。(= *With
good nutrition, you can live a long life.*)

Eat healthy foods. 要吃健康的食物。(= *Have a
healthy diet.*)

Always stay hydrated. (一定要攝取足夠的水分。) 也可
說成：Drink enough water. (要喝足夠的水。) Don't
get dehydrated. (不要脫水。)

> 中國人說：「要多喝水。」外國人常說：***Always
> stay hydrated***.

Mental health matters. 心理健康很重要。(= *Mental
health is important.*)

Think healthy thoughts. (要有健康的思想。) 也可說
成：Think positively. (想法要正面。)

Healthy minds thrive. 心理健康才會成功。(= *With
good mental health, you will flourish.*)

【Life Is Beautiful 結尾語】

So nice talking to you!
很高興能和你們談話！

It was my pleasure!
這是我的榮幸！

Can't wait to see you again!
我等不及要再次見到大家！

** so〔so〕*adv.* 很；非常
　nice〔naɪs〕*adj.* 好的
　pleasure〔ˋplɛʒɚ〕*n.* 樂趣；榮幸

【英語演講】

Life Is Beautiful

Good to see you all.
Life can be a beautiful thing.
Here's how to make it happen.

PART 1・Unit 1~9
英文録音QR碼

First of all, **_a_***lways find the beauty in life.*

Life is beautiful.
Life is sweet.
Life is precious.

Find the beauty.
Seek beauty everywhere.
Savor good things.

Dance through life.
Have no regrets.
Enjoy life fully.

Second, **_b_***e thankful for what you have.*

Life's a blessing.
Appreciate your blessings.
Count your blessings.

Express gratitude daily.
Gratitude is everything.
Always be thankful.

Don't be greedy.
Enough is enough.
Always be content.

Third*, time is valuable.*

Use time wisely.
Make time worthwhile.
Make life meaningful.

Value every second.
Cherish every moment.
Don't be idle.

Live passionately now.
Live fearlessly today.
Embrace life's surprises.

Fourth*, focus on the present moment.*

Always be present.
Focus on now.
Live for today.

Don't rush anything.
Enjoy the journey.
Take it in.

Breathe and observe.
Savor the moment.
Enjoy your life.

***Fifth**, **f**ind true love.*

Love is beautiful.
Love creates miracles.
Life needs love.

Learn to love.
Share your love.
Open your heart.

Care for others.
Love your friends.
Seek true relationships.

***Sixth**, **s**tay positive.*

Believe in positivity.
Choose happy thoughts.
Seek silver linings.

Don't be negative.
Let negativity go.
Never lose hope.

Change your outlook.
Attitude is everything.
Perspective matters most.

Seventh, *don't take life too <u>seriously</u>.*

Always keep calm.
Don't stress out.
Don't overdo it.

Keep life simple.
Simplify your thoughts.
Enjoy life's simplicity.

Always be relaxed.
Take it easy.
Just chill out.

Above all, enjoy nature's beauty.

Get lost outdoors.
Wander and wonder.
Find hidden treasures.

Appreciate nature's wonders.
Savor the view.
Embrace every sunrise.

Revel in nature.
Watch the sunset.
Go touch dirt.

Last but not least, a healthy life means
  everything.

Health empowers individuals.
Wellness breeds success.
Health comes first.

Nutrition fuels longevity.
Eat healthy foods.
Always stay hydrated.

Mental health matters.
Think healthy thoughts.
Healthy minds thrive.

So nice talking to you!
It was my pleasure!
Can't wait to see you again!

PART 1 總整理

Unit 1

Life is beautiful.
人生很美。
Life is sweet. 生活很甜。
Life is precious.
生命珍貴。

Find the beauty.
找到美好之事。
Seek beauty everywhere.
遍尋美好之處。
Savor good things.
品味美好事物。

Dance through life.
舞動人生。
Have no regrets.
勿留遺憾。
Enjoy life fully.
好好享受。

Unit 2

Life's a blessing.
活著是一大幸福。
Appreciate your blessings.
要重視你的幸福。
Count your blessings.
想想自己多幸福。

Express gratitude daily.
每天感謝。
Gratitude is everything.
感激爲上。
Always be thankful. 永遠感謝。

Don't be greedy. 不要貪心。
Enough is enough. 適可而止。
Always be content. 知足常樂。

Unit 3

Use time wisely. 好好利用時間。
Make time worthwhile.
讓時間有價值。
Make life meaningful.
讓生活有意義。

Value every second.
重視每一秒。
Cherish every moment.
珍惜每一刻。
Don't be idle. 勿遊手好閒。

Live passionately now.
現在就熱情地活。
Live fearlessly today.
今天無恐懼地活。
Embrace life's surprises.
擁抱生命的驚喜。

Unit 4

Always be present.
活在當下。
Focus on now. 專注現在。
Live for today. 活在今天。

Don't rush anything.
勿操之過急。
Enjoy the journey.
要享受過程。
Take it in. 要好好體會。

Breathe and observe.
活在當下。
Savor the moment.
品味當下。
Enjoy your life. 享受人生。

Unit 5

Love is beautiful.
愛是美麗的。
Love creates miracles.
愛創造奇蹟。
Life needs love.
人生需要愛。

Learn to love. 要學會去愛。
Share your love. 分享你的愛。
Open your heart.
打開你的心。

Care for others.
要關心他人。
Love your friends.
愛你的朋友。
Seek true relationships.
尋求真關係。

Unit 6

Believe in positivity.
相信正面能量。
Choose happy thoughts.
選擇快樂想法。
Seek silver linings.
尋找一線希望。

Don't be negative.
不要悲觀消極。
Let negativity go.
放下負面情緒。
Never lose hope.
絕不失去希望。

Change your outlook.
改變你的觀點。
Attitude is everything.
態度就是一切。
Perspective matters most.
眼光最為重要。

BOOK 2・PART 1

Unit 7

Always keep calm.
常保持冷靜。
Don't stress out. 勿壓力過大。
Don't overdo it. 不要太累了。

Keep life simple.
保持生活簡單。
Simplify your thoughts.
簡化你的想法。
Enjoy life's simplicity.
享受簡單生活。

Always be relaxed.
務必放鬆。
Take it easy. 輕鬆一點。
Just chill out. 放鬆一下。

Unit 8

Get lost outdoors. 到戶外亂逛。
Wander and wonder.
漫遊且好奇。
Find hidden treasures.
找隱藏寶藏。

Appreciate nature's wonders.
欣賞自然奇景。
Savor the view.
細細體會美景。
Embrace every sunrise.
擁抱每個日出。

Revel in nature.
享受自然。
Watch the sunset.
欣賞日落。
Go touch dirt.
接近自然。

Unit 9

Health empowers
　individuals.
健康給人力量。
Wellness breeds success.
健康創造成功。
Health comes first.
健康最為重要。

Nutrition fuels longevity.
營養能促進長壽。
Eat healthy foods.
要吃健康的食物。
Always stay hydrated.
一定要補充水分。

Mental health matters.
心理健康很重要。
Think healthy thoughts.
要有健康的思想。
Healthy minds thrive.
心理健康才成功。

BOOK 2 \ PART 2

How to Stay Healthy
如何保持健康

PART 2・Unit 1~9
英文錄音QR碼

BOOK 2・PART 2

UNIT ❶

How to Eat Healthy (I)
怎麼樣吃才健康 (I)

Cook at home.
在家煮飯。

Eat family meals.
吃家常菜。

Eat seasonal foods.
吃當季食。

** ───────

healthy〔ˈhɛlθɪ〕*adj.* 健康的
cook〔kʊk〕*v.* 烹飪；做菜
family〔ˈfæməlɪ〕*adj.* 家庭的
meal〔mil〕*n.* 一餐　　***family meal*** ①家常菜
　②餐廳的員工餐【在餐廳營業前，工作人員會
　坐在一起吃飯，就像大家庭一樣】
seasonal〔ˈsiznḷ〕*adj.* 季節性的

Use less oil.

少一點油。

Use less salt.

少一點鹽。

Use less sugar.

少一點糖。

** ————————————

use〔juz〕v. 使用
less〔lɛs〕adj. 較少的
oil〔ɔɪl〕n. 油
salt〔sɔlt〕n. 鹽
sugar〔'ʃʊgɚ〕n. 糖

Plan meals ahead.

事先計劃餐點。

Diversify your meals.

餐點要多樣化。

Enjoy variety daily.

每天吃不同菜。

**

---

plan〔plæn〕*v.* 計劃

meal〔mil〕*n.* 一餐

ahead〔ə'hɛd〕*adv.* 預先;事前

diversify〔daɪ'vɝsə,faɪ〕*v.* 使多樣化

enjoy〔ɪn'dʒɔɪ〕*v.* 享受

variety〔və'raɪətɪ〕*n.* 多樣性;變化

daily〔'delɪ〕*adv.* 每天
  (= *every day*)

【Unit 1 背景説明】

Cook at home. 在家煮飯。(= *Prepare your meals at home.* = *Cook your own meals.* = *Do your own cooking.*)

Eat family meals. ①要吃家常菜。(= *Eat home-cooked meals.*) ②要像個大家庭一樣地吃飯。(= *Eat together as a family.*)

Eat seasonal foods. 吃當季的食物。(= *Eat things that are in season.*)

Use less oil. (少油。) 也可説成：Don't use so much oil. (不要用這麼多油。) Cook with less oil. (用較少的油來煮。)

Use less salt. 少鹽。(= *Don't use so much salt.* = *Use less salt when cooking.*)

Use less sugar. 少糖。(= *Don't use so much sugar.* = *Cook with less sugar.*)

Plan meals ahead. (事先計劃餐點。) 也可説成：Know what you want to cook each day. (每天都要知道你想要煮什麼。)

Diversify your meals. (餐點要多樣化。) 也可説成：Eat different kinds of food. (要吃不同種類的食物。) Don't eat the same thing every day. (不要每天都吃一樣的東西。)

Enjoy variety daily. 每天享用各種不同的食物。(= *Eat something different every day.*)

BOOK 2 · PART 2

UNIT **2**

How to Eat Healthy (II)
怎麼樣吃才健康 **(II)**

Choose white meat.
選擇白肉。

Eat more chicken.
多吃雞肉。

Eat more fish.
多吃魚肉。

**

choose〔tʃuz〕*v.* 選擇

meat〔mit〕*n.* 肉

white meat 白肉【尤指雞身上的肉】

chicken〔'tʃɪkɪn〕*n.* 雞；雞肉

fish〔fɪʃ〕*n.* 魚；魚肉

Choose lean meat.

要選擇瘦肉。

Choose low-fat milk.

選低脂牛奶。

Eat mixed nuts.

吃綜合堅果。

**
_____

choose〔tʃuz〕*v.* 選擇

lean〔lin〕*adj.* 瘦的

meat〔mit〕*n.* 肉   *lean meat* 瘦肉

fat〔fæt〕*n.* 脂肪

low-fat〔'lo,fæt〕*adj.* 低脂的

milk〔mɪlk〕*n.* 牛奶

mixed〔mɪkst〕*adj.* 混合的

nut〔nʌt〕*n.* 堅果

mixed nuts 綜合堅果

BOOK 2・PART 2

Eat in moderation.

吃東西適量。

Always eat slowly.

要細嚼慢嚥。

Don't fill up.

不要吃到飽。

**

moderation〔͵mɑdə'reʃən〕*n.* 適度；適中
in moderation 適度地；有節制地
slowly〔'slolɪ〕*adv.* 慢地
fill up 裝滿；填滿；吃飽

【Unit 2 背景説明】

Choose white meat. (要選擇白肉。) 也可説成：Eat white meat. (要吃白肉。)

Eat more chicken.　要多吃雞肉。(= *Eat more poultry*.)

Eat more fish.　多吃魚肉。(= *Make fish a bigger part of your diet*.)

Choose lean meat.　要選擇瘦肉。(= *Eat lean meat*.) 也可説成：Eat meat low in fat. (要吃低脂的肉。)

Choose low-fat milk. (要選擇低脂牛奶。) 也可説成：Drink low-fat milk. (要喝低脂牛奶。)

Eat mixed nuts. (要吃綜合堅果。) 也可説成：Eat a variety of nuts. (要吃各種不同的堅果。)

Eat in moderation. (吃東西要適量。) 也可説成：Don't eat too much or too little. (不要吃太多或太少。)

Always eat slowly. (總是慢慢吃；要細嚼慢嚥。) 也可説成：Never eat too fast. (絕不要吃得太快。)

Don't fill up. (不要吃到飽。) 也可説成：Stop eating before you feel full. (在你覺得飽之前，就不要再吃了。)

UNIT ❸ *How to Eat Healthy (Ⅲ)*
怎麼樣吃才健康 (III)

If you always feel cold, you must eat hot-natured foods.

如果你總是很怕冷，你就必須吃熱性食物。

Date, durian, almond.

棗子，榴槤，杏仁。

Longan, lichee, cherry.

龍眼，荔枝，櫻桃。

Peach, guava, olive.

桃子，番石榴，橄欖。

**
---
nature (ˈnetʃɚ) *n.* 性質
hot-natured (ˈhatˈnetʃɚd) *adj.* 熱性的
date (det) *n.* 棗子　durian (ˈdurɪən) *n.* 榴槤
almond (ˈamənd, ˈæmənd) *n.* 杏仁
longan (ˈlaŋgən) *n.* 龍眼
lichee (ˈlitʃi) *n.* 荔枝　cherry (ˈtʃɛrɪ) *n.* 櫻桃
peach (pitʃ) *n.* 桃子
guava (ˈgwavə) *n.* 番石榴　olive (ˈalɪv) *n.* 橄欖

If you always feel hot, you must
  eat cold-natured foods.

如果你總是很怕熱，你就必須吃寒性食物。

Pear, pomelo, persimmon.

水梨，柚子，柿子。

Plum, melon, watermelon.

李子，香瓜，西瓜。

Strawberry, mulberry, banana.

草莓，桑椹，香蕉。

** ────────────────────

cold-natured (ˈkoldˈnetʃəd) *adj.* 寒性的
pear (pɛr) *n.* 梨子   pomelo (ˈpɑməlo) *n.* 柚子
persimmon (pəˈsɪmən) *n.* 柿子
plum (plʌm) *n.* 李子   melon (ˈmɛlən) *n.* 香瓜
watermelon (ˈwɔtəˌmɛlən) *n.* 西瓜
strawberry (ˈstrɔˌbɛrɪ) *n.* 草莓
mulberry (ˈmʌlˌbɛrɪ) *n.* 桑椹
banana (bəˈnænə) *n.* 香蕉

BOOK 2・PART 2

Cold-Natured Foods (*II*)
寒性食物 (II)

Starfruit, grapefruit, dragon fruit. 楊桃，葡萄柚，火龍果。

Tomato, tangerine, kiwi.
蕃茄，橘子，奇異果。

Loquat, mangosteen, wax apple. 枇杷，山竹，蓮霧。

** ────────────

starfruit (ˈstɑrˌfrut) *n.* 楊桃
grapefruit (ˈgrepˌfrut) *n.* 葡萄柚
dragon fruit (ˈdrægən ˌfrut) *n.* 火龍果
tomato (təˈmeto) *n.* 蕃茄
tangerine (ˈtændʒəˌrin) *n.* 橘子
kiwi (ˈkiwɪ) *n.* 奇異果
loquat (ˈlokwɑt) *n.* 枇杷
mangosteen (ˈmæŋgəˌstin) *n.* 山竹
wax (wæks) *n.* 蠟
wax apple (ˈwæks ˌæpl̩) *n.* 蓮霧

UNIT ④

The Benefits of Exercise (I)
運動的好處 (I)

Exercise every day.
每天都要運動。

Get quality sleep.
會有優質睡眠。

Improve your flexibility.
改善身體彈性。

**

exercise〔'ɛksə‚saɪz〕*v. n.* 運動

quality〔'kwɑlətɪ〕*n.* 品質 *adj.* 品質好的

sleep〔slip〕*n.* 睡眠

improve〔ɪm'pruv〕*v.* 改善

flexibility〔‚flɛksə'bɪlətɪ〕*n.* 彈性；靈活性

Burn excess calories.

燃燒多餘熱量。

Lose some fat.

減少一些脂肪。

Maintain your weight.

維持你的體重。

**

burn〔bɝn〕*v.* 燃燒
excess〔'ɛksɛs〕*adj.* 過多的；多餘的
　〔ɪk'sɛs〕*n.* 多餘
calorie〔'kælərɪ〕*n.* 卡路里【熱量單位】
lose〔luz〕*v.* 失去；減少
fat〔fæt〕*n.* 脂肪
maintain〔men'ten〕*v.* 維持
weight〔wet〕*n.* 體重

Prevent chronic diseases.

預防慢性疾病。

Enhance your immunity.

會增加免疫力。

Boost your metabolism.

提高新陳代謝。

**————————————

prevent〔prɪˋvɛnt〕*v.* 預防

chronic〔ˋkrɑnɪk〕*adj.* 慢性的

disease〔dɪˋziz〕*n.* 疾病

enhance〔ɪnˋhæns〕*v.* 增加；提高

immunity〔ɪˋmjunətɪ〕*n.* 免疫力

boost〔bust〕*v.* 提高

metabolism〔məˋtæbəͺlɪzm̩〕*n.* 新陳代謝

【Unit 4 背景説明】

Exercise every day. 要每天運動。(= *Get some exercise every day*.)

Get quality sleep. (會有優質睡眠。) 也可説成：Sleep well. (會睡得好。)

Improve your flexibility. 改善你身體的彈性。(= *Enhance your flexibility*.)

Burn excess calories. 燃燒多餘的卡路里。(= *Burn off extra calories*.)

Lose some fat. 減少一些脂肪。(= *Reduce the amount of fat you have*.) 也可説成：Improve your BMI. (改善你的身體質量指數。)

Maintain your weight. 維持你的體重。(= *Don't gain weight and don't lose weight*.)

Prevent chronic diseases. 預防慢性病。(= *Avoid chronic diseases*.)

Enhance your immunity. 增加你的免疫力。(= *Strengthen your immune system.* = *Make your immune system stronger*.)

Boost your metabolism. 提高你的新陳代謝。(= *Increase your metabolism*.)

UNIT ❺

The Benefits of Exercise (*II*)
運動的好處 (II)

Work out daily.

要每天運動。

Consistent exercise pays.

常運動值得。

Always be active.

要動個不停。

** ———————

> ***work out*** 運動
>
> daily〔'delɪ〕*adv.* 每天（= *every day*）
>
> consistent〔kən'sɪstənt〕*adj.* 持續的
>
> exercise〔'ɛksəˌsaɪz〕*n.* 運動
>
> pay〔pe〕*v.* 值得；划得來
>
> always〔'ɔlwez〕*adv.* 總是；一直
>
> active〔'æktɪv〕*adj.* 積極的；活躍的；
> 　在活動中的

Improve your circulation.

改善血液循環。

Protect your joints.

保護你的關節。

Strengthen your heart.

強化你的心臟。

** ————————————————————

improve〔ɪmˋpruv〕v. 改善

circulation〔͵sɝkjəˋleʃən〕n. 循環

protect〔prəˋtɛkt〕v. 保護

joint〔dʒɔɪnt〕n. 關節

strengthen〔ˋstrɛŋθən〕v. 強化

heart〔hɑrt〕n. 心臟

Build strong muscles.

會增強肌肉。

Increase lung capacity.

增加肺活量。

Detox your body.

讓身體排毒。

** ―――――――――――――――

build〔bɪld〕*v.* 建造；構成；形成；發展

strong〔strɔŋ〕*adj.* 強壯的

muscle〔'mʌsḷ〕*n.* 肌肉

increase〔ɪn'kris〕*v.* 增加

lung〔lʌŋ〕*n.* 肺

capacity〔kə'pæsətɪ〕*n.* 容量

detox〔'ditɑks〕*v.* 使排毒

BOOK 2・PART 2

【Unit 5 背景説明】

Work out daily.　要每天運動。(= *Exercise every day*.)

Consistent exercise pays.　持續運動很值得。
(= *Exercising regularly pays off*.) 也可説成：
Exercising regularly has benefits. (持續運動有好
處。)

Always be active.　要動個不停。(= *Stay active*. = *Keep moving*.) 也可説成：Don't be sedentary. (不要坐著
不動。)

Improve your circulation.　改善你的血液循環。
(= *Improve your blood circulation*.)

Protect your joints. (保護你的關節。) 也可説成：
Take care of your joints. (照顧你的關節。)

Strengthen your heart.　強化你的心臟。(= *Make your heart stronger*.)

Build strong muscles. (鍛練強壯的肌肉。) 也可説成：
Get stronger. (會變得更強壯。)

Increase lung capacity.　增加肺活量。(= *Improve your lung capacity*.)

Detox your body.　讓你的身體排毒。(= *Get the toxins out of your system*. = *Get the poisons out of your system*.)

UNIT 6

Mind Your Posture

注意你的姿勢

Have good posture.

有良好姿勢。

Don't ever hunch.

絕不要彎腰。

Don't ever slouch.

絕不要駝背。

**

mind〔maɪnd〕v. 注意

posture〔'pastʃɚ〕n. 姿勢;姿態

don't ever 絕不(= *never*)

hunch〔hʌntʃ〕v. 弓背;彎腰　n. 直覺

slouch〔slautʃ〕v. 垂頭彎腰地走(坐或站)

Keep heads up.

頭要抬起來。

Keep shoulders back.

胸要挺起來。

Always stand tall.

要抬頭挺胸。

** ————————————————

keep〔kip〕*v.* 保持；使保持

head〔hɛd〕*n.* 頭　　up〔ʌp〕*adv.* 向上

shoulders〔'ʃoldəz〕*n. pl.* 肩膀

back〔bæk〕*adv.* 向後

tall〔tɔl〕*adv.* 得意洋洋地

always〔'ɔlwez〕*adj.* 總是；一直

stand tall 昂然挺立

　【比較】walk tall 昂首闊步

Sit up straight.

要能坐直。

Stand up straight.

要能站直。

Stride with confidence.

跨大步走。

** ───────────

sit up 坐直；坐正

straight〔stret〕*adv.* 直直地；直立地

stand up straight 直起腰來；站直；抬頭挺胸

stride〔straɪd〕*v.* (有精神地或威風地)

　　跨大步走

confidence〔'kɑnfədəns〕*n.* 自信；信心

with confidence 滿懷信心地

【Unit 6 背景説明】

Have good posture. (要有良好的姿勢。) 也可說
成：*Don't ever hunch*. (絕不要彎腰。) (= *Don't
hunch*.) *Don't ever slouch*. (絕不要駝背。)
(= *Don't slouch*.) 也可說成：Sit up straight.
(坐直。) Stand up straight. (站直。)

Keep heads up. 是慣用句，表示「頭要抬起來。」
(= *Keep your heads up*.) 也可說成：Heads up.
(抬頭。) Don't look down. (不要往下看。)

Keep shoulders back. 保持肩膀向後，也就是「要
挺胸；胸要挺起來。」(= *Pull your shoulders
back*.) 也可說成：Shoulders back. (挺胸。)
Stand up straight. (要站直。)

Always stand tall. (一定要抬頭挺胸。) 也可說
成：Always stand up straight. (一定要站直。)
Have good posture. (要有良好的姿勢。)

Sit up straight. (要坐直。) *Stand up straight*.
(要站直。) 也可說成：Don't slouch. (不要彎
腰駝背。)

Stride with confidence. (要充滿自信地跨大步走。)
也可說成：Walk confidently. (要充滿自信地走。)

UNIT 7

Listen to Your Body
傾聽你身體的聲音

Respond to signals.

回應身體信號。

Eat when hungry.

餓了就要吃飯。

Drink when thirsty.

渴了就要喝水。

** ─────────────

respond〔rɪ'spɑnd〕*v.* 回應 < *to* >
signal〔'sɪgnḷ〕*n.* 信號
hungry〔'hʌŋgrɪ〕*adj.* 飢餓的
drink〔drɪŋk〕*v.* 喝
thirsty〔'θɝstɪ〕*adj.* 口渴的

Rest when tired.

疲倦就要休息。

Sleep when exhausted.

筋疲力盡則睡。

Stretch when stiff.

僵硬時則拉筋。

**

rest〔 rɛst 〕*v. n.* 休息

tired〔 taɪrd 〕*adj.* 疲倦的

sleep〔 slip 〕*v.* 睡覺

exhausted〔 ɪgˈzɔstɪd 〕*adj.* 筋疲力盡的

stretch〔 strɛtʃ 〕*v.* 伸展；伸懶腰；

　伸展手腳

stiff〔 stɪf 〕*adj.* 僵硬的

Breathe when stressed.

壓力大深呼吸。

Move when energized.

有活力就要動。

Exercise when restless.

煩躁時做運動。

** ─────────────────

breathe〔 brið 〕 *v.* 呼吸

stressed〔 strɛst 〕 *adj.* 感到有壓力的

move〔 muv 〕 *v.* 動；移動；活動身體

energized〔'ɛnɚ͵dʒaɪzd 〕 *adj.* 有活力的；
   精力充沛的

exercise〔'ɛksɚ͵saɪz 〕 *v.* 運動

restless〔'rɛstlɪs 〕 *adj.* 煩躁不安的；
   急躁的（ = *worried* = *uneasy* ）

【Unit 7 背景說明】

Respond to signals. 要回應身體的信號。(= *Act according to the signals you get.* = *Act according to what your body says.*)

Eat when hungry. 餓的時候就吃東西。(= *Eat when you are hungry.* = *Whenever you're hungry, eat something.*) 副詞子句中，句意很明顯時，主詞和 be 動詞可同時省略。

Drink when thirsty. 渴的時候就喝水。(= *Drink when you are thirsty.*) 也可說成：Whenever you are thirsty, drink something. (每當你渴的時候，就要喝點東西。)

Rest when tired. 疲倦的時候休息。(= *Rest when you are tired.*) 也可說成：When you are tired/ fatigued, take a rest.(當你疲倦的時候，就要休息。)

Sleep when exhausted. 筋疲力盡的時候睡覺。(= *Sleep when you are exhausted.* = *When you are exhausted, go to sleep/go to bed/ take a nap.*)

Stretch when stiff. 僵硬的時候就要伸展。

(= *Stretch when you are stiff.*) 也可説成：

Stretch your muscles when they are stiff.

(當肌肉僵硬時，就要伸展。)

Breathe when stressed. 有壓力時深呼吸。

(= *Breathe when you are stressed.* = *Take deep breaths when you feel stressed.* = *Take deep breaths when you feel under pressure.*)

Move when energized. 有活力時動一動。

(= *Move when you are energized.* = *When you have energy, move.* = *Be active when you have energy.*)

Exercise when restless. 焦躁不安時就運動。

(= *Exercise when you are restless.* = *When you feel restless, do some exercise.*) 因爲運動能轉移注意力。

UNIT **8**

The Secrets to Longevity (I)
長壽的祕訣 **(I)**

Find your purpose.
找到你的目標。

Set clear goals.
設定明確志向。

Chase your dreams.
追求你的夢想。

**

secret〔'sikrɪt〕*n.* 祕密;祕訣 < *to* >
longevity〔lɑn'dʒɛvətɪ〕*n.* 長壽
purpose〔'pɝpəs〕*n.* 目的;目標
set〔sɛt〕*v.* 設定　　clear〔klɪr〕*adj.* 清楚的
goal〔gol〕*n.* 目標
chase〔tʃes〕*v.* 追逐;追求
dream〔drim〕*n.* 夢;夢想

Dreams fuel action.

夢想使人行動。

Dreams increase lifespan.

夢想增加壽命。

Targets increase vitality.

目標增加活力。

**

fuel〔ˋfjuəl〕*v.* 對…供給燃料；為…加油
action〔ˋækʃən〕*n.* 行動
increase〔ɪnˋkris〕*v.* 增加
lifespan〔ˋlaɪfˏspæn〕*n.* 壽命
target〔ˋtɑrgɪt〕*n.* 目標
vitality〔vaɪˋtælətɪ〕*n.* 生命力；活力

Goals foster resilience.

目標培養韌性。

Objectives sustain endurance.

目標維持耐力。

Longevity demands direction.

長壽需要方向。

**

goal〔gol〕*n.* 目標
foster〔'fɑstɚ, 'fɔstɚ〕*v.* 養育；培養；促進
resilience〔rɪ'zɪlɪəns〕*n.* 復原力；韌性
objective〔əb'dʒɛktɪv〕*n.* 目的；目標
sustain〔sə'sten〕*v.* 維持
endurance〔ɪn'djʊrəns〕*n.* 忍耐力；持久力
longevity〔lɑn'dʒɛvətɪ〕*n.* 長壽
demand〔dɪ'mænd〕*v.* 需要
direction〔də'rɛkʃən〕*n.* 方向

【Unit 8 背景説明】

Find your purpose.（要找到你的目標。）也可説成：
Know your purpose in life.（要知道你的人生目標。）

Set clear goals.（要設定明確的目標。）也可説成：
Have clear objectives.（要有明確的目標。）

Chase your dreams.（要追求你的夢想。）也可説成：
Pursue what you want.（要追求你想要的。）

Dreams fuel action.（夢想使人行動。）也可説成：
Having a dream makes one more active.（有夢想使人更積極主動。）

Dreams increase lifespan.　夢想增加壽命。（*= Having a dream helps one live longer.*）

Targets increase vitality.　目標增加活力。（*= Having a target makes one more energetic.*）

Goals foster resilience.　目標培養韌性。（*= Having a goal makes one more resilient/stronger/tougher.*）

Objectives sustain endurance.（目標維持耐力。）也可説成：Having an objective helps you persevere.（有目標能幫助你堅持下去。）

Longevity demands direction.（長壽需要方向。）也可説成：A long life needs a goal.（長壽需要有目標。）

UNIT ❾

The Secrets to Longevity (*II*)
長壽的祕訣 **(II)**

Stay socially active.
活躍於社交圈。

Go to parties.
要多參加派對。

Create strong networks.
建立強大人脈。

** ───────────────

stay〔ste〕*v.* 保持
socially〔'soʃəlɪ〕*adv.* 在社交上
active〔'æktɪv〕*adj.* 活躍的
go to 參加（ *= attend* ）
party〔'pɑrtɪ〕*n.* 派對
create〔krɪ'et〕*v.* 創造
strong〔strɔŋ〕*adj.* 強有力的
network〔'nɛt,wɜk〕*n.* 網路；關係網；
　(*pl.*) 人脈

Find your tribe.

要找到你的同好。

Find like-minded friends.

找志同道合朋友。

Discover shared passions.

發現共同的愛好。

** —————————————

tribe〔traɪb〕*n.* 部落；一大夥人；同夥；

同一類東西

like-minded〔'laɪk'maɪndɪd〕*adj.* 志趣相

投的；看法相同的

discover〔dɪ'skʌvɚ〕*v.* 發現

shared〔ʃɛrd〕*adj.* 共享的；共有的；共同的

passion〔'pæʃən〕*n.* 熱情；愛好

Build solid partnerships.

建立穩固合夥關係。

Build meaningful connections.

建立有意義的人脈。

Connections bring longevity.

人脈越多，壽命越長。

**————————

build〔bɪld〕*v.* 建立

solid〔'salɪd〕*adj.* 堅固的

partnership〔'partnɚ‚ʃɪp〕*n.* 合夥關係

meaningful〔'minɪŋfəl〕*adj.* 有意義的

connection〔kə'nɛkʃən〕*n.* 關連；關係；
（*pl.*）人脈

bring〔brɪŋ〕*v.* 帶來

longevity〔lan'dʒɛvətɪ〕*n.* 長壽

【Unit 9 背景説明】

Stay socially active. 在社交上要保持活躍，也就是「要持續活躍於社交圈。」也可說成：Get involved in social activities.（要參與社交活動。）

Go to parties.（要參加派對。）也可說成：Attend social events.（要參加社交活動。）（=*Participate in social activities*. = *Engage in social activities*.）

Create strong networks.（要創造強大的人脈。）也可說成：Develop close connections with many people.（要和很多人培養密切的關係。）Have a durable network of contacts.（要建立持久的人脈。）

Find your tribe. 要找到你的部落，引申為「要找到你的同好。」也可說成：Find people you feel comfortable with.（要找到你相處起來舒服的人。）Find people you identify with.（要找到你認同的人。）

Find like-minded friends.（要找到志同道合的朋友。）也可說成：Make friends with people who think like you.（要和與你想法相同的人交朋友。）

Discover shared passions.（要發現共同的愛好。）
也可說成：Find out what passions/dreams
that you and others have in common.（要發現
你和其他人有什麼共同的愛好/夢想。）

Build solid partnerships.（要建立穩固的合夥關
係。）也可說成：Develop strong relationships.
（要培養穩固的關係。）

Build meaningful connections.（建立有意義的
人脈。）也可說成：Develop meaningful
relationships.（要培養有意義的關係。）Develop
deep relationships.（要培養深厚的關係。）

Connections bring longevity. 人脈帶來長壽；人脈
越多，壽命越長。(= *Relationships will help you
live longer*. = *You'll live longer if you have a
social network*.)

PART 2　總整理

PART 2・Unit 1~9
中英文錄音QR碼

Unit 1

Cook at home.　在家煮飯。
Eat family meals.　吃家常菜。
Eat seasonal foods.　吃當季食。

Use less oil.　少一點油。
Use less salt.　少一點鹽。
Use less sugar.　少一點糖。

Plan meals ahead.
事先計劃餐點。
Diversify your meals.
餐點要多樣化。
Enjoy variety daily.
每天吃不同菜。

Unit 2

Choose white meat.　選擇白肉。
Eat more chicken.　多吃雞肉。
Eat more fish.　多吃魚肉。

Choose lean meat.　要選擇瘦肉。
Choose low-fat milk.
選低脂牛奶。
Eat mixed nuts.　吃綜合堅果。

Eat in moderation.　吃東西適量。
Always eat slowly.　要細嚼慢嚥。
Don't fill up.　不要吃到飽。

Unit 3

*If you always feel cold,
　you must eat hot-natured
　foods.*
　如果你總是很怕冷，你就必
　須吃熱性食物。

Date, durian, almond.
棗子，榴槤，杏仁。
Longan, lichee, cherry.
龍眼，荔枝，櫻桃。
Peach, guava, olive.
桃子，番石榴，橄欖。

*If you always feel hot, you
　must eat cold-natured
　foods.*
　如果你總是很怕熱，你就必
　須吃寒性食物。

Pear, pomelo, persimmon.
水梨，柚子，柿子。
Plum, melon, watermelon.
李子，香瓜，西瓜。
Strawberry, mulberry,
　banana.
草莓，桑椹，香蕉。

Cold-Natured Foods (*II*)
寒性食物 (II)

Starfruit, grapefruit,
  dragon fruit.
楊桃，葡萄柚，火龍果。
Tomato, tangerine, kiwi.
蕃茄，橘子，奇異果。
Loquat, mangosteen, wax
  apple. 枇杷，山竹，蓮霧。

Unit 4

Exercise every day.
每天都要運動。
Get quality sleep.
會有優質睡眠。
Improve your flexibility.
改善身體彈性。

Burn excess calories.
燃燒多餘熱量。
Lose some fat.
減少一些脂肪。
Maintain your weight.
維持你的體重。

Prevent chronic diseases.
預防慢性疾病。
Enhance your immunity.
會增加免疫力。
Boost your metabolism.
提高新陳代謝。

Unit 5

Work out daily. 要每天運動。
Consistent exercise pays.
常運動值得。
Always be active. 要動個不停。

Improve your circulation.
改善血液循環。
Protect your joints.
保護你的關節。
Strengthen your heart.
強化你的心臟。

Build strong muscles.
會增強肌肉。
Increase lung capacity.
增加肺活量。
Detox your body. 讓身體排毒。

Unit 6

Have good posture.
有良好姿勢。
Don't ever hunch. 絕不要彎腰。
Don't ever slouch. 絕不要駝背。

Keep heads up. 頭要抬起來。
Keep shoulders back.
胸要挺起來。
Always stand tall. 要抬頭挺胸。

Sit up straight. 要能坐直。
Stand up straight. 要能站直。
Stride with confidence.
跨大步走。

Unit 7

Respond to signals.
回應身體信號。
Eat when hungry.
餓了就要吃飯。
Drink when thirsty.
渴了就要喝水。

Rest when tired. 疲倦就要休息。
Sleep when exhausted.
筋疲力盡則睡。
Stretch when stiff.
僵硬時則拉筋。

Breathe when stressed.
壓力大深呼吸。
Move when energized.
有活力就要動。
Exercise when restless.
煩躁時做運動。

Unit 8

Find your purpose.
找到你的目標。
Set clear goals. 設定明確志向。
Chase your dreams.
追求你的夢想。

Dreams fuel action.
夢想使人行動。
Dreams increase lifespan.
夢想增加壽命。
Targets increase vitality.
目標增加活力。

Goals foster resilience.
目標培養韌性。
Objectives sustain
    endurance.
目標維持耐力。
Longevity demands
    direction. 長壽需要方向。

Unit 9

Stay socially active.
活躍於社交圈。
Go to parties.
要多參加派對。
Create strong networks.
建立強大人脈。

Find your tribe.
要找到你的同好。
Find like-minded friends.
找志同道合朋友。
Discover shared passions.
發現共同的愛好。

Build solid partnerships.
建立穩固合夥關係。
Build meaningful
    connections.
建立有意義的人脈。
Connections bring
    longevity.
人脈越多，壽命越長。

BOOK 2・PART 2

BOOK 2 \ PART 3

Have an Amazing Life
擁有很棒的人生

PART 3 · Unit 1~9
英文錄音QR碼

UNIT ❶

Be Your Best Self
做最好的自己

You're not alone.
你不孤單。

You're worth it.
你有價值。

You're not worthless.
非無價值。

** ────────────

self〔sɛlf〕*n.* 自己
alone〔əˈlon〕*adj.* 獨自的；孤獨的
worth〔wɝθ〕*adj.* 值得…的
worth it 值得的
worthless〔ˈwɝθlɪs〕*adj.* 無價值的；沒用的

Keep moving forward.

持續進步。

Keep pushing forward.

持續前進。

Keep pushing through.

堅持到底。

** ────────────

keep〔kip〕*v.* 持續

keep + V-ing 持續…

move〔muv〕*v.* 移動

forward〔'fɔrwɚd〕*adv.* 向前

move forward 前進

push〔puʃ〕*v.* 推

push forward 向前推進；奮勇前進

push through 擠過去；設法完成

You have potential.

你有潛力。

Take small steps.

一步步來。

You can overcome.

你能克服。

** ────────────

potential〔pə'tɛnʃəl〕*n.* 潛力

small〔smɔl〕*adj.* 小的

step〔stɛp〕*n.* 一步

take a step 走一步

overcome〔͵ovɚ'kʌm〕*v.* 克服；

　得勝（= *win*）

【Unit 1 背景説明】

You're not alone*.*（你不孤單。）也可説成：We're with you.（我們都與你同在。）

You're worth it*.*（你是值得的；你有價值。）也可説成：You're valuable.（你很珍貴。）

You're not worthless*.*（你並非沒有價值。）也可説成：You're not a loser.（你不是個輸家。）You have value.（你有價值。）

Keep moving forward*.* 要持續前進。（= *Keep going.*）

Keep pushing forward*.* 要持續奮勇前進。（= *Continue to advance.*）

Keep pushing through*.*（要設法把事情完成。）也可説成：Stick it out.（要堅持到底。）Persist.（要堅持。）Persevere.（要堅忍。）

You have potential*.*（你有潛力。）也可説成：You have ability.（你有能力。）（= *You're capable.*）

Take small steps*.*（要小幅邁進。）也可説成：Go slow.（慢慢來。）Take it one step at a time.（一步一腳印。）Take it one day at a time.（順其自然，隨遇而安。）

You can overcome*.*（你能克服。）也可説成：You can overcome anything.（你能克服任何事。）

UNIT ❷

Pursue What You Want
追求你想要的

Keep chasing dreams.

持續追夢。

Keep seeking opportunities.

尋找機會。

Keep pursuing excellence.

追求卓越。

＊＊ ────────────

pursue〔pɚ'su〕*v.* 追求　　***keep + V-ing*** 持續⋯
chase〔tʃes〕*v.* 追逐；追尋；追求
dream〔drim〕*n.* 夢；夢想
seek〔sik〕*v.* 尋求；尋找
opportunity〔͵ɑpɚ'tjunətɪ〕*n.* 機會
excellence〔'ɛksləns〕*n.* 優秀；卓越

Keep challenging yourself.

持續挑戰自我。

Face challenges bravely.

勇於面對挑戰。

Face fears courageously.

勇於面對恐懼。

** ──────────────

keep* + *V-ing 持續…

challenge〔'tʃælɪndʒ〕*v. n.* 挑戰

face〔fes〕*v.* 面對

bravely〔'brevlɪ〕*adv.* 勇敢地

fear〔fɪr〕*n.* 恐懼

courageously〔kə'redʒəslɪ〕*adv.* 勇敢地

Recognize your worth.

自知之明。

Don't discount yourself.

勿貶自己。

Never stop trying.

百折不撓。

** ─────────

recognize〔'rɛkəg͵naɪz〕*v.* 認得；認清

worth〔wɝθ〕*n.* 價值

discount〔'dɪskaʊnt, dɪs'kaʊnt〕*v.* 對…

打折扣；不全相信；忽視

never〔'nɛvɚ〕*adv.* 絕不

stop + *V-ing* 停止…

try〔traɪ〕*v.* 嘗試；努力

【Unit 2 背景説明】

Keep chasing dreams. 持續追求夢想。
(= *Follow your dreams*.)

Keep seeking opportunities. 持續尋找機會。
(= *Always look for new opportunities*.)

Keep pursuing excellence. 持續追求卓越。
(= *Strive for excellence*. = *Seek greatness*.)

Keep challenging yourself. (持續挑戰自我。)
也可説成：Continue trying to improve. (持
續努力求進步。) Keep growing. (持續成長。)

Face challenges bravely. (勇於面對挑戰。) 也
可説成：Be courageous in the face of
difficulty. (勇敢面對困難。)

Face fears courageously. 勇於面對恐懼。
(= *Be brave when you have to deal with
something that makes you nervous*.)

Recognize your worth. 認清自己的價值。
(= *Know your value*.)

Don't discount yourself. 不要貶低自己。
(= *Don't put yourself down*.)

Never stop trying. (絕不停止努力。) 也可説成：
Never give up. (絕不放棄。)

UNIT ❸

You Are Remarkable

你很棒

You're a fighter.

你是鬥士。

You're a warrior.

你是戰士。

Persevere and succeed.

堅忍成功。

**

remarkable〔rɪ'mɑrkəbḷ〕*adj.* 出色的；很棒的

fighter〔'faɪtɚ〕*n.* 戰士；鬥士；武士

warrior〔'wɔrɪɚ〕*n.* 武士；勇士；戰士

persevere〔͵pɝsə'vɪr〕*v.* 堅忍

succeed〔sək'sid〕*v.* 成功

Your light shines.

你在發光發亮。

Keep shining bright.

持續光輝燦爛。

Keep holding on.

持續堅持下去。

** ─────────────

light〔laɪt〕*n.* 光；光線

shine〔ʃaɪn〕*v.* 發光；發亮；照耀

keep + V-ing 持續…

bright〔braɪt〕*adv.* 明亮地

shine bright 燦爛

hold on 繼續下去；持續；堅持

You are cherished.

你被人疼愛。

Love surrounds you.

你被愛包圍。

You deserve happiness.

你值得幸福。

**

cherish〔'tʃɛrɪʃ〕*v.* 珍惜

love〔lʌv〕*n.* 愛

surround〔sə'raʊnd〕*v.* 環繞；包圍

deserve〔dɪ'zɝv〕*v.* 應得

happiness〔'hæpɪnɪs〕*n.* 快樂；幸福

【Unit 3 背景説明】

You're a fighter.（你是鬥士。）也可説成：*You're a warrior*.（你是戰士。）You're a winner.（你是贏家。）You're a survivor.（你很會求生存。）You're tough.（你很頑強。）

Persevere and succeed. 堅忍就會成功。(= *Keep at it and win*.)

Your light shines.（你正在發光發亮。）也可説成：People see your good work.（人們看到你良好的表現。）

Keep shining bright.（要持續光輝燦爛。）也可説成：Keep going.（要持續努力。）Keep doing what you're doing.（要持續做你正在做的事。）Keep doing good.（要持續好好表現。）

Keep holding on.（要持續堅持。）也可説成：Don't give up.（不要放棄。）

You are cherished.（你受人珍惜。）也可説成：You are valued.（你受重視。）You are loved.（你受人喜愛。）

Love surrounds you. 你被愛包圍。(= *Love is all around you*.)也可説成：Everyone loves you.（每個人都愛你。）

You deserve happiness. 你應該獲得幸福。(= *You've earned the right to be happy*.)

UNIT 4

How to Say Thank You
如何說謝謝

I'm so thankful.
我很感謝。

I'm truly grateful.
眞的感謝。

I'm deeply appreciative.
深表感激。

**

so〔so〕*adv.* 很;非常
thankful〔'θæŋkfəl〕*adj.* 感謝的
truly〔'trulɪ〕*adv.* 眞地
grateful〔'gretfəl〕*adj.* 感激的
deeply〔'diplɪ〕*adv.* 深深地
appreciative〔ə'priʃɪ,etɪv〕*adj.* 感激的

Thanks a lot.

非常感謝。

Thanks a million.

萬分感謝。

Thanks a bunch.

非常感激。

** ────────────────

thanks〔θæŋks〕*n. pl.* 感謝

a lot 非常

million〔'mɪljən〕*n.* 百萬;非常多;無數

bunch〔bʌntʃ〕*n.* 一堆;一把

a bunch 許多;大量

I feel blessed.

我有福氣。

Words fail me.

難以言喻。

It's beyond words.

難以言表。

** ————————————

blessed〔'blɛsɪd〕*adj.* 幸福的

words〔wɜdz〕*n. pl.* 言詞；話

fail〔fel〕*v.* 使失望；對⋯派不上用場

words fail me 我驚訝得說不出話來；
我不知道說什麼才好

beyond〔bɪ'jɑnd〕*prep.* 超出⋯的範圍

beyond words 難以用言語形容

【Unit 4 背景説明】

I'm so thankful. 我非常感謝。(= *I'm very thankful*.)

I'm truly grateful. 我眞的很感激。(= *I really appreciate it*.)

I'm deeply appreciative. (我深表感激。) 也可説成：I can't thank you enough. (我再怎麼感謝你也不爲過。)

Thanks a lot. 非常感謝。(= *Thanks very much*.)

Thanks a million. 萬分感謝。(= *Thanks a billion*. = *Thanks a lot*.)

Thanks a bunch. 非常感謝。(= *Thanks a bundle*. = *Thanks very much*.)

I feel blessed. (我覺得很幸福。) 也可説成：I feel fortunate. (我覺得很幸運。) (= *I feel lucky*.)

Words fail me. 我說不出話來。(= *I'm speechless*.)；我不知道該說什麼。(= *I don't know what to say*.)

It's beyond words. (這是用言語無法形容的。) 也可説成：I cannot express it. (我不知道如何表達。)

BOOK 2 · PART 3

UNIT 5

Show Your Appreciation
表示感激

I appreciate it.
我很感謝。

I appreciate everything.
感謝一切。

Truly appreciative here.
真心感謝。

**　———————————

show〔ʃo〕*v.* 表示
appreciation〔ə,priʃɪ'eʃən〕*n.* 感激
appreciate〔ə'priʃɪ,et〕*v.* 欣賞；重視；感激
truly〔'trulɪ〕*adv.* 真地
appreciative〔ə'priʃɪ,etɪv〕*adv.* 感激的
here〔hɪr〕*adv.* 在這裡【可指 me（我）或 us（我們）】

I value you.

我重視你。

I cherish you.

我珍惜你。

I treasure you.

我珍愛你。

** ————————

value〔'væljʊ〕*v.* 重視

cherish〔'tʃɛrɪʃ〕*v.* 珍惜

treasure〔'trɛʒɚ〕*v.* 珍愛；珍視；珍藏

    n. 寶藏；寶貴的人；難得的人（= *gem*）

I owe you.

我欠你的。

You're so kind.

你很善良。

You're truly amazing.

你太棒了。

**

owe〔o〕*v.* 欠

so〔so〕*adv.* 很；非常

kind〔kaɪnd〕*adj.* 仁慈的；親切的

truly〔'trulɪ〕*adv.* 眞地

amazing〔ə'mezɪŋ〕*adj.* 令人驚訝的；
令人驚喜的；很棒的

【Unit 5 背景説明】

I appreciate it. 我很感激。(= *I'm grateful.*)

I appreciate everything. (我感激一切。) 也可説成：
I'm thankful for everything you've done. (我
感激你所做的一切。)

Truly appreciative here. 我眞的很感激。(= *I'm
truly appreciative here.*) here 在此指「我」，即
「説話者本人」(the speaker)。

I value you. 我重視你。(= *I appreciate you.*)

I cherish you. (我珍惜你。) 也可説成：You're
valuable. (你很珍貴。)

I treasure you. (我珍愛你。) 也可説成：You're
a treasure. (你很珍貴。)(= *You're a gem.*)

I owe you. (我欠你一次。) 也可説成：I'll return
the favor someday. (有一天我會報答這個恩惠。)
You did me a big favor. (你幫了我很大的忙。)

You're so kind. 你人眞好。(= *You're very nice.*) 也
可説成：You're very thoughtful. (你非常體貼。)

You're truly amazing. 你眞的很棒。(= *You're
wonderful.* = *You're awesome.*)

UNIT 6

My Mistake
是我的錯

It's my fault.
是我的錯。

I'm to blame.
我該受責。

I'm sincerely sorry.
我很抱歉。

** ―――――――――

mistake〔məˈstek〕*n.* 錯誤
fault〔fɔlt〕*n.* 過錯
blame〔blem〕*v.* 責備
be to blame 該受責備
sincerely〔sɪnˈsɪrlɪ〕*adv.* 眞誠地
sorry〔ˈsɔrɪ〕*adj.* 抱歉的

I was wrong.

我真錯了。

You were right.

你是對的。

Please forgive me.

請原諒我。

**　———————————

wrong〔 rɔŋ 〕*adj.* 錯誤的

right〔 raɪt 〕*adj.* 對的

forgive〔 fɚˈɡɪv 〕*v.* 原諒

It wasn't intentional.
並非有意。

I wasn't thinking.
我沒想通。

I regret it.
我很後悔。

**

intentional〔ɪnˈtɛnʃənḷ〕*adj.* 有意的；
故意的
think〔θɪŋk〕*v.* 想；思考
regret〔rɪˈɡrɛt〕*v.* 後悔

【Unit 6 背景說明】

It's my fault. (那是我的錯。) 也可説成：My bad.
(是我的錯。) My mistake. (是我的錯。)

I'm to blame. (我該受責備。) 也可説成：I'm
responsible. (我該負責。) This one is on me.
(我的錯，我來負責。)

I'm sincerely sorry. 我真的很抱歉。(= *I'm truly
sorry.*)

I was wrong. 我錯了。(= *I was mistaken.*)

You were right. 你是對的。(= *You were correct.
= You had it right.*)

Please forgive me. 請原諒我。(= *Please excuse me.*)

It wasn't intentional. (那不是故意的。) 也可説成：
I didn't mean it. (我不是有意的。) I didn't do
it on purpose. (我不是故意那麼做的。) It was an
accident. (那是個意外。)

I wasn't thinking. (我當時沒想清楚。) 也可説成：
I was careless. (我當時不小心。)

I regret it. (我很後悔。) 也可説成：I'm sorry.
(我很抱歉。)

⸢UNIT ❼

See the World
看看這個世界

Be a traveler.
成爲旅人。

Be a globe-trotter.
走遍天涯。

Explore the world.
探索世界。

** ─────────

traveler〔'trævḷɚ〕 *n.* 旅行者;旅客;遊客

globe〔glob〕 *n.* 地球

trot〔trɑt〕 *v.* 走;慢跑;急行

globe-trotter〔'glob͵trɑtɚ〕 *n.* 周遊列國者;
環球旅行者

explore〔ɪk'splor〕 *v.* 探險;探索

See the unseen.

見未見的。

Explore unfamiliar places.

探索未知。

Discover hidden paradises.

尋祕仙境。

**────────────

unseen〔ʌn'sin〕*adj.* 未被看見的

explore〔ɪk'splor〕*v.* 探險;探索

unfamiliar〔͵ʌnfə'mɪljɚ〕*adj.* 不熟悉的

discover〔dɪ'skʌvɚ〕*v.* 發現;找到

hidden〔'hɪdn̩〕*adj.* 隱藏的;隱密的

paradise〔'pærə͵daɪs〕*n.* 天堂;樂園;
　　像天堂一樣的地方

Forget about comfort.

別管舒適。

Escape your routine.

逃脫慣例。

Find inspiration everywhere.

遍尋靈感。

** ───────

forget〔fɚ'gɛt〕*v.* 忘記

forget about 忘記；對…不放在心上

comfort〔'kʌmfɚt〕*n.* 舒適

escape〔ə'skep〕*v.* 逃離

routine〔ru'tin〕*n.* 例行公事；慣例

inspiration〔͵ɪnspə'reʃən〕*n.* 激勵；靈感；啓發

everywhere〔'ɛvrɪ͵hwɛr〕*adv.* 到處

【Unit 7 背景説明】

Be a traveler.（要成為旅行者；要去旅行。）也可
説成：Travel to many places.（要去很多地方
旅行。）Travel often.（要常常旅行。）

Be a globe-trotter.（要成為環球旅行者；要行遍天
下。）也可説成：Travel around the world.（要
環遊世界。）Travel widely.（要周遊四方。）

Explore the world.　要探索世界。(＝*See the
world.*) 也可説成：Travel.（要去旅行。）Go
to new places.（要去沒去過的地方。）

See the unseen.　要看沒看過的。(＝*See new
things.＝See things no one else has.*)

Explore unfamiliar places.　要探索不熟悉的地方。
(＝*Explore new places.＝Explore some place
you know nothing about.*) 也可説成：Go
places no one has been before.（要去以前沒有
人去過的地方。）Go places no one knows
about.（要去沒有人知道的地方。）

Discover hidden paradises.（要找到隱密的仙境。）
也可説成：Find great places that few people
know.（要找到很少人知道的很棒的地方。）Find
wonderful new places.（要找到很很棒的，沒去
過的地方。）

Forget about comfort. 別管舒適。(= *Don't*
worry about comfort.) 也可説成：Don't let a
lack of comfort stop you.（不要讓缺乏舒適阻擋
你。）Go somewhere you're unfamiliar with.
（去你不熟悉的地方。）

Escape your routine.（逃脫慣例。）也可説成：
Break your routine.（打破慣例。）Do
something different.（做不一樣的事。）Do
something you don't usually do.（做你平常
不會做的事。）

Find inspiration everywhere.（要到處尋找靈感。）
也可説成：Be inspired by everything you see.
（要因爲你所看見的每件事物而受到啓發。）

⌐ UNIT **8**

Travel Does You Good
旅行對你有益

Traveling is healthy.
旅行有益健康。

Taste exotic cuisine.
品味異國料理。

Relax and rejuvenate.
放鬆恢復活力。

＊＊ ─────────────

travel〔'trævl̩〕*v. n.* 旅行
do *sb.* ***good*** 對某人有益
healthy〔'hɛlθɪ〕*adj.* 健康的；有益健康的
taste〔test〕*v.* 品嚐
exotic〔ɪg'zɑtɪk〕*adj.* 有異國風味的
cuisine〔kwɪ'zin〕*n.* 烹飪；菜餚
relax〔rɪ'læks〕*v.* 放鬆
rejuvenate〔rɪ'dʒuvə‚net〕*v.* 返老還童；恢復活力

Seek unforgettable experiences.

尋求難忘經驗。

Collect lifelong memories.

收集終生回憶。

Create lifelong friendships.

建立終生友誼。

**

seek〔sik〕*v.* 尋求;尋找

unforgettable〔ˌʌnfɚˈgɛtəbl̩〕*adj.* 難忘的

experience〔ɪkˈspɪrɪəns〕*n.* 經驗

collect〔kəˈlɛkt〕*v.* 收集

lifelong〔ˈlaɪfˌlɔŋ〕*adj.* 終生的

memory〔ˈmɛmərɪ〕*n.* 記憶;回憶

create〔krɪˈet〕*v.* 創造

friendship〔ˈfrɛndʃɪp〕*n.* 友誼

Embrace new cultures.

接受新的文化。

Expand your perspective.

擴展你的眼界。

Foster personal growth.

促進個人成長。

** ————————————————

embrace〔ɪmˈbres〕*v.* 擁抱；欣然接受

culture〔ˈkʌltʃɚ〕*n.* 文化

expand〔ɪkˈspænd〕*v.* 擴大；擴展；增加

perspective〔pɚˈspɛktɪv〕*n.* 正確的眼光；
看法；眼界

foster〔ˈfɑstɚ, ˈfɔstɚ〕*v.* 培育；產生

personal〔ˈpɝsn̩l〕*adj.* 個人的

growth〔groθ〕*n.* 成長

【Unit 8 背景説明】

Traveling is healthy.（旅行有益健康。）也可説成：
Traveling is good for you.（旅行對你有益。）
Traveling is a healthy pastime.（旅行是有益健康
的消遣。）

Taste exotic cuisine.（品嚐異國料理。）也可説成：
Try new foods.（嘗試新的食物。）

Relax and rejuvenate.（放鬆並恢復活力。）也可説
成：Rest and restore your energy.（休息並恢復你
的活力。）Rest and recharge.（休息並再次充電。）

Seek unforgettable experiences.（要尋求難忘的
經驗。）也可説成：Look for memorable
experiences.（要尋找難忘的經驗。）Look for
new and amazing things to do.（要尋找新的而
且很棒的事情來做。）

Collect lifelong memories.（要收集終生的回憶。）
也可説成：Do memorable things.（要做一些難
忘的事。）Do things that you will never forget.
（要做一些你絕不會忘記的事。）

BOOK 2, PART 3

Create lifelong friendships. (要建立終生的友誼。)
也可說成 : Make friends for life. (要結交終生的
朋友。) Make friends that you will keep
forever. (要結交一輩子的朋友。)

Embrace new cultures. (要接受新的文化。) 也可
說成 : Be excited about seeing a different
culture. (要對看到不同的文化感到興奮。)
Throw yourself into a new culture. (要讓自
己置身於新的文化中。)

Expand your perspective. 要擴展你的眼界。
(= *Widen your view.* = *Broaden your mind.*
= *Be broad-minded.*)

Foster personal growth. 促進個人的成長。
(= *Nurture your personal growth.*) 也可說成 :
Develop yourself. (要發展自我。)

UNIT ❾

Be Adventurous
勇於冒險

Embrace limitless possibilities.

擁抱無限可能。

Embrace endless wonders.

擁抱無限驚奇。

Let curiosity guide.

讓好奇心引導。

** ———————————————

adventurous〔əd'vɛntʃərəs〕*adj.* 愛冒險的
embrace〔ɪm'bres〕*v.* 擁抱；欣然接受
limitless〔'lɪmɪtlɪs〕*adj.* 無限的
possibility〔ˌpɑsə'bɪlətɪ〕*n.* 可能性；可能（的事）
endless〔'ɛndlɪs〕*adj.* 無休止的；無窮盡的
wonder〔'wʌndɚ〕*n.* 奇觀；奇蹟；驚奇；奇事
curiosity〔ˌkjʊrɪ'ɑsətɪ〕*n.* 好奇心
guide〔gaɪd〕*v.* 引導

Embrace the unfamiliar.

擁抱不熟悉事。

Conquer unfamiliar cities.

征服陌生城市。

Experience unfamiliar dishes.

體驗陌生美食。

** ───────────

embrace〔ɪm'bres〕*v.* 擁抱；欣然接受

unfamiliar〔͵ʌnfə'mɪljɚ〕*adj.* 不熟悉的

the unfamiliar 不熟悉的事物

(= *unfamiliar things*)

conquer〔'kɑŋkɚ〕*v.* 征服

city〔'sɪtɪ〕*n.* 城市

experience〔ɪk'spɪrɪəns〕*v.* 經歷；體驗

n. 經驗　　dish〔dɪʃ〕*n.* 菜餚

Savor diverse flavors.

品嚐多樣口味。

Embrace cultural diversity.

接納各種文化。

Always celebrate diversity.

為多樣化歡呼。

** ———————————————

savor〔ˈsevɚ〕*v.* 品嚐

diverse〔dəˈvɝs, daɪ-〕*adj.* 各種的；不同的

flavor〔ˈflevɚ〕*n.* 口味

embrace〔ɪmˈbres〕*v.* 擁抱；欣然接受

cultural〔ˈkʌltʃərəl〕*adj.* 文化的

diversity〔dəˈvɝsətɪ, daɪ-〕*n.* 多樣性；多樣化

celebrate〔ˈsɛləˌbret〕*v.* 慶祝；頌揚；讚美

【Unit 9 背景說明】

Embrace limitless possibilities. (擁抱無限的可能。) 也可說成：Appreciate all the chances you have. (要重視你所擁有的所有機會。)
Welcome new opportunities. (歡迎新的機會。)
Welcome new experiences. (歡迎新的經驗。)

Embrace endless wonders. (擁抱無限驚奇。) 也可說成：Welcome the world's unending marvels. (歡迎全世界無止盡的奇蹟。)

Let curiosity guide. (讓好奇心引導。) 也可說成：Follow your interests. (跟著你的興趣走。)
Pursue interesting things. (要追求有趣的事。)
Be curious. (要有好奇心。)

Embrace the unfamiliar. (要接受不熟悉的事物。) 也可說成：Don't be afraid of new things. (不要害怕新的事物。) Welcome new experiences. (要歡迎新的經驗。)

Conquer unfamiliar cities.（要征服陌生的城市。）
也可説成：Explore new cities.（要探索新的城
市。）Get comfortable in new places.（在新的
地方要感到自在。）

Experience unfamiliar dishes.（要體驗不熟悉的
菜餚。）也可説成：Try new foods.（要嘗試新的
食物。）

Savor diverse flavors. 要品嚐不同的口味。(=*Enjoy
a variety of flavors.*) 也可説成：Enjoy new
foods.（要享用新的食物。）

Embrace cultural diversity.（要接受各種文化。）
也可説成：Appreciate different cultures.（要
欣賞不同的文化。）Appreciate cultural
differences.（要欣賞文化的差異。）

Always celebrate diversity. 要為多樣化歡呼。
(=*Rejoice in variety.*) 也可説成：Appreciate
the variety the world offers.（要欣賞這個世界
提供的多樣性。）

BOOK 2・PART 3

PART 3・Unit 1~9
中英文錄音QR碼

PART 3 總整理

Unit 1

You're not alone.
你不孤單。
You're worth it. 你有價值。
You're not worthless.
非無價值。

Keep moving forward.
持續進步。
Keep pushing forward.
持續前進。
Keep pushing through.
堅持到底。

You have potential.
你有潛力。
Take small steps. 一步步來。
You can overcome.
你能克服。

Unit 2

Keep chasing dreams.
持續追夢。
Keep seeking
opportunities. 尋找機會。
Keep pursuing excellence.
追求卓越。

Keep challenging yourself.
持續挑戰自我。
Face challenges bravely.
勇於面對挑戰。
Face fears courageously.
勇於面對恐懼。

Recognize your worth.
自知之明。
Don't discount yourself.
勿貶自己。
Never stop trying.
百折不撓。

Unit 3

You're a fighter.
你是鬥士。
You're a warrior.
你是戰士。
Persevere and succeed.
堅忍成功。

Your light shines.
你在發光發亮。
Keep shining bright.
持續光輝燦爛。
Keep holding on.
持續堅持下去。

You are cherished.
你被人疼愛。
Love surrounds you.
你被愛包圍。
You deserve happiness.
你值得幸福。

Unit 4

I'm so thankful.　我很感謝。
I'm truly grateful.
真的感謝。
I'm deeply appreciative.
深表感激。

Thanks a lot.　非常感謝。
Thanks a million.
萬分感謝。
Thanks a bunch.　非常感激。

I feel blessed.　我有福氣。
Words fail me.　難以言喻。
It's beyond words.
難以言表。

Unit 5

I appreciate it.　我很感謝。
I appreciate everything.
感謝一切。
Truly appreciative here.
真心感謝。

I value you.　我重視你。
I cherish you.　我珍惜你。
I treasure you.　我珍愛你。

I owe you.　我欠你的。
You're so kind.　你很善良。
You're truly amazing.
你太棒了。

Unit 6

It's my fault.　是我的錯。
I'm to blame.　我該受責。
I'm sincerely sorry.
我很抱歉。

I was wrong.　我真錯了。
You were right.　你是對的。
Please forgive me.
請原諒我。

It wasn't intentional.
並非有意。
I wasn't thinking.
我沒想通。
I regret it.　我很後悔。

Unit 7

Be a traveler.　成為旅人。
Be a globe-trotter.
走遍天涯。
Explore the world.
探索世界。

See the unseen.
見未見的。
Explore unfamiliar places.
探索未知。
Discover hidden
    paradises. 尋祕仙境。

Forget about comfort.
別管舒適。
Escape your routine.
逃脫慣例。
Find inspiration
    everywhere. 遍尋靈感。

Unit 8

Traveling is healthy.
旅行有益健康。
Taste exotic cuisine.
品味異國料理。
Relax and rejuvenate.
放鬆恢復活力。

Seek unforgettable
    experiences.
尋求難忘經驗。
Collect lifelong memories.
收集終生回憶。
Create lifelong friendships.
建立終生友誼。

Embrace new cultures.
接受新的文化。
Expand your perspective.
擴展你的眼界。
Foster personal growth.
促進個人成長。

Unit 9

Embrace limitless
    possibilities.
擁抱無限可能。
Embrace endless
    wonders.
擁抱無限驚奇。
Let curiosity guide.
讓好奇心引導。

Embrace the unfamiliar.
擁抱不熟悉事。
Conquer unfamiliar cities.
征服陌生城市。
Experience unfamiliar
    dishes. 體驗陌生美食。

Savor diverse flavors.
品嚐多樣口味。
Embrace cultural
    diversity. 接納各種文化。
Always celebrate
    diversity. 爲多樣化歡呼。

BOOK 3 　 PART 1

Tips for Good Emotional Health

情緒健康的秘訣

PART 1・Unit 1~9
英文錄音QR碼

UNIT 1

Be Optimistic
要樂觀

Always stay positive.

保持樂觀。

Think positive thoughts.

正面思考。

Say positive words.

要說好話。

**

optimistic〔͵ɑptə'mɪstɪk〕*adj.* 樂觀的

always〔'ɔlwez〕*adv.* 總是；一直

stay〔ste〕*v.* 保持　positive〔'pɑzətɪv〕*adj.*
　正面的；積極的；樂觀的；好的

think〔θɪŋk〕*v.* 想；心懷…（想法）

thought〔θɔt〕*n.* 思想；想法

words〔wɜdz〕*n. pl.* 言詞；話

See the good.

看好的一面。

Radiate high spirits.

要散發朝氣。

Radiate hopeful energy.

散發正能量。

** ——————

good〔gʊd〕*n.* 善；優點；長處；好事

radiate〔'redɪ/et〕*v.* 散發；輻射

spirit〔'spɪrɪt〕*n.* 精神

high spirits 歡欣；快樂；興高采烈

hopeful〔'hopfəl〕*adj.* 充滿希望的

energy〔'ɛnə·dʒɪ〕*n.* 能量

Rise above fear.

不要恐懼。

Rise above doubt.

不要懷疑。

Rise above negativity.

不要悲觀。

** ────────────

rise〔raɪz〕*v.* 上升

rise above 高出；超越；克服；擺脫；
不受…影響

fear〔fɪr〕*n.* 恐懼

doubt〔daʊt〕*n.* 懷疑

negativity〔͵nɛgə'tɪvətɪ〕*n.* 負面；否定；
消極的態度

【Unit 1 背景説明】

Always stay positive. 總是保持樂觀。(= *Remain positive. = Stay optimistic.*)

Think positive thoughts. 要正面思考。(= *Think postitive. = Think happy thoughts.*) 也可説成：
Think optimistic thoughts. (要有樂觀的想法。)
Have a positive attitude. (要有樂觀的態度。)

Say positive words. 要說好話。(= *Say positive things. = Say optimistic things.*) 也可説成：
Don't make negative comments. (不要有負面的評論。)

See the good. 要看好的一面。(= *See the positive. = See the sunny side of things. = Look on the bright side of things.*)

Radiate high spirits. (要散發快樂。) 也可説成：
Be cheerful in everything you do. (做任何事都要快樂。) Be energetic in everything you do. (做任何事都要充滿活力。)

Radiate hopeful energy. （要散發充滿希望的能
量。）也可說成：Spread good vibes. （要散發
正能量。） Spread optimism. （要散發樂觀。）
（ = *Spread positivity.* ） Spread confidence.
（要散發自信。）

Rise above fear. 要克服恐懼；不要恐懼。
（ = *Overcome fear.* ）也可說成：Defeat
anxiety. （要戰勝焦慮。）

Rise above doubt. 要克服懷疑；不要懷疑。
（ = *Overcome doubt.* ）也可說成：Don't let
doubt hold you back. （不要讓懷疑阻礙你。）

Rise above negativity. 要克服負面情緒；不要
悲觀。（ = *Overcome negativity.* ）也可說成：
Conquer pessimism. （要征服悲觀。） Don't
let negativity hold you back. （不要讓負面
情緒阻礙你。）

UNIT ❷

Don't Just Whine
不要只會抱怨

Don't ever complain.
切勿抱怨。

Complaining achieves nothing.
埋怨無益。

Complaining solves nothing.
牢騷無用。

** ───────────

just〔dʒʌst〕*adv.* 僅；只

whine〔hwaɪn〕*v.* 抱怨（= *complain*）

don't ever 絕不（= *never*）

complain〔kəm'plen〕*v.* 抱怨

achieve〔ə'tʃiv〕*v.* 達成

solve〔sɑlv〕*v.* 解決

Complaining is pointless.

抱怨無意義。

Complaining doesn't help.

抱怨沒有用。

Seek positive solutions.

尋找好解方。

** ——————————

complain〔kəm'plen〕*v.* 抱怨

pointless〔'pɔɪntlɪs〕*adj.* 無意義的

help〔hɛlp〕*v.* 有幫助；有用

seek〔sik〕*v.* 尋求；尋找

positive〔'pɑzətɪv〕*adj.* 正面的；積極的；
　樂觀的；好的

solution〔sə'luʃən〕*n.* 解決之道

Stop being critical.

停止批評。

Change your mindset.

改變心態。

Make things better.

情況變好。

** ─────────────────

stop* + *V-ing 停止⋯

critical 〔ˈkrɪtɪkḷ 〕 *adj.* 批評的；吹毛求疵的

change 〔 tʃendʒ 〕 *v.* 改變

mindset 〔ˈmaɪndˌsɛt 〕 *n.* 心態

make 〔 mek 〕 *v.* 使

things 〔 θɪŋz 〕 *n. pl.* 事情；情況

【Unit 2 背景說明】

Don't ever complain*.* 絕對不要抱怨。(= *Never complain.* = *Never grumble.* = *Never whine.*)

Complaining achieves nothing*.* (抱怨無法達成任何事。) 也可說成：Complaining doesn't help. (抱怨沒有用。)

Complaining solves nothing*.* 抱怨無法解決任何問題。(= *Complaining doesn't resolve problems.*)

Complaining is pointless*.* 抱怨沒有意義。(= *Complaining is meaningless.*)

Complaining doesn't help*.* 抱怨沒有用。(= *Complaining is useless.* = *Complaining is of no use.*)

Seek positive solutions*.* 要尋找有效的解決方法。(= *Look for a real solution.* = *Look for a solution that will work.*)

Stop being critical*.* 停止批評。(= *Stop being judgmental.*) 也可說成：Stop being disapproving. (不要一直反對。)

Change your mindset*.* (改變你的心態。) 也可說成：Change your attitude. (改變你的態度。)

Make things better*.* 讓情況變得更好。(= *Improve things.* = *Improve the situation.*)

BOOK 3 · PART 1

UNIT ❸

Share Your Positivity
分享你的正能量

Spread positive vibes.
傳播正面能量。

Spread sunshine everywhere.
到處散播陽光。

Spread kindness everywhere.
到處散播善意。

** _____

positivity〔͵pɑzə'tɪvətɪ〕*n.* 正面；積極
spread〔sprɛd〕*v.* 散播
positive〔'pɑzətɪv〕*adj.* 正面的；積極的；
　樂觀的；好的
vibes〔vaɪbz〕*n. pl.*（給人的）印象；情緒上的
　激動；氣氛【源自 vibrations】
positive vibes 正能量（= *positive energy*）
sunshine〔'sʌn͵ʃaɪn〕*n.* 陽光；快樂；幸福
kindness〔'kaɪndnɪs〕*n.* 仁慈；善意

Spread the happiness.

散播快樂。

Embrace the light.

擁抱光明。

Shine your light.

發光發亮。

** ───────────────

spread〔sprɛd〕*v.* 散播

happiness〔'hæpɪnɪs〕*n.* 快樂；幸福

embrace〔ɪm'bres〕*v.* 擁抱

light〔laɪt〕*n.* 光

shine〔ʃaɪn〕*v.* 照耀；發光；用…照明

Keep faith alive.

保持信心。

Believe in miracles.

相信奇蹟。

Stay optimistic daily.

天天樂觀。

** ───────────────

keep〔kip〕*v.* 使保持

faith〔feθ〕*n.* 信念；信心

alive〔ə'laɪv〕*adj.* 活著的；仍然存在的

believe in 相信；信任

miracle〔'mɪrəkḷ〕*n.* 奇蹟

stay〔ste〕*v.* 保持

optimistic〔ˌɑptə'mɪstɪk〕*adj.* 樂觀的

daily〔'delɪ〕*adv.* 每天（= *every day*）

【**Unit 3 背景説明**】

Spread positive vibes. 要散播正能量。
(= *Spread good vibes.* = *Spread positive energy.*) 也可説成 : Inspire others to be optimistic. (要激勵別人樂觀。)

Spread sunshine everywhere. (到處散播陽光；到處散播快樂。) 也可説成 : Always be cheerful. (要總是很快樂。) Always be positive. (要總是很樂觀。)(= *Always be optimistic.*)

Spread kindness everywhere. (到處散播善意。) 也可説成 : Always be compassionate. (要總是很有同情心。) Always be nice. (要總是很親切。) Always be considerate. (要總是很體貼。)

Spread the happiness. 散播快樂。(= *Share your happiness.*) 也可説成 : Make others happy. (要使別人快樂。)

Embrace the light. (擁抱光明。) 也可説成 : Be positive. (要樂觀。)(= *Be optimistic.*) Welcome positivity. (要歡迎正能量。)

Shine your light.（讓你的光輝照耀；散發你的光芒。）也可説成：Be radiant.（要散發光芒。）Do good deeds.（要做好事。）Be kind.（要善良。）Be positive.（要樂觀。）

Keep faith alive. 要保持信念；要保持信心。（＝*Keep believing.*＝*Don't stop believing.*）也可説成：Don't doubt.（不要懷疑。）

Believe in miracles. 相信會有奇蹟。（＝*Believe in wonders.*）也可説成：Believe that wonders can happen.（相信奇蹟會發生。）Believe that anything can happen.（相信任何事都可能發生。）

Stay optimistic daily.（每天保持樂觀。）也可説成：Keep a positive outlook.（要有樂觀的看法。）Always be optimistic.（要一直都很樂觀。）

UNIT ❹

Let Bygones Be Bygones
過去的就讓它過去

Forgive and forget.
【諺】既往不咎。

Let go gracefully.
優雅放下。

Choose forgiveness daily.
選擇原諒。

** ────────────

bygones〔'baɪ,gɑnz〕*n. pl.* 過去的事
forgive〔fɚ'gɪv〕*v.* 原諒
forget〔fɚ'gɛt〕*v.* 忘記　　***let go*** 放手；
　　放下（不再想過去的某事或因之而惱怒）
gracefully〔'gresfəlɪ〕*adv.* 優雅地
choose〔tʃuz〕*v.* 選擇
forgiveness〔fɚ'gɪvnɪs〕*n.* 原諒
daily〔'delɪ〕*adv.* 每天（= *every day*）

Release old pain.

放下舊傷。

Release old grudges.

放下怨恨。

Release past burdens.

放下既往。

**───────────

release〔rɪˋlis〕*v.* 釋放；放開；

放手；放下

old〔old〕*adj.* 舊的；從前的

pain〔pen〕*n.* 痛苦

grudge〔grʌdʒ〕*n.* 怨恨

past〔pæst〕*adj.* 過去的

burden〔ˋbɝdn̩〕*n.*（精神上的）負擔

Embrace new beginnings.

擁抱新的開始。

Grant yourself freedom.

給你自己自由。

Forgiveness brings liberation.

原諒帶來解脫。

**————————————

embrace〔ɪmˊbres〕*v.* 擁抱；欣然接受

beginning〔bɪˊɡɪnɪŋ〕*n.* 開始

grant〔ɡrænt〕*v.* 給予

freedom〔ˊfridəm〕*n.* 自由

forgiveness〔fɚˊɡɪvnɪs〕*n.* 原諒；寬恕

liberation〔͵lɪbəˊreʃən〕*n.* 解放；解脫

【Unit 4 背景説明】

Forgive and forget. (【諺】既往不咎。) 也可説
成:Pardon others. (要原諒別人。) Don't hold
on to resentment. (不要一直憎恨。) Don't hold
grudges. (不要懷恨在心。)

Let go gracefully. (優雅地放下。) 也可説成:Let
it go. (就算了吧。) Forget about it. (忘了吧;
算了吧。) Don't hold on to bad feelings. (不
要一直有不好的感覺。)

Choose forgiveness daily. (每天選擇原諒。)
也可説成:Always forgive others. (總是原諒
別人。)

Release old pain. (釋放以前的痛苦;放下以前的傷
痛。) 也可説成:Let go of your sorrows. (放
下你的悲傷。) Let go of your resentment. (放
下你的憤恨。)

Release old grudges. (放下以前的怨恨。) 也可説
成:Don't hold grudges. (不要懷恨在心。)
Forgive and forget. (【諺】既往不咎。)

Release past burdens. （放下過去的負擔。）也可
説成：Let go of the past. （要放下過去。）Let
go of the things that troubled you. （放下困擾
你的事。）

Embrace new beginnings. 擁抱新的開始。
（ = *Welcome a fresh start.* = *Welcome a new
start.* ）

Grant yourself freedom. 給你自己自由。(= *Let
yourself be free.* = *Allow yourself to be free.*)

Forgiveness brings liberation. （原諒帶來解脫。）
也可説成：Forgiving will set you free. （原諒會
讓你自由。）When you forgive others, you
will be free. （當你原諒別人時，你就會自由。）

UNIT ❺

Never Seek Vengeance

絕不要報仇

Forgive and grow.

原諒才能成長。

Forgive and thrive.

原諒才能成功。

Forgive and heal.

寬恕才能療癒。

❋❋ ────────────

seek〔sik〕*v.* 尋求

vengeance〔'vɛndʒəns〕*n.* 復仇

forgive〔fə'gɪv〕*v.* 原諒;寬恕

grow〔gro〕*v.* 成長

thrive〔θraɪv〕*v.* 興盛;繁榮;成功
  (= *prosper* = *flourish* = *succeed*)

heal〔hil〕*v.* 治癒;痊癒

Don't get even.

不要報仇。

Don't take revenge.

不要報復。

Let karma work.

善惡有報。

** ───────────

even〔ˋivən〕 *adj.* 均衡的；同樣的；
　不相上下的

get even 報復

revenge〔rɪˋvɛndʒ〕 *n.* 報復；報仇

take revenge 報復；報仇（= *seek revenge*
　= *get even* = *retaliate*）

karma〔ˋkɑrmə〕 *n.* 命運；因果報應；
　羯磨；業【宗教名詞】

work〔wɜk〕 *v.* 工作；做事；起作用

Let God avenge.
要讓上帝來復仇。

Justice is God's.
正義是上帝的事。

God settles all.
上帝會解決一切。

** ———————————————

let〔lɛt〕v. 讓

God〔gɑd〕n. 上帝

avenge〔ə'vɛndʒ〕v. 復仇；報仇；報復
【avenge 通常指為伸張正義而採取正當的
報復，而 revenge 通常指為私怨而報仇，
常帶有強烈的惡意】

justice〔'dʒʌstɪs〕n. 公平；正義

settle〔'sɛtl̩〕v. 解決（問題、爭議、糾紛等）

【Unit 5 背景說明】

Forgive and grow. （原諒才能成長。）也可說成：
You will mature when you pardon others.
（當你原諒別人，你就會變成熟。）

Forgive and thrive. 原諒才能成功。(= *You will
succeed when you pardon others*.)

Forgive and heal. （原諒才能療癒。）也可說成：
You will feel better when you forgive
others. （當你原諒別人，你會感覺更好。）

Don't get even. 不要報仇。(= *Don't retaliate.*
= *Don't seek revenge*.)

Don't take revenge. 不要報復。(= *Don't try to
get even. = Don't retaliate*.)

Let karma work. 讓因果報應來做這工作。(= *Let
karma do the work*.) 也可說成：Let fate
handle it. （讓命運來處理。）

Let God avenge. （讓上帝來復仇。）也可說成：
Leave it up to God to set things right. （交由
上帝來導正情況。）(= *Leave it to God to make
it right*.)

Justice is God's. （實現公平正義的是上帝的事。）
也可說成：Only God can judge. （只有上帝能
審判。）

God settles all. 上帝會解決一切。(= *God will
resolve everything*.)

UNIT **6**

Forgiveness Is Good for You
寬恕對你有益

Forgiveness has power.
寬恕很有力量。

Embrace compassion's power.
擁抱同情力量。

Embrace forgiving hearts.
擁抱寬恕的心。

** ————————————

forgiveness〔fɚ'gɪvnɪs〕*n.* 原諒；寬恕
power〔'pauɚ〕*n.* 力量
embrace〔ɪm'bres〕*v.* 擁抱；欣然接受；利用
compassion〔kəm'pæʃən〕*n.* 同情
forgiving〔fɚ'gɪvɪŋ〕*adj.* 原諒別人的；寬大的
heart〔hɑrt〕*n.* 心；人

Break the cycle.

打破循環。

Release the anger.

放下憤怒。

Release the hate.

放下仇恨。

** ——————————————

break〔brek〕*v.* 打破

cycle〔ˈsaɪkḷ〕*n.* 循環

release〔rɪˈlis〕*v.* 釋放；放開；
   放下；放手

anger〔ˈæŋgɚ〕*n.* 生氣；憤怒

hate〔het〕*n.* 仇恨；憎恨

Inner peace emerges.
內心的平靜出現。

Second chances arise.
第二次機會出現。

Rewrite your story.
重寫你自己故事。

** ———————————

inner〔'ɪnɚ〕*adj.* 內心的

peace〔pis〕*n.* 和平；平靜

emerge〔ɪ'mɝdʒ〕*v.* 出現

chance〔tʃæns〕*n.* 機會

second chance 第二次機會

arise〔ə'raɪz〕*v.* 產生；出現

rewrite〔ri'raɪt〕*v.* 重寫；改寫

story〔'storɪ〕*n.* 故事

【Unit 6 背景説明】

Forgiveness has power. (寬恕很有力量。) 也可
説成：Forgiving others is powerful. (原諒別人
很有力量。) Pardoning others has a big effect.
(原諒別人有很大的影響力。)

Embrace compassion's power. (擁抱同情的力
量。) 也可説成：Welcome the strength of
kindness. (要歡迎善良的力量。) Use the
strength of kindness. (要運用善良的力量。)

Embrace forgiving hearts. (擁抱寬恕的心。) 也
可説成：Encourage others to be forgiving.
(鼓勵別人要寬恕。) Welcome people who are
forgiving. (要歡迎寬大的人。)

Break the cycle. (打破循環；打破惡性循環。)
也可説成：Don't continue the pattern of
behavior. (不要繼續那種行為模式。) Don't
repeat that pattern of behavior. (不要重複
那種行為模式。)【在此是指不要一直冤冤相報，
以牙還牙】

Release the anger.（放下憤怒。）也可說成：Let go of your hate.（放下你的仇恨。）Let go of your anger.（放下你的憤怒。）

Release the hate.（放下仇恨。）也可說成：Let go of your animosity.（要放下你的敵意。）

Inner peace emerges.（內心的平靜會出現。）也可說成：You will feel serene.（你會覺得平靜。）（= *You will feel calm.*）

Second chances arise.（第二次機會會出現。）也可說成：New opportunities will appear.（新的機會會出現。）You will have a chance to correct your mistakes.（你會有機會改正你的錯誤。）

Rewrite your story.（重寫你的故事。）也可說成：Change.（要改變。）Change your life.（改變你的人生。）Change the course of your life.（改變你人生的歷程。）

UNIT 7

Control Your Anger
控制你的憤怒

Don't get angry.
不要生氣。

Don't get mad.
不要抓狂。

Don't get upset.
不要憤怒。

**

---

control〔kən'trol〕*v.* 控制

anger〔'æŋgɚ〕*n.* 生氣；憤怒

get〔gɛt〕*v.* 變得

angry〔'æŋgrɪ〕*adj.* 生氣的

get angry 生氣

mad〔mæd〕*adj.* 發瘋的；生氣的

upset〔ʌp'sɛt〕*adj.* 不高興的

Don't lose control.

不要失去控制。

Control your temper.

控制你的脾氣。

Control your emotions.

控制你的情緒。

**——————

lose〔luz〕*v.* 失去
control〔kən'trol〕*n. v.* 控制
lose control 失控
temper〔'tɛmpɚ〕*n.* 脾氣
emotion〔ɪ'moʃən〕*n.* 情緒

Avoid getting furious.

避免暴怒。

Avoid getting annoyed.

避免惱火。

Refrain from rage.

忍住憤怒。

** ───────────────

avoid〔əˋvɔɪd〕v. 避免

avoid* + *V-ing 避免⋯

get〔gɛt〕v. 變得

furious〔ˋfjʊrɪəs〕*adj.* 狂怒的

annoyed〔əˋnɔɪd〕*adj.* 惱怒的

refrain〔rɪˋfren〕v. 抑制;忍住;避免

refrain from 抑制;忍住

rage〔redʒ〕*n.* 憤怒

【Unit 7 背景説明】

Don't get angry. (不要生氣。) 也可説成：*Don't get mad*. (不要抓狂。) *Don't get upset*. (不要不高興。) Keep your temper. (要控制你的脾氣。)

Don't lose control. (不要失控。) 也可説成：*Control your temper*. (要控制你的脾氣。) (= *Keep your temper*.) *Control your emotions*. (要控制你的情緒。)

Avoid getting furious. 避免暴怒。(= *Avoid getting mad*.) 也可説成：Try not to get mad. (試著不要抓狂。)

Avoid getting annoyed. 避免惱怒。(= *Avoid getting upset*.) 也可説成：Try not to get irritated. (試著不要被激怒。)

Refrain from rage. 忍住憤怒。(= *Avoid getting angry*.) 也可説成：Don't lose your temper. (不要發脾氣。)

(UNIT 8)

Anger Is Unhealthy
憤怒不健康

Anger breeds regret.
憤怒產生後悔。

Anger extinguishes love.
憤怒使愛熄滅。

Anger suffocates happiness.
憤怒扼殺快樂。

** ────────────

anger〔'æŋgɚ〕*n.* 生氣;憤怒
unhealthy〔ʌn'hɛlθɪ〕*adj.* 不健康的
breed〔brid〕*v.* 產生
regret〔rɪ'grɛt〕*n.* 後悔
extinguish〔ɪk'stɪŋgwɪʃ〕*v.* 使熄滅
suffocate〔'sʌfə,ket〕*v.* 使窒息而死;使悶死
happiness〔'hæpɪnɪs〕*n.* 快樂;幸福

Anger shatters connections.

憤怒粉碎人脈。

Anger damages relationships.

憤怒傷害關係。

Anger hinders communication.

憤怒阻礙溝通。

**———————————

anger〔ˈæŋgə〕*n.* 生氣；憤怒

shatter〔ˈʃætə〕*v.* 使粉碎；使破碎

connections〔kəˈnɛkʃənz〕*n. pl.* 關係；人脈

damage〔ˈdæmɪdʒ〕*v.* 破壞

relationship〔rɪˈleʃənˌʃɪp〕*n.* 關係

hinder〔ˈhɪndə〕*v.* 阻礙

communication〔kəˌmjunəˈkeʃən〕*n.* 溝通

Anger impacts health.

憤怒重擊健康。

Anger hurts hearts.

憤怒傷害心臟。

Health deteriorates rapidly.

健康快速惡化。

** ——————————————

anger〔'æŋgɚ〕*n.* 生氣；憤怒

impact〔ɪm'pækt〕*v.* 影響

〔'ɪmpækt〕*n.* 影響；撞擊

health〔hɛlθ〕*n.* 健康

hurt〔hɝt〕*v.* 傷害

heart〔hɑrt〕*n.* 心臟

deteriorate〔dɪ'tɪrɪə,ret〕*v.* 惡化

rapidly〔'ræpɪdlɪ〕*adv.* 快速地

【Unit 8 背景說明】

Anger breeds regret. 憤怒產生後悔。(= *Anger leads to regret.*)

Anger extinguishes love. 憤怒使愛熄滅；憤怒會讓愛消失。(= *Anger kills love.*)

Anger suffocates happiness. 憤怒使快樂窒息；憤怒會讓人不快樂。(= *Anger prevents happiness.*)

Anger shatters connections. 憤怒使關係破碎。(= *Anger ends relationships.*)

Anger damages relationships. (憤怒破壞關係。) 也可說成：Anger hurts relationships. (憤怒傷害關係。)

Anger hinders communication. (憤怒阻礙溝通。) 也可說成：Anger makes communication difficult. (憤怒會使溝通變得困難。)

Anger impacts health. (憤怒影響健康。) (= *Anger affects your health.*)

Anger hurts hearts. (憤怒傷害心臟。) 也可說成：Anger is bad for your heart. (憤怒對你的心臟不好。)

Health deteriorates rapidly. (健康會快速惡化。) 也可說成：You will lose your health quickly. (你會很快就失去你的健康。)

UNIT **9**

What Conquers Anger?
什麼能征服憤怒？

Patience conquers anger.
耐心征服憤怒。

Love conquers hatred.
眞愛征服仇恨。

Kindness conquers hostility.
善意征服敵意。

**

conquer〔'kɑŋkɚ〕*v.* 征服
anger〔'æŋgɚ〕*n.* 生氣；憤怒
patience〔'peʃəns〕*n.* 耐心
hatred〔'hetrɪd〕*n.* 仇恨
kindness〔'kaɪndnɪs〕*n.* 仁慈；善意
hostility〔hɑs'tɪlətɪ〕*n.* 敵意

Take a break.

休息一下。

Take deep breaths.

做深呼吸。

Count to ten.

一數到十。

** ────────

break〔brek〕*n.* 休息

take a break 休息一下

deep〔dip〕*adj.* 深的

breath〔brɛθ〕*n.* 呼吸

take a deep breath 做個深呼吸

count〔kaʊnt〕*v.* 數

Humor builds bridges.

幽默搭起橋樑。

Smiles dissolve tension.

微笑化解緊張。

Emotional intelligence prevails.

情商好是贏家。

** ─────────────

humor (ˈhjumɚ) *n.* 幽默
build (bɪld) *v.* 建立　　bridge (brɪdʒ) *n.* 橋
smile (smaɪl) *n.* 微笑
dissolve (dɪˈzɑlv) *v.* 使溶解；使消失
tension (ˈtɛnʃən) *n.* 緊張
emotional (ɪˈmoʃənl̩) *adj.* 情緒的
intelligence (ɪnˈtɛlədʒəns) *n.* 智力
emotional intelligence 情商；情緒商數
　(= *EI* = *emotional intelligence quotient* = *EQ*)
prevail (prɪˈvel) *v.* 盛行；佔優勢；獲勝

【Unit 9 背景説明】

Patience conquers anger. 耐心能征服憤怒。
(= *Patience can defeat anger.*)

Love conquers hatred. 愛能征服仇恨。(= *Love can destroy hatred.*)

Kindness conquers hostility. 善意能征服敵意。
(= *Kindness can overcome hostility.*)

Take a break. 休息一下。(= *Take a rest.* = *Take five.* = *Take ten.*)

Take deep breaths. 做深呼吸。(= *Breathe deeply.*)

Count to ten. 從一數到十。(= *Count one to ten.* = *Count from one to ten.* = *Count one, two, three, four, five, six, seven, eight, nine, ten.*)

Humor builds bridges. (幽默搭起橋樑。) 也可説成：Humor can help you connect with people. (幽默能幫助你和別人建立關係。)

Smiles dissolve tension. (微笑能化解緊張。) 也可説成：A smile can make a situation less tense. (微笑能使情況較不緊張。)

Emotional intelligence prevails. (情商好是贏家。)(= *Someone with a high EQ always comes out ahead.*)

PART 1 · Unit 1~9
中英文錄音QR碼

PART 1 總整理

Unit 1

Always stay positive.
保持樂觀。
Think positive thoughts.
正面思考。
Say positive words.
要說好話。

See the good. 看好的一面。
Radiate high spirits.
要散發朝氣。
Radiate hopeful energy.
散發正能量。

Rise above fear.
不要恐懼。
Rise above doubt.
不要懷疑。
Rise above negativity.
不要悲觀。

Unit 2

Don't ever complain.
切勿抱怨。
Complaining achieves
    nothing. 埋怨無益。
Complaining solves
    nothing. 牢騷無用。

Complaining is pointless.
抱怨無意義。
Complaining doesn't help.
抱怨沒有用。
Seek positive solutions.
尋找好解方。

Stop being critical.
停止批評。
Change your mindset.
改變心態。
Make things better.
情況變好。

Unit 3

Spread positive vibes.
傳播正面能量。
Spread sunshine
    everywhere.
到處散播陽光。
Spread kindness
    everywhere.
到處散播善意。

Spread the happiness.
散播快樂。
Embrace the light. 擁抱光明。
Shine your light. 發光發亮。

Keep faith alive. 保持信心。
Believe in miracles.
相信奇蹟。
Stay optimistic daily.
天天樂觀。

Unit 4

Forgive and forget.
【諺】既往不咎。
Let go gracefully. 優雅放下。
Choose forgiveness daily.
選擇原諒。

Release old pain. 放下舊傷。
Release old grudges.
放下怨恨。
Release past burdens.
放下既往。

Embrace new beginnings.
擁抱新的開始。
Grant yourself freedom.
給你自己自由。
Forgiveness brings
    liberation. 原諒帶來解脫。

Unit 5

Forgive and grow.
原諒才能成長。
Forgive and thrive.
原諒才能成功。
Forgive and heal.
寬恕才能療癒。

Don't get even. 不要報仇。
Don't take revenge.
不要報復。
Let karma work.
善惡有報。

Let God avenge.
要讓上帝來復仇。
Justice is God's.
正義是上帝的事。
God settles all.
上帝會解決一切。

Unit 6

Forgiveness has power.
寬恕很有力量。
Embrace compassion's
    power. 擁抱同情力量。
Embrace forgiving hearts.
擁抱寬恕的心。

Break the cycle. 打破循環。
Release the anger.
放下憤怒。
Release the hate.
放下仇恨。

Inner peace emerges.
內心的平靜出現。
Second chances arise.
第二次機會出現。
Rewrite your story.
重寫你自己故事。

BOOK 3・PART 1

Unit 7

Don't get angry.
不要生氣。
Don't get mad.
不要抓狂。
Don't get upset.
不要憤怒。

Don't lose control.
不要失去控制。
Control your temper.
控制你的脾氣。
Control your emotions.
控制你的情緒。

Avoid getting furious.
避免暴怒。
Avoid getting annoyed.
避免惱火。
Refrain from rage.
忍住憤怒。

Unit 8

Anger breeds regret.
憤怒產生後悔。
Anger extinguishes love.
憤怒使愛熄滅。
Anger suffocates
happiness.
憤怒扼殺快樂。

Anger shatters connections.
憤怒粉碎人脈。
Anger damages relationships.
憤怒傷害關係。
Anger hinders
communication. 憤怒阻礙溝通。

Anger impacts health.
憤怒重擊健康。
Anger hurts hearts.
憤怒傷害心臟。
Health deteriorates rapidly.
健康快速惡化。

Unit 9

Patience conquers anger.
耐心征服憤怒。
Love conquers hatred.
真愛征服仇恨。
Kindness conquers hostility.
善意征服敵意。

Take a break. 休息一下。
Take deep breaths. 做深呼吸。
Count to ten. 一數到十。

Humor builds bridges.
幽默搭起橋樑。
Smiles dissolve tension.
微笑化解緊張。
Emotional intelligence
prevails. 情商好是贏家。

BOOK 3　\\　**PART 2**

A to Z of Compliments
各種稱讚

PART 2・Unit 1~9
英文錄音QR碼

UNIT ❶

You look awesome.

你看起來很棒。

You look amazing.

你看來很厲害。

You look astonishing.

你眞令人驚豔。

**

look〔luk〕v. 看起來

awesome〔'ɔsəm, 'asəm〕adj. 令人敬畏的；
很棒的【美國人多唸成〔'asəm〕】

amazing〔ə'mezɪŋ〕adj. 驚人的；很棒的

astonishing〔ə'stanɪʃɪŋ〕adj. 令人驚訝的

You look excellent.

你看來很優秀。

You look exceptional.

你很與眾不同。

You look extraordinary.

你看來很特別。

**

excellent〔ˈɛksḷənt〕*adj.* 優秀的；極好的

exceptional〔ɪkˈsɛpʃənḷ〕*adj.* 卓越的；
  傑出的；出眾的；優秀的
  【exception〔ɪkˈsɛpʃən〕*n.* 例外】

extraordinary〔ɪkˈstrɔrdṇˌɛrɪ〕*adj.* 非凡的；
  特別的；令人驚奇的
  (↔ ordinary〔ˈɔrdṇˌɛrɪ〕*adj.* 普通的)

You look fantastic.

你看起來真棒。

You look fabulous.

你看起來很棒。

You look fascinating.

你看來很迷人。

** ────────────

fantastic〔fæn'tæstɪk〕*adj.* 極好的；
很棒的
fabulous〔'fæbjələs〕*adj.* 極好的；
絕佳的
fascinating〔'fæsn̩,etɪŋ〕*adj.* 迷人的

【Unit 1 背景説明】

You look awesome. 你看起來很棒。(= *You look great.*)

You look amazing. 你看起來令人驚訝；你看起來很棒。(= *You look wonderful.*)

You look astonishing. 你看起來令人驚訝；你看起來很棒。(= *You look astounding.*)

You look excellent. 你看起來很優秀；你看起來很棒。(= *You look marvelous.*)

You look exceptional. 你看起來與眾不同。(= *You look outstanding.*)

You look extraordinary. 你看起來很特別。(= *You look remarkable.*)

You look fantastic. 你看起來很棒。(= *You look wonderful.*)

You look fabulous. 你看起來很漂亮。(= *You look marvelous.*)

You look fascinating. 你看起來很迷人。(= *You look charming.* = *You look enchanting.*)

UNIT ❷

You look great.
你看起來非常棒。

You look gorgeous.
你看起來真漂亮。

You look glorious.
你看來光彩奪目。

** ————————————————

look〔lʊk〕*v.* 看起來
great〔gret〕*adj.* 極好的；很棒的
gorgeous〔ˈgɔrdʒəs〕*adj.* 非常漂亮的
glorious〔ˈglorɪəs〕*adj.* 光輝的；燦爛的

You look marvelous.

你看起來真棒。

You look majestic.

你看來真高貴。

You look magnificent.

你看來太棒了。

**

marvelous〔'mɑrvḷəs〕*adj.* 令人驚嘆的；
很棒的

majestic〔mə'dʒɛstɪk〕*adj.* 有威嚴的；
莊嚴的；雄偉的

magnificent〔mæg'nɪfəsṇt〕*adj.* 壯麗的；
極好的；很棒的

You look smart.

你看來很時髦。

You look stunning.

你看來很漂亮。

You look spectacular.

你很引人注目。

**

smart〔smɑrt〕*adj.* 聰明的;整潔

漂亮的;時髦的

stunning〔ˈstʌnɪŋ〕*adj.* 使人嚇呆的;

極漂亮的;極迷人的

spectacular〔spɛkˈtækjələ〕*adj.* 壯觀的;

令人驚嘆的;引人注目的

【Unit 2 背景說明】

You look great. 你看起來很棒。(= *You look wonderful.* = *You look awesome.*)

You look gorgeous. 你看起來非常漂亮。(= *You look magnificent.*)

You look glorious. 你看起來光輝燦爛。(= *You look splendid.*)

You look marvelous. 你看起來令人驚嘆；你看起來很棒。(= *You look excellent.*)

You look majestic. 你看起來莊重威嚴；你看起來很高貴。(= *You look elegant.*)

You look magnificent. 你看起來很棒。(= *You look splendid.*)

You look smart. 字面的意思是「你看起來很聰明。」在此引申為「你看起來很時髦。」(= *You look fashionable.*)

You look stunning. 你看起來很漂亮；你看起來很迷人。(= *You look wonderful.*)

You look spectacular. 你看起來很引人注目。(= *You look impressive.*)

UNIT ❸

You look super.

你看起來超好。

You look superb.

你看起來極好。

You look spiffy.

你看來很時髦。

** ─────────────

look〔lʊk〕*v.* 看起來
super〔'supɚ〕*adj.* 超級的;極好的
superb〔sʊ'pɝb〕*adj.* 極好的
spiffy〔'spɪfɪ〕*adj.* 出色的;時髦的

You look terrific.

你看起來很棒。

You look tremendous.

你看起來極好。

You look top-notch.

你看來最高檔。

**

terrific〔təˋrɪfɪk〕*adj.* 很棒的
tremendous〔trɪˋmɛndəs〕*adj.* 巨大的；極好的
top〔tɑp〕*adj.* 最頂端的
notch〔nɑtʃ〕*n.* (V 字形的) 刻痕；切口；
　　等級；檔次
top-notch〔ˌtɑpˋnɑtʃ〕*adj.* 頂呱呱的；第一流的
　　【據說 top-notch 來自於一個農場遊戲，遊戲的
　　裝置是一根水平放置的杆子和兩根刻了凹槽
　　（ notch ）的垂直杆子，農夫們站在杆子下，然
　　後向上扔鐵桶，每過一次，水平杆子的高度就
　　向上放一個凹槽的高度，能扔到最高凹槽（ top-
　　notch ）的人，就是第一名】

You look wonderful.

你看起來真棒。

You look wondrous.

你看起來極棒。

You look wicked.

你看來棒呆了。

**

wonderful〔ˈwʌndɚfəl〕*adj.* 極好的；
很棒的
wondrous〔ˈwʌndrəs〕*adj.* 令人驚奇的；
不可思議的；極棒的；絕妙的
wicked〔ˈwɪkɪd〕*adj.* 邪惡的；優秀的；
極好的；很棒的（= *excellent*）

【Unit 3 背景説明】

You look super. 你看起來超級好。(= *You look marvelous.*)

You look superb. 你看起來超級棒。(= *You look magnificent.*)

You look spiffy. 你看起來很時髦。(= *You look classy.* = *You look fashionable.*)

You look terrific. 你看起來很棒。(= *You look great.*)

You look tremendous. 你看起來非常好。(= *You look wonderful.*)

You look top-notch. 你看起來真棒。(= *You look excellent.*)

You look wonderful. 你看起來很棒。(= *You look great.* = *You look awesome.*)

You look wondrous. 你看起來超棒。(= *You look remarkable.*)

You look wicked. 字面的意思是「你看起來很邪惡。」在此引申爲「你看起來很棒。」(= *You look excellent.* = *You look neat.* = *You look cool.*)

UNIT ④

Great Minds Think Alike

英雄所見略同

We agree completely.

我們完全同意。

We concur wholeheartedly.

我們全心贊成。

We think alike.

我們想法相同。

**

mind〔 maɪnd 〕*n.* 心;精神;頭腦;想法;人

alike〔 ə'laɪk 〕*adv.* 同樣地

agree〔 ə'gri 〕*v.* 同意;意見一致

completely〔 kəm'plitlɪ 〕*adv.* 完全地

concur〔 kən'kɝ 〕*v.* 意見一致;一致同意

wholeheartedly〔'hol'hɑrtɪdlɪ 〕*adv.* 誠心

誠意地;由衷地;衷心地

We have consensus.

我們都有共識。

We are like-minded.

我們志同道合。

We're in harmony.

我們和諧一致。

** ―――――――――――

consensus〔kən'sɛnsəs〕 *n.*（意見的）
一致；共識

like-minded〔'laɪk'maɪndɪd〕 *adj.* 看法
相同的；志趣相投的

harmony〔'hɑrmənɪ〕 *n.* 協調；和諧；
一致

in harmony 和諧；一致

BOOK 3 · PART 2

We're in sync.

我們步調一致。

We're in accord.

我們意見一致。

We're in agreement.

我們意見相同。

** ————————————

sync〔sɪŋk〕*n.* 同步調
　【是 synchronization 的非正式說法，發
　音和 sink〔sɪŋk〕*v.* 下沈 相同】
in sync 同步；一致
accord〔əˋkɔrd〕*n.* 一致；符合
in accord 一致；符合
agreement〔əˋgrimənt〕*n.* 同意；
　意見一致
in agreement 意見一致

【Unit 4 背景說明】

We agree completely. 我們完全同意;我們的意見
完全一致。(= *We are in complete agreement.*
= ***We concur wholeheartedly***.)

We think alike. 我們的想法相同。(= *We think the
same.* = *We have the same idea/ideas.*)

We have consensus. (我們有共識。) 也可説成:
We're in agreement. (我們意見一致。)

We are like-minded. 我們想法相同。(= *We think
the same.*)

We're in harmony. (我們和諧一致。) 也可説成:
We concur. (我們意見一致。) We have no
disagreement. (我們沒有意見不合。)

We're in sync. (我們步調一致。) 也可説成:
We're in accord. (我們意見一致。) ***We're in
agreement***. (我們意見相同。) We agree. (我們
都同意;我們意見一致。) We have the same
opinion. (我們意見相同。) We think the same.
(我們的想法相同。)

UNIT ⑤

I totally agree.
我完全同意。

Couldn't agree more.
再同意不過。

Complete agreement here.
完全認同你。

** ──────────────

totally〔ˈtotl̩〕*adv.* 完全地

agree〔əˈgri〕*v.* 同意

couldn't agree more 不能同意更多；
非常同意

complete〔kəmˈplit〕*adj.* 完全的

agreement〔əˈgrimənt〕*n.* 同意；意見一致

here〔hɪr〕*adv.* 在這裡【可指 me（我）
或 us（我們）】

I second that.

我支持。

I'm on board.

我同意。

I'm with you.

我附議。

** ——————————

second〔ˈsɛkənd〕*v.* 贊成；附議；支持

board〔bord〕*n.* 木板；甲板

on board 在車（船、飛機）上；是其中
  的一部分；在同一個陣線上；參與；
  同意；支持

with〔wɪθ〕*prep.* 支持

That's spot on.

完全正確。

Exactly my thoughts!

正合我意！

Right on point.

你說得對。

** ————————————

spot on 確切的；準確的（= *exactly right*
= *perfectly accurate*）【源自英國的軍
事用語】

exactly〔 ɪgˈzæktlɪ 〕*adv.* 正是

thought〔 θɔt 〕*n.* 想法

right〔 raɪt 〕*adv.* 完全；非常

on point 非常好；完美（= *excellent*）

【Unit 5 背景説明】

I totally agree.（我完全同意。）也可説成：We are in total agreement.（我們的意見完全一致。）

Couldn't agree more. 不能同意更多；我非常同意。(= *I couldn't agree more.*)

Complete agreement here. 我完全同意。
(= *There is complete agreement here.*
= *I agree completely.*)

I second that. 我贊成；我支持。(= *I approve of that.* = *I support that.*)

I'm on board.（我同意；我支持。）也可説成：I agree.（我同意。）I'm willing.（我願意。）

I'm with you. 我支持你。(= *I support you.*)

That's spot on. 完全正確。(= *That's exactly right.*)

Exactly my thoughts! 正是我的想法！(= *That's what I think!*) 如果指某一特定想法，則可説成：Exactly my thought!（那正是我的想法！）
(= *Exactly my thinking!*)

Right on point. 完全正確。(= *Spot on.* = *On target.*) 源自 That's right on point. 或 You're right on point. 在此引申爲「你説得對。」(= *You're exactly right.*)

UNIT **6**

I support you.

我支持你。

I second you.

我贊同你。

I back you.

我認同你。

**

support〔səˈport〕*v.* 支持
second〔ˈsɛkənd〕*v.* 贊成；支持
back〔bæk〕*v.* 支持（= *second* = *support*）

I got you.

我會挺你。

I endorse you.

我肯定你。

I'm behind you.

我支持你。

**

I got you. 我支持你。

　(= *I've got your back.*)

endorse〔ɪn'dɔrs〕*v.* 背書；認可；

　贊成；支持

behind〔bɪ'haɪnd〕*prep.* 在…後面；

　做…的後盾；支持

BOOK 3 · PART 2

I'm your friend.

我是你的朋友。

I'm your ally.

我是你的盟友。

I'm your supporter.

我是你支持者。

** ───────────

ally〔'ælaɪ〕*n.* 盟友；盟邦
supporter〔sə'pɔrtɚ〕*n.* 支持者

【**Unit 6 背景説明**】

I support you. 我支持你。(= ***I second you***. = ***I
back you***.) 也可説成：I approve. (我賛成。)
I endorse you. (我替你背書；我支持你。)

I got you. 我挺你；我支持你。(= ***I've got your
back***. = ***I back you***. = ***I support you***.) 也可説
成：You can count on me. (你可以依賴我。)

I endorse you. (我替你背書；我支持你。) 也可説
成：I publicly support you. (我公開支持你。)

I'm behind you. 我做你的後盾；我支持你。
(= *I support you*.)

I'm your friend. 我是你的朋友。(= *I'm your
ally*.)

I'm your ally. 我是你的盟友；我支持你。
(= *I support you*.)

I'm your supporter. 我是你的支持者；我支持你。
(= *I support you*.)

UNIT **7**

A Beautiful Sight
美麗的景色

What a view!

好美的景色!

What a vision!

好美的視野!

What a vista!

好美的景觀!

** ───────────────

sight〔saɪt〕*n.* 景色;景象
what〔hwɑt〕*pron.*【用於感嘆句】多麼
view〔vju〕*n.* 景色
vision〔'vɪʒən〕*n.* 視力;夢一般的事物;美景
vista〔'vɪstə〕*n.* 遠景;景色(= *view*)

What a sight!

美麗動人的景色！

What a scene!

多麼壯麗的景象！

What incredible scenery!

難以置信的風景！

**————————

sight〔saɪt〕*n.* 景色；景象

scene〔sin〕*n.* 景色；景象

incredible〔ɪnˈkrɛdəbḷ〕*adj.* 令人難以
置信的

scenery〔ˈsinərɪ〕*n.* 風景【集合名詞】

What a spectacle!

多麼壯觀的景象！

What a picture!

多麼美麗的畫面！

What a landscape!

多麼迷人的景色！

** ————————————

spectacle〔ˈspɛktəkl̩〕*n.* 景象；奇觀；
壯觀的場面
picture〔ˈpɪktʃɚ〕*n.* 畫；圖片；美景
landscape〔ˈlændskep〕*n.* 風景；景色

【**Unit 7 背景說明**】

What a view! What a vision! What a vista!
這三句話意思相同，都等於 What a great sight!
（多麼棒的景色！）

What a sight! What a scene! What incredible
scenery! 這三句話意思相同，也可說成：This is
such a beautiful sight!（這真是非常美麗的景
色！）

What incredible scenery!（多麼令人難以置信的
風景！）也可說成：What a beautiful view!
（多麼美麗的景色！）

What a spectacle! 多麼壯觀的景象！（ = *What a*
vision! = *What a sight!* ）

What a picture! 多麼美麗的畫面！（ = *What a*
view! = *What a vision!* ）

What a landscape! 多麼漂亮的風景！（ = *What a*
beautiful landscape! = *What beautiful*
scenery! ）

UNIT **8**

I'm in awe!
我肅然起敬！

Eyes wide open!
我大開眼界！

Lost in admiration!
我著迷讚嘆！

**

awe〔ɔ〕*n.* 敬畏

in awe 心存敬畏

wide〔waɪd〕*adv.* 張大地；充分張開地

wide open 張得很大的

lost〔lɔst〕*adj.* 迷失的；著迷的

admiration〔͵ædmə'reʃən〕*n.* 讚嘆；
  欽佩；讚賞

Heaven on earth!

天堂在人間！

Nature's finest work!

自然的傑作！

This is perfection!

這就是完美！

** ————————————

heaven〔'hɛvən〕*n.* 天堂

earth〔ɝθ〕*n.* 地球

nature〔'netʃɚ〕*n.* 大自然

fine〔faɪn〕*adj.* 好的

work〔wɝk〕*n.* 作品

perfection〔pɚ'fɛkʃən〕*n.* 完美；極致

This is magical!

這真神奇！

This is paradise!

這是天堂！

Beyond all expectations!

超乎期待！

** ———————————

magical〔ˈmædʒɪkl̩〕*adj.* 神奇的；
　不可思議的

paradise〔ˈpærəˌdaɪs〕*n.* 天堂；樂園

beyond〔bɪˈjɑnd〕*prep.* 超過…的範圍

expectation〔ˌɛkspɛkˈteʃən〕*n.* 預期；期待

beyond expectation 超出預期

beyond all expectations 超出所有的期待；
　比所期待的要好

【Unit 8 背景説明】

I'm in awe!（我心存敬畏；我肅然起敬！）也可説成：I'm amazed!（我非常驚訝！）

Eyes wide open! 眼睛張得很大，也就是「大開眼界！」是慣用句，源自 My eyes are wide open!（我大開眼界！）也可説成：I can't look away!（我無法移開視線！）

Lost in admiration! 迷失在讚嘆中，引申爲「著迷讚嘆！」源自 I'm lost in admiration!（我著迷讚嘆！）也可説成：I can do nothing but admire it!（我只能對它讚嘆！）I can't stop admiring it!（我無法停止讚嘆！）

Heaven on earth!「在地球上的天堂！」也就是「人間天堂！」源自 It's heaven on earth!（它是人間天堂！）(*= It's paradise!*) 也可説成：Perfect!（太完美了！）(*= Perfection!*)

Nature's finest work! 這是大自然最好的作品！(*= This is nature's finest work!*) 也可説成：An amazing natural sight!（很棒的自然美景！）

It's an outstanding natural sight!（它是很出色的自然美景！）

This is perfection! 這真是完美！（ = *This is perfect!*）也可說成：This is exquisite!（這真是精美！）

This is magical!（這真是神奇！）也可說成：
This is enchanting!（這真是迷人！）
This is amazing!（這真令人驚訝！）
This is phenomenal!（這真是太棒了！）

This is paradise! 這是天堂！（ = *This is heaven!*）也可說成：This is perfect!（這真是完美！）

Beyond all expectations!（超出預期！）源自 It's beyond all expectations!（這真是超乎預期；這比預期的好！）也可說成：More than I ever expected!（超出我的預期！）It's better than I ever imagined!（這比我所能想像的還要好！）

UNIT ⑨

I'm very touched.

我很感動。

I'm so moved.

我太感動。

I'm deeply affected.

深受感動。

** ————————————

touched〔tʌtʃt〕*adj.* 感動的

so〔so〕*adv.* 很；非常

moved〔muvd〕*adj.* 感動的

deeply〔'diplɪ〕*adv.* 深深地

affect〔ə'fɛkt〕*v.* 影響；使受感動

You impress me.

我很佩服你。

I'm so impressed.

我非常佩服。

You're very impressive.

你很難忘記。

**
---

impress〔ɪmˋprɛs〕*v.* 使印象深刻；
　使佩服 .
so〔so〕*adv.* 很；非常
impressive〔ɪmˋprɛsɪv〕*adj.* 令人印
　象深刻的

You inspire me.

你激勵了我。

You motivate me.

你激發了我。

You're incredibly talented.

你很有才華。

** ———————————————

inspire〔ɪn'spaɪr〕*v.* 激勵；給予靈感

motivate〔'motə,vet〕*v.* 激勵

incredibly〔ɪn'krɛdəblɪ〕*adv.* 令人難以
　置信地；非常地；驚人地

talented〔'tæləntɪd〕*adj.* 有才能的

【Unit 9 背景説明】

I'm very touched. (我非常感動。) 也可説成：*I'm so moved*. (我很感動。) *I'm deeply affected*. (我深受感動。) I'm impressed. (我印象深刻；我非常佩服。)

You impress me. (你使我印象深刻；你令我佩服。) 也可説成：*I'm so impressed*. (我非常佩服。) *You're very impressive*. (你令人印象非常深刻。) You're great. (你很棒。) You're splendid. (你非常好。) You're awesome. (你太棒了。)

You inspire me. 你激勵了我。(= *You motivate me*.) 也可説成：You encourage me. (你鼓勵了我。)

You're incredibly talented. (你很有才華。) 也可説成：You're really gifted. (你眞的很有天分。) You're really accomplished. (你眞的很有才華。)

PART 2　總整理

Unit 1

You look awesome.
你看起來很棒。
You look amazing.
你看來很厲害。
You look astonishing.
你真令人驚豔。

You look excellent.
你看來很優秀。
You look exceptional.
你很與眾不同。
You look extraordinary.
你看來很特別。

You look fantastic.
你看起來真棒。
You look fabulous.
你看起來很棒。
You look fascinating.
你看來很迷人。

Unit 2

You look great.
你看起來非常棒。
You look gorgeous.
你看起來真漂亮。
You look glorious.
你看來光彩奪目。

You look marvelous.
你看起來真棒。
You look majestic.
你看來真高貴。
You look magnificent.
你看來太棒了。

You look smart.
你看來很時髦。
You look stunning.
你看來很漂亮。
You look spectacular.
你很引人注目。

Unit 3

You look super.
你看起來超好。
You look superb.
你看起來極好。
You look spiffy.
你看來很時髦。

You look terrific.
你看起來很棒。
You look tremendous.
你看起來極好。
You look top-notch.
你看來最高檔。

You look wonderful.
你看起來真棒。
You look wondrous.
你看起來極棒。
You look wicked.
你看來棒呆了。

Unit 4

We agree completely.
我們完全同意。
We concur wholeheartedly.
我們全心贊成。
We think alike.
我們想法相同。

We have consensus.
我們都有共識。
We are like-minded.
我們志同道合。
We're in harmony.
我們和諧一致。

We're in sync.
我們步調一致。
We're in accord.
我們意見一致。
We're in agreement.
我們意見相同。

Unit 5

I totally agree. 我完全同意。
Couldn't agree more.
再同意不過。
Complete agreement here.
完全認同你。

I second that. 我支持。
I'm on board. 我同意。
I'm with you. 我附議。

That's spot on. 完全正確。
Exactly my thoughts!
正合我意！
Right on point. 你說得對。

Unit 6

I support you. 我支持你。
I second you. 我贊同你。
I back you. 我認同你。

I got you. 我會挺你。
I endorse you. 我肯定你。
I'm behind you. 我支持你。

I'm your friend.
我是你的朋友。
I'm your ally.
我是你的盟友。
I'm your supporter.
我是你支持者。

Unit 7

What a view!
好美的景色！
What a vision!
好美的視野！
What a vista!
好美的景觀！

What a sight!
美麗動人的景色！
What a scene!
多麼壯麗的景象！
What incredible scenery!
難以置信的風景！

What a spectacle!
多麼壯觀的景象！
What a picture!
多麼美麗的畫面！
What a landscape!
多麼迷人的景色！

Unit 8

I'm in awe!
我肅然起敬！
Eyes wide open!
我大開眼界！
Lost in admiration!
我著迷讚嘆！

Heaven on earth!
天堂在人間！
Nature's finest work!
自然的傑作！
This is perfection!
這就是完美！

This is magical!
這真神奇！
This is paradise!
這是天堂！
Beyond all expectations!
超乎期待！

Unit 9

I'm very touched. 我很感動。
I'm so moved. 我太感動。
I'm deeply affected.
深受感動。

You impress me.
我很佩服你。
I'm so impressed.
我非常佩服。
You're very impressive.
你很難忘記。

You inspire me. 你激勵了我。
You motivate me.
你激發了我。
You're incredibly talented.
你很有才華。

BOOK 3 · PART 2

BOOK 3　PART 3

The Importance of Cooperation

合作的重要

PART 3・Unit 1~9
英文錄音QR碼

UNIT ❶

The Power of Unity
團結的力量

United we shine.
團結我們閃耀。

United we soar.
團結我們高飛。

United we succeed.
團結我們成功。

** ────────────

unity〔'junətɪ〕*n.* 團結

united〔jʊ'naɪtɪd〕*adj.* 團結的

shine〔ʃaɪn〕*v.* 發光；發亮；表現突出；
　出眾

soar〔sɔr, sor〕*v.* 高飛；翱翔；暴漲

succeed〔sək'sid〕*v.* 成功

United we achieve.

團結我們實現。

United we advance.

團結我們進步。

United we ascend.

團結我們上升。

** ——————————

united〔juˈnaɪtɪd〕*adj.* 團結的

achieve〔əˈtʃiv〕*v.* 達成;實現

advance〔ədˈvæns〕*v.* 進步

ascend〔əˈsɛnd〕*v.* 上升;升級;
晉升;登上較高的等級;登上較高
的職位

United we win.

團結我們會贏。

United we prevail.

團結我們獲勝。

United we triumph.

團結我們戰勝。

** ─────────────

united〔ju'naɪtɪd〕*adj.* 團結的

win〔wɪn〕*v.* 贏；獲勝；成功

prevail〔prɪ'vel〕*v.* 佔優勢；獲勝

triumph〔'traɪəmf〕*v.* 得勝；成功；

得意洋洋

【Unit 1 背景説明】

United we shine. United we soar. United we succeed. 這三句話的句首都省略了 If we are，關鍵字 <u>s</u>hine-<u>s</u>oar-<u>s</u>ucceed 字首都是 **s**。

United we shine.（團結我們就會發光發亮。）也可説成：When we work together, we excel.（當我們團結合作，就會勝過別人。）

United we soar.（團結我們就能展翅高飛。）也可説成：When we work together, we improve.（當我們團結合作，就會變得更好。）

United we succeed. 團結我們就會成功。(= *When we work together, we are successful.*)

United we achieve. United we advance. United we ascend. 這三句話的句首都省略了 If we are，關鍵字 <u>a</u>chieve-<u>a</u>dvance-<u>a</u>scend 字首都是 **a**。

United we achieve.（團結我們就能實現目標。）也可説成：United we succeed.（團結我們就能成功。）(= *Together we will succeed.*)

United we advance.　團結我們就會進步。(= *United we improve.* = *United we progress.* = *Together we will progress.*)

United we ascend.　團結我們就能上升；團結我們就會進步。(= *United we rise.* = *United we soar.* = *United we advance.*)

United we win.　United we prevail.　United we triumph. 這三句話意思相同，句首都省略了 If we are。

United we win. (團結我們就會贏。) 也可說成：
　United we prevail. (團結我們就會獲勝。)
　United we triumph. (團結我們就能成功。)
　(= *United we dominate.* = *Together we will triumph.*)

UNIT ❷

Together we stand.

一起我們站穩。

Together we grow.

一起我們成長。

Together we prosper.

一起我們發達。

** ———————————

together〔təˋgɛðɚ〕*adv.* 一起

stand〔stænd〕*v.* 站立；持續存在

grow〔gro〕*v.* 成長

prosper〔ˋprɑspɚ〕*v.* 興盛；繁榮；成功

Together we're strong.
一起我們很強大。

Together we're powerful.
一起我們有力量。

Together we're resilient.
一起我們有韌性。

** ────────────

together〔təˋgɛðə〕*adv.* 一起

strong〔strɔŋ〕*adj.* 強壯的；堅強的

powerful〔ˋpaʊəfəl〕*adj.* 強有力的

resilient〔rɪˋzɪlɪənt〕*adj.* 有彈力的；
迅速恢復精神的；有韌性的

Together we're unstoppable.

團結勢不可擋。

Together we're unbeatable.

團結無人能敵。

Together we're invincible.

團結所向披靡。

** ───────────────

together〔 təˋgɛðɚ 〕*adv.* 一起
unstoppable〔 ʌnˋstɑpəbḷ 〕*adj.* 無法阻擋的
unbeatable〔 ʌnˋbitəbḷ 〕*adj.* 無法打敗的；
　難以戰勝的；無與倫比的；不能超越的
invincible〔 ɪnˋvɪnsəbḷ 〕*adj.* 不能征服的；
　無敵的

【**Unit 2 背景說明**】

> ***Together we stand.*** 一起我們就會屹立不搖。
> (= *United we stand.*) 也可說成：United we
> stand, divided we fall. (【諺】團結則立，分散
> 則倒。) Together we endure. (一起我們就能
> 持續下去。)

> ***Together we grow.*** (一起我們就會成長。) 也可說
> 成：Together we advance. (一起我們進步。)
> (= *Together we progress.*)

> ***Together we prosper.*** 一起我們就會成功。
> (= *Together we thrive.* = *Together we flourish.*
> = *Together we succeed.* = *Together we blossom.*
> = *Together we shine.*)

> ***Together we're strong.*** (一起我們會很強大。) 也
> 可說成：There is strength in numbers. (【諺】
> 人多勢眾。) United we have power. (團結我們
> 就有力量。)

Together we're powerful. 一起我們會很有力量。
(= *Together we're mighty.*) 也可説成：United
we have strength. (團結我們就有力量。)

Together we're resilient. 一起我們會很有韌性。
(= *Together we're tough.*)

Together we're unstoppable. (一起我們無人能
擋。) 也可説成：When we work together, no
one can stop us. (當我們一起合作，沒有人能阻
止我們。) When we work together, we are
unbeatable. (當我們一起合作，我們就不會被打
敗。)

Together we're unbeatable. 一起我們不會被打
敗。(= *Together we're undefeatable.* = *Together
we're indominable.*)

Together we're invincible. 一起我們就所向無敵。
(= *Together we're bulletproof.* = *Together
we're indestructible.* = *Together we're
invulnerable.*)

UNIT ❸

One for all.

我爲人人。

All for one.

人人爲我。

Strength in numbers.

【諺】人多勢衆。

** ———————————

All for one and one for all. 人人爲我，

　我爲人人。

strength 〔 strɛŋθ 〕 *n.* 力量

number 〔'nʌmbɚ 〕 *n.* 總數；人數；

　(*pl.*) 許多；大批

We're a team.

我們是團隊。

We're a unit.

我們是一體。

We're an alliance.

我們是同盟。

**————————————————

team〔tim〕*n.* 團隊

unit〔'junɪt〕*n.* 單位；一團

  (= *group* = *squad* = *team*)

alliance〔ə'laɪəns〕*n.* 聯盟；同盟

  (= *union*)；同盟國

Teamwork makes magic.

團隊合作創造神蹟。

Teamwork creates miracles.

團隊合作創造奇蹟。

Teamwork works wonders.

團隊合作造成奇蹟。

** ─────────────

teamwork〔'tim͵wɝk〕*n.* 團隊合作；
　協同合作；配合

magic〔'mædʒɪk〕*n.* 魔法；魔術

make magic 創造奇蹟

create〔krɪ'et〕*v.* 創造

miracle〔'mɪrəkl̩〕*n.* 奇蹟

wonder〔'wʌndɚ〕*n.* 奇蹟

work wonders 創造奇蹟（= *create miracles*
　= *make magic*）

【Unit 3 背景説明】

One for all.（我爲人人。）也可説成：Each member of the group supports the group.（團體的每個成員都支持團體。）Each of us supports the group.（我們每個人都支持團體。）

All for one.（人人爲我。）也可説成：All the members of the group support each individual in the group.（團體的所有成員都支持團體中的每個人。）We all support one another.（我們全都互相支持。）

All for one and one for all. 這句話是出自大仲馬《三劍客》（Three Musketeers）的座右銘，也是瑞士聯邦的傳統國家建國格言。

Strength in numbers.（人多力量大；人多勢眾。）源自諺語：There is strength in numbers.（數多則有力；人多勢眾。）也可説成：We're strong when we're together.（當我們在一起時，我們會很強大。）

We're a team.（我們是團隊。）也可説成：*We're a unit*.（我們是個團體。）*We're an alliance*.（我們是同盟。）We are united.（我們團結在一起。）We work together.（我們一起合作。）We're all in this together.（我們一起做這件事。）

Teamwork makes magic. Teamwork creates miracles. Teamwork works wonders. 這三句話意思相同。

Teamwork makes magic.（團隊合作能讓魔法發生。）也可説成：Teamwork is magical.（團隊合作很神奇。）When we work together, we can do anything.（當我們一起合作，我們能完成任何事。）

Teamwork creates miracles. 團隊合作能創造奇蹟。（= *Teamwork works wonders*.）也可説成：Teamwork is miraculous.（團隊合作令人驚奇。）（= *With teamwork we can do miraculous things*.）Together we can do anything.（我們一起能完成任何事。）

UNIT ④

The Power of Generosity
慷慨的力量

Be generous now.
現在就要慷慨。

Be generous today.
今天就要慷慨。

Be generous daily.
每天都要慷慨。

** ——————————

power〔'pauɚ〕*n.* 力量
generosity〔͵dʒɛnə'rɑsətɪ〕*n.* 慷慨；大方
generous〔'dʒɛnərəs〕*adj.* 慷慨的；大方的
daily〔'delɪ〕*adv.* 每天（= *every day*）

Generosity changes lives.

慷慨改變人生。

Generosity inspires generosity.

慷慨激發慷慨。

Generosity promotes unity.

慷慨促進團結。

** ——————————

generosity〔ˌdʒɛnəˈrɑsətɪ〕*n.* 慷慨；大方

change〔tʃendʒ〕*v.* 改變

lives〔laɪvz〕*n. pl.* 生活；人生【單數是 life】

inspire〔ɪnˈspaɪr〕*v.* 激勵

promote〔prəˈmot〕*v.* 促進

unity〔ˈjunətɪ〕*n.* 團結

Share without hesitation.

毫不猶豫分享。

Share without reservation.

毫無保留分享。

Share blessings generously.

慷慨分享幸福。

** ────────────

share〔ʃɛr〕*v.* 分享
hesitation〔͵hɛzə'teʃən〕*n.* 猶豫
reservation〔͵rɛzɚ'veʃən〕*n.* 保留
blessing〔'blɛsɪŋ〕*n.* 幸福;幸運的事
generously〔'dʒɛnərəslɪ〕*adv.* 慷慨地;
　　大方地

【Unit 4 背景説明】

Be generous now. (現在就要慷慨。) 也可説成：
Give at this moment. (現在就要付出。)

Be generous today. (今天就要慷慨。) 也可説成：
Be willing to give today. (今天就要願意付出。)

Be generous daily. (每天都要慷慨。) 也可説成：Be
willing to give every day. (每天都要願意付出。)

Generosity changes lives. (慷慨改變人生。) 也
可説成：Being generous can make a big
difference in someone's life. (慷慨可能會使某
人的一生大不相同。)

Generosity inspires generosity. 慷慨激發慷慨。
(= *Being generous inspires other people to be
generous, too*.)

Generosity promotes unity. 慷慨促進團結。
(= *Generosity makes people feel united*.) 也可
説成：Generosity increases cooperation. (慷
慨能促進合作。)

Share without hesitation. (要毫不猶豫地分享。)
也可説成：Don't hesitate to share what you
have. (要毫不猶豫地分享你所擁有的。) ***Share
without reservation***. (要毫無保留地分享。)

Share blessings generously. (要慷慨地分享幸福。)
也可説成：Be generous when you share what
you have. (要慷慨地分享你所擁有的。)

UNIT ❺

Give with love.

充滿愛意地給。

Give with joy.

充滿喜悅地給。

Give with kindness.

充滿善意地給。

**
_____

give〔gɪv〕*v.* 給與;付出

love〔lʌv〕*n.* 愛

joy〔dʒɔɪ〕*n.* 喜悅;高興

kindness〔'kaɪndnɪs〕*n.* 仁慈;善意

Give without reward.

付出不求回報。

Give without regret.

付出毫不後悔。

Give without reluctance.

付出心甘情願。

** ─────────────

give〔gɪv〕*v.* 給與；付出
reward〔rɪ'wɔrd〕*n.* 報酬；獎賞
regret〔rɪ'grɛt〕*n.* 後悔；遺憾
reluctance〔rɪ'lʌktəns〕*n.* 不情願；勉強

Give without counting.

付出毫無算計。

Give without demand.

付出沒有要求。

Give without expectations.

付出不要期望。

** ——————————

give〔gɪv〕*v.* 給與;付出

count〔kaʊnt〕*v.* 數;計算

demand〔dɪ'mænd〕*n.* 要求

expectation〔,ɛkspɛk'teʃən〕*n.* 期待;期望

【Unit 5 背景説明】

Give with love. 要充滿愛意地給。(= *Give to others lovingly.*)

Give with joy. 要充滿喜悅地給。(= *Give to others joyfully.*) 也可説成：Give happily.（要快樂地給。）(= *Be happy to give.*)

Give with kindness. 要充滿善意地給。(= *Give kindly.* = *Give to others kindly.*)

關鍵字 <u>r</u>eward-<u>r</u>egret-<u>r</u>eluctance 都是 r 開頭的字。

Give without reward. (要沒有回報地付出；付出不求回報。) 也可説成：Don't take any compensation for what you give. (付出不要拿任何的補償。)

Give without regret. (要毫不後悔地付出。) 也可説成：Never be sorry that you gave. (不要對你的付出感到遺憾。) (= *Don't be sorry to have given.*)

Give without reluctance. 要毫不勉強地付出；要心甘情願地付出。(= *Give willingly*.) 也可說成：Give without hesitation. (要毫不猶豫地付出。)

關鍵字 <u>c</u>ounting-<u>d</u>emand-<u>e</u>xpectations 字首是 c-d-e。

Give without counting. (要沒有算計地付出。) 也可說成：Don't calculate how much you give. (不要計算你付出多少。) Don't keep track of what you have given. (不要記錄你付出了什麼。)

Give without demand. (要沒有要求地付出。) 也可說成：When you give something, don't ask for anything in return. (當你付出時，不要要求任何回報。)

Give without expectations. (要沒有期望地付出。) 也可說成：Don't expect anything in return. (不要期待有任何回報。)

UNIT 6

Be a light.
成爲一盞明燈。

Be a giver.
當一位付出者。

Be an inspiration.
成爲激勵大師。

**

light〔laɪt〕*n.* 光；燈；發光體；
　領導人物
giver〔'gɪvɚ〕*n.* 付出者
inspiration〔ˌɪnspə'reʃən〕*n.* 激勵；
　靈感；給予激勵的人

Think of others.

想到別人。

Look after others.

照顧別人。

Always be kind.

永存好心。

**

think of 想到

others〔ˈʌðəz〕*pron.* 別人

look after 照顧

always〔ˈɔlwez〕*adv.* 總是；一直

kind〔kaɪnd〕*adj.* 仁慈的；親切的

Share your wealth.

分享財富。

Share your resources.

分享資源。

Make others smile.

讓別人笑。

** ———————————————

share〔ʃɛr〕v. 分享

wealth〔wɛlθ〕n. 財富

resource〔rɪˈsors〕n. 資源【常用複數】

make〔mek〕v. 使

smile〔smaɪl〕v. 微笑；笑

【Unit 6 背景説明】

Be a light. (要成爲一盞燈；要成爲領導人物。) 也可説成： Be a leader. (要成爲領導者。) Be an expert. (要成爲專家。)

Be a giver. (要成爲付出者；要願意付出。) 也可説成： Be generous. (要慷慨。)

Be an inspiration. (要成爲激勵大師。) 也可説成： Be an influence. (要成爲有影響力的人。) Be a role model. (要成爲模範。)

Think of others. (要想到別人。) 也可説成： Be considerate. (要體貼。)

Look after others. 要照顧別人。(= *Care for others*. = *Take care of others*.)

Always be kind. (一定要善良。) 也可説成： Be kind-hearted every day. (每天都要好心。) Be warm-hearted every day. (每天都要熱心。) Be thoughtful every day. (每天都要體貼。) Be generous every day. (每天都要慷慨。)

Share your wealth. (分享你的財富。) 也可説成： Give money to others. (要給別人錢。)

Share your resources. (分享你的資源。) 也可説成： Give some of what you have to others. (要把你所擁有的一部分給別人。)

Make others smile. (要讓別人笑。) 也可説成： Make others happy. (要讓別人快樂。)

UNIT 7

Don't Be a Scrooge
不要小氣

Don't be frugal.
不要過份節儉。

Don't be miserly.
不要吝嗇小氣。

Share your money.
有錢大家享用。

**

scrooge〔skrudʒ〕*n.* 吝嗇鬼；守財奴
frugal〔'frugḷ〕*adj.* 節儉的
miserly〔'maɪzɚlɪ〕*adj.* 吝嗇的；小氣的
share〔ʃɛr〕*v.* 分享

Mind the big.

注重大事。

Embrace the big.

在意大事。

Ignore the small.

忽略小事。

** —————————

mind〔maɪnd〕*v.* 介意；注意

big〔bɪg〕*adj.* 大的；重要的

the big 大事（ = *big things* ）

embrace〔ɪm'bres〕*v.* 擁抱；欣然
　接受；看到

ignore〔ɪg'nor〕*v.* 忽視

small〔smɔl〕*adj.* 小的；微不足道的；
　無關緊要的

the small 小事（ = *small things* ）

Overlook small matters.

不計較小事情。

Overlook tiny details.

不計較小細節。

Ignore minor things.

不在意小事情。

** ────────────────

overlook〔͵ovɚˋluk〕*v.* 忽視

matter〔ˋmætɚ〕*n.* 事情

tiny〔ˋtaɪnɪ〕*adj.* 微小的

detail〔ˋditel〕*n.* 細節

ignore〔ɪgˋnor〕*v.* 忽視（*= overlook = disregard*）

minor〔ˋmaɪnɚ〕*adj.* 較不重要的；次要的

【Unit 7 背景説明】

Don't be frugal. 不要節儉。(= *Don't be so thrifty.*) 也可説成：Don't be a penny-pincher.
（不要一毛不拔。）

Don't be miserly. 不要吝嗇；不要小氣。(= *Don't be stingy.* = *Don't be tight-fisted.*) 也可説成：Be generous.（要慷慨。）

Share your money.（分享你的錢；有錢大家用。）也可説成：Give away some of your money.（要送出一些錢。）Donate some of your money.（要捐一些錢。）

Mind the big. 要注意大事。(= *Pay attention to the big things.*)

Embrace the big. 要注意重要的事。(= *Appreciate the important things.* = *Pay attention to the important things.*)

Ignore the small. (要忽略小事。) 也可説成：
Don't waste your time on unimportant
things. (不要浪費你的時間在不重要的事情上。)
Don't worry about trivial things. (不要擔心
瑣碎的事。)

Overlook small matters. (要忽視小事。) 也可説
成：Forget about unimportant things. (忘掉
不重要的事。)

Overlook tiny details. (要忽視微小的細節。)
也可説成：Don't waste your time on
unimportant things. (不要浪費你的時間在不
重要的事情上。)

Ignore minor things.　忽視較不重要的事。
(= *Ignore unimportant things*.) 也可説成：
Disregard trivial things. (要忽視瑣碎的事。)

UNIT 8

Offer to pay.

要主動付帳。

Your treat today.

今天你請客。

It's your chance.

是你的機會。

** ────────

offer〔'ɔfɚ〕*v.* 提供;主動提出;提議
pay〔pe〕*v.* 付錢
treat〔trit〕*v.* 對待;請(客) *n.* 特別款待
one's treat 某人請客
chance〔tʃæns〕*n.* 機會

Foot the bill.

要去買單。

Settle the tab.

要去付帳。

Eagerly cover expenses.

搶著付錢。

**

foot〔fʊt〕*v.* 支付（帳單或費用）　*n.* 腳

bill〔bɪl〕*n.* 帳單

settle〔'sɛtl̩〕*v.* 解決；支付（= *pay*）

tab〔tæb〕*n.* （待付的）帳單；帳款

eagerly〔'igəlɪ〕*adv.* 渴望地；急切地

cover〔'kʌvɚ〕*v.* 支付

expense〔ɪk'spɛns〕*n.* 花費；費用

Offer a meal.

要請人吃飯。

Give a present.

要送人禮物。

You'll take off.

會飛黃騰達。

**

offer〔ˋɔfɚ〕*v.* 提供
meal〔mil〕*n.* 一餐
present〔ˋprɛznt〕*n.* 禮物
take off 起飛;突然開始成功

【Unit 8 背景説明】

Offer to pay. 要提議付錢。(= *Suggest that you pay.*)

Your treat today. 今天你要請客。(= *It's your treat today.*) 也可説成：It's your turn to pay the bill. (今天輪到你付帳。) Pay the bill. (要付帳。) (= *Pick up the tab.*)

It's your chance. 這是你的機會。(= *This is your opportunity.*)

Foot the bill. 要付帳。(= *Pay the bill.*)

Settle the tab. 要付錢。(= *Pick up the tab.* = *Pick up the check.* = *Pay the bill.* = *Foot the bill.*)

Eagerly cover expenses. 要急切地支付費用；要搶著付錢。(= *Cover the expenses enthusiastically.* = *Pick up the tab enthusiastically.*)

Offer a meal. 要提供餐點；要請人吃飯。(= *Provide a meal.*) 也可説成：Pay for others' meals. (付錢請人吃飯。) Pay the tab. (要付帳。)

Give a present. 要送個禮物。(= *Give a gift.*)

You'll take off. 你會飛黃騰達；你會成功。(= *You'll succeed.*)

UNIT ❾

Don't fear losses.

不要怕吃虧。

Share and enjoy.

要樂於分享。

Spend without fear.

花錢不手軟。

** ————————————————

fear〔 fɪr 〕*v. n.* 害怕
loss〔 lɔs 〕*n.* 損失
share〔 ʃɛr 〕*v.* 分享
enjoy〔 ɪnˈdʒɔɪ 〕*v.* 享受
spend〔 spɛnd 〕*v.* 花費;花錢

Enjoy being needed.

喜歡被需要。

Cherish being utilized.

珍惜被利用。

Appreciate being useful.

感謝我有用。

** ———————————————

enjoy〔ɪnˈdʒɔɪ〕*v.* 享受；喜歡

enjoy + *V-ing* 享受…；喜歡…

need〔nid〕*v.* 需要

cherish〔ˈtʃɛrɪʃ〕*v.* 珍惜

utilize〔ˈjutḷˌaɪz〕*v.* 利用

appreciate〔əˈpriʃɪˌet〕*v.* 欣賞；
　重視；感激

useful〔ˈjusfəl〕*adj.* 有用的

Never exploit others.

絕不剝削他人。

Never use others.

絕不利用他人。

Never take advantage.

絕不佔人便宜。

＊＊ ────────────

never〔'nɛvɚ〕*adv.* 絕不

exploit〔ɪk'splɔɪt〕*v.* 剝削；利用

others〔'ʌðɚz〕*pron.* 別人

use〔juz〕*v.* 使用；利用；運用

advantage〔əd'væntɪdʒ〕*n.* 利益；
　好處；優點

take advantage 利用；佔便宜

【Unit 9 背景説明】

Don't fear losses. 不要害怕損失，在此引申爲「不要怕吃虧。」也可説成：Don't worry about the expense. (不要擔心花費。)

Share and enjoy. 要樂於分享。(= *Give and enjoy yourself.* = *Take pleasure in giving.*)
也可説成：Take pleasure in being generous.
(要以慷慨爲樂。)

Spend without fear. (不要怕花錢。) 也可説成：Spend freely. (要隨意地花錢。)

Enjoy being needed. 享受被需要。(= *Take pleasure in knowing that you are needed.*)

Cherish being utilized. (珍惜被利用。) 也可説成：Enjoy being useful. (高興自己有用。)

Appreciate being useful. 感激能派上用場。(= *Appreciate the fact that you are useful.*)

Never exploit others. (絶不要剝削別人。) 也可説成：***Never use others.*** (絶不要利用別人。)
Don't manipulate others. (不要操縱別人。)

Never take advantage. 絶不佔人便宜。(= *Never take advantage of others.*)

PART 3 總整理

Unit 1

United we shine.
團結我們閃耀。
United we soar.
團結我們高飛。
United we succeed.
團結我們成功。

United we achieve.
團結我們實現。
United we advance.
團結我們進步。
United we ascend.
團結我們上升。

United we win. 團結我們會贏。
United we prevail.
團結我們獲勝。
United we triumph.
團結我們戰勝。

Unit 2

Together we stand.
一起我們站穩。
Together we grow.
一起我們成長。
Together we prosper.
一起我們發達。

Together we're strong.
一起我們很強大。
Together we're powerful.
一起我們有力量。
Together we're resilient.
一起我們有韌性。

Together we're
  unstoppable.
團結勢不可擋。
Together we're
  unbeatable.
團結無人能敵。
Together we're
  invincible.
團結所向披靡。

Unit 3

One for all. 我為人人。
All for one. 人人為我。
Strength in numbers.
【諺】人多勢眾。

We're a team.
我們是團隊。
We're a unit. 我們是一體。
We're an alliance.
我們是同盟。

Teamwork makes magic.
團隊合作創造神蹟。
Teamwork creates
  miracles.
團隊合作創造奇蹟。
Teamwork works
  wonders.
團隊合作造成奇蹟。

Unit 4

Be generous now.
現在就要慷慨。
Be generous today.
今天就要慷慨。
Be generous daily.
每天都要慷慨。

Generosity changes lives.
慷慨改變人生。
Generosity inspires
  generosity.
慷慨激發慷慨。
Generosity promotes
  unity. 慷慨促進團結。

Share without hesitation.
毫不猶豫分享。
Share without reservation.
毫無保留分享。
Share blessings
  generously. 慷慨分享幸福。

Unit 5

Give with love.
充滿愛意地給。
Give with joy.
充滿喜悅地給。
Give with kindness.
充滿善意地給。

Give without reward.
付出不求回報。
Give without regret.
付出毫不後悔。
Give without reluctance.
付出心甘情願。

Give without counting.
付出毫無算計。
Give without demand.
付出沒有要求。
Give without expectations.
付出不要期望。

Unit 6

Be a light. 成爲一盞明燈。
Be a giver. 當一位付出者。
Be an inspiration.
成爲激勵大師。

Think of others. 想到別人。
Look after others.
照顧別人。
Always be kind. 永存好心。

Share your wealth.
分享財富。
Share your resources.
分享資源。
Make others smile.
讓別人笑。

Unit 7

Don't be frugal.
不要過份節儉。
Don't be miserly.
不要吝嗇小氣。
Share your money.
有錢大家享用。

Mind the big.　注重大事。
Embrace the big.　在意大事。
Ignore the small.　忽略小事。

Overlook small matters.
不計較小事情。
Overlook tiny details.
不計較小細節。
Ignore minor things.
不在意小事情。

Unit 8

Offer to pay.　要主動付帳。
Your treat today.
今天你請客。
It's your chance.
是你的機會。

Foot the bill.　要去買單。
Settle the tab.　要去付帳。
Eagerly cover expenses.
搶著付錢。

Offer a meal.　要請人吃飯。
Give a present.
要送人禮物。
You'll take off.
會飛黃騰達。

Unit 9

Don't fear losses.
不要怕吃虧。
Share and enjoy.
要樂於分享。
Spend without fear.
花錢不手軟。

Enjoy being needed.
喜歡被需要。
Cherish being utilized.
珍惜被利用。
Appreciate being useful.
感謝我有用。

Never exploit others.
絕不剝削他人。
Never use others.
絕不利用他人。
Never take advantage.
絕不佔人便宜。

BOOK 4　PART 1

The Most Important Things
最重要的東西

PART 1 · Unit 1~9
英文録音QR碼

UNIT 1

The Importance of Choice
選擇的重要

Choosing matters most.
抉擇最爲重要。

Choice before effort.
選擇大於努力。

Selection outweighs labor.
取捨勝於實幹。

**

choice〔tʃɔɪs〕*n.* 選擇
choose〔tʃuz〕*v.* 選擇
matter〔'mætɚ〕*v.* 重要
most〔most〕*adv.* 最；最爲（= *the most*）
before〔bɪ'for〕*prep.* 在…之前；比…優先
effort〔'ɛfɚt〕*n.* 努力
selection〔sə'lɛkʃən〕*n.* 選擇
outweigh〔aʊt'we〕*v.* 比…重；比…重要
labor〔'lebɚ〕*n.* 勞動；辛勞；努力

Choose your tribe.

選擇你的社交圈。

Choose compatible companions.

選合得來的同伴。

Choose top-notch circles.

選擇高端人脈圈。

**────────────

choose〔tʃuz〕*v.* 選擇

tribe〔traɪb〕*n.* 部落；同夥；一大群人；
　一大幫人

compatible〔kəmˈpætəbḷ〕*adj.* 能相容的；
　合得來的

companion〔kəmˈpænjən〕*n.* 同伴

top〔tɑp〕*adj.* 頂端的

notch〔nɑtʃ〕*n.*（V 字形的）刻痕；凹槽；等級

top-notch〔ˌtɑpˈnɑtʃ〕*adj.* 頂呱呱的；一流的

circle〔ˈsɝkḷ〕*n.* 圓圈；（具有共同利益或興趣
　的人所形成的）圈子

Choose mentors well.

善於選擇師父。

Choose your journey.

選擇你的旅途。

Choose your destiny.

選擇你的命運。

** ───────────────

choose〔tʃuz〕*v.* 選擇
mentor〔'mɛntor〕*n.* 良師;導師;師父
journey〔'dʒɝnɪ〕*n.* 旅程
destiny〔'dɛstənɪ〕*n.* 命運

【Unit 1 背景説明】

Choosing matters most. （選擇最重要。）主詞 Choosing 是動名詞，視爲單數。用 most 或 the most 都可，意思相同。也可説成：Being able to choose is the most important thing.（能夠選擇是最重要的。）What you choose is the most important thing.（你選擇什麼是最重要的。）

Choice before effort. 沒有動詞，是慣用句，表「選擇比努力優先。」也可説成：Making a choice is more important than making an effort.（選擇比努力重要。）

Selection outweighs labor. 選擇比努力重要。（= *Choosing is more important than effort.*）也可説成：Making the right choice is more important than working hard.（做正確的選擇比努力更重要。）

Choose your tribe. 字面的意思是「選擇你的部落。」引申爲「選擇你的社群。」（= *Select your own community.*）；「選擇你的社交圈。」（= *Choose your social circle.*）

Choose compatible companions. (選擇合得來的
同伴。) 也可說成：Choose people you can get
along with well. (選擇能和你和睦相處的人)
Choose people you can work with well. (選
擇能和你好好合作的人。)

Choose top-notch circles. (選擇高檔的朋友圈。)
也可說成：Choose the best group of people.
(選擇最好的一群人。) Join the best groups. (加
入最好的團體。) Associate with best people.
(和最好的人來往。)

Choose mentors well. (好好選擇良師。) 也可說
成：Pick good role models. (挑選好的模範。)
Pick good advisors. (挑選好的顧問。)

Choose your journey. (選擇你的旅程。) 也可說
成：Decide what you want. (決定你想要什麼。)
Decide what you want to do in life. (決定在
人生中你想要做什麼。)

Choose your destiny. (選擇你的命運。) 也可說
成：Control your destiny. (掌控你的命運。)
Decide your own future. (決定你自己的未來。)

UNIT ❷

Health Is Everything
健康最重要

Health is wealth.
健康是財富。

Health is strength.
健康是力量。

Health is happiness.
健康是幸福。

** ───────

health〔hɛlθ〕*n.* 健康

everything〔'ɛvrɪ,θɪŋ〕*pron.* 一切事物；
　最重要的東西

wealth〔wɛlθ〕*n.* 財富

strength〔strɛŋθ〕*n.* 力量

happiness〔'hæpɪnɪs〕*n.* 快樂；幸福

Health brings vitality.

健康帶來活力。

Health brings productivity.

健康有生產力。

Health brings prosperity.

健康帶來興盛。

** ————————————

health〔hɛlθ〕*n.* 健康
bring〔brɪŋ〕*v.* 帶來
vitality〔vaɪˈtælətɪ〕*n.* 活力
productivity〔ˌprodʌkˈtɪvətɪ〕*n.* 生產力
prosperity〔prɑsˈpɛrətɪ〕*n.* 繁榮;
　興盛;成功

Good health matters.

健康非常重要。

Physical health matters.

身體健康重要。

Mental health first.

心理健康第一。

** ──────────────────

health〔hɛlθ〕*n.* 健康

matter〔'mætɚ〕*v.* 重要

physical〔'fɪzɪkḷ〕*adj.* 身體的

mental〔'mɛntḷ〕*adj.* 心理的

first〔fɝst〕*adj.* 第一的；居首位的

　　adv. 居首位；第一

【Unit 2 背景說明】

Health is wealth. (【諺】健康就是財富。) 也可說成：Health is the most valuable thing one can have. (健康是一個人所能擁有的最珍貴的東西。) We can achieve anything if we have good health. (如果我們擁有良好的健康，就能達成任何事。)

Health is strength. (健康就是力量。) 也可說成：Good health leads to a strong body. (良好的健康造就強壯的身體。) We need good health to be strong. (我們需要良好的健康才會強壯。)

Health is happiness. (健康就是快樂。) 也可說成：If we are healthy, we can be happy. (如果我們健康，就能快樂。) Without good health, it is difficult to be happy. (沒有良好的健康，很難快樂。)

Health brings vitality. 健康帶來活力。(= *Good health brings energy*.) 也可說成：Good health gives strength. (良好的健康給人力量。)

Health brings productivity. (健康帶來生產力。)
也可説成：Having good health makes you
more productive. (擁有良好的健康使你更有生
產力。)

Health brings prosperity. (健康帶來成功。) 也
可説成：With good health, we can be
prosperous. (擁有良好的健康，我們才能成功。)

Good health matters.　良好的健康很重要。
(*= Good health is important.*)

Physical health matters.　身體健康很重要。
(*= Being physically healthy is important.*)

Mental health first. (心理健康第一。) 是慣用句，
源自 Mental health is first. (心理健康第一。)
Place mental health first. (要把心理健康放在第
一位。) 也可説成：Mental health is most
important. (心理健康最重要。) Mental health
is more important. (心理健康更重要。)

UNIT ❸

Kindness Counts
善良很重要

Kindness is powerful.
善良很有力量。

Kindness is radiant.
善良光芒四射。

Kindness is rewarding.
善良會有回報。

**

kindness〔'kaɪndnɪs〕*n.* 仁慈；善意；善良

count〔kaʊnt〕*v.* 重要

powerful〔'paʊəfəl〕*adj.* 有力量的；
　強而有力的

radiant〔'redɪənt〕*adj.* 光芒四射的；容光
　煥發的；洋溢著幸福的

rewarding〔rɪ'wɔrdɪŋ〕*adj.* 值得做的；
　有益的；有報酬的

Kindness breeds happiness.
善良產生快樂。

Kindness bridges divides.
善良消除分歧。

Kindness breaks barriers.
善意打破障礙。

** ─────────

kindness〔'kaɪndnɪs〕*n.* 仁慈；善意；善良

breed〔brid〕*v.* 產生

happiness〔'hæpɪnɪs〕*n.* 快樂；幸福

bridge〔brɪdʒ〕*v.* 架橋於；填補（空隙）；
彌合（差距）；消除（分歧）

divide〔də'vaɪd〕*n.* （重大的）分歧
v. 劃分；分割 *bridge divides* 消除分歧

break〔brek〕*v.* 打破

barrier〔'bærɪɚ〕*n.* 障礙（物）；阻礙；隔閡
break barriers 消除障礙

Show kindness daily.

每天展現善意。

Show kindness freely.

隨時表現善意。

Practice kindness sincerely.

真誠實踐善良。

** ————————————————

show〔ʃo〕v. 展現

kindness〔'kaɪndnɪs〕n. 仁慈；善意；善良

daily〔'delɪ〕adv. 每天 (= every day)

freely〔'frilɪ〕adv. 自由地；無拘束地；
　　大量地；無節制地

practice〔'præktɪs〕v. 實行

practice kindness 行善

sincerely〔sɪn'sɪrlɪ〕adv. 真誠地

【Unit 3 背景説明】

Kindness is powerful. （善良很有力量。）也可説成：
Kindness is persuasive. （善良很有說服力。）

Kindness is radiant. （善良光芒四射。）也可説成：
Kindness is joyful. （善良令人快樂。）

Kindness is rewarding. （善良會有回報。）也可説成：
It is fulfilling to be kind. （善良令人有成就感。）
Being kind makes you feel good. （善良會使你感
覺很好。）

Kindness breeds happiness. （善良產生快樂。）也可
説成：If we are kind, we can be happy. （如果我
們善良，我們就會快樂。）Being kind makes others
happy. （善良會使別人快樂。）

Kindness bridges divides. （善良消除分歧。）也可説成：
Kindness can mend fences. （善良可以解決紛爭。）

Kindness breaks barriers.　善意消除障礙。（= *Kindness
overcomes obstacles*. ）

Show kindness daily.　每天展現善意。（= *Be kind every
day*. ）

Show kindness freely. （隨時表現善意。）也可説成：
Never hesitate to be kind. （要毫不猶豫地對人好。）

Practice kindness sincerely. （要眞誠地實踐善良。）也
可説成：Be genuinely kind. （要眞的善良。）

UNIT 4

The Power of Positivity

樂觀的力量

Choose optimism daily.

天天選擇樂觀。

Choose joy daily.

天天選擇快樂。

Positive vibes prevail.

正能量會勝利。

** ————————

power〔ˈpauɚ〕*n.* 力量

positivity〔ˌpɑzəˈtɪvətɪ〕*n.* 正面;積極;樂觀

choose〔tʃuz〕*v.* 選擇

optimism〔ˈɑptəˌmɪzəm〕*n.* 樂觀

daily〔ˈdelɪ〕*adv.* 每天 (= *every day*)

joy〔dʒɔɪ〕*n.* 喜悅;高興;快樂

positive〔ˈpɑzətɪv〕*adj.* 正面的

vibes〔vaɪbz〕*n. pl.* (給人的) 印象;情緒上的
激動;氣氛;氛圍 (= *vibrations*)

prevail〔prɪˈvel〕*v.* 獲勝;佔優勢;盛行

Smile through storms.

笑對風雨。

Smile through challenges.

笑對挑戰。

Embrace the sun.

擁抱太陽。

**

smile〔smaɪl〕*v.* 微笑；笑

through〔θru〕*prep.* 穿越；通過

storm〔stɔrm〕*n.* 暴風雨

challenge〔'tʃælɪndʒ〕*n.* 挑戰

embrace〔ɪm'bres〕*v.* 擁抱；欣然接受

sun〔sʌn〕*n.* 太陽；太陽般光輝奪目的事物

See light ahead.

看見前方光明。

See rainbows after.

看見雨後彩虹。

Hope illuminates shadows.

希望照亮黑暗。

**

light〔laɪt〕*n.* 光
ahead〔ə'hɛd〕*adv.* 在前面
rainbow〔'ren,bo〕*n.* 彩虹
after〔'æftɚ〕*adv.* 之後；後來
hope〔hop〕*n.* 希望
illuminate〔ɪ'lumə,net〕*v.* 照亮
shadow〔'ʃædo〕*n.* 影子；陰暗處

【Unit 4 背景説明】

Choose optimism daily.（每天選擇樂觀。）也可説成：Be optimistic every day.（要每天樂觀。）（= *Be positive every day*.）

Choose joy daily.（每天選擇快樂。）也可説成：Be joyful every day.（要每天快樂。）（= *Be happy every day*.）

Positive vibes prevail.（正能量佔優勢。）也可説成：Positive energy will win the day.（正能量會成功獲得支持。）Optimism will win.（樂觀會獲勝。）

Smile through storms. 要微笑度過風雨；要逆來順受。（= *Grin and bear it*.）也可説成：Be positive no matter what happens.（無論發生什麼事，都要樂觀。）（= *Be optimistic no matter what happens*.）

Smile through challenges.（要微笑度過挑戰。）也可説成：Remain positive in the face of difficulty. (面對困難依然要樂觀。) (= *Be optimistic in the face of difficulty.*)

Embrace the sun. (要擁抱太陽。) 也可説成：
Focus on the positive. (要專注於正面的事物。)
Appreciate the good things in life. (要欣賞生命中美好的事物。)

See light ahead. (看見前方的光明。) 和 *See rainbows after*. (看見雨後的彩虹。) 都表示
「一直充滿希望。」(= *Remain hopeful.*)
Believe things will get better. (相信一切都會變得更好。)

Hope illuminates shadows. (希望照亮黑暗。)
也可説成：Hope overcomes difficulty.
(希望能克服困難。) Hope overcomes fear.
(希望能克服恐懼。) Everything looks
better with hope. (有了希望，一切看起來更美好。)

UNIT 5

Money Talks
金錢萬能

Wealth is power.
財富是力量。

Cash is king.
現金是王道。

Money is freedom.
有錢就自由。

**

talk〔tɔk〕v. 說話；有說服力

Money talks. 【諺】財大就氣粗；有錢就有
　勢；金錢萬能。　　wealth〔wɛlθ〕n. 財富

power〔ˈpaʊɚ〕n. 力量

cash〔kæʃ〕n. 現金　　king〔kɪŋ〕n. 國王

freedom〔ˈfridəm〕n. 自由

Money is essential.

錢是必要的。

Money is influential.

錢有影響力。

Money talks loudly.

金錢是萬能。

**

---

essential〔ə'sɛnʃəl〕*adj.* 必要的;
非常重要的
influential〔͵ɪnflʊ'ɛnʃəl〕*adj.* 有影響力的
talk〔tɔk〕*v.* 說話;有說服力
loudly〔'laʊdlɪ〕*adv.* 大聲地

Money tests friendships.
金錢考驗友誼。

Money tests relationships.
金錢考驗關係。

Money undermines trust.
金錢破壞信任。

** ─────────────

test〔tɛst〕*v.* 測驗;考驗

friendship〔'frɛndʃɪp〕*n.* 友誼

relationship〔rɪ'leʃən͵ʃɪp〕*n.* 關係

undermine〔͵ʌndɚ'maɪn〕*v.* 暗中破壞;
（逐漸地）損害

trust〔trʌst〕*n.* 信任

【Unit 5 背景說明】

Wealth is power.（財富就是力量。）也可說成：
With money, you have more power.（有了
錢，你會更有力量。）Money gives one power.
（金錢給人力量。）

Cash is king.（現金爲王。）也可說成：Hold on
to your cash.（要守住你的現金。）是投資者在股
市熊市的一種保存資本避險策略。在經濟最壞時候，
多持有現金，能應付基本生活，在股市下跌時，可
逢低買進，迎接牛市重臨，這便是「有現金成王，
無現金成寇」的道理。

Money is freedom.（金錢就是自由。）也可說成：
With money, you have more freedom.（有了
錢，你會更自由。）Money gives one freedom.
（金錢給人自由。）

Money is essential.（錢是必要的。）也可說成：
Money is necessary.（錢是必需的。）Without
money, you can't do anything.（沒有錢，你無
法做任何事。）

Money is influential.（錢有影響力。）也可說成：
Money is powerful.（金錢力量大。）

Money is compelling. (錢有說服力。) (= *Money is persuasive.*)

Money talks loudly. 金錢說話說得很大聲，引申爲「金錢萬能。」源自諺語 Money talks. (金錢萬能。) 也可說成：Money is powerful. (金錢力量大。) People pay attention to money. (人們很注意錢。)

Money tests friendships. (金錢考驗友誼。) 也可說成：Money can challenge friendships. (金錢可以挑戰友誼。) Money can cause problems in a friendship. (金錢可能在友誼中製造問題。)

Money tests relationships. (金錢考驗關係。) 也可說成：Money can challenge relationships. (金錢可以挑戰關係。) Money can cause problems in a relationship. (金錢可能在一段關係中製造問題。)

Money undermines trust. (金錢破壞信任。) 也可說成：Money can cause distrust. (金錢會造成不信任。) Money can make people feel less secure in a relationship. (金錢可能會使人在一段關係中覺得較沒有安全感。)

UNIT ⑥

The Value of Time
時間的重要

Time is money.
【諺】時間就是金錢。

Time is precious.
時間是珍貴的。

Time is priceless.
時間是無價的。

BOOK 4・PART 1

** ————————————

value〔'væljʊ〕 *n.* 價值;重要性
precious〔'prɛʃəs〕 *adj.* 珍貴的
priceless〔'praɪslɪs〕 *adj.* 無價的

Time flies by.

時光飛逝。

Time is fleeting.

光陰似箭。

Time is unstoppable.

時間不停。

**

fly〔flaɪ〕*v.* 飛

by〔baɪ〕*adv.* 由旁邊（經）過

fly by （時間）飛逝

fleeting〔'flitɪŋ〕*adj.* 短暫的；迅速的

　【fleet〔flit〕*n.* 艦隊；船隊】

unstoppable〔ʌn'stɑpəbḷ〕*adj.* 止不住的；

　不可阻擋的；制止不了的

Time tells all.

時間說明一切。

Time tests all.

時間考驗一切。

Time heals all.

時間治療一切。

**

tell〔tɛl〕*v.* 說；傳達；告訴；顯示

test〔tɛst〕*v.* 檢驗；考驗

heal〔hil〕*v.* 治癒

【**Unit 6** 背景説明】

Time is money. (【諺】時間就是金錢。) 也可説成：
Time waits for no one. (時間不等人。)
Hurry up. (趕快。)

Time is precious. 時間很珍貴。(= *Time is valuable*.)

Time is priceless. 時間是無價的。(= *Time is invaluable*. = *Time is beyond price*.)

Time flies by. (時光飛逝。) 也可説成：How time flies. (時間過得真快。) Time waits for no man. (歲月不待人。)

Time is fleeting. 時間過得很快；光陰似箭。(= *Time passes quickly*.) 也可説成：The clock is ticking. (時間緊迫。)

Time is unstoppable. (時間是不可阻擋的。) 也可説成：Time passes nonstop. (時間會不停地過去。) Time never stops. (時間從不停止。)

Time tells all. 時間說明一切。(= *Time will tell.*)
也可說成 : The truth will come out. (真相會大
白。) You'll know the answer in the future.
(未來你會知道答案。)

Time tests all. (時間考驗一切。) 也可說成 : Time
will prove everything. (時間會證明一切。)
Time will make it plain. (時間會明確說明。)

Time heals all. 時間治療一切。(= *Time cures
all.*) 也可說成 : Time is the best healer. (【諺】
時間是最好的治療者;時間會治療一切。) Time
heals all wounds. (時間會治好所有的傷口。)
Everything gets better with time. (隨著時間的
過去,一切都會變好。) With time, the pain will
fade away. (痛苦會隨著時間的過去而消失。)

UNIT **7**

The Value of Knowledge
知識的重要

Knowledge is power.
【諺】知識就是力量。

Knowledge is liberty.
知識就是自由。

Knowledge is opportunity.
知識就是機會。

** ─────────────

value〔'væljʊ〕*n.* 價值；重要性
knowledge〔'nɑlɪdʒ〕*n.* 知識
power〔'paʊɚ〕*n.* 力量
liberty〔'lɪbɚtɪ〕*n.* 自由
opportunity〔,ɑpɚ'tjunətɪ〕*n.* 機會

Knowledge is invaluable.

知識是無價的。

Knowledge is indispensable.

知識不可或缺。

Knowledge is key.

知識非常重要。

** ——————————

knowledge〔'nɑlɪdʒ〕 *n.* 知識

invaluable〔ɪn'væljuəb!〕 *adj.* 無價的；

非常貴重的（ = *priceless* ）

indispensable〔͵ɪndɪ'spɛnsəb!〕 *adj.* 不可

或缺的

key〔ki〕 *adj.* 極重要的；關鍵性的

n. 鑰匙；關鍵 < *to* >

Knowledge opens doors.

知識打開大門。

Knowledge breeds confidence.

知識產生自信。

Knowledge shapes destiny.

知識塑造命運。

** ————————

knowledge (ˈnɑlɪdʒ) *n.* 知識

open (ˈopən) *v.* 打開

open doors 創造機會

breed (brid) *v.* 產生

confidence (ˈkɑnfədəns) *n.* 自信；信心

shape (ʃep) *v.* 塑造；決定

destiny (ˈdɛstənɪ) *n.* 命運

【Unit 7 背景説明】

Knowledge is power. 【諺】知識就是力量。
(= *Knowledge is strength.*) 也可説成：Having more knowledge gives one more power. (擁有更多的知識，會讓人更有力量。)

Knowledge is liberty. 知識就是自由。
(= *Knowledge is freedom.*) 也可説成：The more you know, the freer you will be. (你懂得越多，就越自由。) With knowledge, you can be free. (有了知識，你就可以自由。) With knowledge, you can do what you want. (有了知識，你就可以做你想做的事。)

Knowledge is opportunity. (知識就是機會。)
也可説成：The more you know, the more opportunities you will have. (你懂得越多，擁有的機會就越多。)

Knowledge is invaluable. 知識是無價的。
(= *Knowledge is priceless.*)

Knowledge is indispensable. 知識是不可或缺的。
(= *Knowledge is essential.*) 也可説成：One

can't succeed without knowledge. (沒有知識，無法成功。)

Knowledge is key. (知識非常重要。) 也可說成：Knowledge is the key that unlocks all doors. (知識是開啓所有門的鑰匙。) Knowledge is the key to success. (知識是成功的關鍵。)【key 後有修飾語時，前面加 the】

Knowledge opens doors. 知識能打開門，引申爲「知識創造機會。」也可說成：Knowledge is opportunity. (知識就是機會。) Knowledge leads to opportunities. (知識產生機會。) The more you know, the more opportunities you will have. (你懂得越多，擁有的機會就越多。)

Knowledge breeds confidence. (知識產生自信。) 也可說成：The more you know, the more confident you will be. (你懂得越多，就會越有自信。)

Knowledge shapes destiny. (知識塑造命運。) 也可說成：What you know shapes your future. (你的知識能決定你的未來。)

BOOK 4・PART 1

UNIT **8**

What Is Love? 愛是什麼？

Love is blind.

【諺】愛是盲目的。

Love is boundless.

愛沒有界限。

Love is limitless.

愛是無限的。

BOOK 4・PART 1

**

love〔lʌv〕*n.* 愛

blind〔blaɪnd〕*adj.* 瞎的；盲的；失明的；
　盲目的

boundless〔'baʊndlɪs〕*adj.* 無限的；
　無窮的；無止境的

limitless〔'lɪmɪtlɪs〕*adj.* 無限的；無限制的

Love conquers all.

愛能征服一切。

Love conquers fear.

愛能征服恐懼。

Love endures hardships.

愛能忍受苦難。

** ────────────────

conquer〔ˈkɑŋkɚ〕v. 征服

fear〔fɪr〕n. 恐懼

endure〔ɪnˈdjʊr〕v. 忍受

hardship〔ˈhɑrdʃɪp〕n. 艱難；辛苦；困苦

Love embraces differences.

愛能擁抱差異。

Love embraces flaws.

愛能擁抱缺點。

Love is magical.

愛是非常神奇。

** ─────────────────

embrace〔ɪmˋbres〕*v.* 擁抱;欣然接受
difference〔ˋdɪfərəns〕*n.* 不同;差異
flaw〔flɔ〕*n.* 瑕疵;缺點
magical〔ˋmædʒɪkḷ〕*adj.* 神奇的

【Unit 8 背景説明】

Love is blind. (【諺】愛情是盲目的。) 也可説成：
We see no faults in the person we love. (我們看不到愛人的缺點。) People do foolish things when in love. (人在戀愛時會做傻事。) Love blinds reason. (愛情蒙蔽理智。)

Love is boundless. 愛沒有界限。(= *Love has no limits.*) 也可説成：Love is unlimited. (愛是沒有限制的。)

Love is limitless. (愛是沒有限制的。) 也可説成：Love has no limits. (愛沒有限制。) Love is infinite. (愛是無限的。) Love is boundless. (愛沒有界限。)

Love conquers all. (愛能征服一切。) 也可説成：Love overcomes all obstacles. (愛能克服所有的阻礙。) Love overcomes all challenges. (愛能克服所有的挑戰。) Love always wins. (真愛一定會獲勝。)

BOOK 4・PART 1

Love conquers fear. （愛能征服恐懼。）也可說
成：Love overcomes fear.（愛能克服恐懼。）
Love makes people fearless.（愛讓人無所畏
懼。）

Love endures hardships. （愛能忍受艱難困苦。）
也可說成：Love is resilient.（愛很有韌性。）
Love survives no matter what.（無論如何，
愛都能存活。）Love survives despite
difficulties.（無論多困難，愛都能存活。）

Love embraces differences. （愛能擁抱差異。）
也可說成：Love accepts differences.（愛能接
受差異。）Love is tolerant.（愛是寬容的。）

Love embraces flaws. （愛能擁抱缺點。）也可說
成：Love is accepting.（愛能包容。）Love is
blind.（愛情是盲目的。）

Love is magical. 愛是神奇的。(= *Love is
miraculous.*) 也可說成：Love creates
miracles.（愛能創造奇蹟。）Love can do
anything.（愛無所不能。）

UNIT **9**

Carpe Diem

及時行樂；把握時機

Seize the day.

把握今天。

Seize your destiny.

掌握命運。

Seize your passion.

擁抱熱情。

BOOK 4 · PART 1

** ————————————

carpe diem〔͵kɑrpe ′diəm〕及時行樂；
　把握時機（= *seize the day*）

seize〔siz〕*v.* 抓住；掌握；把握

the day 今天；當時

destiny〔′dɛstənɪ〕*n.* 命運

passion〔′pæʃən〕*n.* 熱情；愛好

Embrace life fully.

全心擁抱生活。

Embrace the now.

擁抱此時此刻。

Embrace the unknown.

擁抱未知事物。

** ——————————

embrace〔ɪm'bres〕*v.* 擁抱;欣然
　接受;利用
fully〔'fʊlɪ〕*adv.* 充分地
the now 現在（ = *the present* ）
unknown〔ʌn'non〕*adj.* 未知的
the unknown 未知的人或物;未知的世界

Live with abandon.

隨心所欲地活。

Live without fear.

毫無恐懼地活。

Live without regrets.

無遺憾地生活。

**

---

abandon〔ə'bændən〕*n.*（自由）奔放；
隨心所欲　*v.* 抛棄

fear〔fɪr〕*n.* 害怕；恐懼；畏懼

regret〔rɪ'grɛt〕*n. v.* 後悔；遺憾

【**Unit 9 背景說明**】

Seize the day. 要抓住今天；要把握時機。(= *Grab the chance.* = *Take the opportunity.*) 也可説成：Make the most of an opportunity. (要善加利用機會。) Strike while the iron is hot. (【諺】打鐵趁熱。)

Seize your destiny. 要掌握你的命運。(= *Pursue your destiny.*) 也可説成：Pursue your future. (要追求你的未來。)

Seize your passion. (要掌握你的熱情；要追求你的愛好。) 也可説成：Go after what you want. (要追求你想要的。) Pursue your vocation. (要發展你的事業。)

Embrace life fully. (要充分地擁抱生活。) 也可説成：Appreciate life. (要重視生活。) Appreciate the life you have. (要重視你所擁有的生活。)

Embrace the now. (要擁抱現在。) 也可説成：Live in the present. (要活在當下。) Focus on the present. (要專注於現在。) 不可説成：*Embrace now.* (誤)

Embrace the unknown. （要擁抱未知的事物。）

也可説成：Don't fear the unknown. （不要害怕未知的事物。） Welcome new adventures.

（要歡迎新的冒險經驗。）

Live with abandon. （要隨心所欲地生活。）也可説成：Be unrestrained. （要無拘無束。） Live without restraint. （要無拘無束地生活。）（= *Live without inhibition.*） Don't fear risk. （不要害怕危險。） Be reckless. （要不顧一切。）（= *Live recklessly.*）

Live without fear. （要毫無恐懼地生活。）也可説成：Be fearless. （要無所畏懼。）

Live without regrets. （要毫無遺憾地生活。）也可説成：Don't hesitiate to do something you want to do. （想做什麼就要毫不猶豫地去做。）

Don't regret anything you do. （不要後悔你做的任何事。）

PART 1 總整理

Unit 1

Choosing matters most.
抉擇最為重要。
Choice before effort.
選擇大於努力。
Selection outweighs labor.
取捨勝於實幹。

Choose your tribe.
選擇你的社交圈。
Choose compatible
   companions.
選合得來的同伴。
Choose top-notch circles.
選擇高端人脈圈。

Choose mentors well.
善於選擇師父。
Choose your journey.
選擇你的旅途。
Choose your destiny.
選擇你的命運。

Unit 2

Health is wealth. 健康是財富。
Health is strength.
健康是力量。
Health is happiness.
健康是幸福。

Health brings vitality.
健康帶來活力。
Health brings productivity.
健康有生產力。
Health brings prosperity.
健康帶來興盛。

Good health matters.
健康非常重要。
Physical health matters.
身體健康重要。
Mental health first.
心理健康第一。

Unit 3

Kindness is powerful.
善良很有力量。
Kindness is radiant.
善良光芒四射。
Kindness is rewarding.
善良會有回報。

Kindness breeds
   happiness. 善良產生快樂。
Kindness bridges divides.
善良消除分歧。
Kindness breaks barriers.
善意打破障礙。

Show kindness daily.
每天展現善意。
Show kindness freely.
隨時表現善意。
Practice kindness sincerely.
真誠實踐善良。

Unit 4

Choose optimism daily.
天天選擇樂觀。
Choose joy daily.
天天選擇快樂。
Positive vibes prevail.
正能量會勝利。

Smile through storms.
笑對風雨。
Smile through challenges.
笑對挑戰。
Embrace the sun. 擁抱太陽。

See light ahead. 看見前方光明。
See rainbows after.
看見雨後彩虹。
Hope illuminates shadows.
希望照亮黑暗。

Unit 5

Wealth is power. 財富是力量。
Cash is king. 現金是王道。
Money is freedom.
有錢就自由。

Money is essential.
錢是必要的。
Money is influential.
錢有影響力。
Money talks loudly.
金錢是萬能。

Money tests friendships.
金錢考驗友誼。
Money tests relationships.
金錢考驗關係。
Money undermines trust.
金錢破壞信任。

Unit 6

Time is money.
【諺】時間就是金錢。
Time is precious.
時間是珍貴的。
Time is priceless.
時間是無價的。

Time flies by. 時光飛逝。
Time is fleeting.
光陰似箭。
Time is unstoppable.
時間不停。

Time tells all.
時間說明一切。
Time tests all.
時間考驗一切。
Time heals all.
時間治療一切。

Unit 7

Knowledge is power.
【諺】知識就是力量。
Knowledge is liberty.
知識就是自由。
Knowledge is opportunity.
知識就是機會。

Knowledge is invaluable.
知識是無價的。
Knowledge is
  indispensable.
知識不可或缺。
Knowledge is key.
知識非常重要。

Knowledge opens doors.
知識打開大門。
Knowledge breeds
  confidence.
知識產生自信。
Knowledge shapes destiny.
知識塑造命運。

Unit 8

Love is blind.
【諺】愛是盲目的。
Love is boundless.
愛沒有界限。
Love is limitless.
愛是無限的。

Love conquers all.
愛能征服一切。
Love conquers fear.
愛能征服恐懼。
Love endures hardships.
愛能忍受苦難。

Love embraces differences.
愛能擁抱差異。
Love embraces flaws.
愛能擁抱缺點。
Love is magical.
愛是非常神奇。

Unit 9

Seize the day.　把握今天。
Seize your destiny.　掌握命運。
Seize your passion.
擁抱熱情。

Embrace life fully.
全心擁抱生活。
Embrace the now.
擁抱此時此刻。
Embrace the unknown.
擁抱未知事物。

Live with abandon.
隨心所欲地活。
Live without fear.
毫無恐懼地活。
Live without regrets.
無遺憾地活。

BOOK 4 \ PART 2

You Deserve a Great Life
你值得擁有很棒的生活

PART 2・Unit 1~9
英文錄音QR碼

UNIT ❶

Know Your Value
要知道自己的價值

You are worthy.
你有價值。

You are mighty.
你很強大。

You are outstanding.
你很傑出。

** ————————

value〔'væljʊ〕*n.* 價值
worthy〔'wɜðɪ〕*adj.* 值得的；值得尊敬的；
　值得欽佩的；值得支持的
mighty〔'maɪtɪ〕*adj.* 強大的；強有力的；
　偉大的
outstanding〔'aʊt'stændɪŋ〕*adj.* 傑出的

You are incredible.
你太棒了。

You are unbelievable.
超乎想像。

You are remarkable.
你不簡單。

** ———————————————

incredible〔ɪnˈkrɛdəbḷ〕*adj.* 令人難以
置信的；極好的

unbelievable〔ˌʌnbɪˈlivəbḷ〕*adj.* 令人
難以置信的；非常驚人的

remarkable〔rɪˈmɑrkəbḷ〕*adj.* 值得注
意的；出色的；非凡的；卓越的

BOOK 4・PART 2

Impossible is nothing.

沒有不可能。

Achieve the impossible.

達成不可能。

Dream big dreams.

要敢做大夢。

**

impossible〔ɪm'pɑsəbḷ〕*adj.* 不可能的

nothing〔'nʌθɪŋ〕*pron.* 無事;無物;
　無價值的事物

achieve〔ə'tʃiv〕*v.* 達成

the impossible 不可能的事
　(= *impossible things*)

dream〔drim〕*v.* 做 (夢)　　*n.* 夢;夢想

【Unit 1 背景説明】

You are worthy. 你很有價值。(= *You are valuable. = You are precious.*) 也可説成：You are commendable. (你值得稱讚。)

You are mighty. 你很強大。(= *You are powerful. = You are strong.*) 也可説成：You are great. (你很偉大。) You are capable. (你很有能力。)

You are outstanding. 你很傑出。(= *You are remarkable. = You are exceptional. = You are amazing.*)

You are incredible. 你令人無法置信，引申爲「你太棒了。」(= *You are amazing. = You are fantastic. = You are remarkable. = You are extraordinary.*)

You are unbelievable. 你令人無法置信。(= *You are incredible. = You are exceptional. = You are amazing.*)

You are remarkable. 你很出色。(= *You are outstanding.* = *You are amazing.*)

Impossible is nothing. 不可能根本不算什麼，也就是「你可以輕易做到。」(= *You can do it easily.*) 也可說成：Anything is possible. (任何事都有可能。)

Achieve the impossible. 要達成不可能的事。(= *Do what seems impossible.*) 也可說成：Achieve great things. (要達成偉大的事。) Do great things. (要做大事。)

Dream big dreams. 要有遠大的夢想。(= *Dream big.*) 也可說成：Be ambitious. (要有志氣。) Have high standards. (要有很高的標準。) Set a high bar. (要設定崇高的目標。)

(UNIT ❷

Never Stop Changing
絕不停止改變

Change is good.
改變是好事。

Change is progress.
改變是進步。

Never fear change.
絕不怕改變。

** ————————————

never〔ˈnɛvɚ〕*adv.* 絕不
stop + V-ing 停止⋯
change〔tʃendʒ〕*n. v.* 改變
progress〔ˈprɑgrɛs〕*n.* 進步
fear〔fɪr〕*v.* 害怕

BOOK 4・PART 2

Dare to begin.

勇於開始。

Dare to try.

勇於嘗試。

Find your courage.

要有勇氣。

** ————————————

dare〔dɛr〕*v.* 敢

begin〔bɪˈgɪn〕*v.* 開始

try〔traɪ〕*v.* 嘗試

courage〔ˈkɝɪdʒ〕*n.* 勇氣

Try, try, try!

一試再試！

Just keep trying.

持續努力。

Persevere and persist.

不屈不撓。

** ———————————

try〔traɪ〕*v.* 嘗試；努力

just〔dʒʌst〕*adv.* 只要；就

keep + V-ing 持續⋯

keep trying 不斷嘗試；持續努力

persevere〔͵pɝsə'vɪr〕*v.* 堅忍；堅持；

　不屈不撓

persist〔pə'sɪst〕*v.* 堅持

BOOK 4・PART 2

【Unit 2 背景説明】

Change is good.（改變很好。）也可説成：
Change is a positive thing.（改變是好事。）
It's beneficial to change.（改變有好處。）
New things are beneficial.（新的事物有好處。）

Change is progress. 改變是進步。（= *Change is advancement.*）也可説成：Change is a way to move forward.（改變是進步的方式。）

Never fear change. 絕不要害怕改變。（= *Don't be afraid of change.*）也可説成：Don't be afraid of new things.（不要害怕新事物。）Don't be afraid of new ideas.（不要害怕新的想法。）

Dare to begin.（要敢開始。）也可説成：Have the courage to start.（要有勇氣開始。）Have the courage to take the first step.（要有勇氣踏出第一步。）

Dare to try.（要敢嘗試。）也可説成：Have the courage to try.（要有勇氣嘗試。）Have the courage to do it.（要有勇氣去做。）

Find your courage. (要找到你的勇氣。) 也可説成：Have courage. (要有勇氣。) Be brave. (要勇敢。)

Try, try, try! 要一試再試！(= *Keep trying!*) 也可説成：Don't give up! (不要放棄！) 源自諺語：If at first you don't succeed, try, try, try again. (再接再勵，終會成功。)

Just keep trying. 要持續努力。(= *Keep making efforts.*) 也可説成：Don't give up. (不要放棄。)

Persevere and persist. (不屈不撓，堅持到底。) 也可説成：Continue. (要繼續下去。) Endure. (要忍耐。) Insist. (要堅持。) Keep going. (要繼續前進。)

UNIT ❸

Enjoy Life　享受生活

Take life easy.

悠然自得。

Keep it simple.

保持簡單。

Don't overthink it.

勿想太多。

＊＊ ────────────

take〔tek〕*v.* 認為；對待；處理
easy〔'izɪ〕*adv.* 輕鬆地；安逸地
take life easy 輕鬆看待生活；放輕鬆
keep〔kip〕*v.* 使保持
simple〔'sɪmpḷ〕*adj.* 簡單的
overthink〔,ovɚ'θɪŋk〕*v.* 思考過度；
　想得太多

Life is good.

人生美好。

Life is awesome.

人生太棒。

Love your life.

熱愛生活。

**

life〔 laɪf 〕*n.* 人生；生活；生命
awesome〔'ɔsəm 〕*adj.* 很棒的
love〔 lʌv 〕*v.* 愛

Sing out loud.

放聲歌唱。

Smell the roses.

享受生活。

Laugh to exhaustion.

笑至疲憊。

**

sing〔sɪŋ〕*v.* 唱歌

out loud 出聲地

smell〔smɛl〕*v.* 聞

rose〔roz〕*n.* 玫瑰

laugh〔læf〕*v.* 笑

exhaustion〔ɪgˋzɔstʃən〕*n.* 筋疲力盡

【Unit 3 背景説明】

Take life easy. 輕鬆看待生活，也就是「要放輕鬆。」
(= *Take it easy.* = *Relax.*) 也可説成：Don't
stress. (不要緊張。)

Keep it simple. (要保持簡單。) 也可説成：Don't
complicate things. (不要把事情複雜化。)

Don't overthink it. 不要想太多。(= *Don't think
about it too much.* = *Don't think too much.*)

Life is good. (人生很美好。) 也可説成：Life is
great. (人生很棒。)

Life is awesome. 人生很棒。(= *Life is wonderful.*
= *Life is excellent.*)

Love your life. (要愛你的生活。) 也可説成：Enjoy
your life. (要享受你的生活。) Be happy with
your life. (要對你的生活感到滿意。)

Sing out loud. (放聲歌唱。) 也可説成：Sing.
(唱歌。) Sing a song. (唱一首歌。)

【比較】**Sing out loud**. (唱出聲音來。)

(= *Sing aloud*.)

Sing loudly. (大聲唱。)

Smell the roses. (聞聞玫瑰花香;享受生活。)源
自 Stop and smell the roses. (停下來,享受生
活。)這句話出自 1960 年代一位高爾夫球選手
Walter Hagen 的自傳:"Don't hurry. Don't
worry. And be sure to smell the flowers
along the way." (不要急。不要擔心。一定要聞
聞沿途的花香。)也可說成:Live for the day.
(要為今天而活。) Enjoy the moment. (要享受
此刻。)

Laugh to exhaustion. (要笑到筋疲力盡為止。)
也可說成:Laugh until you're tired. (要笑到
你累了為止。) Laugh until you can't laugh
anymore. (要笑到不能笑為止。)

UNIT ④

Keep Your Eye on the Prize
盯住目標，心無旁騖

You're very capable.
你很有能力。

You're very strong.
你非常堅強。

You can endure.
你能夠忍受。

** ———————

keep *one's* **eye on** 盯住
prize〔praɪz〕*n.* 獎品
capable〔ˈkepəbḷ〕*adj.* 有能力的
strong〔strɔŋ〕*adj.* 強壯的；堅強的
endure〔ɪnˈdjʊr〕*v.* 忍耐；忍受

Keep your focus.

保持專注。

Keep your determination.

保持決心。

Keep it burning.

持續熱情。

** ───────────────

keep〔kip〕*v.* 保持；使持續

focus〔'fokəs〕*n.* 焦點；關注；注意；
　集中目標

determination〔dɪ,tɜmə'neʃən〕*n.* 決心

burn〔bɜn〕*v.* 燃燒

Stay on track.

保持目標。

Stay the course.

堅持到底。

Always stay disciplined.

保持自律。

**

stay〔ste〕v. 停留；保持

track〔træk〕n. 軌道

stay on track 保持專注

course〔kors〕n. 路線；方向；

（競賽的）跑道

stay the course 堅持到底

discipline〔'dɪsəplɪn〕n. 紀律；訓練

v. 訓練

disciplined〔'dɪsəplɪnd〕adj. 受過訓練的；

遵守紀律的

【Unit 4 背景説明】

You're very capable. (你很有能力。) 也可説成：
You're very competent. (你很能幹。) You're
very skilled. (你非常熟練。)

You're very strong. 你非常堅強。(= *You're very*
tough.) 也可説成：You're very powerful. (你
非常有力量。)

You can endure. 你能夠忍受。(= *You can bear*
it.) 也可説成：You can persevere. (你不屈不
撓。) You'll survive. (你會存活下去。) You
can survive it. (你能安然度過。) You can do
it. (你能做到。)

Keep your focus. 保持你的專注。(= *Maintain*
your focus. = *Keep your eye on the prize.*)
也可説成：Keep your mind on what you're
doing. (專注於你正在做的事。) Don't lose
sight of your goal. (不要沒看見你的目標。)

Keep your determination.（保持你的決心。）也
可說成：Be determined.（要堅決。）（= *Be
resolute.*）Don't give up.（不要放棄。）

Keep it burning.（要讓它持續燃燒。）也可說成：
Keep it going.（要讓它持續下去。）Keep your
determination alive.（要使你的決心保持不衰。）

Stay on track. 待在軌道上，引申為「專心點；別
分心；保持專注。」（= *Keep your focus.*）也可說
成：Stay on target.（瞄準目標。）。；

Stay the course. 待在跑道上，引申為「堅持到底。」
（= *See it through.* = *Persist.* = *Persevere.*）也可
說成：Keep trying.（持續努力。）

Always stay disciplined. 一定要保持紀律。
（= *Always be disciplined.*）也可說成：Always
be self-controlled.（一定要自制。）Always
be well-organized.（一定要很有條理。）

UNIT **5**

Focus on the Good
專注於生活中的美好

No bad days.
無糟糕日子。

No sad days.
無悲傷日子。

No more trouble.
不再有煩惱。

**

focus on 專注於
good〔gʊd〕*n.* 好事
bad〔bæd〕*adj.* 壞的；不愉快的；倒楣的
sad〔sæd〕*adj.* 悲傷的
no more 不再有
trouble〔ˋtrʌbḷ〕*n.* 麻煩；煩惱

Ignore the hate.
莫再仇恨。

Ignore the criticism.
忽視批評。

Embrace the love.
擁抱愛意。

** ———————————

ignore〔ɪgˋnor〕v. 忽視

hate〔het〕n. 憎恨

criticism〔ˋkrɪtə͵sɪzəm〕n. 批評

embrace〔ɪmˋbres〕v. 擁抱；欣然接受

love〔lʌv〕n. 愛

Be the light.

成為光芒。

Sparkle and shine.

閃耀生輝。

Just keep smiling.

保持微笑。

**

light〔laɪt〕*n.* 光線；光輝；光芒

sparkle〔'spɑrkḷ〕*v.* 閃耀；發亮

shine〔ʃaɪn〕*v.* 發光；發亮

just〔dʒʌst〕*adv.* 只；就

keep* + *V-ing 持續…

smile〔smaɪl〕*v.* 微笑；笑

【Unit 5 背景説明】

No bad days. 沒有不好的日子。(= *There are no bad days*.) 也可説成：No difficult days. (沒有辛苦的日子。) (= *No hard days*.) No awful days. (沒有糟糕的日子。) No stressful days. (沒有充滿壓力的日子。)

No sad days. (沒有悲傷的日子。) 也可説成：
No miserable days. (沒有悲慘的日子。)
No disappointing days. (沒有令人失望的日子。)
No depressing days. (沒有令人沮喪的日子。)
No unhappy days. (沒有不快樂的日子。)

No more trouble. 不會再有煩惱。(= *There will be no more trouble*.) 也可説成：No more problems. (不會再有問題。)

Ignore the hate.　Ignore the criticism.
Embrace the love. 這三句話的 the 可以省略。

Ignore the hate. (忽視仇恨。) 也可説成：Pay no attention to hate. (不要在意仇恨。) Pay no attention to hateful ideas. (不要有仇恨的想法。)

Pay no attention to hateful people. (不要在意充滿恨意的人。)

Ignore the criticism. (忽視批評。) 也可說成：
Pay no attention to the criticism. (不要在意批評。) Pay no attention to negative comments. (不要在意負面的評論。)

Embrace the love. (擁抱愛意。) 句中的 the love 是指 love (愛)、praise (稱讚)，或 good wishes from others (別人的祝福)。也可說成：Accept the love. (接受愛。) Accept the praise. (接受讚美。)

Be the light. (要成為光芒。) 也可說成：Be optimistic. (要樂觀。) Be the one who cheers up others. (要成為能激勵別人的人。)

Sparkle and shine. (要發光、發亮。) 也可說成：Excel. (要勝過別人。) Be enthusiastic. (要有熱忱。) Be full of energy. (要充滿活力。)

Just keep smiling. (要保持微笑。) 也可說成：Don't stop smiling. (不要停止微笑。)

UNIT **6**

Be a Good Person
做個好人

Do good deeds.
做好事。

Always be good.
做好人。

Always add value.
會增值。

** ——————————

good〔gud〕*adj.* 好的；善良的

deed〔did〕*n.* 行為

good deed 好事

always〔'ɔlwez〕*adv.* 總是；一直

add〔æd〕*v.* 增加

value〔'væljʊ〕*n.* 價值

Do what's right.

做對的事。

Don't expect rewards.

不求回報。

Act without expectation.

施恩莫念。

**

---

right〔raɪt〕*adj.* 對的;正確的

expect〔ɪk'spɛkt〕*v.* 期待

reward〔rɪ'wɔrd〕*n.* 報酬;獎賞

act〔ækt〕*v.* 採取行動

expectation〔͵ɛkspɛk'teʃən〕*n.* 期待

Give to receive.

有捨有得。

Give without remembering.

付出勿念。

Receive without forgetting.

收穫勿忘。

**

give〔gɪv〕*v.* 給與；付出
receive〔rɪ'siv〕*v.* 收到；得到
remember〔rɪ'mɛmbɚ〕*v.* 記得
forget〔fɚ'gɛt〕*v.* 忘記

【Unit 6 背景説明】

Do good deeds. 要做好事。(= *Do good things*.)

也可説成：Help others. (要幫助別人。)

Be kind. (要仁慈。)

Always be good. (要永遠善良。) 也可説成：

Be decent. (要高尚。) Don't be bad.

(不要當壞人。)

Always add value. (會不斷增加價值。) 指的是你

做的好事會增值。也可説成：Always be useful.

(要一直對人有所幫助。) Always make things

better. (要總是使情況變得更好。) Always leave

things better than you found them. (要讓事情

比在你發現它們時更好。) Make the world a

better place. (要讓世界變得更好。)

Do what's right. (要做對的事。) 也可説成：

Do the right thing. (要做正確的事。)

Don't expect rewards. 不要期待回報。

(= *Don't expect to be repaid*.)

Act without expectation. 採取行動，不要有任何期待，也就是老子所說的「要無欲而爲。」也可說成：Do things for others without expecting anything in return. (爲別人做事不要期待任何回報。)

Give to receive. (付出才會獲得。) 也可說成：If you give to others, you will also benefit. (如果你對別人付出，你也會獲益。)

Give without remembering. (付出不要記得。) 也可說成：Forget about what you do for others. (要忘記你爲別人做的事。) Forget about what you give to others. (要忘記你給別人的東西。)

Receive without forgetting. (獲得不要忘記。) 也可說成：Never forget what others do for you. (絕不要忘記別人爲你做的事。) Never forget what others give to you. (絕不要忘記別人給你的東西。)

UNIT **7**

Get Involved 要參與

Show up often.
時常出現。

Make yourself known.
使己出名。

Expand your network.
拓展人脈。

** ———————————

involved〔ɪnˋvɑlvd〕*adj.* 參與的
show up 出現
known〔non〕*adj.* 為人所知的
expand〔ɪkˋspænd〕*v.* 拓展
network〔ˋnɛt͵wɝk〕*n.* 網路；關係網；
　聯絡網

Do something impressive.
要做創舉。

Leave a contribution.
留下貢獻。

Leave your mark.
留名青史。

** ───────────────

impressive〔ɪmˈprɛsɪv〕*adj.* 令人印象
深刻的；令人欽佩的
leave〔liv〕*v.* 留下
contribution〔͵kɑntrəˈbjuʃən〕*n.* 貢獻
mark〔mɑrk〕*n.* 痕跡；記號
leave your mark 留下你的印記；
留下深遠的影響；名垂青史

BOOK 4・PART 2

Leave an impression.

魅力無限。

Be sought after.

受人追捧。

Be remembered forever.

永垂不朽。

** ————————————————

leave〔liv〕*v.* 留下

impression〔ɪm'prɛʃən〕*n.* 印象

seek〔sik〕*v.* 尋求【三態變化：seek-
sought-sought】

seek after 想要獲得

sought after （因品質高或稀有而）
熱門的；廣受歡迎的

remember〔rɪ'mɛmbɚ〕*v.* 記得

forever〔fɚ'ɛvɚ〕*adv.* 永遠

【Unit 7 背景說明】

Show up often. (要常常出現。) 也可說成：Be available. (要有空參加聚會。) Always be ready to help. (要總是願意幫忙。) Attend lots of events. (要參加很多活動。)

Make yourself known. 主要的意思是「做自我介紹。」在此是指「要讓自己很有名。」(= *Make yourself well-known*.) 也可說成：Draw attention to yourself. (要讓人注意到你。) Stand out. (要很突出。)

Expand your network. (要拓展你的人際網路； 要拓展人脈。) 也可說成：Get to know more people. (要能認識更多的人。) Expand your contacts. (要拓展你的人脈。)

Do something impressive. (要做令人印象深刻的 事。) 也可說成：Do something remarkable. (要做了不起的事。)(= *Do remarkable things*.)

Leave a contribution. (要留下貢獻。) 也可說 成：Make a contribution. (要有貢獻。)

Have an impact. (要產生影響。) (= *Have an influence.*) Play an important role. (要扮演重要的角色。)

Leave your mark*.* 要留下你的印記，引申為「要留下深遠的影響。」也可說成：Be successful. (要很成功。) Make a difference. (要產生影響。) Do something memorable. (要做令人難忘的事。)

Leave an impression*.* (要讓人留下印象。) 也可說成：Leave a good impression on others. (要讓人留下好印象。) Be memorable. (要令人難忘。)

Be sought after*.* 要受人歡迎。(= *Be popular.*) 也可說成：Be wanted. (要讓大家搶著要。) Be someone others want. (要做一個大家都想要的人。)

Be remembered forever*.* (要讓人永遠記得。) 也可說成：Be unforgettable. (要令人難忘。) (= *Be memorable.*)

UNIT **8**

Determine Your Own Future
決定你自己的未來

Live with purpose.
活著有目標。

Live with intention.
活著有目的。

Follow your heart.
跟著良心走。

** ───────

determine〔dɪˋtɜmɪn〕*v.* 決定
future〔ˋfjutʃə〕*n.* 未來
purpose〔ˋpɜpəs〕*n.* 目的；意圖
intention〔ɪnˋtɛnʃən〕*n.* 意圖；打算
　（= *purpose*）
follow〔ˋfɑlo〕*v.* 跟隨；聽從
heart〔hɑrt〕*n.* 心

Trust the process.

信任過程。

Trust your journey.

相信旅程。

Enjoy the ride.

享受旅途。

** ———————————

trust〔trʌst〕v. 信任；相信

process〔'prɑsɛs〕n. 過程

journey〔'dʒɝnɪ〕n. 旅行；旅程

enjoy〔ɪn'dʒɔɪ〕v. 享受

ride〔raɪd〕n. 騎乘；乘車旅行；
旅行；行程

Create your life.

開創你的生活。

Create your destiny.

創造你的命運。

Achieve your dreams.

實現你的夢想。

＊＊ _____

create〔krɪ'et〕*v.* 創造

destiny〔'dɛstənɪ〕*n.* 命運

achieve〔ə'tʃiv〕*v.* 達成

dream〔drim〕*n.* 夢；夢想

【Unit 8 背景説明】

Live with purpose. 活著要有目的；活著要有目標。
(= *Live with intention*.) 也可説成：Have a
reason for living. (要有活著的理由。) Make
your life meaningful. (要讓你的人生有意義。)

Follow your heart. (跟著你內心的感覺走。) 也可
説成：Do what feels right to you. (做你覺得
對的事。) Do what you want to do. (做你想
做的事。)

Trust the process. 要信任過程。(= *Believe in the
process*.) 也可説成：Believe that the process
will work. (要相信這個過程會有用。)

Trust your journey. (要信任你的旅行。) 也可説
成：Believe that your journey will be
successful. (要相信你的旅行會成功。) 在此的
journey (旅行) 是指 your life (你的人生)、
your career (你的事業)，或任何你正在做的事。

Enjoy the ride. (享受這段旅程。) 也可說成：
Enjoy the process. (享受這個過程。)
Enjoy the journey. (享受這次旅行。)
Enjoy the moment. (享受這一刻。)

Create your life. (創造你的人生。) 也可說成：
Make the life you want. (創造你想要的生活。)
Decide your own life. (決定你自己的人生。)

Create your destiny. (創造你的命運。) 也可
說成：Decide your fate. (決定你的命運。)
Decide your future. (決定你的未來。)

Achieve your dreams. (達成你的夢想。) 也可
說成：Realize your goals. (實現你的目標。)
Get what you want in life. (要得到你人生中
想要的東西。)

UNIT **9**

Go After What You Want
追求你想要的

Follow your dreams.
追求夢想。

Pursue your passion.
追求熱情。

Embrace your ambition.
擁抱雄心。

** ————————————

go after 追求
follow (ˈfalo) *v.* 跟隨；追求
  (= *chase* = *go after*)
dream (drim) *n.* 夢；夢想
pursue (pɚˈsu) *v.* 追求；實行；從事
passion (ˈpæʃən) *n.* 熱情；愛好
embrace (ɪmˈbres) *v.* 擁抱；欣然接受
ambition (æmˈbɪʃən) *n.* 雄心；抱負；志向

Strive for greatness.

追求偉大。

Make an effort.

付出努力。

Keep making progress.

持續進步。

**

strive〔straɪv〕*v.* 努力
greatness〔'gretnɪs〕*n.* 偉大；崇高
effort〔'ɛfət〕*n.* 努力
make an effort 努力
keep + V-ing 持續…
progress〔'prɑgrɛs〕*n.* 進步
make progress 進步

BOOK 4・PART 2

Visualize your success.
想像成功。

Realize your dreams.
實現夢想。

Live your dreams.
活出夢想。

** ────────────

visualize〔ˈvɪʒʊəlˌaɪz〕v. 使形象化；
　使能被看見；使顯現；想像
success〔səkˈsɛs〕n. 成功
realize〔ˈriəˌlaɪz〕v. 了解；實現
dream〔drim〕n. 夢；夢想
live〔lɪv〕v.（在生活中）表現；實踐

【Unit 9 背景説明】

Follow your dreams. 追求你的夢想。(= *Pursue your dreams.* = *Go after your dream.*)

Pursue your passion. 追求你的熱情，引申為「做你喜歡做的事。」也可說成：Pursue what you want. (追求你想要的。)

Embrace your ambition. 擁抱你的志向，引申為「致力於達成你的抱負，實現你的理想。」(= *Commit yourself to achieving your ambition.*)

Strive for greatness. 要為偉大而努力；要追求卓越。(= *Try to be the best.*)

Make an effort. 要努力。(= *Try.*)

Keep making progress. 要持續進步。(= *Continue advancing.* = *Continue moving forward.*)

Visualize your success. 想像你的成功。(= *See yourself being successful.*) 也可說成：Have a clear understanding of what success means to you. (要清楚了解成功對你的意義。)

Realize your dreams. 實現你的夢想。(= *Make your dreams a reality.*)

Live your dreams. (活出你的夢想。) 也可說成：Live according to your dreams. (要按照你的夢想來過生活。)

PART 2 總整理

PART 2 · Unit 1~9
中英文錄音QR碼

Unit 1

You are worthy. 你有價值。
You are mighty. 你很強大。
You are outstanding.
你很傑出。

You are incredible.
你太棒了。
You are unbelievable.
超乎想像。
You are remarkable.
你不簡單。

Impossible is nothing.
沒有不可能。
Achieve the impossible.
達成不可能。
Dream big dreams.
要敢做大夢。

Unit 2

Change is good.
改變是好事。
Change is progress.
改變是進步。
Never fear change.
絕不怕改變。

Dare to begin. 勇於開始。
Dare to try. 勇於嘗試。
Find your courage.
要有勇氣。

Try, try, try! 一試再試！
Just keep trying.
持續努力。
Persevere and persist.
不屈不撓。

Unit 3

Take life easy. 悠然自得。
Keep it simple.
保持簡單。
Don't overthink it.
勿想太多。

Life is good. 人生美好。
Life is awesome.
人生太棒。
Love your life. 熱愛生活。

Sing out loud. 放聲歌唱。
Smell the roses. 享受生活。
Laugh to exhaustion.
笑至疲憊。

Unit 4

You're very capable.
你很有能力。
You're very strong.
你非常堅強。
You can endure.
你能夠忍受。

Keep your focus.
保持專注。
Keep your determination.
保持決心。
Keep it burning.
持續熱情。

Stay on track.
保持目標。
Stay the course.
堅持到底。
Always stay disciplined.
保持自律。

Unit 5

No bad days.
無糟糕日子。
No sad days.
無悲傷日子。
No more trouble.
不再有煩惱。

Ignore the hate.
莫再仇恨。
Ignore the criticism.
忽視批評。
Embrace the love.
擁抱愛意。

Be the light. 成為光芒。
Sparkle and shine.
閃耀生輝。
Just keep smiling.
保持微笑。

Unit 6

Do good deeds. 做好事。
Always be good. 做好人。
Always add value.
會增值。

Do what's right. 做對的事。
Don't expect rewards.
不求回報。
Act without expectation.
施恩莫念。

Give to receive. 有捨有得。
Give without
　remembering. 付出勿念。
Receive without forgetting.
收穫勿忘。

BOOK 4・PART 2

Unit 7

Show up often.
時常出現。
Make yourself known.
使己出名。
Expand your network.
拓展人脈。

Do something impressive.
要做創舉。
Leave a contribution.
留下貢獻。
Leave your mark.
留名青史。

Leave an impression.
魅力無限。
Be sought after.
受人追捧。
Be remembered forever.
永垂不朽。

Unit 8

Live with purpose.
活著有目標。
Live with intention.
活著有目的。
Follow your heart.
跟著良心走。

Trust the process. 信任過程。
Trust your journey.
相信旅程。
Enjoy the ride. 享受旅途。

Create your life.
開創你的生活。
Create your destiny.
創造你的命運。
Achieve your dreams.
實現你的夢想。

Unit 9

Follow your dreams.
追求夢想。
Pursue your passion.
追求熱情。
Embrace your ambition.
擁抱雄心。

Strive for greatness.
追求偉大。
Make an effort. 付出努力。
Keep making progress.
持續進步。

Visualize your success.
想像成功。
Realize your dreams.
實現夢想。
Live your dreams. 活出夢想。

BOOK 4 \ PART 3

How to Succeed in Society
如何在社會上成功

PART 3 · Unit 1~9
英文錄音QR碼

UNIT **1**

Be a Go-Getter
要積極進取

Seek new adventures.
尋求新冒險。

Embrace new opportunities.
擁抱新機會。

Welcome new challenges.
歡迎新挑戰。

**

go-getter〔'go͵gɛtɚ〕*n.* 有衝勁和進取心的人
seek〔sik〕*v.* 尋求
adventure〔əd'vɛntʃɚ〕*n.* 冒險;冒險經歷
embrace〔ɪm'bres〕*v.* 擁抱;欣然接受
opportunity〔͵ɑpɚ'tjunətɪ〕*n.* 機會
welcome〔'wɛlkəm〕*v.* 歡迎
challenge〔'tʃælɪndʒ〕*n.* 挑戰

Take risks daily.

每天勇於冒險。

Take risks fearlessly.

無所畏懼冒險。

Always challenge yourself.

始終挑戰自己。

**———————

risk〔rɪsk〕*n.* 風險;危險

take a risk 冒險

daily〔'delɪ〕*adv.* 每天 (= *every day*)

fearlessly〔'fɪrlɪslɪ〕*adv.* 不怕地;無畏地;
　勇敢地

always〔'ɔlwez〕*adv.* 總是;一直

challenge〔'tʃælɪndʒ〕*v.* 挑戰

Strive for more.

追求更多。

Learn and grow.

學習成長。

Push yourself further.

鞭策自己。

**————————————

strive〔straɪv〕*v.* 努力

strive for 為追求⋯而努力

grow〔gro〕*v.* 成長

push〔puʃ〕*v.* 推；催促；逼迫

push oneself 推自己一下；突破自我

further〔ˈfɝðɚ〕*adv.* 更進一步地

BOOK 4・PART 3

【Unit 1 背景説明】

Seek new adventures. (尋求新的冒險經歷。) 也可説成：Be adventurous. (要喜歡冒險。)

Embrace new opportunities. (欣然接受新的機會。) 也可説成：Welcome new opportunities. (歡迎新的機會。)

Welcome new challenges. (歡迎新的挑戰。) 也可説成：Don't fear new trials. (不要害怕新的考驗。)

Take risks daily. 要每天冒險。(= *Make taking chances part of your routine*.)

Take risks fearlessly. 要不怕冒險。(= *Don't be afraid to take a chance*.)

Always challenge yourself. (要一直挑戰自己。) 也可説成：Test yourself. (要考驗自己。) Keep trying to improve. (要一直努力改進。)

Strive for more. (要努力追求更多。) 也可説成：Try to get/learn/do/develop more. (要努力得到 / 學習 / 做 / 發展更多。)

Learn and grow. (要學習並成長。) 也可説成：Keep improving. (要持續進步。) (= *Keep advancing*. = *Keep progressing*. = *Keep moving forward*.)

Push yourself further. (要突破自我。) 也可説成：Push yourself. (要鞭策自己。) Try hard. (要努力。) Put your all into it. (要全力以赴。)

UNIT ❷

Don't Fear Love
不要害怕去愛

Love is pure.
愛是純潔的。

Love is kind.
愛是仁慈的。

Love is patient.
愛是有耐性。

** ———————————

fear〔fɪr〕*v.* 害怕

love〔lʌv〕*n. v.* 愛

pure〔pjʊr〕*adj.* 純粹的

kind〔kaɪnd〕*adj.* 仁慈的;親切的;好心的

patient〔'peʃənt〕*adj.* 有耐心的

Spread love always.

永遠散播愛。

Spread your warmth.

要散播溫暖。

Share your heart.

分享你的心。

**————————————

spread〔sprɛd〕*v.* 散播
always〔ˈɔlwez〕*adv.* 總是；一直
warmth〔wɔrmθ〕*n.* 溫暖
share〔ʃɛr〕*v.* 分享
heart〔hɑrt〕*n.* 心；感情；愛情；同情心

Love is unconditional.

愛是無條件的。

Love is infinite.

愛是無止盡的。

Love always wins.

有愛一定獲勝。

** ————————————

unconditional〔͵ʌnkən'dɪʃənḷ〕*adj.*
無條件的
infinite〔'ɪnfənɪt〕*adj.* 無限的
always〔'ɔlwez〕*adv.* 總是；一直
win〔wɪn〕*v.* 贏；獲勝

【**Unit 2 背景説明**】

Love is pure. 愛是純粹的。(= *Love is absolute*.) 也可説成：Love is unconditional. (愛是無條件的。) Love is divine. (愛是神聖的。) Love is wholesome. (愛是有益健康的。)

Love is kind. 愛是仁慈的。(= *Love is nice*.) 也可説成：Love is generous. (愛是慷慨的。) Love is compassionate. (愛是有同情心的。)

Love is patient. (愛是有耐心的。) 也可説成：Love endures. (愛能忍耐。)

Spread love always. (要總是散播愛。) 也可説成：Always show your love. (要總是展現你的愛。) Always share your love. (要總是分享你的愛。)

Spread your warmth. (要散播你的溫暖。) 也可説成：Be kind. (要仁慈。) Be loving. (要充滿愛。) Be compassionate. (要有同情心。) Show your love. (要展現你的愛。)

Share your heart. (要分享你的心意。) 句中的 your heart 是指 your feelings (你的感情) 或 your love (你的愛)。也可説成：Share your love. (要分享你的愛。) Share your feelings. (要分享你的感情。)

Love is unconditional. 愛是無條件的。(= *Love is unqualified.*) 也可說成：Love is absolute. (愛是純粹的。)

Love is infinite. 愛是無限的。(= *Love is limitless.*) 也可說成：Love is endless. (愛是無止盡的。)

Love always wins. (有愛一定獲勝。) 也可說成：Love cannot be defeated. (愛不會被打敗。) You will always succeed with love. (有愛一定會成功。)

UNIT ❸

Be a Team Player
要有團隊精神

United we stand.
團結則立。

Together we rise.
一起崛起。

Together we thrive.
一起成功。

** ———————————

team player 具有團隊精神的人

united〔juˋnaɪtɪd〕*adj.* 團結的

stand〔stænd〕*v.* 站立;繼續存在(= *survive*)

together〔təˋgɛðɚ〕*adv.* 一起

rise〔raɪz〕*v.* 上升;升高;變得重要(成功或有權力)

thrive〔θraɪv〕*v.* 繁榮;興盛;成功(= *succeed*)

Unity creates power.

團結創造力量。

Unity creates progress.

團結創造進步。

Teamwork breeds success.

團結就會成功。

**────────────

unity〔'junətɪ〕*n.* 團結
create〔krɪ'et〕*v.* 創造
power〔'pauə〕*n.* 力量
progress〔'prɑgrɛs〕*n.* 進步 〔prə'grɛs〕*v.*
teamwork〔'tim͵wɝk〕*n.* 團隊合作
breed〔brid〕*v.* 孕育;產生
success〔sək'sɛs〕*n.* 成功

We're better together.

我們一起更好。

We're stronger together.

我們一起更強。

Harmonious teamwork prevails.

團隊戰勝一切。

＊＊ ————————————

together〔tə'gɛðɚ〕 *adv.* 一起

strong〔strɔŋ〕 *adj.* 強壯的；堅強的

harmonious〔hɑr'monɪəs〕 *adj.* 和諧的

teamwork〔'tim,wɝk〕 *n.* 團隊合作

prevail〔prɪ'vel〕 *v.* 普遍；佔優勢；勝過；
　戰勝；優勝（= *succeed*）

【Unit 3 背景說明】

United we stand.（團結我們就會繼續存在。）源自諺語：United we stand, divided we fall.（團結則立，分散則倒。）也可說成：Together we cannot be defeated.（一起我們不會被打敗。）

Together we rise.（一起我們就會崛起。）也可說成：United we will progress.（團結我們就會進步。）

Together we thrive.（一起我們就會成功。）也可說成：If we work together, we will succeed.（如果我們合作，我們就會成功。）

Unity creates power.（團結創造力量。）也可說成：We are powerful when we are united.（當我們團結在一起，我們會很有力量。）Togetherness makes us stronger.（團結使我們更強大。）

Unity creates progress.（團結創造進步。）也可說成：When we are united, we will progress.（當我們團結在一起，我們就會進步。）Togetherness helps us advance.（團結幫助我們進步。）

Teamwork breeds success. (團結孕育成功。)
也可説成：If we work together, we will be
successful. (如果我們合作，我們就會成功。)
(= *Working together enables us to succeed.*)

We're better together. (我們一起會更好。) 也可
説成：We are more valuable together. (我們
一起會更有價值。) We are more effective
together. (我們一起會更有效力。)

We're stronger together. 我們一起會更強大。
(= *Together we can be more powerful.*) 也可
説成：We are more powerful when we work
together. (當我們一起合作，我們會更有力量。)

Harmonious teamwork prevails. (和諧的團隊
合作能佔優勢。) 也可説成：Good teamwork
always wins. (良好的團隊合作一定會獲勝。)
Good teamwork leads to success. (良好的
團隊合作能夠成功。)

UNIT 4

Be Agreeable
要討人喜歡

Arguing is useless.
爭論無用。

Arguing is meaningless.
爭論無義。

Winners don't argue.
勝者不爭。

** —————————

agreeable〔ə'griəbḷ〕*adj.* 令人愉快的

argue〔'ɑrgju〕*v.* 爭論

useless〔'juslɪs〕*adj.* 無用的

meaningless〔'minɪŋlɪs〕*adj.* 無意義的

winner〔'wɪnɚ〕*n.* 勝利者；優勝者；贏家

End the quarrel.

結束爭吵。

End the dispute.

解決爭端。

Be the peacemaker.

當和事佬。

** ——————————————

end 〔 ɛnd 〕 *v.* 結束

quarrel 〔'kwɔrəl 〕 *n. v.* 爭吵

dispute 〔 dɪ'spjut 〕 *n. v.* 爭論；爭執

peacemaker 〔'pis,mekɚ 〕 *n.* 調停者；

仲裁人；和事佬

Learn to forgive.

學習原諒。

Bury the hatchet.

停止爭吵。

Become friends again.

重修舊好。

**

forgive〔fə'gɪv〕v. 原諒
bury〔'bɛrɪ〕v. 埋葬
hatchet〔'hætʃɪt〕n. 小斧頭；戰斧
bury the hatchet 和解；言歸於好
again〔ə'gɛn〕adv. 再次

BOOK 4・PART 3

【Unit 4 背景説明】

Arguing is useless.（爭論是沒有用的。）也可説成：
Arguing is a waste of time.（爭論是在浪費時間。）

Arguing is meaningless. 爭論是沒有意義的。
(= *There is no point in arguing.*)

Winners don't argue.（贏家不會爭論。）也可説成：
If you want to win, don't argue.（如果你想贏，就不要爭論。）If you argue, you can't win.（如果你爭論，你就不會贏。）

End the quarrel. 結束爭吵。(= *Stop quarreling.*)

End the dispute. 結束爭論。(= *Stop arguing.* = *Stop fighting.*)

Be the peacemaker. 要當和事佬。(= *Be the one to make peace.* = *Be the one to end the argument.*)

Learn to forgive.（學習原諒。）也可説成：Forgive and forget.（【諺】既往不咎。）Pardon others.（要原諒別人。）Let bygones be bygones.（【諺】既往不咎。）

Bury the hatchet. 休戰；和解；言歸於好；化干戈為玉帛。【源自北美印地安人於休戰時將戰斧埋於土中之習俗】
也可説成：Make peace.（要和解。）

Become friends again.（要再度成為朋友。）也可説成：Repair your relationship.（要修補你們的關係。）

UNIT **5**

Treasure Your Friends
珍惜你的朋友

Friends are invaluable.
朋友無價。

Friends over wealth.
朋友勝財。

Cherish your friendships.
珍惜友誼。

** ———————————————

treasure〔ˈtrɛʒɚ〕*v.* 珍惜
invaluable〔ɪnˈvæljəbl̩〕*adj.* 無價的；珍貴的
over〔ˈovɚ〕*prep.* 在…之上；比…重要
wealth〔wɛlθ〕*n.* 財富
cherish〔ˈtʃɛrɪʃ〕*v.* 珍惜
friendship〔ˈfrɛndʃɪp〕*n.* 友誼

Remember gratitude always.

常記感恩。

Stay true always.

常保眞誠。

Little things count.

湧泉相報。

**————————————

remember〔rɪˋmɛmbɚ〕*v.* 記得

gratitude〔ˋgrætəˌtjud〕*n.* 感激

always〔ˋɔlwez〕*adv.* 總是;一直

stay〔ste〕*v.* 保持

true〔tru〕*adj.* 眞的;忠實的;忠誠的

little〔ˋlɪtḷ〕*adj.* 小的

count〔kaʊnt〕*v.* 重要

Appreciate every deed.

感激每善。

Return the favor.

知恩圖報。

Return kindness tenfold.

十倍報恩。

** ———————————

appreciate〔ə'priʃɪˌet〕v. 感激（他人所做
的事）(= be thankful for = be grateful for)

deed〔did〕n.（尤指很壞或很好的）事情；
行為   return〔rɪ'tɝn〕v. 報答

favor〔'fevə〕n. 恩惠

kindness〔'kaɪndnɪs〕n. 親切；仁慈；善意；
親切的行為

tenfold〔'tɛnˌfold〕adv. 十倍地

【**Unit 5 背景説明**】

Friends are invaluable. 朋友是無價的；朋友是很珍貴的。(= *Friends are priceless*.)

Friends over wealth. 朋友比財富重要。(= *Friends are more important than wealth*.) 也可説成：Value your friends more than wealth. (要重視你的朋友甚於財富。)

Cherish your friendships. 要珍惜你的友誼。(= *Treasure your friendships*.) 也可説成：Value your friendships. (要重視你的友誼。)

Remember gratitude always. 要一直記得感恩。(= *Remember to always be grateful*.)

Stay true always. 要一直保持忠誠。(= *Always be loyal*.)

Little things count. 小事很重要。(= *Small things matter*.)

Appreciate every deed. (要感激每一個行為。) 也可説成：Appreciate everything others do for you. (要感激別人為你做的每一件事。)

Return the favor. 要報答恩惠。(= *Return the kindness*.)

Return kindness tenfold. 要十倍地報答恩惠。(= *Return the favor ten times over*.) 也可説成：Be even kinder in return. (要湧泉相報。)

BOOK 4 · PART 3

UNIT ❻

Choose Your Mentors Well
選擇好的師父

Follow the best.
追隨最好。

Have role models.
崇拜模範。

Learn from them.
見賢思齊。

**

mentor〔ˈmɛntɔr〕*n.* 良師；導師；顧問
follow〔ˈfalo〕*v.* 跟隨；仿效
the best 最好的人 (= *the best person*; *the best people*)　role〔rol〕*n.* 角色
model〔ˈmɑdl〕*n.* 模特兒；模範；榜樣；典範
role model 模範；行爲榜樣
learn from 向…學習

Learn from champions.

向冠軍學習。

Take their advice.

聽取其勸告。

Follow their suggestions.

聽從其建議。

**

champion〔'tʃæmpɪən〕*n.* 冠軍；出類
　拔萃的人

advice〔əd'vaɪs〕*n.* 勸告；建議

take one's advice 聽從某人的勸告

follow〔'fɑlo〕*v.* 遵守；聽從

suggestion〔səg'dʒɛstʃən〕*n.* 建議

Reach new heights.

更上層樓。

Aim for excellence.

追求卓越。

Aspire to greatness.

渴望偉大。

**─────────

reach〔ritʃ〕v. 達到

height〔haɪt〕n. 高度；(pl.) 高處【*new heights* 在此指 a new, higher level（一個新的、更高的層級）】

aim〔em〕v. 瞄準　　*aim for* 瞄準；致力於

excellence〔ˈɛksləns〕n. 優秀；卓越

aspire〔əˈspaɪr〕v. 渴望

aspire to sth. 渴望某事

greatness〔ˈgretnɪs〕n. 偉大；崇高；著名

【**Unit 6 背景説明**】

Follow the best.（要追隨最好的人。）也可説成：
Imitate the most successful people.（要仿效
最成功的人。）Follow the example of the best
people.（要以最優秀的人為榜樣。）

Have role models.（要有模仿的榜樣。）也可説成：
Have someone to look up to.（要有值得尊敬的
人。）Have people to emulate.（要有可以模仿
的人。）

Learn from them.（要向他們學習。）也可説成：
Learn from the example of role models.
（要以楷模為榜樣來學習。）

Learn from champions.（要向冠軍學習；要向出類
拔萃的人學習。）也可説成：Learn from the best.
（要向最好的人學習。）Follow the example of
winners.（要以優勝者為榜樣。）

Take their advice.　要聽從他們的勸告。(= *Follow*
their advice.）也可説成：Take their
suggestions.（要聽從他們的建議。）

Follow their suggestions．（要聽從他們的建議。）
也可說成：Do as they say.（要按照他們所說的
做。）

Reach new heights．要達到新高峰。（＝*Attain
new heights*.）也可說成：Reach the next
level.（要達到下一個等級。）Advance further
than ever before.（要比以前更進步。）

Aim for excellence．（要追求卓越。）也可說成：
Strive to be excellent.（要努力變得優秀。）
Strive to be superb.（要努力變得很棒。）Strive
to be outstanding.（要努力變得傑出。）Aim
high.（要有遠大的志向。）

Aspire to greatness．（要渴望偉大。）也可說成：
Be ambitious.（要有抱負。）Set your sights
high.（要設定崇高的目標。）

BOOK 4・PART 3

UNIT 7

Don't Hold Back Your Praise
要毫無保留地稱讚

Remember to compliment.
記得誇獎別人。

It costs nothing.
它不花一毛錢。

It means everything.
但卻意義重大。

** ───────────

hold back 克制；保留
remember〔rɪ'mɛmbɚ〕*v.* 記得
compliment〔'kɑmplə,mɛnt〕*v.* 稱讚
　〔'kɑmpləmənt〕*n.*　　cost〔kɔst〕*v.* 花費
nothing〔'nʌθɪŋ〕*pron.* 無事；無物
mean〔min〕*v.* 意思是；具有…重要性
everything〔'ɛvrɪ,θɪŋ〕*pron.* 一切事物；
　重要的事物　　***mean everything*** 很重要

Often compliment sincerely.

經常眞誠稱讚。

Praise people everywhere.

到處稱讚人們。

Everyone deserves compliments.

人人應得讚美。

**

---

compliment〔ˈkɑmpləˌmɛnt〕v. 稱讚
〔ˈkɑmpləmənt〕n.

sincerely〔sɪnˈsɪrlɪ〕adv. 眞誠地

praise〔prez〕v. n. 稱讚

everywhere〔ˈɛvrɪˌhwɛr〕adv. 到處

deserve〔dɪˈzɝv〕v. 應得

Kind words matter.

好聽的話重要。

Praise lifts spirits.

讚美振奮人心。

Compliments create connection.

讚美創造人脈。

**————————

kind〔kaɪnd〕*adj.* 親切的；仁慈的；好心的

words〔wɜdz〕*n. pl.* 言詞；話

matter〔'mætɚ〕*v.* 重要

praise〔prez〕*n. v.* 稱讚

lift〔lɪft〕*v.* 使振奮；振作（精神）

spirit〔'spɪrɪt〕*n.* 精神

compliment〔'kɑmpləmənt〕*n.* 稱讚

create〔krɪ'et〕*v.* 創造

connection〔kə'nɛkʃən〕*n.* 連結；人際關係

【Unit 7 背景説明】

Remember to compliment. (記得要稱讚。) 也可
說成： Don't forget to compliment people.
(不要忘記稱讚別人。) Don't forget to give
compliments. (不要忘記稱讚。)

It costs nothing. (它不花一毛錢。) 也可説成：
It's easy to do. (它很容易做。) It takes no
time or money. (它不用花時間或金錢。)

It means everything. (它意義重大。) 也可説成：
It's meaningful to others. (它對別人有意義。)
It's important to others. (它對別人很重要。)

Often compliment sincerely. 要經常真誠地稱讚。
(= *Compliment often, sincerely.* = *Give*
genuine compliments often.)

Praise people everywhere. (要到處稱讚人們。)
也可説成： Praise everyone. (要稱讚每個人。)
(= *Give compliments to everyone.*)

Everyone deserves compliments. 每個人都應該得到稱讚。(= *We all deserve praise.*)

Kind words matter. (好話很重要。) 也可説成：Kind words make a difference. (好話能產生影響。) It's important to say nice things. (說好話很重要。)

Praise lifts spirits. (稱讚能提振精神。) 也可説成：Being praised makes people feel better. (被稱讚會使人覺得更好。)

Compliments create connection. 稱讚能創造連結，也就是「稱讚能創造人際關係；稱讚能創造人脈。」也可説成：Giving compliments can help you connect with people. (稱讚能幫助你和別人建立關係。) Praise brings people together. (稱讚使人們更友好。)

UNIT 8

Mind Your P's and Q's
謹言慎行

Politeness is powerful.

禮貌就有力量。

Respect is powerful.

尊敬就有力量。

Show your respect.

表現你的尊重。

** ─────────────

mind your p's and q's 注意你的言談舉止
politeness〔pəˈlaɪtnɪs〕*n.* 禮貌（= *courtesy*）
powerful〔ˈpaʊəfəl〕*adj.* 強有力的；有力量的
respect〔rɪˈspɛkt〕*n.* 尊敬；尊重
show〔ʃo〕*v.* 顯示；展現

Always say please.

一定要說「請」。

Say thank you.

一定要說「謝謝」。

Communicate with kindness.

親切地溝通。

**————————————

always〔ˋɔlwez〕*adv.* 總是;一直

please〔pliz〕*adv.* 請

communicate〔kəˋmjunəˏket〕*v.* 溝通

kindness〔ˋkaɪndnɪs〕*n.* 親切;仁慈;體貼

with kindness 親切地 (*= kindly*)

Watch your words.

要注意措辭。

Mind your manners.

要注意禮貌。

Courtesy really matters.

禮貌很重要。

**————————

watch〔watʃ〕v. 注意

words〔wɝdz〕n. pl. 言詞;話

mind〔maɪnd〕v. 注意

manners〔'mænɚz〕n. pl. 禮貌

courtesy〔'kɝtəsɪ〕n. 禮貌(= politeness
= manners)

really〔'rɪəlɪ〕adv. 真地

matter〔'mætɚ〕v. 重要

【Unit 8 背景説明】

Politeness is powerful.（禮貌很有力量。）也可説成：
　Courtesy is effective.（禮貌很有效果。）

Respect is powerful.（尊敬很有力量。）也可説成：
　Being respectful is very effective.（恭敬很有
　效果。）

Show your respect.（要表現你的尊重。）也可説成：
　Be respectful.（要很恭敬。）

Always say please.（一定要說「請」。）也可説成：
　Never forget to say please.（絕不要忘記說「請」。）

Say thank you.（要說「謝謝」。）也可説成：Always
　say thank you.（一定要說「謝謝」。）Remember
　to say thank you.（記得要說「謝謝」。）Thank
　others.（要感謝別人。）

Communicate with kindness.（要親切地溝通。）
　也可説成：Be kind when you talk to others.
　（和別人說話的時候要親切。）

Watch your words.（要注意你說的話。）也可説成：
　Be careful of what you say.（要小心你說的話。）

Mind your manners.（要注意你的禮貌。）也可説
　成：Be polite.（要有禮貌。）

Courtesy really matters. 禮貌眞的很重要。
　(= *Politeness is very important*.)

UNIT **9**

Be Sincere 要真誠

Always be honest.

保持誠實。

Speak the truth.

要說真話。

Tell the truth.

要講實話。

**

sincere〔sɪn'sɪr〕*adj.* 真誠的

always〔'ɔlwez〕*adv.* 總是；一直

honest〔'ɑnɪst〕*adj.* 誠實的

speak〔spik〕*v.* 說

truth〔truθ〕*n.* 事實；實話

tell〔tɛl〕*v.* 說

Always be fair.

永遠公正無私。

Consider everyone involved.

考量每人利益。

Meet everyone's needs.

滿足每人需求。

** ────────────

always〔'ɔlwez〕*adv.* 總是；一直
fair〔fɛr〕*adj.* 公平的
consider〔kən'sɪdɚ〕*v.* 考慮到
involved〔ɪn'vɑlvd〕*adj.* 牽涉在內的；有關的
meet〔mit〕*v.* 滿足（= *satisfy*）
need〔nid〕*n.* 需要

Always be helpful.

要樂於助人。

Improve your relationships.

要改善關係。

Build better friendships.

建立好友誼。

**　——————————————

always〔ˈɔlwez〕*adv.* 總是；一直
helpful〔ˈhɛlpfəl〕*adj.* 有幫助的；有用的；
　主動幫忙的
improve〔ɪmˈpruv〕*v.* 改善
relationship〔rɪˈleʃənˌʃɪp〕*n.* 關係；
　人際關係
build〔bɪld〕*v.* 建立
friendship〔ˈfrɛndʃɪp〕*n.* 友誼

【Unit 9 背景說明】

Always be honest. 一定要誠實。(= *Always be truthful.*)

Speak the truth. 要說實話。(= **Tell the truth.** = *State the truth.* = *Say what's true.* = *Just be honest.* = *Just be truthful.*)

Always be fair. (一定要公平。) 也可說成：Always be just. (一定要公正。)

Consider everyone involved. (要考慮到每個參與其中的人。) 也可說成：Take everyone into account. (要考慮到每個人。)

Meet everyone's needs. 要滿足每個人的需要。(= *Satisfy everyone's needs.* = *Accommodate everyone's needs.*) 也可說成：Meet/Satisfy/Accommodate the needs of everyone. 意思相同。

Always be helpful. (一定要樂於助人。) 也可說成：Always be useful. (一定要對人有幫助。)

Improve your relationships. 要改善你的人際關係。(= *Make your relationships better.*)

Build better friendships. (要建立更好的友誼。) 也可說成：Improve your friendships. (要改善你的友誼。)

PART 3・Unit 1~9
中英文錄音QR碼

BOOK 4・PART 3

PART 3 總整理

Unit 1

Seek new adventures.
尋求新冒險。
Embrace new
　opportunities.
擁抱新機會。
Welcome new challenges.
歡迎新挑戰。

Take risks daily.
每天勇於冒險。
Take risks fearlessly.
無所畏懼冒險。
Always challenge yourself.
始終挑戰自己。

Strive for more.　追求更多。
Learn and grow.　學習成長。
Push yourself further.
鞭策自己。

Unit 2

Love is pure.　愛是純潔的。
Love is kind.　愛是仁慈的。
Love is patient.
愛是有耐性。

Spread love always.
永遠散播愛。
Spread your warmth.
要散播溫暖。
Share your heart.
分享你的心。

Love is unconditional.
愛是無條件的。
Love is infinite.
愛是無止盡的。
Love always wins.
有愛一定獲勝。

Unit 3

United we stand.　團結則立。
Together we rise.
一起崛起。
Together we thrive.
一起成功。

Unity creates power.
團結創造力量。
Unity creates progress.
團結創造進步。
Teamwork breeds success.
團結就會成功。

We're better together.
我們一起更好。
We're stronger together.
我們一起更強。
Harmonious teamwork
　prevails. 團隊戰勝一切。

Unit 4

Arguing is useless.
爭論無用。
Arguing is meaningless.
爭論無義。
Winners don't argue.
勝者不爭。

End the quarrel. 結束爭吵。
End the dispute. 解決爭端。
Be the peacemaker.
當和事佬。

Learn to forgive.
學習原諒。
Bury the hatchet. 停止爭吵。
Become friends again.
重修舊好。

Unit 5

Friends are invaluable.
朋友無價。
Friends over wealth.
朋友勝財。
Cherish your friendships.
珍惜友誼。

Remember gratitude
　always. 常記感恩。
Stay true always. 常保真誠。
Little things count.
湧泉相報。

Appreciate every deed.
感激每善。
Return the favor.
知恩圖報。
Return kindness tenfold.
十倍報恩。

Unit 6

Follow the best. 追隨最好。
Have role models.
崇拜模範。
Learn from them.
見賢思齊。

Learn from champions.
向冠軍學習。
Take their advice.
聽取其勸告。
Follow their suggestions.
聽從其建議。

Reach new heights.
更上層樓。
Aim for excellence.
追求卓越。
Aspire to greatness.
渴望偉大。

Unit 7

Remember to compliment.
記得誇獎別人。
It costs nothing.
它不花一毛錢。
It means everything.
但卻意義重大。

Often compliment
　sincerely. 經常真誠稱讚。
Praise people everywhere.
到處稱讚人們。
Everyone deserves
　compliments.
人人應得讚美。

Kind words matter.
好聽的話重要。
Praise lifts spirits.
讚美振奮人心。
Compliments create
　connection.
讚美創造人脈。

Unit 8

Politeness is powerful.
禮貌就有力量。
Respect is powerful.
尊敬就有力量。
Show your respect.
表現你的尊重。

Always say please.
一定要說「請」。
Say thank you.
一定要說「謝謝」。
Communicate with
　kindness. 親切地溝通。

Watch your words.
要注意措辭。
Mind your manners.
要注意禮貌。
Courtesy really matters.
禮貌很重要。

Unit 9

Always be honest.
保持誠實。
Speak the truth. 要說真話。
Tell the truth. 要講實話。

Always be fair.
永遠公正無私。
Consider everyone
　involved. 考量每人利益。
Meet everyone's needs.
滿足每人需求。

Always be helpful.
要樂於助人。
Improve your
　relationships. 要改善關係。
Build better friendships.
建立好友誼。

BOOK 5 \ PART 1

Live a Positive Life
活出積極人生

PART 1・Unit 1~9
英文錄音QR碼

UNIT 1

Make Every Day a Great Day
要讓每一天都很棒

Wake up happy.

起床快樂。

Savor the present.

品味此刻。

Enjoy every moment.

享受當下。

**

great〔gret〕*adj.* 很棒的
wake up 起床
happy〔'hæpɪ〕*adj.* 快樂的
savor〔'sevɚ〕*v.* 品味
present〔'prɛznt〕*n.* 現在
enjoy〔ɪn'dʒɔɪ〕*v.* 享受
moment〔'momənt〕*n.* 時刻

Rise and grind.

起床工作。

Get to work.

開始工作。

Be awesome today.

過好今天。

**

rise〔raɪz〕*v.* 起床

grind〔graɪnd〕*v.* 磨粉;努力

get to work 開始工作

awesome〔ˈɔsəm〕*adj.* 很棒的

Make today count.

今天要過得有意義。

Make yourself proud.

要讓自己感到驕傲。

Be greater today.

今天要過得更美好。

**

make〔mek〕v. 使；讓
count〔kaʊnt〕v. 有重要意義；有價值
proud〔praʊd〕adj. 驕傲的
great〔gret〕adj. 極好的；很棒的

【Unit 1 背景説明】

Wake up happy. (起床時要很快樂。) 是慣用句。
也可説成：Be in a good mood when you
wake up. (起床時要心情好。) 在這裡的 happy
是指 in a happy state (處於快樂的狀態)，而
Wake up happily. (快樂地起床。)(= *Be happy
about waking up.*) 在此句意不合。

Savor the present. (品味現在。) 也可説成：
Appreciate the present. (重視現在。) Live in
the moment. (活在當下。)

Enjoy every moment. 享受每一刻。(= *Delight in
the time you have.*) 也可説成：Take pleasure
in everything you do. (做每一件事都要樂在
其中。)

Rise and grind. 起床工作。(= *Get up and get to
work.*) 也可説成：Rise and shine. (快起床。)

Get to work. 開始工作。(= *Start working.*)

BOOK 5・PART 1

Be awesome today.　今天一定要很棒。(= *Be wonderful today*.) 也可説成 : Do something awesome today.（今天要做一些很棒的事。）

Make today count. (要讓今天過得有意義。) 也可説成 : Do something meaningful today.（今天要做些有意義的事。）

Make yourself proud. (要讓自己感到驕傲。) 也可説成 : Do something you can be proud of.（要做你會感到驕傲的事。）

Be greater today.　今天要更棒。(= *Be better today*. = *Improve today*.) 也可説成 : Do something better today.（今天要做一些更好的事。）Be better than you were yesterday.（要比昨天的你更好。）

UNIT ❷

Live with Purpose
生活有目標

Organize your life.
規劃你的人生。

Live your potential.
發揮你的潛力。

Have meaningful goals.
要有重要目標。

** ————————————————

organize〔ˋɔrgənˏaɪz〕*v.* 組織；籌畫
live〔lɪv〕*v.* 過（生活）；表現；實踐
potential〔pəˋtɛnʃəl〕*n.* 潛力
meaningful〔ˋminɪŋfəl〕*adj.* 有意義的
goal〔gol〕*n.* 目標

Do meaningful work.

做有意義的工作。

Love your job.

愛你的工作。

Make enough money.

賺足夠的錢。

**

meaningful〔ˋminɪŋfəl〕*adj.* 有意義的

job〔dʒɑb〕*n.* 工作

make〔mek〕*v.* 賺（錢）

enough〔əˋnʌf〕*adj.* 足夠的

Find your fire.

找到你的熱情。

Master your skill.

精通你的技能。

Live, work, create.

享受生活、努力工作、創造發明。

** ———————————————

fire〔faɪr〕*n.* 火；熱情（= *passion*）

master〔'mæstɚ〕*v.* 精通

skill〔skɪl〕*n.* 技能

live〔lɪv〕*v.* 活著；享受生活

create〔krɪ'et〕*v.* 創造

【Unit 2 背景説明】

Organize your life. （規劃你的人生。）也可説成：Get organized. （要很有條理。）

Live your potential. 要發揮你的潛力。（= *Live up to your potential*. = *Achieve your potential*. = *Fulfill your potential*. = *Realize your potential*. ）

Have meaningful goals. （要有有意義的目標。）也可説成：Strive to do something meaningful. （要努力做些有意義的事。）

Do meaningful work. （要做有意義的工作。）也説成：Have a meaningful job. （要有有意義的工作。）Do something meaningful. （要做有意義的事。）

Find your fire. 要找到你的熱情。（= *Find your passion*. ）也可説成：Find what motivates you. （要找到能激勵你的事。）

Master your skill. （要精通你的技能。）也可説成：Be an expert at what you do. （要成爲你所做的事的專家。）

Live, work, create. 要享受生活、努力工作、創造發明。（= *Live, exert yourself, invent something*. ）

UNIT ❸

Live Happily

要快樂生活

Remember to live.

記得享受人生。

Keep it fun.

讓它充滿樂趣。

Feed your soul.

滿足你的心靈。

BOOK 5・PART 1

** ——————————

happily〔ˈhæpɪlɪ〕*adv.* 快樂地
remember〔rɪˈmɛmbɚ〕*v.* 記得
live〔lɪv〕*v.* 活著；享受人生（= *enjoy life*）
keep〔kip〕*v.* 使保持
fun〔fʌn〕*adj.* 有趣的；令人愉快的
feed〔fid〕*v.* 餵養；滿足
soul〔sol〕*n.* 靈魂；心靈

Appreciate the moment.
重視當下。

Cherish the moment.
珍惜此刻。

Be extremely grateful.
感恩知足。

** ——————————————

appreciate〔ə'priʃɪ‚et〕*v.* 重視;欣賞;
感激

moment〔'momənt〕*n.* 時刻;此刻

cherish〔'tʃɛrɪʃ〕*v.* 珍惜

extremely〔ɪk'strimlɪ〕*adv.* 極度地;非常

grateful〔'gretfəl〕*adj.* 感激的

Live, learn, love.

活著、學習、去愛。

Never look back.

勿想過去。

There's always hope.

永存希望。

BOOK 5・PART 1

** ———————————

live〔lɪv〕*v.* 活著;享受人生

learn〔lɜn〕*v.* 學習

love〔lʌv〕*v.* 愛

never〔'nɛvɚ〕*adv.* 絕不

look back 回頭看;回顧

always〔'ɔlwez〕*adv.* 總是;一直

hope〔hop〕*n.* 希望

【Unit 3 背景說明】

Keep it fun. 要使它一直很有趣。(= *Don't let the fun stop*.)

Feed your soul. 要滿足你的心靈。(= *Do something for your spirit*.) 也可說成：Do things that make you happy. (要做會使你快樂的事。)

Appreciate the moment. (要重視現在。) 也可說成：Live in the present. (要活在當下。)

Cherish the moment. (珍惜此刻。) 也可說成：Appreciate the present. (重視現在。) Treasure what you have right now. (珍惜你現在擁有的一切。)

Be extremely grateful. 要非常感激。(= *Be very thankful*.)

Never look back. (絕不要回頭看；絕不要回顧過去。) 也可說成：Don't think about the past. (不要想過去。)

There's always hope. (總是會有希望。) 也可說成：There is still hope. (仍然有希望。) Hope never disappears. (希望絕不會消失。) Hope will always exist. (希望會永遠存在。)

UNIT ④

Choose Happiness 選擇快樂

Nourish your body.
滋養身體。

Nourish your soul.
滋養心靈。

Create positive habits.
養好習慣。

**　BOOK 5・PART 1**

** _____

choose〔tʃuz〕*v.* 選擇
happiness〔'hæpɪnɪs〕*n.* 快樂
nourish〔'nɝɪʃ〕*v.* 滋養
body〔'bɑdɪ〕*n.* 身體
soul〔sol〕*n.* 靈魂；心靈
create〔krɪ'et〕*v.* 創造
positive〔'pɑzətɪv〕*adj.* 正面的；積極的；
　樂觀的；好的　　habit〔'hæbɪt〕*n.* 習慣

Happiness is everywhere.
快樂無處不在。

Happiness is homemade.
快樂是自製的。

Think happy thoughts.
要有快樂思維。

**

happiness〔ˈhæpɪnɪs〕*n.* 快樂；幸福
everywhere〔ˈɛvrɪˌhwɛr〕*adv.* 到處
homemade〔ˈhomˈmed〕*adj.* 自製的
think〔θɪŋk〕*v.* 想；心懷（…想法）
thought〔θɔt〕*n.* 想法

Great things await.

好事等你。

Expect great things.

期待好事。

Blue skies ahead.

前途無量。

BOOK 5・PART 1

**

great〔gret〕*adj.* 極好的;很棒的

await〔ə'wet〕*v.* 等待著

expect〔ɪk'spɛkt〕*v.* 期待

blue〔blu〕*adj.* 藍色的;蔚藍的

sky〔skaɪ〕*n.* (某種狀態的) 天空

ahead〔ə'hɛd〕*adv.* 在前面

【Unit 4 背景説明】

Nourish your body.（滋養你的身體。）也可説成：
Do good things for your physical health.（要
爲你的身體健康做些好事。）Eat healthy food.
（要吃健康的食物。）

Nourish your soul.（滋養你的心靈。）也可説成：
Do good things for your soul.（要爲你的心靈
做些好事。）Take care of your spirit.（要照顧
你的精神。）

Create positive habits. 要創造正面的習慣，也就是
「要創造好的習慣。」(= *Establish good habits*.)
也可説成：Develop good behaviors.（要培養好
的行爲。）Develop a good lifestyle.（要培養良
好的生活方式。）

Happiness is everywhere.（快樂到處都有。）也可
説成：You can find happiness everywhere.
（你到處都找得到快樂。）You can find happiness
all around you.（你可以發現快樂就在你的周圍。）

Happiness is homemade.（快樂是自製的。）也可說成：You can make your own happiness.（你可以製造自己的快樂。）

Think happy thoughts.（要有快樂的想法。）也可說成：Be optimistic.（要樂觀。）

Great things await.（美好的事物在等待著你。）也可說成：The future is full of wonderful things.（未來充滿了很棒的事物。）The future is bright.（未來一片光明。）

Expect great things.（要期待很棒的事情。）也可說成：Great things will happen.（會有很棒的事情發生。）Look forward to good things in the future.（要期待未來會有好事。）

Blue skies ahead. 前方有藍天。(= *There are blue skies ahead.*) 是慣用句，源自 1926 年 Irving Berlin 的同名歌曲。前方有藍天，引申爲「一切都很好。」(= *Everything is good.*) 也可說成：The future looks good.（前景看好。）Things are looking up.（情況越來越好。）You have no limits.（你沒有任何限制；你前途無量。）

UNIT **5**

Be a Good Example
成為模範

Don't be selfish.
不要自私。

Learn to give.
學會付出。

Maintain your integrity.
保持正直。

**

example〔ɪgˈzæmpḷ〕*n.* 例子；榜樣；模範
selfish〔ˈsɛlfɪʃ〕*adj.* 自私的
give〔gɪv〕*v.* 給與；付出
maintain〔menˈten〕*v.* 維持；保持
integrity〔ɪnˈtɛgrətɪ〕*n.* 正直

Lead the way.

引領道路。

Light the way.

點亮道路。

Lead by example.

以身作則。

** ────────────

lead〔lid〕*v.* 引導;領導

way〔we〕*n.* 路

lead the way 先行;帶路;示範

light〔laɪt〕*v.* 給…點燈;照亮

light the way 照亮道路

example〔ɪgˋzæmpḷ〕*n.* 例子;榜樣;模範

lead by example 以身作則

Aspire to inspire.

渴望激勵他人。

Inspire someone today.

今天激勵某人。

Everybody needs inspiration.

人人需要激勵。

** ───────────────────

aspire〔ə'spaɪr〕v. 渴望

inspire〔ɪn'spaɪr〕v. 激勵；給予靈感

need〔nid〕v. 需要

inspiration〔ˌɪnspə'reʃən〕n. 激勵；靈感

【**Unit 5 背景説明**】

Don't be selfish.（不要自私。）也可説成：Don't be greedy.（不要貪心。）Don't be stingy.（不要小氣。）

Learn to give.（學會付出。）也可説成：Be a giver.（要願意付出。）Be charitable.（要慈善。）Be generous.（要慷慨。）Learn to be generous.（要學會慷慨。）

Maintain your integrity.（要保持你的正直。）也可説成：Stay honest.（要保持誠實。）Be honorable.（要品德高尚。）

Lead the way. Light the way. Lead by example. 這三句話意思相同，第一個字都是 L 開頭。

Lead the way.（要帶路。）也可説成：Be a leader.（要當領導者。）Be a role model.（要當個模範。）（= *Be an example*.）

Light the way.（要照亮道路。）也可説成：Lead the way.（要帶路。）Be a guide.（要當嚮導。）Be a role model.（要成爲模範。）

BOOK 5・PART 1

Lead by example*.* 要以身作則。(= *Be a role model.*) 也可說成：Show others how it's done. (要告訴別人該怎麼做。)

Aspire to inspire*.* 要渴望激勵他人。(= *Aim to inspire others.* = *Try to inspire others.* = *Want to encourage others.*) 也可說成：Seek to encourage others. (要試圖鼓勵別人。) Seek to motivate others. (要試圖激勵別人。)

Inspire someone today*.* 今天就激勵某個人。(= *Motivate someone today.* = *Encourage someone today.*)

Everybody needs inspiration*.* 每個人都需要激勵。(= *Everybody needs encouragement.* = *Everybody needs motivation.*) 也可說成：We all need encouragement. (我們全都需要鼓勵。) We all need motivation. (我們全都需要激勵。)

UNIT 6

Surround Yourself with Positive People 要和樂觀的人在一起

Avoid hateful people.

避開損友。

Make new friends.

結交新友。

Make friendships last.

友誼永存。

BOOK 5・PART 1

**　**

**　**

surround〔səˈraʊnd〕*v.* 使環繞

positive〔ˈpɑzətɪv〕*adj.* 正面的；積極的；樂觀的

avoid〔əˈvɔɪd〕*v.* 避開

hateful〔ˈhetfəl〕*adj.* 充滿恨意的

make friends 交朋友　　make〔mek〕*v.* 使；讓

friendship〔ˈfrɛndʃɪp〕*n.* 友誼

last〔læst〕*v.* 持續；存在

Let it be.

就這樣吧。

Let it go.

隨它去吧。

Nobody is perfect.

人無完人。

**

let〔lɛt〕v. 讓

be〔bi〕v. 存在（= *exist*）；處於（某種狀態）

let it be 就這樣吧

let it go 隨它去吧

nobody〔'no͵bɑdɪ〕*pron.* 沒有人；無人

perfect〔'pɝfɪkt〕*adj.* 完美的

Love is eternal.

愛是永不止息。

Love is unbeatable.

愛是所向無敵。

Love your enemies.

要愛你的敵人。

** ―――――――――――

love〔lʌv〕*n.* 愛

eternal〔ɪ'tɜnḷ〕*adj.* 永恆的

unbeatable〔ʌn'bitəbḷ〕*adj.* 無法戰

　　勝的；不能超越的

enemy〔'ɛnəmɪ〕*n.* 敵人

【Unit 6 背景説明】

Avoid hateful people. (要避開充滿恨意的人。) 也可説成: Don't spend time with people who are bitter/spiteful. (不要和充滿恨意的人在一起。)

Make new friends. (結交新朋友。) 也可説成:
Make more friends. (結交更多的朋友。)
Make other friends. (結交其他的朋友。)

Make friendships last. (要讓友誼持續存在。) 也可説成: Keep your friendships. (要維持你的友誼。)

Let it be. 就這樣吧;隨它去吧;任由它去。(= *Let it go*. = *Forget about it*. = *Don't interfere*.)

Nobody is perfect. (沒有人是完美的。) 也可説成:
Everyone makes mistakes. (每個人都會犯錯。)

Love is eternal. (愛是永恆的。) 也可説成: Love never dies. (愛絕不會消失。) Love never ends. (愛永不止息。)

Love is unbeatable. (愛是無法戰勝的;愛是不能超越的。) 也可説成: Love always wins. (有愛一定勝利。) Love cannot be defeated. (愛不會被打敗。)

Love your enemy. (要愛你的敵人。) 這句話出自「聖經」。也可説成: Love everyone, even those who wish to hurt you. (要愛每個人,即使是那些想傷害你的人。)

UNIT **7**

Be Proactive　要積極主動

Take a step.
採取步驟。

Make a move.
採取行動。

Accept a challenge.
接受挑戰。

BOOK 5・PART 1

** ─────────────

proactive〔proˈæktɪv〕*adj.* 主動的；積極的

step〔stɛp〕*n.* 一步；步驟

take a step 採取步驟

move〔muv〕*n.* 移動；動作

make a move 採取行動

accept〔əkˈsɛpt〕*v.* 接受

challenge〔ˈtʃælɪndʒ〕*n.* 挑戰

Go for it.

大膽一試。

Just do it.

做就對了。

Make it happen.

讓它成真。

**

go for it 大膽試一試

just〔dʒʌst〕*adv.* 就

just do it 做就對了

happen〔'hæpən〕*v.* 發生

make it happen 成功實現；付諸行動

Take action now.
現在就採取行動。

Ready, set, go!
預備、準備、行動！

Decide, commit, succeed!
決定、投入、成功！

BOOK 5・PART 1

** ————————————

action〔'ækʃən〕*n.* 行動

take action 採取行動

ready〔'rɛdɪ〕*adj.* 準備好的

set〔sɛt〕*adj.* 準備好的

go〔go〕*v.* 出發；開始

decide〔dɪ'saɪd〕*v.* 決定；決心

commit〔kə'mɪt〕*v.* 承諾；投入

succeed〔sək'sid〕*v.* 成功

【Unit 7 背景説明】

Take a step. (採取步驟。) 也可説成：Take action.
(採取行動。) Begin. (開始。)

Make a move. 開始行動；採取步驟。(= *Take
action.* = *Take a step.*) 也可説成：Start. (開始。)

Accept a challenge. (接受挑戰。) 也可説成：Take
a risk. (要勇於冒險。)

Go for it. Just do it. Make it happen. 這三句話
意思相同。

Go for it. 大膽試一試；去做吧。(= *Try it.*) 也可説
成：Take a chance. (要冒險一試。)

Just do it. 做就對了；去做吧。(= *Go for it.* = *Take
action.*) 也可説成：Don't delay. (不要拖延。)
Don't hesitate. (不要猶豫。)

Make it happen. 讓它實現；去做吧。(= *Achieve
it.* = *Get it done.*)

Take action now. 現在就採取行動。(= *Do it now.*
= *Do something now.*)

Ready, set, go! 源自 Get ready, get set, go!
(準備好，準備就緒，開始行動！) (= *Get ready
and start!*)

UNIT ❽

Grab the Chance　要抓住機會

Life doesn't stop.

生命不停。

Life won't wait.

歲月不待。

Now or never.

機不可失。

** ───────

　grab〔græb〕*v.* 抓住

　chance〔tʃæns〕*n.* 機會

　life〔laɪf〕*n.* 人生；生活；生命

　stop〔stɑp〕*v.* 停止　　wait〔wet〕*v.* 等

　never〔'nɛvɚ〕*adv.* 絕不；永不

　now or never　要就現在，不然就永遠

　　沒機會了；機不可失

Believe in yourself.

相信自己。

Never stop dreaming.

夢想不停。

Passion, strength, fire.

熱情、力量、活力。

BOOK 5・PART 1

** ─────────────

believe in 相信；信任【believe 則
是「相信（某人的話）」】

never〔ˋnɛvɚ〕*adv.* 絕不

stop* + *V-ing 停止…

dream〔drim〕*v.* 做夢；夢想

passion〔ˋpæʃən〕*n.* 熱情

strength〔strɛŋθ〕*n.* 力量

fire〔faɪr〕*n.* 火；熱情

Winners never quit.

贏者不棄。

Quitters never win.

棄者不贏。

Success breeds success.

一次成功，次次成功。

** ————————

winner〔'wɪnɚ〕 *n.* 優勝者；贏家

quit〔kwɪt〕 *v.* 停止；放棄

quitter〔'kwɪtɚ〕 *n.* 輕易放棄的人

win〔wɪn〕 *v.* 贏；獲勝；成功

success〔sək'sɛs〕 *n.* 成功

breed〔brid〕 *v.* 孕育；產生

【Unit 8 背景説明】

Life doesn't stop.（生命不會停止。）也可説成：
Life won't stop for you.（生命不會爲了你停
下來。）Life goes on.（生命會不斷向前進。）

Life won't wait.（生命不會等人；歲月不待人。）
也可説成：Time and tide wait for no man.
（【諺】歲月不待人。）Life goes on.（生命會不斷
向前進。）

Now or never. 是慣用句，「要就現在，不然就永遠沒
機會了；機不可失；勿失良機。」也可説成：Do it
now or give it up.（現在就做，否則就放棄。）
Take action or forget about it.（要採取行動，
否則就算了吧。）

Believe in yourself.（要相信自己。）也可説成：
Have confidence.（要有信心。）Know that
you can do it.（要知道你做得到。）

Never stop dreaming.（絕對不要停止夢想。）也可
説成：Don't give up your dreams.（不要放棄

你的夢想。）Follow your dreams.（要追求你的夢想。）

***Passion*, *strength*, *fire*.** 是慣用句，源自 Have passion, strength, and fire.（要有熱情、力量，和活力。）

***Winners never quit*.** 贏家絕不會放棄。（= *Those who win never give up*.）也可說成：Those who succeed never give up.（成功的人絕不會放棄。）

***Quitters never win*.**（輕易放棄的人絕對不會贏。）也可說成：People who quit can never succeed.（放棄的人絕對不會成功。）If you quit, you can't succeed.（如果你放棄，你就不會成功。）

***Success breeds success*.**（成功孕育成功；成功為成功之母；一次成功，次次成功。）也可說成：One success leads to another.（成功會造就成功。）Nothing succeeds like success.（【諺】一事如意，事事順利。）

UNIT **9**

Innovate 要創新

New is good.
新即是好。

Keep making changes.
不斷改變。

Forget the past.
忘了過去。

** ———————————

innovate〔ˈɪnəˌvet〕*v.* 創新

new〔nju〕*adj.* 新的　　*n.* 新事物

keep + *V-ing* 持續…

change〔tʃendʒ〕*n.* 改變

make a change 改變

forget〔fəˈgɛt〕*v.* 忘記

past〔pæst〕*n.* 過去

Do it differently.

要有不同的做法。

Use your creativity.

運用你的創造力。

Creativity takes courage.

創意需要勇氣。

** ———————————

differently〔ˈdɪfərəntlɪ〕*adv.* 不同地

use〔juz〕*v.* 使用;運用

creativity〔͵krieˈtɪvətɪ〕*n.* 創造力

take〔tek〕*v.* 需要

courage〔ˈkɝɪdʒ〕*n.* 勇氣

Let's make history.

創造歷史。

Let's move mountains.

締造奇蹟。

Legends never die.

永垂不朽。

**

let's + *V*. 我們…吧

history〔ˈhɪstrɪ〕*n.* 歷史

make history 創造歷史

move〔muv〕*v.* 移動

mountain〔ˈmaʊntn̩〕*n.* 山

move mountains 移動山脈；竭盡全力；
　創造奇蹟

legend〔ˈlɛdʒənd〕*n.* 傳說；傳奇故事；
　傳奇人物

【Unit 9 背景説明】

New is good. (新即是好。) 也可説成：New things are good. (新的事物很好。) Progress is good. (進步很好。) It's good to try new things. (嘗試新事物很好。)

Keep making changes. (要持續改變；要不斷改變。) 也可説成：Continue to grow. (要繼續成長。)

Forget the past. (忘了過去。) 也可説成：Don't dwell on the past. (不要老是想著過去。) (= *Don't think about the past*.) Never look back. (絕不要回顧過去。)

Do it differently. (要用不同的方法來做。) 也可説成：Do it another way. (要用另一個方法來做。)

Use your creativity. (要運用你的創造力。) 也可説成：Be creative. (要有創意。)

BOOK 5・PART 1

Creativity takes courage. 創意需要勇氣。
(= *You have to have courage to be creative.*)
也可說成：You have to be brave to be
creative. (要有創意必須要勇敢。)

Let's make history. (我們來創造歷史吧。) 也可
說成：Let's do something memorable. (我們
來做一些值得紀念的事吧。)

Let's move mountains. 我們來移動高山吧，引申
為「我們來創造奇蹟吧。」源自聖經：Faith will
move mountains. (信念能移動高山。) 中國古
代也有「愚公移山」的故事。也可說成：Let's do
the impossible. (我們來做不可能的事吧。)

Legends never die. (傳奇人物永遠不死；英雄永
遠不死。) (= *Heroes never die.*) 這句話源自
2017 年的一首同名歌曲。也可說成：If we do
something great, we will never be forgotten.
(如果我們做了偉大的事，就絕不會被遺忘。)

PART 1 總整理

PART 1・Unit 1~9
中英文錄音QR碼

Unit 1

Wake up happy.
起床快樂。
Savor the present. 品味此刻。
Enjoy every moment.
享受當下。

Rise and grind. 起床工作。
Get to work. 開始工作。
Be awesome today.
過好今天。

Make today count.
今天要過得有意義。
Make yourself proud.
要讓自己感到驕傲。
Be greater today.
今天要過得更美好。

Unit 2

Organize your life.
規劃你的人生。
Live your potential.
發揮你的潛力。
Have meaningful goals.
要有重要目標。

Do meaningful work.
做有意義的工作。
Love your job. 愛你的工作。
Make enough money.
賺足夠的錢。

Find your fire.
找到你的熱情。
Master your skill.
精通你的技能。
Live, work, create.
享受生活、努力工作、創造發明。

Unit 3

Remember to live.
記得享受人生。
Keep it fun. 讓它充滿樂趣。
Feed your soul.
滿足你的心靈。

Appreciate the moment.
重視當下。
Cherish the moment.
珍惜此刻。
Be extremely grateful.
感恩知足。

BOOK 5・PART 1

Live, learn, love.
活著、學習、去愛。
Never look back. 勿想過去。
There's always hope.
永存希望。

Unit 4

Nourish your body.
滋養身體。
Nourish your soul. 滋養心靈。
Create positive habits.
養好習慣。

Happiness is everywhere.
快樂無處不在。
Happiness is homemade.
快樂是自製的。
Think happy thoughts.
要有快樂思維。

Great things await.
好事等你。
Expect great things.
期待好事。
Blue skies ahead. 前途無量。

Unit 5

Don't be selfish. 不要自私。
Learn to give. 學會付出。
Maintain your integrity.
保持正直。

Lead the way. 引領道路。
Light the way. 點亮道路。
Lead by example.
以身作則。

Aspire to inspire.
渴望激勵他人。
Inspire someone today.
今天激勵某人。
Everybody needs
  inspiration.
人人需要激勵。

Unit 6

Avoid hateful people.
避開損友。
Make new friends.
結交新友。
Make friendships last.
友誼永存。

Let it be. 就這樣吧。
Let it go. 隨它去吧。
Nobody is perfect.
人無完人。

Love is eternal.
愛是永不止息。
Love is unbeatable.
愛是所向無敵。
Love your enemies.
要愛你的敵人。

Unit 7

Take a step. 採取步驟。
Make a move. 採取行動。
Accept a challenge.
接受挑戰。

Go for it. 大膽一試。
Just do it. 做就對了。
Make it happen. 讓它成真。

Take action now.
現在就採取行動。
Ready, set, go!
預備、準備、行動！
Decide, commit, succeed!
決定、投入、成功！

Unit 8

Life doesn't stop.
生命不停。
Life won't wait. 歲月不待。
Now or never. 機不可失。

Believe in yourself.
相信自己。
Never stop dreaming.
夢想不停。
Passion, strength, fire.
熱情、力量、活力。

Winners never quit.
贏者不棄。
Quitters never win.
棄者不贏。
Success breeds success.
一次成功，次次成功。

Unit 9

New is good.
新即是好。
Keep making changes.
不斷改變。
Forget the past.
忘了過去。

Do it differently.
要有不同的做法。
Use your creativity.
運用你的創造力。
Creativity takes courage.
創意需要勇氣。

Let's make history.
創造歷史。
Let's move mountains.
締造奇蹟。
Legends never die.
永垂不朽。

BOOK 5・PART 1

BOOK 5 \ PART 2

Take Care of Yourself
好好照顧自己

PART 2・Unit 1~9
英文錄音QR碼

UNIT ❶

Relaxation Is Key
放鬆很重要

Remember to rest.
記得要休息。

Have some downtime.
有休息時間；機器也要休息。

Everyone needs rest.
人人需休息。

** ———————————————

relaxation 〔,rilæks'eʃən〕 *n.* 放鬆

key 〔 ki 〕 *adj.* 重要的

remember 〔 rɪ'mɛmbɚ 〕 *v.* 記得

rest 〔 rɛst 〕 *v. n.* 休息

downtime 〔'daʊn,taɪm 〕 *n.* 停機時間；休息
時間（ = *opportunity for rest and relaxation* ）

Let yourself rest.

自己休息。

Restore your energy.

恢復能量。

Recharge your batteries.

好好充電。

** ―――――――――

let〔lɛt〕*v.* 讓

rest〔rɛst〕*v.* 休息

restore〔rɪ'stor〕*v.* 恢復

energy〔'ɛnɚdʒɪ〕*n.* 活力;精力

recharge〔ri'tʃɑrdʒ〕*v.* 給(電池)再充電

battery〔'bætərɪ〕*n.* 電池

recharge one's batteries 再充電;
恢復體力

Close your eyes.

閉上眼睛。

Sit and breathe.

坐著呼吸。

Do a meditation.

進行冥想。

**

close〔kloz〕*v.* 閉上

sit〔sɪt〕*v.* 坐

breathe〔brið〕*v.* 呼吸

meditation〔ˌmɛdəˈteʃən〕*n.* 沈思；冥想

BOOK 5・PART 2

【Unit 1 背景說明】

Remember to rest.（記得要休息。）也可說成：
Don't forget to take a break.（不要忘記要休
息一下。）

Have some downtime. 要有一些休息時間。(= *Set
aside some time for rest.*) 也可說成：Take a
break.（要休息一下。）Relax.（要放輕鬆。）

Everyone needs rest. 每個人都需要休息。(= *We
all need to take breaks.*) 也可說成：We all
need to relax.（我們都需要放輕鬆。）

Let yourself rest. 要讓自己休息。(= *Allow
yourself to rest.*)

Restore your energy. 恢復你的活力。(= *Regain
your energy.* = *Refresh yourself.*)

Recharge your batteries. 恢復你的體力。
(= *Restore your energy.*)

Sit and breathe.（坐著呼吸。）也可說成：Sit
down and focus on your breathing.（坐下
來，專心呼吸。）Sit down and relax.（坐下
來，放輕鬆。）

Do a meditation. 沈思冥想。(= *Meditate.*) 也可
說成：Do meditation.（進行冥想。）

UNIT ❷

Best Sleep Tips (I)
優質睡眠指南 (I)

Avoid big meals.
避免暴飲暴食。

Avoid afternoon coffee.
避免午後咖啡。

Avoid screen time.
避看電子螢幕。

** ————————————

sleep〔slip〕*n.* 睡眠;睡覺

tip〔tɪp〕*n.* 祕訣　avoid〔ə'vɔɪd〕*v.* 避免

big〔bɪg〕*adj.* 豐盛的　meal〔mil〕*n.* 一餐

afternoon〔ˌæftə'nun〕*adj.* 下午的;午後用的

coffee〔'kɔfɪ, 'kɑfɪ〕*n.* 咖啡【現在美國人唸

〔'kɑfɪ〕較普遍】　screen〔skrin〕*n.* 螢幕

screen time (看電腦、電視、手機等的)螢幕時間

BOOK 5・PART 2

Get enough exercise.

獲得充分運動。

Get enough sunlight.

獲得足夠陽光。

Get enough air.

保持空氣流通。

** ———————————

enough〔ə'nʌf〕*adj.* 足夠的
exercise〔'ɛksəˌsaɪz〕*n.* 運動
sunlight〔'sʌnˌlaɪt〕*n.* 陽光
air〔ɛr〕*n.* 空氣

Don't eat late.

不要吃得太晚。

Don't work late.

不要工作太晚。

Drink calming tea.

要飲用安神茶。

**

eat〔it〕*v.* 吃；吃東西；吃飯

late〔let〕*adv.* 晚地

eat late 很晚才吃飯

work late 工作到很晚

calm〔kɑm〕*v.* 使平靜；使（心神）鎮定

tea〔ti〕*n.* 茶

【 Unit 2 背景説明 】

Avoid big meals. (避免吃大餐。) 也可説成：
Don't eat too much. (不要吃太多。) Don't
eat a lot before going to sleep. (睡前不要吃
很多。)

Avoid afternoon coffee. 要避免下午喝咖啡。
(= *Don't drink coffee in the afternoon*.)

Avoid screen time. 要避免螢幕時間，也就是
「要避免看電子螢幕。」也可説成：Don't use
electronic devices before bed. (睡前不要使
用電子裝置。) Don't spend too much time
staring at a screen. (不要花太多時間盯著螢幕。)

Get enough exercise. (要有充分的運動。) 也可説
成：Stay active. (要保持運動。) Be physically
active. (身體要活動。)

Get enough sunlight. (要獲得足夠的陽光。) 也
可説成：Get outside. (要去外面。) Get some
sunshine. (要曬點太陽。)

Get enough air.（要獲得足夠的空氣。）也可說成：Get enough fresh air.（要獲得足夠的新鮮空氣。）Go outside.（要去外面。）

Don't eat late.（不要很晚才吃飯。）也可說成：Don't eat late at night.（晚上不要太晚吃飯。）Don't eat before bed.（不要睡前吃東西。）

Don't work late.（不要工作到很晚。）也可說成：Don't work too late.（不要工作得太晚。）Don't do overtime.（不要加班。）（= *Don't work overtime*.）Leave on time.（要準時離開。）

Drink calming tea.（要喝能使人鎮定的茶；要喝安神茶。）也可說成：Drink herbal tea.（要喝花草茶。）Drink caffeine-free tea.（要喝不含咖啡因的茶。）

UNIT ❸

Best Sleep Tips (II)
優質睡眠指南 (II)

Sleep in darkness.
在黑暗中入睡。

Sleep in silence.
在安靜中入睡。

Lower the temperature.
降低一些溫度。

**

sleep〔slip〕*n. v.* 睡覺；睡眠

tip〔tɪp〕*n.* 祕訣

darkness〔'dɑrknɪs〕*n.* 黑暗

silence〔'saɪləns〕*n.* 沈默；無聲；寂靜；安靜

lower〔'loɚ〕*v.* 降低

temperature〔'tɛmpərətʃɚ〕*n.* 溫度

Take a bath.

要懂得泡澡。

Wear comfortable pajamas.

著舒適睡衣。

Wear comfortable socks.

穿舒適襪子。

＊＊

bath〔bæθ〕*n.* 洗澡

take a bath 洗澡；泡澡

wear〔wɛr〕*v.* 穿

comfortable〔'kʌmfətəbḷ〕*adj.* 舒服的；
　舒適的

pajamas〔pə'dʒɑməz〕*n. pl.* 睡衣；睡衣褲

socks〔sɑks〕*n. pl.* 短襪

Avoid drinking alcohol.

避免喝酒。

Practice deep breathing.

做深呼吸。

Follow a schedule.

按表操作；作息正常。

**

avoid〔 ə'vɔɪd 〕v. 避免

alcohol〔 'ælkə,bɔl 〕n. 酒；酒精

practice〔 'præktɪs 〕v. 實行；練習

deep〔 dip 〕adj. 深的

breathe〔 brið 〕v. 呼吸

follow〔 'falo 〕v. 遵守

schedule〔 'skɛdʒul 〕n. 時間表

【**Unit 3 背景說明**】

Sleep in darkness. (要在黑暗中入睡。) 也可説
成：Sleep in a dark room. (要在黑暗的房間
睡覺。) Sleep in a dark place. (要在黑暗的
地方睡覺。)

Sleep in silence. (要在寂靜中入睡。) 也可説成：
Sleep in a quiet room. (要在安靜的房間睡覺。)
Sleep in a quiet place. (要在安靜的地方睡覺。)

Lower the temperature. (要降低溫度。) 也可説
成：Keep the temperature cool. (溫度要保持
涼爽。)【溫度低有助於一夜好眠】Sleep in a cool
room. (要在涼爽的房間睡覺。) Sleep in a cool
place. (要在涼爽的地方睡覺。)

Take a bath. (要洗澡；要泡澡。) 也可説成：Take
a hot bath. (要洗個熱水澡。) Soak in the tub.
(要泡在浴缸裡。)「淋浴」則是 take a shower。

Wear comfortable pajamas. (要穿舒適的睡衣。)
pajamas (睡衣；睡衣褲) 須用複數形。也可説成：

BOOK 5・PART 2

Sleep in something comfortable. (要穿著舒適
的衣服睡覺。)

Wear comfortable socks. (要穿舒服的襪子。)
也可說成 : Sleep with your socks on. (要穿
著襪子睡覺。) Wear socks to bed. (要穿著襪
子睡覺。)

Avoid drinking alcohol. (要避免喝酒。) 也可說
成 : Don't drink too much alcohol. (不要喝太
多酒。) Don't drink alcohol before bed. (睡
覺前不要喝酒。)

Practice deep breathing. (要做深呼吸。) 也可說
成 : Take deep breaths. (要做深呼吸。)
Breathe deeply. (要深呼吸。)

Follow a schedule. (要遵守時間表。) 也可說成 :
Stick to a routine. (要堅持例行公事;要遵守慣
例。) Develop good habits. (要培養好習慣。)

UNIT ④

Follow Your Own Star
跟隨你心中最閃耀的那顆星

Find your passion.
找到你的熱愛。

Follow your passion.
追隨你的熱情。

Live your purpose.
活出你的使命。

**────────────

follow〔ˈfalo〕*v.* 跟隨

star〔star〕*n.* 星星

passion〔ˈpæʃən〕*n.* 熱情;愛好

live〔lɪv〕*v.*(在生活中)表現;實踐

purpose〔ˈpɝpəs〕*n.* 目的;意圖;目標

Passion creates energy.
熱情創造活力。

Make magic happen.
要讓奇蹟出現。

Make dreams happen.
要讓夢想成眞。

**

passion〔'pæʃən〕*n.* 熱情；愛好

create〔krɪ'et〕*v.* 創造

energy〔'ɛnə·dʒɪ〕*n.* 能量；活力

make〔mek〕*v.* 使

magic〔'mædʒɪk〕*n.* 魔法【在此指「很
棒的事」(wonderful things)】

happen〔'hæpən〕*v.* 發生

dream〔drim〕*n.* 夢；夢想

Embrace your why.

接受爲何而生；擁抱天職。

Pursue your why.

追尋爲何而在；追尋目標。

Preserve your passion.

保存你的熱情；維持熱情。

** ———————————

embrace〔ɪm'bres〕v. 擁抱；欣然接受

why〔hwaɪ〕n. 理由；原因

pursue〔pɚ'su〕v. 追求

preserve〔prɪ'zɝv〕v. 保存；維護；維持

passion〔'pæʃən〕n. 熱情

【Unit 4 背景説明】

Find your passion.（要找到你的熱愛。）也可説成：Find out what you really want to do.（要了解你眞正想做的是什麼。）Find out what makes you happy.（要找出能讓你快樂的事。）

Follow your passion. 要追隨你的熱情；要做你眞正想要的事。(= *Do what you really want to do*.) 也可説成：Do what makes you happy.（要做能讓你快樂的事。）

Live your purpose.（要活出你的使命；要實現你的目標。）也可説成：Remember your purpose every day.（每天都要記得你的目標。）Live according to your purpose.（要按照你的目標生活。）句中的 your purpose 是指 your calling（你的天職）、your reason for being（你存在的理由）。

Passion creates energy.（熱情創造活力。）也可説成：Passion gives you energy.（熱情能給你活力。）If you are passionate, you will have more energy.（如果你很熱情，你就會更有活力。）

Make magic happen.（要讓魔法發生；要讓奇蹟出現。）也可說成：Make good things happen.（要讓好事發生。）Do good things.（要做好事。）

Make dreams happen. 要讓夢想實現。(= *Make dreams come true.*) 也可說成：Achieve your goals.（要達成你的目標。）

Embrace your why.（欣然接受你存在的原因。）也可說成：Understand your purpose.（要了解你存在的目的。）Don't fight your calling.（不要對抗你的天職。）

Pursue your why.（追尋你存在的理由。）也可說成：Try to fulfill your purpose.（要努力達成你的目標。）Always remember why you're here.（一定要記得你存在的理由。）

Preserve your passion. 要維持你的熱情。(= *Remain passionate.*) 也可說成：Don't give up on what you care about.（不要放棄你在乎的事。）Continue to feel passionate.（要持續覺得充滿熱情。）

UNIT ⑤

Never Stop Learning
絕不停止學習

Knowledge is powerful.
知識很有力量。

Gain information everywhere.
隨地獲取資訊。

Improve your life.
改善自身生活。

**

never〔ˈnɛvə〕*adv.* 絕不　　***stop + V-ing*** 停止…
knowledge〔ˈnɑlɪdʒ〕*n.* 知識
powerful〔ˈpauəfəl〕*adj.* 有力量的；強而有力的
gain〔gen〕*v.* 獲得
information〔ˌɪnfəˈmeʃən〕*n.* 資訊
everywhere〔ˈɛvrɪˌhwɛr〕*adv.* 到處
improve〔ɪmˈpruv〕*v.* 改善

Learning shapes futures.

學習塑造未來。

Be a student.

要成爲學習者。

Create your future.

創造你的未來。

** ─────────────

learning〔ˋlɜnɪŋ〕 *n.* 學習；學問；學識

shape〔ʃep〕 *v.* 塑造；決定；影響

future〔ˋfjutʃɚ〕 *n.* 未來

create〔krɪˋet〕 *v.* 創造

Mindset determines fate.

心態決定命運。

Thirst for more.

渴望獲得更多。

Own your fate.

掌握你的命運。

**

mindset (ˈmaɪndˌsɛt) *n.* 心態
determine (dɪˈtɝmɪn) *v.* 決定
fate (fet) *n.* 命運
thirst (θɝst) *v. n.* 渴望 < *for* >　　*n.* 口渴
own (on) *v.* 擁有；控制；支配
　(= *determine* ; *control*)

【Unit 5 背景説明】

Knowledge is powerful. 知識很有力量。
(= *Knowledge is mighty.*) 也可説成：
Knowledge is power. (【諺】知識就是力量。)
The more you know, the more you can do.
(你懂得越多，能做的事就更多。) The more you
know, the more power you have. (你懂得越
多，就越有力量。)

Gain information everywhere. (要到處獲得資
訊。) 也可説成：Always learn. (要不斷學習。)
Learn from every experience. (要從每個經驗
中學習。)

Improve your life. 改善你的生活。(= *Make your
life better.*) 也可説成：Enrich your life. (充實
你的生活。)

Learning shapes futures. (學習塑造未來。) 也可
説成：What you learn will determine your
future. (你所學的會決定你的未來。)

Be a student. (要當個學生。) 也可説成:Be a learner. (要當個學習者。) Focus on learning. (要專注於學習。)

Create your future. (要創造你的未來。) 也可説成:Determine your own future. (要決定你自己的未來。) (= *Decide your own future*.)

Mindset determines fate. (心態決定命運。) 也可說成:Your attitude will decide your future. (你的態度會決定你的未來。) Your attitude will determine what happens to you. (你的態度會決定你會發生什麼事。)

Thirst for more. 要渴望獲得更多。(= *Desire more*. = *Want more*.) 也可説成:Be ambitious. (要有抱負;要志向遠大。)

Own your fate. 擁有你的命運,引申為「要掌握自己的命運。」也可説成:Determine your own fate. (要決定你自己的命運。) Control your future. (要掌控你的未來。)

UNIT ❻

Failure Is a Beginning, Not the End 失敗是個開始，不是結束

Fail every day.
每天都會失敗。

Failure builds success.
失敗造就成功。

Learn from mistakes.
錯誤中能學習。

**─────────────

failure〔ˋfeljɚ〕*n.* 失敗　　fail〔fel〕*v.* 失敗
build〔bɪld〕*v.* 建立；建造
success〔səkˋsɛs〕*n.* 成功
learn from 向…學習
mistake〔məˋstek〕*n.* 錯誤

Fall seven times.

倒下七次。

Get up eight.

爬起八次。

That's the secret.

就是祕訣。

**

fall〔fɔl〕*v.* 跌倒

time〔taɪm〕*n.* 次

get up 站起來

secret〔'sikrɪt〕*n.* 祕密；祕訣

Dare to fail.

勇於失敗。

Continue with courage.

勇敢繼續。

Achieve great things.

成就大業。

** ──────────────

dare〔dɛr〕*v.* 敢

fail〔fel〕*v.* 失敗

continue〔kənˈtɪnju〕*v.* 繼續

courage〔ˈkɝɪdʒ〕*n.* 勇氣

with courage 勇敢地

achieve〔əˈtʃiv〕*v.* 達成

great〔gret〕*adj.* 大的；偉大的；很棒的

great thing 大事

【Unit 6 背景説明】

Fail every day. (要每天失敗。) 也可説成 : Make mistakes every day. (要每天犯錯。) Always make mistakes. (要一直犯錯。) Be willing to fail. (要願意失敗。) Be willing to make mistakes. (要願意犯錯。)

Failure builds success. 失敗造就成功。 (= *Failure leads to success*.) 也可説成 : Success comes from failure. (成功來自 失敗。)

Learn from mistakes. (從錯誤中學習。) 也可説 成 : Don't make the same mistakes twice. (不要犯兩次同樣的錯誤。)

Fall seven times. (跌倒七次。) 也可説成 : Fail seven times. (失敗七次。)

Get up eight. 源自 Get up eight times. (起來八 次。) 也可説成 : Start again eight times. (重新 開始八次。) (= *Start over eight times*.) 源自日 本諺語 "Nana korboi ya oki" (倒下七次，爬起

八次)，說明堅忍不拔的概念，無論你被打倒幾次，
都必須再爬起來。

That's the secret. 那就是祕訣。(= *That's the
trick.*) 也可說成：That's the key. (那就是
關鍵。)

Dare to fail. (要勇於失敗。) 也可說成：Don't
be afraid to fail. (不要害怕失敗。)

Continue with courage. (要有勇氣繼續。) 也可
說成：Go on bravely. (要勇敢地繼續。) Be
courageous enough to keep going. (要夠勇
敢，能持續前進。)

Achieve great things. (要達成偉大的事。) 也可
說成：Do great things. (要做大事。) Do
remarkable things. (要做了不起的事。)

UNIT ❼

Be a Good Listener
要善於傾聽

Listen to learn.

傾聽才能學習。

Listen to understand.

傾聽才能了解。

Listen to sympathize.

傾聽才有同感。

** ─────────

listener (ˈlɪsn̩ɚ) *n.* 傾聽者
listen (ˈlɪsn̩) *v.* 注意聽;傾聽
understand (ˌʌndɚˈstænd) *v.* 了解
sympathize (ˈsɪmpəˌθaɪz) *v.* 同情;
　有同感;有共鳴;贊成

Clear your mind.

頭腦清楚。

Be fully present.

專注當下。

Don't be distracted.

切勿分心。

**

clear〔klɪr〕*v.* 使（頭腦）清楚

mind〔maɪnd〕*n.* 心；精神；頭腦；想法

fully〔'fʊlɪ〕*adv.* 完全地

present〔'prɛznt〕*adj.* 出席的；在場的

　【在此指「專注的」（mindful）】

distract〔dɪ'strækt〕*v.* 使分心

Don't interrupt others.

不要打斷他人談話。

Use body language.

使用肢體語言。

Ask open-ended questions.

問開放式問題，不問是非題。

** ——————————————

interrupt〔͵ɪntəˊrʌpt〕*v.* 打斷（談話）

use〔juz〕*v.* 使用；運用

body〔ˊbɑdɪ〕*n.* 身體

language〔ˊlæŋgwɪdʒ〕*n.* 語言

body language 肢體語言

ask〔æsk〕*v.* 問

open-ended〔ˊopənˏɛndɪd〕*adj.* 開放
　式的；無結論的

question〔ˊkwɛstʃən〕*n.* 問題

【Unit 7 背景説明】

Listen to learn*.* 傾聽才能學習。(= *Listen in order to learn. = Listen, and you will learn something. = Learn by listening.*)

Listen to understand*.* 傾聽才能了解。(= *Listen in order to understand. = Listen, and you will understand.*)

Listen to sympathize*.* 傾聽才能同情。(= *Listen in order to sympathize. = Listen, and you will be able to sympathize. = Show your sympathy by listening.*)

Clear your mind*.* 要使你的頭腦清楚，也就是「思路要清晰。」也可説成：Chill out. (要冷靜。) Calm down. (冷靜下來。)

Be fully present*.* 要完全在場，引申爲「要專注於當下。」(= *Stay in the moment.*) 也可説成：Be fully conscious. (要完全了解。) Be mindful. (要注意。)

Don't be distracted. (不要分心。) 也可說成：
Focus. (要專注。) Concentrate. (要專心。)
Focus on what you're doing. (要專注於你正在
做的事。) Concentrate on what's happening.
(要專心注意發生了什麼事。)

Don't interrupt others. 不要打斷別人；不要插
嘴。(= *Don't cut others off.* = *Don't speak out
of turn.*)

Use body language. (要使用肢體語言。) 也可說
成：Use gestures. (要用手勢。) Make
gestures. (要做手勢。)

Ask open-ended questions. (要問開放式的問題。)
也可說成：Ask questions that people can
elaborate on. (要問別人可以詳細說明的問題。)
Don't ask yes-or-no questions. (不要問是非
題。) 問開放式的問題能知道更多資訊 (to elicit
information)，能鼓勵別人說話 (to encourage
others to talk)。

UNIT 8

Laughter Is the Best Medicine
笑是最好的藥

Laugh every day.
每天都要笑。

Find the humor.
要找到幽默。

Humor heals us.
幽默能療癒。

** ——————————

laughter〔'læftɚ〕*n.* 笑
medicine〔'mɛdəsn̩〕*n.* 藥
laugh〔læf〕*v.* 笑　　find〔faɪnd〕*v.* 找到
humor〔'hjumɚ〕*n.* 幽默；可笑
heal〔hil〕*v.* 治癒

Laugh with friends.

和友同笑。

Laugh at yourself.

嘲笑自己。

Make life better.

生活更好。

** ─────────────

laugh〔læf〕*v.* 笑

laugh at 嘲笑

make〔mek〕*v.* 使

life〔laɪf〕*n.* 人生；生活；生命

Laughter brings joy.

笑能快樂。

Laughter relieves stress.

笑能減壓。

Laugh and heal.

笑能療癒。

**

laughter〔ˈlæftɚ〕*n.* 笑

bring〔brɪŋ〕*v.* 帶來

joy〔dʒɔɪ〕*n.* 快樂；高興；喜悅

relieve〔rɪˈliv〕*v.* 減輕

stress〔strɛs〕*n.* 壓力

　（*= pressure = tension*）

laugh〔læf〕*v.* 笑

heal〔hil〕*v.* 治癒；痊癒

【Unit 8 背景說明】

Laugh every day. (要每天笑。) 也可說成：Enjoy every day. (要享受每一天。) Have fun every day. (每天都要過得愉快。)

Find the humor. (要找到幽默。) 也可說成：Look for the funny side of things. (要尋找事物有趣的一面。)

Humor heals us. (幽默能療癒我們。) 也可說成：Laughing makes us feel better. (笑能讓我們感覺更好。)

Laugh with friends. 和朋友一起笑。(= *Laugh along with your friends.*)

Laugh at yourself. (嘲笑自己。) 也可說成：Find the humor in what you do. (要找到你所做的事的幽默之處。)

Make life better. (讓生活更好。) 也可說成：Improve your life. (改善你的生活。)

Laughter brings joy. 笑能帶來快樂。(= *Laughter makes people happy.*)

Laughter relieves stress. 笑能減輕壓力。(= *Laughter fights tension.*)

Laugh and heal. (要大笑並且痊癒。) 也可說成：Laugh and feel better. (常笑就會感覺更好。) If you laugh more, you will feel better. (如果你更常笑，就會感覺更好。)

UNIT ❾

Family Is Most Important
家人最重要

Cherish your parents.
愛父母。

Stay close by.
在身旁。

Don't go far.
不遠遊。

** ——————————————

family〔ˈfæməlɪ〕*n.* 家庭；家人
cherish〔ˈtʃɛrɪʃ〕*v.* 珍惜
parents〔ˈpɛrənts〕*n. pl.* 父母
stay〔ste〕*v.* 停留
close〔klos〕*adj.* 接近的　*adv.* 接近地
close by 在旁邊；在附近
far〔fɑr〕*adv.* 遙遠地

Respect your parents.

尊敬父母。

Keep them updated.

知道近況。

Keep them informed.

持續更新。

** ————————————

respect〔rɪ'spɛkt〕*v.* 尊敬;尊重

parents〔'pɛrənts〕*n. pl.* 父母

keep〔kip〕*v.* 使保持

update〔ʌp'det〕*v.* 為…提供最新資訊

informed〔ɪn'fɔrmd〕*adj.* 了解情況的;
　　見多識廣的

Honor your parents.

尊重父母。

Share your location.

分享行蹤。

Share your whereabouts.

告知動向。

** ———————————————

honor〔'ɑnɚ〕*v.* 尊敬；給予榮譽

parents〔'pɛrənts〕*n. pl.* 父母

share〔ʃɛr〕*v.* 分享；告訴

location〔lo'keʃən〕*n.* 位置；地點

whereabouts〔'hwɛrə‚baʊts〕*n. pl.* 行蹤；
下落；去向

【Unit 9 背景說明】

Cherish your parents. Stay close by. Don't go far. 這三句話的意思是「父母在，不遠遊。」

Cherish your parents. 要珍惜你的父母。(= *Treasure your parents.*)

Stay close by. 要待在附近。(= *Stay near.* = *Stay nearby.*)

Don't go far. (不要去遠方。) 也可說成：Remain near. (要待在附近。) (= *Remain nearby.*)

Respect your parents. 要尊敬你的父母。(= *Honor your parents.*)

Keep them updated. (要讓他們知道最新的消息。) 也可說成：Tell them your news. (要告訴他們你的消息。)

Keep them informed. 要讓他們了解情況。(= *Keep them in the know.*)

父母在，不遠遊，「遊必有方」。

Honor your parents. 要尊敬你的父母。(= *Respect your parents.*)

Share your location. 要分享你的位置，也就是「要告訴他們你的位置。」(= *Tell them your location.*)

Share your whereabouts. 要分享你的行蹤，也就是「要告訴他們你的行蹤。」也可說成：Tell them where you are. (要告訴他們你在哪裡。)

PART 2　總整理

PART 2・Unit 1~9
中英文錄音QR碼

Unit 1

Remember to rest.
記得要休息。
Have some downtime.
有休息時間；機器也要休息。
Everyone needs rest.
人人需休息。

Let yourself rest.　自己休息。
Restore your energy.
恢復能量。
Recharge your batteries.
好好充電。

Close your eyes.　閉上眼睛。
Sit and breathe.　坐著呼吸。
Do a meditation.
進行冥想。

Unit 2

Avoid big meals.
避免暴飲暴食。
Avoid afternoon coffee.
避免午後咖啡。
Avoid screen time.
避看電子螢幕。

Get enough exercise.
獲得充分運動。
Get enough sunlight.
獲得足夠陽光。
Get enough air.
保持空氣流通。

Don't eat late.
不要吃得太晚。
Don't work late.
不要工作太晚。
Drink calming tea.
要飲用安神茶。

Unit 3

Sleep in darkness.
在黑暗中入睡。
Sleep in silence.
在安靜中入睡。
Lower the temperature.
降低一些溫度。

Take a bath.　要懂得泡澡。
Wear comfortable pajamas.
著舒適睡衣。
Wear comfortable socks.
穿舒適襪子。

Avoid drinking alcohol.
避免喝酒。
Practice deep breathing.
做深呼吸。
Follow a schedule.
按表操作；作息正常。

Unit 4

Find your passion.
找到你的熱愛。
Follow your passion.
追隨你的熱情。
Live your purpose.
活出你的使命。

Passion creates energy.
熱情創造活力。
Make magic happen.
要讓奇蹟出現。
Make dreams happen.
要讓夢想成真。

Embrace your why.
接受為何而生；擁抱天職。
Pursue your why.
追尋為何而在；追尋目標。
Preserve your passion.
保存你的熱情；維持熱情。

Unit 5

Knowledge is powerful.
知識很有力量。
Gain information everywhere.
隨地獲取資訊。
Improve your life.
改善自身生活。

Learning shapes futures.
學習塑造未來。
Be a student. 要成為學習者。
Create your future.
創造你的未來。

Mindset determines fate.
心態決定命運。
Thirst for more.
渴望獲得更多。
Own your fate.
掌握你的命運。

Unit 6

Fail every day. 每天都會失敗。
Failure builds success.
失敗造就成功。
Learn from mistakes.
錯誤中能學習。

Fall seven times. 倒下七次。
Get up eight. 爬起八次。
That's the secret. 就是祕訣。

Dare to fail. 勇於失敗。
Continue with courage.
勇敢繼續。
Achieve great things.
成就大業。

Unit 7

Listen to learn.
傾聽才能學習。
Listen to understand.
傾聽才能了解。
Listen to sympathize.
傾聽才有同感。

Clear your mind. 頭腦清楚。
Be fully present. 專注當下。
Don't be distracted.
切勿分心。

Don't interrupt others.
不要打斷他人談話。
Use body language.
使用肢體語言。
Ask open-ended questions.
問開放式問題，不問是非題。

Unit 8

Laugh every day.
每天都要笑。
Find the humor. 要找到幽默。
Humor heals us.
幽默能療癒。

Laugh with friends.
和友同笑。
Laugh at yourself.
嘲笑自己。
Make life better.
生活更好。

Laughter brings joy.
笑能快樂。
Laughter relieves stress.
笑能減壓。
Laugh and heal. 笑能療癒。

Unit 9

Cherish your parents.
愛父母。
Stay close by. 在身旁。
Don't go far. 不遠遊。

Respect your parents.
尊敬父母。
Keep them updated.
知道近況。
Keep them informed.
持續更新。

Honor your parents.
尊重父母。
Share your location.
分享行蹤。
Share your whereabouts.
告知動向。

BOOK 5 \ PART 3

Keys to a Successful Life
成功人生的關鍵

PART 3 · Unit 1~9
英文錄音QR碼

UNIT ❶

How to Make a Fortune
如何發財

Find a mentor.
找個師父。

Learn new skills.
學新技能。

Start a business.
開始創業。

**　━━━━━━━━━

make〔mek〕*v.* 賺（錢）
fortune〔'fɔrtʃən〕*n.* 財富；巨款
make a fortune 發財；賺大錢
mentor〔'mɛntor〕*n.* 良師；師父
skill〔skɪl〕*n.* 技能
start〔stɑrt〕*v.* 開始；創立
business〔'bɪznɪs〕*n.* 生意；事業；企業

Save and invest.

存錢投資。

Invest in assets.

投資資產。

Build passive income.

建立被動收入。

**————————————

save〔sev〕*v.* 儲蓄；存錢

invest〔ɪnˈvɛst〕*v.* 投資　　***invest in*** 投資

asset〔ˈæsɛt〕*n.* 資產

build〔bɪld〕*v.* 建立

passive〔ˈpæsɪv〕*adj.* 被動的

income〔ˈɪnˌkʌm〕*n.* 收入

passive income 被動收入（= *unearned income*）【不需要投入時間或只需要相對少的時間，就能創造持續穩定收入的方式，相反的是 earned income（主動收入）】

Work hard consistently.

持續努力工作。

Network relentlessly everywhere.

持續建立人脈。

Improve and grow.

要進步與成長。

＊＊ ───────────

work hard 努力；努力工作

consistently〔kən'sɪstəntlɪ〕*adv.* 不變地；
　始終如一地

network〔'nɛt͵wɜk〕*v.* 建立關係網；
　建立人脈

relentlessly〔rɪ'lɛntlɪslɪ〕*adv.* 不間斷地；
　持續地

everywhere〔'ɛvrɪ͵hwɛr〕*adv.* 到處

improve〔ɪm'pruv〕*v.* 改善；進步

grow〔gro〕*v.* 成長

【**Unit 1** 背景說明】

Find a mentor. (要找到一個良師。) 也可說成： Find an advisor. (要找到一個顧問。) Find a guide. (要找到一位指導者。)

Learn new skills. (學習新技能。) 也可說成： Acquire new abilities. (要獲得新的能力。) Learn how to do new things. (要學習如何做沒做過的事。)

Start a business. 要開始創業。(= *Establish a business*.) 也可說成： Establish a company. (要成立公司。)

Save and invest. 要存錢並投資。(= *Set some money aside and put some money into investments*.) 也可說成： Save your money and put it into something that will make more money. (要把你的錢存起來，投資會賺更多錢的東西。)

Invest in assets. (要投資資產。) 也可說成： Invest in property. (要投資房地產。) Buy real estate. (要買房地產。)

Build passive income. （建立被動收入。）也可說成：Put your money to work for you. （要讓你的錢為你工作。）Secure some income that you don't have to work for. （獲得一些你不需要努力就可擁有的收入。）Increase the amount of income you get from investments. （要增加你從投資獲得的收入。）

Work hard consistently. （要持續努力工作。）也可說成：Always work hard. （要一直努力工作。）Don't slack off. （不要懈怠。）

Network relentlessly everywhere. （要不斷到處建立人脈。）也可說成：Take every opportunity to network. （要把握每一個能建立人脈的機會。）

Improve and grow. （要進步與成長。）也可說成：Better and develop yourself. （要改善並發展自我。）Continue to develop your skills. （要持續培養你的技能。）

UNIT ❷

Helping People Is the Root of Happiness 助人爲快樂之本

Help when possible.

盡力幫忙。

Help without hesitation.

立刻幫忙。

Support with kindness.

善意支持。

** ───────────

root〔rut〕*n.* 根源;來源
possible〔'pasəbḷ〕*adj.* 可能的
when possible 在可能的情況下
hesitation〔͵hɛzə'teʃən〕*n.* 猶豫
support〔sə'port〕*v.* 支持
kindness〔'kaɪndnɪs〕*n.* 仁慈;好意;體貼
with kindness 親切地(= *kindly*)

Offer a hand.

提供幫助。

Lend a hand.

願意幫忙。

Reach out selflessly.

無私協助。

** ───────────

offer〔'ɔfɚ〕*v.* 提供；提議

hand〔hænd〕*n.* 手；幫助

lend〔lɛnd〕*v.* 借（出）

lend a hand 幫忙；協助

reach out 伸手；伸出援手

selflessly〔'sɛlflɪslɪ〕*adv.* 無私地

Stand by friends.

支持朋友。

Always be there.

永在身旁。

Be readily available.

隨找隨到。

**

stand by 站在（某人）那一邊；

繼續支持（或幫助）

always〔ˈɔlwez〕*adv.* 總是

be there 願意隨時提供幫助

readily〔ˈrɛdɪlɪ〕*adv.* 樂意地；立即地；

容易地

available〔əˈveləbḷ〕*adj.* 可獲得的；有空的

BOOK 5・PART 3

【Unit 2 背景説明】

Help when possible. 儘可能幫忙。(= *Help whenever you can.*)

Help without hesitation. 要毫不猶豫地幫忙。(= *Don't hesitate to help others.*) 也可説成 : Be willing to help others. (要願意幫助別人。)

Support with kindness. (要親切地支持。) 也可説成 : Help others by being kind to them. (要親切地幫助別人。)

Offer a hand. (要提供幫助。) 也可説成 : Offer to help. (要願意幫忙。)

Lend a hand. 要幫忙。(= *Help.*)

Reach out selflessly. (要無私地伸出援手。) 也可説成 : Offer to help without expecting anything in return. (要願意不求回報地幫忙。)

Stand by friends. 要支持朋友。(= *Support your friends.*) 也可説成 : Be loyal to friends. (要對朋友忠實。)

Always be there. (總是願意隨時提供幫助。) 也可説成 : Don't desert your friends. (不要拋棄你的朋友。)

Be readily available. (要可以隨時找到。) 也可説成 : Be available to your friends. (要讓朋友找得到你。) Be willing to help your friends. (要願意幫助你的朋友。)

UNIT ❸

How to Network 如何建立人脈

Attend important events.

參加重要活動。

Meet interesting people.

認識有趣的人。

Engage in conversation.

參與共同談話。

** ───────────

network〔'nɛt,wɝk〕*v.* 建立人際網路；
　建立人脈
attend〔ə'tɛnd〕*v.* 參加
event〔ɪ'vɛnt〕*n.* 事件；（大型）活動
meet〔mit〕*v.* 認識
interesting〔'ɪntrɪstɪŋ〕*adj.* 有趣的
engage〔ɪn'gedʒ〕*v.* 從事；參與 < *in* >
conversation〔,kɑnvɚ'seʃən〕*n.* 會話；談話

Get contact information.

獲取連絡資訊。

Follow up promptly.

立刻後續行動。

Build meaningful relationships.

建立重要關係。

**————————————

contact〔ˈkɑntækt〕*n.* 連絡

information〔ˌɪnfəˈmeʃən〕*n.* 資訊

follow up 採取後續行動

promptly〔ˈprɑmptlɪ〕*adv.* 立刻

build〔bɪld〕*v.* 建立

meaningful〔ˈminɪŋfəl〕*adj.* 有意義的

relationship〔rɪˈleʃənˌʃɪp〕*n.* 關係

Connect with purpose.

有目的地聯繫。

Expand your opportunities.

擴展你的機會。

Open new doors.

找到新的機會。

** ──────────

connect〔kə'nɛkt〕*v.* 連結;聯繫;建立關係

purpose〔'pɝpəs〕*n.* 目的

with purpose 有意地;故意地

expand〔ɪk'spænd〕*v.* 擴展

opportunity〔͵ɑpɚ'tjunətɪ〕*n.* 機會(*= chance*)

open〔'opən〕*v.* 打開

door〔dor〕*n.* 門

open new doors 提供新的機會或可能性
(*= provide new opportunities or possibilities*)

【Unit 3 背景説明】

Attend important events.（要參加重要活動。）也可説成：Go to important events/occasions/meetings/conferences.（要參加重要的活動 / 場合 / 聚會 / 會議。）

Meet interesting people.（要認識有趣的人。）也可説成：Make contact with fascinating people.（要接觸很棒的人。）Connect with fascinating people.（要和很棒的人連絡。）

Engage in conversation.（要參與談話。）也可説成：Talk to people.（要和人談話。）Chat with people.（要和人聊天。）

Get contact information.（要獲得連絡資訊。）也可説成：Find out how to reach people.（要查明如何連絡別人。）Find out how to get in touch with them.（要查明如何和他們連絡。）

Follow up promptly.（要立刻採取後續行動。）也可説成：Follow through right away.（要立刻

完成後續動作。) Send a message right away.
（要立刻傳訊息。）Call them right away.（要
立刻打電話給他們。）

Build meaningful relationships.（要建立有
意義的關係。）也可説成：Establish deep
relationships.（要建立很深的關係。）Develop
deep relationships.（要培養很深的關係。）

Connect with purpose.（要刻意連絡。）也可
説成：Be purposeful when you contact
someone.（要有目的地連絡某人。）

Expand your opportunities.（要擴展你的機會。）
也可説成：Increase your chances.（要增加你的
機會。）

Open new doors. 要開啓新的大門；要找到新的機
會。(= *Find new opportunities.*）也可説成：
Take advantage of new opportunities.（要利
用新的機會。）

UNIT ❹

How to Improve Your Immune System 如何增強你的免疫系統

Eat whole foods.

吃全天然食品。

Drink water often.

要常常多喝水。

Don't skip meals.

不要不吃正餐。

＊＊ ─────────────────

improve〔ɪmˈpruv〕*v.* 改善；增進

immune〔ɪˈmjun〕*adj.* 免疫的

system〔ˈsɪstəm〕*n.* 系統

whole〔hol〕*adj.* 整個的；完整的

skip〔skɪp〕*v.* 跳過；略過；漏掉

meal〔mil〕*n.* 一餐

Get some exercise.

做些運動。

Stay physically active.

保持運動。

Take the stairs.

勤爬樓梯。

** ————————————

exercise (ˈɛksəˌsaɪz) *n.* 運動
stay (ste) *v.* 保持
physically (ˈfɪzɪkl̩ɪ) *adv.* 身體上
active (ˈæktɪv) *adj.* 活動的
take (tek) *v.* 使用
stair (stɛr) *n.* 樓梯
take the stairs 走樓梯

Get enough rest.

充足休息。

Get outdoors daily.

每日外出。

Always breathe deeply.

常深呼吸。

**

enough〔ə'nʌf, ɪ'nʌf〕*adj.* 足夠的

rest〔rɛst〕*n.* 休息

outdoors〔'aʊt'dorz〕*adv.* 到戶外；在戶外

get outdoors 到戶外

daily〔'delɪ〕*adv.* 每天（= *every day*）

always〔'ɔlwez〕*adv.* 總是；一直

breathe〔brið〕*v.* 呼吸

deeply〔'diplɪ〕*adv.* 深深地

【Unit 4 背景説明】

Eat whole foods. (要吃原形食物。) 也可説成: Eat unprocessed foods. (要吃未加工的食物。)

Drink water often. 要常喝水。(= *Drink water frequently*.)

Don't skip meals. (不要不吃正餐。) 也可説成: Don't miss a meal. (不要有任何一餐不吃。) Eat three meals a day. (要一天吃三餐。)

Get some exercise. (要做些運動。) 也可説成: Be active. (要活動。)

Stay physically active. 身體要保持活動,也就是「要保持運動。」也可説成: Remember to move. (記得要活動。)

Take the stairs. (要走樓梯。) 也可説成: Climb the stairs. (要爬樓梯。) Take the stairs instead of the elevator. (要走樓梯,不要搭電梯。)

Get enough rest. (要有足夠的休息。) 也可説成: Sleep enough. (要有充足的睡眠。) Relax enough. (要夠放鬆。)

Get outdoors daily. (要每天到戶外。) 也可説成: Spend some time outside every day. (每天都要待在外面一段時間。)

Always breathe deeply. (要一直深呼吸。) 也可説成: Take deep breaths. (要做深呼吸。)

UNIT ❺

How to Break Up Peacefully
如何和平分手

Don't part angrily.
勿生氣分手。

Avoid legal battles.
避免打官司。

No one wins.
無人可獲勝。

** ———————————

break up 分手
peacefully〔'pisfəlɪ〕*adv.* 和平地
part〔part〕*v.* 分離;離別;分手
angrily〔'æŋgrɪlɪ〕*adv.* 生氣地
avoid〔ə'vɔɪd〕*v.* 避免
legal〔'ligl̩〕*adj.* 法律的
battle〔'bætl̩〕*n.* 戰役;交戰
legal battles 官司　　win〔wɪn〕*v.* 贏;獲勝

Speak with respect.

尊重口吻談話。

Agree to disagree.

同意不同看法。

Fighting isn't worthwhile.

不值得去爭吵。

**

speak〔spik〕v. 說話

respect〔rɪˈspɛkt〕n. 尊敬；敬意

with respect 懷著敬意

agree〔əˈgri〕v. 同意

disagree〔͵dɪsəˈgri〕v. 不同意；意見不合

agree to disagree 同意不同看法

fight〔faɪt〕v. 打架；吵架

worthwhile〔ˈwɝθˈhwaɪl〕*adj.* 值得的

Remember good memories.

記住美好回憶。

Part with compassion.

感同身受分手。

Surrender with love.

因為愛而屈服。

** ————————————

remember〔rɪ'mɛmbɚ〕*v.* 記得

memory〔'mɛmərɪ〕*n.* 回憶

part〔pɑrt〕*v.* 分開;分別;分手

compassion〔kəm'pæʃən〕*n.* 同情;憐憫

surrender〔sə'rɛndɚ〕*v.* 投降;屈服

with love 因為愛;充滿愛地

【Unit 5 背景說明】

Don't part angrily. (不要生氣地分手。) 也可說成：Don't leave angry. (離開時不要生氣。) Stay and work it out. (要留下來把事情解決。)

Avoid legal battles. (避免打官司。) 也可說成：Don't get involved in lawsuits. (不要捲入訴訟。) Don't get involved in legal disputes. (不要捲入法律糾紛。)

No one wins. 沒有人是贏家。(= *There are no winners*.) 也可說成：Everyone loses. (每個人都是輸家。)

Speak with respect. 要恭敬地說話。(= *Speak respectfully*.) 也可說成：Be respectful when you talk to others. (和別人說話時要恭敬。)

Agree to disagree. (同意彼此不同的觀點。) 也可說成：Respect others' opinions. (要尊重別人的意見。) Don't argue about differences. (不要因為意見不同而爭論。)

Fighting isn't worthwhile. 爭吵不值得。(= *It isn't worth it to argue.*) 也可說成：Fighting is not worth the time and effort. (不值得花時間和力氣去爭吵。)

Remember good memories. (記住美好回憶。) 也可說成：Don't forget the good times you've had. (不要忘了你擁有過的美好時光。) Don't forget the good things you've experienced. (不要忘了你經歷過的好事。)

Part with compassion. (要感同身受地分手。) 也可說成：Part with kindness. (要好好地分手。) Leave others kindly. (要好好地離開別人。)

Surrender with love. 要因為愛而屈服。(= *Give in lovingly.*) 也可說成：Give in. (要屈服；要讓步。)

UNIT ❻

How to Be a Better Person
如何成為更好的人

Listen without judging.
傾聽而不批評。

Respect others' opinions.
尊重他人意見。

Respect others' boundaries.
尊重他人界限。

** ———————

listen (ˈlɪsn̩) *v.* 聽；傾聽；注意聽
judge (dʒʌdʒ) *v.* 判斷；批評
respect (rɪˈspɛkt) *v.* 尊敬；尊重
others (ˈʌðəz) *pron.* 別人
opinion (əˈpɪnjən) *n.* 意見
boundary (ˈbaʊndərɪ) *n.* 界限

Spread love generously.

慷慨地散播愛。

Give without expectation.

付出不求回報。

Support those struggling.

支持掙扎的人。

** ─────────────

spread〔sprɛd〕*v.* 散播

love〔lʌv〕*n.* 愛

generously〔'dʒɛnərəslɪ〕*adv.* 慷慨地；
　豐富地

give〔gɪv〕*v.* 給與；付出

expectation〔͵ɛkspɛk'teʃən〕*n.* 期待

support〔sə'port〕*v.* 支持

struggle〔'strʌgḷ〕*v.* 奮鬥；努力；掙扎

BOOK 5・PART 3

Offer sincere apologies.

願意真誠道歉。

Show genuine kindness.

展現真正善意。

Have clear communication.

要清楚地溝通。

＊＊ ────────────

offer〔'ɔfə〕v. 提供

sincere〔sɪn'sɪr〕adj. 真誠的

apology〔ə'pɑlədʒɪ〕n. 道歉

show〔ʃo〕v. 展現

genuine〔'dʒɛnjuɪn〕adj. 真的

kindness〔'kaɪndnɪs〕n. 親切；仁慈；善意

clear〔klɪr〕adj. 清楚的

communication〔kə,mjunə'keʃən〕n. 溝通

【Unit 6 背景説明】

Listen without judging.（傾聽而不批評。）也可説成：Just listen without judging.（只要傾聽而不批評。）Don't be judgmental when someone tells you something.（當有人告訴你某事時，不要批評。）Don't judge when someone confides in you.（當有人向你吐露心事時，不要批評。）

Respect others' opinions.（尊重別人的意見。）也可説成：Value others' views.（重視別人的看法。）Don't criticize others' opinions.（不要批評別人的意見。）Don't argue with others' opinions.（不要爭論別人的看法。）

Respect others' boundaries.（尊重別人的界限。）也可説成：Don't overstep.（不要超越界限。）Listen when someone says no.（當有人拒絕時要聽進去。）

Spread love generously.（要慷慨地散播愛。）也可説成：Be generous with your love.（要慷慨地付出愛。）（= *Give love freely*.）

Give without expectation. 付出不求回報。
(= *Give without expectation of return.*) 也可
說成 : Never expect anything in return. (絕
不要期待任何回報。)

Support those struggling. 支持正在掙扎的人。
(= *Support those who are struggling.*) 也可說
成 : Help people who are having difficulty.
(幫助有困難的人。)

Offer sincere apologies. 提供眞誠的道歉；願意
眞誠地道歉。(= *Apologize sincerely.* = *Give
meaningful apologies.*)

Show genuine kindness. (展現眞正的善意。) 也
可說成 : Be sincerely kind. (要眞誠善良。)

Have clear communication. 要清楚地溝通。
(= *Communicate clearly.*) 也可說成 : Speak
clearly. (要說清楚。) Speak unambiguously.
(說話不要含糊不清。)

UNIT ❼

How to Be an Indispensable Person 如何成為不可或缺的人

Don't make excuses.
不要想找藉口。

Accept responsibility willingly.
願意接受責任。

Face challenges boldly.
勇敢面對挑戰。

** ───────────────

indispensable〔͵ɪndɪˈspɛnsəbḷ〕*adj.* 不可或缺的

excuse〔ɪkˈskjus〕*n.* 藉口

make excuses 找藉口

accept〔əkˈsɛpt〕*v.* 接受

responsibility〔rɪ͵spɑnsəˈbɪlətɪ〕*n.* 責任

willingly〔ˈwɪlɪŋlɪ〕*adv.* 願意地

face〔fes〕*v.* 面對

challenge〔ˈtʃælɪndʒ〕*n.* 挑戰

boldly〔ˈboldlɪ〕*adv.* 大膽地；勇敢地

Don't justify mistakes.

不要替錯誤辯解。

Admit your faults.

要承認你的過錯。

Learn from feedback.

從別人意見學習。

**

---

justify〔'dʒʌstə‚faɪ〕*v.* 使成為正當；

為…辯護

mistake〔mə'stek〕*n.* 錯誤

admit〔əd'mɪt〕*v.* 承認

fault〔fɔlt〕*n.* 過錯

feedback〔'fid‚bæk〕*n.* 反饋；意見反應

Be fully accountable.

負起完全的責任。

Accountability creates opportunity.

負責能創造機會。

Accountability inspires growth.

負責能激勵成長。

**

fully〔ˈfʊlɪ〕*adv.* 完全地

accountable〔əˈkaʊntəbl̩〕*adj.* 應負責任的

accountability〔əˌkaʊntəˈbɪlətɪ〕*n.* 負有
責任或義務

create〔krɪˈet〕*v.* 創造

opportunity〔ˌɑpɚˈtjunətɪ〕*n.* 機會

inspire〔ɪnˈspaɪr〕*v.* 激勵；激發

growth〔groθ〕*n.* 成長

【Unit 7 背景說明】

Don't make excuses. (不要找藉口。) 也可說
成：Don't try to explain it away. (不要想搪
塞過去。)

Accept responsibility willingly. 要願意承擔責
任。(= *Accept your duties readily.*) 也可說成：
Don't shirk your responsibilities. (不要逃避
你的責任。)

Face challenges boldly. (要勇敢面對挑戰。) 也
可說成：Be brave in the face of difficulty.
(要勇於面對困難。)

Don't justify mistakes. (不要替錯誤辯解。) 也可
說成：Don't make excuses. (不要找藉口。)
Don't try to avoid blame. (不要想逃避責任。)

Admit your faults. (要承認你的過錯。) 也可說
成：Acknowledge your mistakes. (要承認你
的錯誤。) Own up to what you did. (要承認
你做的事。)

Learn from feedback*. （ 要從別人的意見中學習。）
也可説成：Learn how to improve from the
criticism of others. （ 從別人的批評中學習如何改
進。）Use others' criticism to improve
yourself. （ 利用別人的批評來改善自己。）

Be fully accountable*.　要負起完全的責任。
(= *Take full responsibility.*)

Accountability creates opportunity*. （ 負責能創
造機會。）也可説成：If you are responsible
for what you do, you will have more
chances. （ 如果你爲自己所做的事負責，你就會有
更多的機會。）

Accountability inspires growth*. （ 負責能激勵成
長。）也可説成：Taking responsibility will
allow you to grow. （ 負責任會讓你成長。）
Being responsible will help you grow. （ 負
起責任會幫助你成長。）

UNIT ❽

Benefits of Traveling.

旅行的好處

Travel the world.

環遊世界。

See the world.

看看世界。

Explore and adventure.

探索冒險。

** ───────────

benefit〔'bɛnəfɪt〕*n.* 利益；好處

travel〔'trævḷ〕*v.* 旅行；在…旅行

world〔wɝld〕*n.* 世界

explore〔ɪk'splor〕*v.* 探索；探險

adventure〔əd'vɛntʃɚ〕*n. v.* 冒險

Traveling increases happiness.

旅行增加快樂。

It relieves stress.

它能紓解壓力。

It improves health.

它能改善健康。

** ———————————

travel〔ˈtrævḷ〕*v. n.* 旅行

increase〔ɪnˈkris〕*v.* 增加

happiness〔ˈhæpɪnɪs〕*n.* 快樂；幸福

relieve〔rɪˈliv〕*v.* 減輕

stress〔strɛs〕*n.* 壓力（ = *pressure* ）

improve〔ɪmˈpruv〕*v.* 改善；增進

health〔hɛlθ〕*n.* 健康

Meet different people.

認識不同的人。

Improve social skills.

提升社交技巧。

Create lifelong memories.

創造終生回憶。

** ————————————

meet〔 mit 〕*v.* 遇見;認識

different〔'dɪfərənt 〕*adj.* 不同的

improve〔 ɪm'pruv 〕*v.* 改善

social〔'soʃəl 〕*adj.* 社交的

skill〔 skɪl 〕*n.* 技巧;技能

create〔 krɪ'et 〕*v.* 創造

lifelong〔'laɪf,lɔŋ 〕*adj.* 終生的;一輩子的

memory〔'mɛmərɪ 〕*n.* 回憶

【Unit 8 背景説明】

Travel the world.（要環遊世界。）
= ***See the world.***（要看看世界。）
= Travel widely.（要到處旅行。）

Explore and adventure.（要探索並冒險。）也可說
　成：Go to new places.（要去新的地方。）Have
　adventures.（要冒險。）Do new things.（要做新
　的事情。）

Traveling increases happiness.（旅行增加快樂。）也
　可說成：The more you travel, the happier you
　will be.（你越常旅行，就會越快樂。）

It relieves stress.（它能減輕壓力。）也可說成：Travel
　helps you decompress.（旅行能幫助你減壓。）

It improves health.（它能增進健康。）也可說成：
　You'll be healthier if you travel.（如果你去旅行，
　你會更健康。）

Meet different people.（認識不同的人。）也可說成：
　Meet new people.（認識新的人。）

Improve social skills.（改善社交技巧。）也可說成：
　Learn how to interact with others better.（學習
　如何與別人有更好的互動。）

Create lifelong memories.（創造終生的回憶。）也可
　說成：Build lasting memories.（創造持久的回憶。）

UNIT 9

How to Stay Positive
如何保持樂觀

Smile more often.

更常微笑。

Smiling is contagious.

笑能傳染。

Smiling brings happiness.

笑能快樂。

** ――――――――

stay〔ste〕*v.* 保持
positive〔ˈpɑzətɪv〕*adj.* 正面的;積極的;
　樂觀的　smile〔smaɪl〕*v.* 微笑;笑
often〔ˈɔfən〕*adv.* 常常
contagious〔kənˈtedʒəs〕*adj.* 傳染性的
bring〔brɪŋ〕*v.* 帶來
happiness〔ˈhæpɪnɪs〕*n.* 快樂;幸福

Laugh out loud.

笑出聲音。

Laughter is medicine.

笑是良藥。

You'll live longer.

能活更久。

** ────────────────

laugh〔læf〕*v.* 笑
loud〔laʊd〕*adv.* 大聲地
out loud 出聲地 (= *aloud*)
laughter〔'læftɚ〕*n.* 笑
medicine〔'mɛdəsn̩〕*n.* 藥
long〔lɔŋ〕*adv.* 長久地

Acknowledge the good.

認同好事。

Express gratitude often.

常表感謝。

Live with gratitude.

常存感激。

**

---

acknowledge〔æk'nɑlɪdʒ〕*v.* 承認

Acknowledge the good. 認同好事。【源自
　作家 Eckhart Tolle 的名言：Acknowledging
　the good that you already have in your life
　is the foundation for all abundance. (認同
　你人生中已經擁有的，是所有富足的基礎。)】

express〔ɪk'sprɛs〕*v.* 表達

gratitude〔'grætə͵tjud〕*n.* 感激

often〔'ɔfən〕*adv.* 常常

with gratitude 感激地；帶著感激之情

【Unit 9 背景説明】

Smile more often. (要更常微笑。) 也可説成：
Smile more. (要多微笑。)

Smiling is contagious. (笑具有傳染性。) 也可説
成：One smile leads to another. (一人微笑，
另一人也會跟著笑。)

Smiling brings happiness. (微笑能帶來快樂。)
也可説成：Smiling makes people happy. (微
笑能使人快樂。)

Laugh out loud. 要笑出聲音來。(= *Laugh aloud*.)
也可説成：Laugh. (要笑。)

Laughter is medicine. (笑是藥。) 也可説成：
It's good medicine. (它是良藥。) 源自諺語：
Laughter is the best medicine. (笑是最好的
藥。) 也可説成：Laughter makes people feel
better. (笑能使人感覺更好。)

You'll live longer. 你會活得更久。(= *You'll have
a long life*.)

Acknowledge the good. (要認同好事。) 也可説
成：Recognize what is good. (要認可好事。)

Express gratitude often. (要常常表達感激。) 也可
説成：Often say thank you. (要常說「謝謝」。)

Live with gratitude. (要充滿感激地活著。) 也可説
成：Be grateful. (要心存感激。)

PART 3 總整理

Unit 1

Find a mentor. 找個師父。
Learn new skills. 學新技能。
Start a business. 開始創業。

Save and invest. 存錢投資。
Invest in assets. 投資資產。
Build passive income.
建立被動收入。

Work hard consistently.
持續努力工作。
Network relentlessly
everywhere. 持續建立人脈。
Improve and grow.
要進步與成長。

Unit 2

Help when possible.
盡力幫忙。
Help without hesitation.
立刻幫忙。
Support with kindness.
善意支持。

Offer a hand. 提供幫助。
Lend a hand. 願意幫忙。
Reach out selflessly.
無私協助。

Stand by friends.
支持朋友。
Always be there.
永在身旁。
Be readily available.
隨找隨到。

Unit 3

Attend important events.
參加重要活動。
Meet interesting people.
認識有趣的人。
Engage in conversation.
參與共同談話。

Get contact information.
獲取連絡資訊。
Follow up promptly.
立刻後續行動。
Build meaningful
relationships.
建立重要關係。

Connect with purpose.
有目的地聯繫。
Expand your opportunities.
擴展你的機會。
Open new doors.
找到新的機會。

Unit 4

Eat whole foods.
吃全天然食品。
Drink water often.
要常常多喝水。
Don't skip meals.
不要不吃正餐。

Get some exercise.
做些運動。
Stay physically active.
保持運動。
Take the stairs.　勤爬樓梯。

Get enough rest.　充足休息。
Get outdoors daily.　每日外出。
Always breathe deeply.
常深呼吸。

Unit 5

Don't part angrily.
勿生氣分手。
Avoid legal battles.
避免打官司。
No one wins.　無人可獲勝。

Speak with respect.
尊重口吻談話。
Agree to disagree.
同意不同看法。
Fighting isn't worthwhile.
不值得去爭吵。

Remember good
　memories.
記住美好回憶。
Part with compassion.
感同身受分手。
Surrender with love.
因為愛而屈服。

Unit 6

Listen without judging.
傾聽而不批評。
Respect others' opinions.
尊重他人意見。
Respect others'
　boundaries.
尊重他人界限。

Spread love generously.
慷慨地散播愛。
Give without expectation.
付出不求回報。
Support those struggling.
支持掙扎的人。

Offer sincere apologies.
願意真誠道歉。
Show genuine kindness.
展現真正善意。
Have clear communication.
要清楚地溝通。

Unit 7

Don't make excuses.
不要想找藉口。
Accept responsibility
willingly. 願意接受責任。
Face challenges boldly.
勇敢面對挑戰。

Don't justify mistakes.
不要替錯誤辯解。
Admit your faults.
要承認你的過錯。
Learn from feedback.
從別人意見學習。

Be fully accountable.
負起完全的責任。
Accountability creates
opportunity.
負責能創造機會。
Accountability inspires
growth. 負責能激勵成長。

Unit 8

Travel the world.
環遊世界。
See the world.
看看世界。
Explore and adventure.
探索冒險。

Traveling increases
happiness. 旅行增加快樂。
It relieves stress.
它能紓解壓力。
It improves health.
它能改善健康。

Meet different people.
認識不同的人。
Improve social skills.
提升社交技巧。
Create lifelong memories.
創造終生回憶。

Unit 9

Smile more often. 更常微笑。
Make others smile.
使人微笑。
Smiling brings happiness.
笑能快樂。

Laugh out loud. 笑出聲音。
Laughter is medicine.
笑是良藥。
You'll live longer. 能活更久。

Acknowledge the good.
認同好事。
Express gratitude often.
常表感謝。
Live with gratitude.
常存感激。

句子索引

句子索引

B

句子索引

句子索引

句子索引

句子索引

句子索引

T

句子索引

U

V

關鍵字索引

關鍵字索引

關鍵字索引

關鍵字索引

【劉毅老師的話】

「完美英語」+「完美中文」，讓你妙語如珠，人人喜歡，人人佩服。

和你的生命有關

劉毅

1. 2013年7月17日，應趙豔花董事長邀請，參加大連「萬人一口氣英語講座」。

2. 偶遇國學大師王麗華老師，她出口成章，妙語如珠，突然感覺到，她很了不起，變得非常漂亮。能夠把所學的中文成語，運用到日常生活中，非常令人佩服，這是我多年來學習的目標。

3. 2022年8月4日，遇到才女王宣雯老師，才能夠把「完美英語」和「完美中文」結合，中英文都出口成章，逐漸付諸實行。

4. 英語是國際語言，我們既然要學，就要學說「完美英語」，說得比美國人還要好，苦練的英文最美。

5. 「完美英語」加上「完美中文」是超級組合，適合中國人，也適合國際人士，你一說出來，就會讓周圍的人震撼不已。

6. 英文要使用，才能記住，看了有感覺的英文，才
會有興趣，才會想要學。

7.
| 完美英語 | + | 完美中文 | + | 心靈雞湯 |

= | 看了感動 | = | 被動使用 | → | 繼續使用，就不會忘記 |

8. 我們每天說無數次「謝謝」，別人沒感覺，自己
也沒感覺，和說 "Thank you." 一樣，外國人沒
感覺，自己也沒感覺。

9.
完美英語	完美中文
Forever grateful.	永遠感激。
Incredibly grateful.	非常感激。
Eternally grateful.	感激不盡。

10. 你可以利用本書的「句子索引」和「關鍵字索引」
找出你想說的句子，例如你知道Knowledge is
power. (知識就是力量。) 就可以找到所有
Knowledge 開頭的句子，像Knowledge opens doors.
Knowledge is opportunity. 等。

天天使用「英文三字經」和「英文二字經」，

→ | 天天進步 | → | 天天有成就感 |

→ | 天天愉快 | → | 身體健康 | → | 長生不老 |

如何推廣「英文三字經」?

1. 「英文三字經」能夠使江西名師肖星老師,從贛州帶了30多位同學,來廈門參加「劉毅英文三字經背誦比賽」。

2. 河南名師趙獻輝老師,原本40位初三同學,快速增加至90位,能夠使學生增加的老師,就是名師,增加越多,身價越高。最主要的原因是使用「英文三字經」為教材。

3. 林寒蕾老師背「英文三字經」,她的小孩3歲,自動地跟著背了起來,也來參加廈門「英文三字經背誦比賽」,真是不可思議。

4. 廈門「英文三字經背誦比賽」,參賽者劉義生老師,今年78歲,背完「英文三字經」之後,舌頭變軟,身體變得更健康,睡得更好。

5.「英文三字經」適合任何年齡，任何程度，當你背到變成直覺，像唸經一樣，你會百毒不侵，快樂如神仙。可在手機上不斷地使用。

6.「英文三字經背誦比賽」，建議可分「成人組」和「兒童組」。

> ▶評分標準：
> ①正常速度背一遍，錯誤最少者。
> ②快速背一遍，速度最快、最清楚者。

7. 請英文老師視情況自行訂定「英文三字經」背誦比賽的時間及辦法。推廣「英文三字經」是做好事，學英文，應該從「說」開始。教學相長，老師受益最大。

8. 劉毅老師期待受到邀請，參加各地「英文三字經背誦比賽」，他喜歡享受各地的熱情、文化，和美食。

劉毅「董事長完美英語班」同學合照

英文三字經
Three-Word English Wisdom

附錄音 QR 碼　售價：990 元

主　　編 / 劉　毅

發 行 所 / 學習出版有限公司

　　　　　TEL (02) 2704-5525

郵 撥 帳 號 / 05127272 學習出版社帳戶

登 記 證 / 局版台業 2179 號

印 刷 所 / 裕強彩色印刷有限公司

台 北 門 市 / 台北市許昌街 17 號 6F

　　　　　TEL (02) 2331-4060

台灣總經銷 / 紅螞蟻圖書有限公司

　　　　　TEL (02) 2795-3656

本公司網址 / www.learnbook.com.tw

電 子 郵 件 / learnbook0928@gmail.com

2023 年 9 月 21 日初版

ISBN 978-986-231-491-3

Speak kindly. 要說好話。

Speak softly. 語氣溫和。

Speak compassionately. 有同情心。

　　每個人都知道要說好話，語氣要溫和，要有同情心，但是脾氣一來，都忘了。但你背「英文二字經」，使用「英文二字經」，能使自己脾氣變得更好，讓人喜歡。

Change inspires. 改變激勵人心。

Change motivates. 改變激發動力。

Change rejuvenates. 改變恢復活力。

改變自己，穿一件新衣服、認
識一個新朋友，都會讓你精神為之
一振。

Spread joy.　散播喜悅。

Spread happiness.　散播快樂。

Spread goodwill.　傳遞善意。

　　你看了一部精彩的電影，介紹
給朋友，你會很快樂，他也會很快
樂。

Live fully.　過得充實。

Live passionately.　熱愛生活。

Live wholeheartedly.　全心生活。

　　要活就要活得充實、活得快樂，不要浪費時間，不要做自己不喜歡做的事。